PLAYBOY SURGEON, TOP-NOTCH DAD

BY

JANICE LYNN

ONE SUMMER IN SANTA FE

BY

MOLLY EVANS

This month, Mills & Boon® Medical™ Romance
goes Stateside!

Introducing...

HOT-SHOT AMERICAN DOCS

From sunny California to the sultry heat
of the Deep South, these maverick doctors
will get your heartbeat racing!

With their dreamy looks, bad-boy attitudes,
and unquestioned talent, these rebel doctors
are just waiting to be tamed...

Meet the women who take on
these oh-so eligible bachelors in:

PLAYBOY SURGEON, TOP-NOTCH DAD
by Janice Lynn

and

ONE SUMMER IN SANTA FE
by Molly Evans

PLAYBOY
SURGEON,
TOP-NOTCH DAD

BY
JANICE LYNN

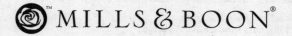
MILLS & BOON

All the characters in this book have no existence outside the imagination of the author, and have no relation whatsoever to anyone bearing the same name or names. They are not even distantly inspired by any individual known or unknown to the author, and all the incidents are pure invention.

® and TM are trademarks owned and used by the trademark owner and/or its licensee. Trademarks marked with ® are registered with the United Kingdom Patent Office and/or the Office for Harmonisation in the Internal Market and in other countries.

First published in Great Britain 2009
Paperback edition 2010
Harlequin Mills & Boon Limited,
Eton House, 18-24 Paradise Road, Richmond, Surrey TW9 1SR

© Janice Lynn 2009

ISBN: 978 0 263 87665 9

Harlequin Mills & Boon policy is to use papers that are natural, renewable and recyclable products and made from wood grown in sustainable forests. The logging and manufacturing process conform to the legal environmental regulations of the country of origin.

Printed and bound in Spain
by Litografia Rosés, S.A., Barcelona

Janice Lynn has a Masters in Nursing from Vanderbilt University, and works as a nurse practitioner in a family practice. She lives in the southern United States with her husband, their four children, their Jack Russell—appropriately named Trouble—and a lot of unnamed dust bunnies that have moved in since she started her writing career. To find out more about Janice and her writing, visit www.janicelynn.com.

Recent titles by the same author:

THE PLAYBOY DOCTOR CLAIMS HIS BRIDE
SURGEON BOSS, SURPRISE DAD
THE DOCTOR'S MEANT-TO-BE MARRIAGE
THE HEART SURGEON'S SECRET SON

To every woman who has ever closed her eyes
and lived the fantasy on the pages.

And to Lindsey Brookes for bringing so much laughter
into my life. I love you, girl!

CHAPTER ONE

How was cardiac nurse Blair Pendergrass supposed to avoid Oz Manning when he kept popping up in every aspect of her life?

Trying not to think of Madison Memorial's hotshot new heart surgeon, she inserted a catheter into her patient Latham Duke's vein. Attaching the intravenous equipment, she taped the tubing to secure the line to the banker's arm.

"You're really good at that." Mr Duke relaxed his clenched fingers now that the IV line was in place. "The last nurse who stuck me about killed me."

Blair smiled. She enjoyed what she did and took great pride in causing as little pain as possible to her patients.

"Let's hope Dr Manning doesn't finish the job that other nurse started." Wrinkles furrowed his pale forehead at the thought of his arteriogram.

Since Oz's arrival, every female in LA—Lower Alabama, that was—had gone gaga over him.

Except Blair. She consciously avoided the six-foot-two heart surgeon who reputedly broke as many hearts as he healed.

She'd written Oz off as a hopeless playboy years ago

when he'd visited his mentor Dr Ted Talbot. Sure, he could charm the habit off a nun with one crook of his little finger, but Blair had learned her lesson with regard to full-of-themselves men.

Been there, done that, had the scars to prove it.

Still, for what Oz was doing for Dr Talbot, she'd tolerate his insufferable womanizing ways.

Her heart squeezed. For nearly half a year Dr Talbot had been battling the metastatic cancer that had started in his colon and aggressively spread to his pancreas, liver and hip.

"I know an arteriogram is a common procedure, but frankly having something rammed through my groin and up into my heart terrifies me," Mr Duke continued on a breathy note. "Especially by a new doctor."

Blair patted his hand. "Although he's new to Madison Memorial, Dr Manning isn't a new doctor. He previously worked at one of the country's leading cardiology clinics."

"So I hear."

"Then you heard right." Blair administered the medication that wouldn't completely put Mr Duke to sleep, but would make him less aware of what was happening. "With Dr Talbot on medical leave—" *oh, how her heart broke at his rapidly declining health* "—Dr Manning is the most highly skilled surgeon on staff. There's no one I'd trust more with my heart," she assured him honestly. Oz's professional résumé was impressive.

"Isn't that sweet," a cocky male voice praised from a few feet away. "I never knew that's how you felt."

She silently cursed Oz's timing.

Meeting his blue gaze, she took in his pleased grin. Dimples dug into his cheeks, adding a boy-next-door charm to his good looks. Blair rolled her eyes. He'd be much easier to deal with if he was cross-eyed, bald, paunchy and dim-witted.

None of those things, Oz's grin widened.

Heat infused her bloodstream as surely as it would Mr Duke's when Oz pushed the dye. Blair had great empathy with the hot, flushing sensation described as the number-one side effect of the dye used to illuminate the vessels.

"Good morning, Latham." Oz's gaze skimmed over the monitors hooked to his patient, who was already visibly relaxing from the medication. "Is Blair treating you well?"

"The best." The man nodded toward his IV. "As gentle as she put this thing in, she's officially my all-time favorite nurse."

"I hear that a lot." Oz flashed a teasing look her way. "Blair being a favorite, especially from men."

Puh-leeze.

Her short, dark hair and plain green eyes made her average in looks. Childbirth had left her hips too wide, her breasts too big, and her body perpetually ten pounds heavier than she wanted it to be.

She hadn't been any man's favorite in a long time.

If ever.

"Beautiful and good at her job, too," Mr Duke mused. "She's a keeper."

"Definitely." Oz raked his gaze over her. When their eyes met something dark flashed in the blue depths.

Blair stepped back, shaken by the intensity of his stare. He loved to tease her, seemed to live to do so, which was why she avoided him as much as possible. But for that brief moment he'd looked serious. Almost dangerous.

"Good thing I'm a catch-and-release kind of guy or I'd be in trouble."

Relieved at his normal cocky tone, she let out the breath she hadn't realized she'd been holding.

Without another glance her way, Oz turned back to the equipment. He warned his patient about the ensuing hot flush and possibly the sensation that he'd need to urinate. When finished, he double-checked Mr Duke's identification bracelet. Satisfied he had the right patient and wasn't missing any allergies, Oz administered the dye.

"Nice." He watched the image on the screen and closely observed his patient's reaction to the medication.

"Is she single?"

Blair blinked. Had Mr Duke really just asked that?

"Yeah—" a tiny tic twitched at Oz's jaw "—but I thought you were married?"

"My son just moved back to Madison. He graduated from business school in December. Yale," the man added proudly. "A real bright boy. Handsome, like his father." He chuckled. "I'd love for him to meet a nice local girl—" he gave Blair a meaningful look, his gaze going to her gloved left hand "—and settle down and get married."

Settle down? Marriage? Ick. Blair almost broke out in hives at the thought. She didn't have time to date, much less get married. She didn't even want to. Her life was full with her five-year-old daughter, Addy, her younger sister, Reesee, and Dr Talbot. There wasn't room for catering to a man's ego and she didn't want to make room. She liked her life as it was—with the exception of Dr Talbot's illness and Oz's annoying presence.

"You should tell your son about the fund-raiser we're doing to help with Dr Talbot's medical expenses," she suggested, tired of being talked about as if she weren't there. "We're hosting a silent auction for donated items, but the main attraction is a bachelor/bachelorette auction."

"That dye wasn't as bad as I feared," Mr Duke admitted. "Bachelor/bachelorette auction?"

"Actually, I should talk to your son about volunteering to be auctioned. A handsome businessman would raise a lot for a good cause."

"You're still short on bachelors?" A frown creased Oz's forehead, but he didn't glance away from his patient. "Even after I contacted Will Majors about volunteering? Stephanie told me he called."

Although Oz had offered to help in any way he could, surprisingly, he had refused to be auctioned. Not when Blair asked, nor when her co-coordinator Stephanie had asked. Blair still couldn't believe Oz hadn't wanted to be auctioned. She'd have thought women fighting over him publicly would be right up his alley.

"We still need two more bachelors to even the numbers out."

"Two bachelors," he mused.

Oz might be talking with her, but his real focus was on what he was doing. He guided the instrument into the patient's femoral artery and up into the heart.

Even during routine procedures, Blair breathed a little shallowly until her patient was resting comfortably post-procedure. She'd never developed the tough skin needed to see the person lying there as just another patient.

Perhaps because her mother had died during a hysterectomy for uterine fibroids when Blair had only been nineteen.

"Ah, problem number one is right there," Oz

murmured, causing Blair's and Mr Duke's heavy-lidded gaze to shift to the computerized screen. "There's a tiny blockage of the right bundle branch. Nothing a stent won't fix."

Mr Duke had closed his eyes, probably in sleep. Blair kept a vigilant eye on the man's vitals. Oz positioned the device to where the artery was significantly narrowed, impeding blood flow and cutting off oxygen to Mr Duke's heart tissue. With single-minded purpose Oz opened the blockage.

The blood flow immediately resumed through the artery.

Oz had a magic touch when it came to healing hearts.

Blair had learned so much from working with Dr Talbot, but she'd told Mr Duke the truth. There wasn't a cardiologist she'd trust more than Oz Manning. He was that good, that talented.

Which seemed at odds with the man who was always teasing, always flirting, always out with one woman after another. Only this visit, with caring for Dr Talbot his primary focus, Oz had curtailed his revolving-door dating.

Before finishing Mr Duke's arteriogram, Oz placed two more stents in diseased arteries. While he worked he explained what he was doing to his patient. He made conversation with the heavy-lidded man as if they were watching a football game on television rather than Oz's life-saving measures inside the man's heart.

Although a big teddy bear outside of work, Dr Talbot was a grizzly during procedures. Blair had grown accustomed to his intensity, to his drill sergeant ways in the cardiac cath lab. Oz's easygoing attitude disoriented her to say the least.

The man disoriented her, period.

Even now, she could smell his musky scent, was keenly aware of his broad shoulders, thick chest and narrow hips. Not to mention that her fingers perpetually itched to trace over the cleft in his strong chin.

Okay, so Oz was attractive. Big deal. She wasn't blind. No matter how attractive he was, she'd never allow a man like him to get close. Never again. Some lessons were learned the hard way and left lasting impressions an entire lifetime wouldn't erase.

Blair swallowed, forcing her mind back to her patient and not his sexy surgeon.

"Unfortunately, I can't repair your mitral valve through the catheter," Oz said, although he'd explain again when his patient was free of the twilight medication. "The damage to the valve is too extensive to seal the leak as we'd hoped."

Although having taken leave from his clinical position in Minnesota, Oz continued researching a valve repair device that didn't require opening the patient's chest. He opted to use the innovative procedure at Madison when patients met the study criteria.

When Oz decreased the anesthetic medication and removed the catheter from the man's femoral artery, Blair placed a weighted device on her patient's groin, keeping pressure on the bleed.

Mr Duke's face had grown pale, but not from blood loss. "Does this mean I have to have open-heart surgery?"

"There isn't a way around it." Oz sat straighter on the wheeled stool. "If you're agreeable, we'll get you on the schedule for tomorrow. Regardless, I recommend doing the surgery within the next few weeks."

The medicine starting to wear off, Mr Duke shook his head. "I can't have surgery that soon. I didn't come prepared to stay. I'll be out of commission for weeks. There are things at home, at the bank, that need doing before I'm incapacitated that long."

"Who's going to do those things when you die from heart disease? Who's going to take care of your family?"

Blair couldn't drag her gaze away from Oz. His lips had thinned. The cleft in his chin seemed deeper, craggier. But his eyes were what held her mesmerized.

In that moment, she glimpsed an unguarded vulnerability she hadn't known he possessed. Somewhere along the line he'd known heartache.

Blair didn't like the quiver of empathy that look elicited within her. Not one bit.

She busied herself checking things she'd already checked.

"Will that happen if I choose not to have surgery?" Mr Duke swallowed hard. "Won't the stents you put in today be enough to keep me going? I wasn't feeling that bad to begin with, just got out of breath easily."

"Maybe nothing will happen if you don't have the surgery." His expression having returned to normal, Oz shrugged. "But odds are you'll go into heart failure or develop another serious heart condition such as atrial fibrillation. The stents have opened up the blocked arteries, but won't correct your leaky valve."

Mr Duke grimaced. "What does this valve do? What does it matter if a little blood leaks?"

"The mitral valve is the valve between your heart's left atrium and left ventricle. When the valve doesn't seal properly, some of the blood that is supposed to be pumped from the ventricle into your aorta washes back into the atrium. That means less blood goes into the aorta. To compensate for the decreased blood available to the body, the left ventricle enlarges so it can work harder to pump more blood."

Mr Duke digested Oz's explanation, taking a moment before he responded. "You told me last week when you did the ultrasound that my heart was enlarged. Is this valve why?"

"The heart is a muscle. If it's working harder, it's going to get bigger, just as your bicep enlarges when you work out."

"If I don't do the surgery, my heart will keep getting worse?"

"Absolutely," Oz said without hesitation. "The longer you wait, the more damaged the valve is going to be, the more extensive the surgery will be. Currently, I can surgically repair the valve, which means you keep your own valve. If we wait, the valve will be so damaged you'll have to have a mechanical replacement."

"A mechanical valve?" The man's brows drew together. "Why mechanical?"

"Because a tissue valve replacement would wear out. You'd be back in surgery in ten to fifteen years. With a mechanical, you'll have to take a blood thinner, but the valve would last your lifetime. Still, the best option is to fix your own valve before you reach that point."

"I need some time." Closing his eyes and taking a deep breath, the man sighed. "I don't have to decide this moment?"

"No." Oz shook his head. "I'll be by to see you later

this morning. Right now, you do everything your lovely nurse tells you to do and you'll be fine."

Blair ignored his silver-tongued compliment.

"Thank you, Dr Manning. I'll think about what you've said and discuss it with my family." Mr Duke held out his hand toward Oz.

"Blair will provide you with some literature and a video on mitral valve repair." Removing his rubber gloves, Oz shook Mr Duke's hand. "If you or your family have any additional questions or want more information, feel free to ask. Blair's part of my cardiac team and knows about as much as I do about the repair procedure."

She doubted that.

Still a little hazy, Mr Duke nodded.

"Be sure to tell your son about the fund-raiser." Oz sent a knowing look toward Blair. "If he's lucky, Blair will bid on him."

Blair gave Oz a cool glare as she continued preparing her patient for transport to the recovery room. No wonder she didn't like him. He was a total flirt, prone to insincere flattery, a womanizer, and an incessant tease.

"Pay him no attention," she advised her patient. "I think he's sniffed anesthesia one time too many."

Oz laughed, deep and throaty, and Blair was suddenly overtaken by an acute attack of loneliness. Loneliness at just how long it had been since she'd spent any real time with a man, just laughing and enjoying together time.

What was she thinking?

She didn't need or want someone like Oz making her question her life. He made her uncomfortable, made her heart pound as if she'd run a marathon in record time, made her lungs feel as if they couldn't get enough air.

All of which just made her like him that much less.

After she had Mr Duke resting in Recovery, she headed back to the cardiac nurses' station.

The devil leaned against the counter, looking sexy as sin and flirting with two nurses. No surprise there.

Kanesha Biles was happily married, but the nursing director was far from immune to Dr Oz. Her dark eyes glittering with delight, she slapped at Oz's arm and giggled at whatever he'd said. Becky stared at him in pure, unadulterated adoration, as if she were ready to sell her soul for a night of his attention.

"Oz Manning, you are bad," Kanesha scolded, shaking her head with an indulgent look on her face.

"You know what they say about bad boys, don't you?" Oz asked, his attention shifting to Blair.

She picked up a hospital memo, careful not to look into eyes so blue they'd been known to stupefy even the most staid of feminine souls. Eyes so blue they reminded her of another man who'd once hurt her by his careless use of the charms he wielded like a sword slaying a woman's defenses. Her defenses.

Just like Chris, Oz knew the effect he had on the opposite sex. He thrived on female attention.

"What do they say, Dr Manning?" Becky urged when Oz let his words hang tantalizingly in the air. "Tell us, please."

Unable to stop herself, Blair glanced toward Oz. He stared straight at her as if he could look into her soul and know every thought, every desire she'd ever had.

"Deep down, bad boys are really, really good."

His silky voice dripped with sin.

With suggestion.

With pure seduction. As if he was speaking directly to Blair and no one else in the world existed.

With…oh, Lord, Blair's lungs threatened to burst. Her knees buckled. She grabbed hold of the nurses' station desk to steady herself.

She didn't like him. She knew he was a playboy who broke women's hearts.

No matter how he wielded power over all things female, Oz was too much like Addy's father for Blair to ever lower the shield protecting her heart.

Still, thank God she wasn't hooked to one of the monitoring devices.

Protective shield or not, all sorts of alarms would be blaring at the traitorous pounding against her rib cage.

CHAPTER TWO

READY for a break, Oz made his way through the lunch line. Carrying his loaded tray, he grabbed a bottled water, then gave the hospital cafeteria checkout cashier his badge to scan.

"How's it going today, Gran?" he asked. The blue-haired lady's real name was Wanda, but Oz had teasingly called her "Gran." The nickname had stuck.

Gran's wrinkled cheeks flushed to a rosy shade of pink. "Not bad. My arthritis is flared a little, but when's it not?"

"You should let Will give you something for that."

Will Majors was Gran's primary care physician and a friend of Oz's. The two had hit it off during Oz's visits and usually spent time windsurfing or sailing. These days both men had other priorities, Dr Talbot being Oz's number one.

"He's tried." The woman chuckled. "But I'm not going to take medications unless I reach the point where I have to. If I don't ease up in a day or two, though, I'll schedule an appointment with Dr Will."

"Take care, Gran, and keep making men pay you to stand there looking beautiful."

Beaming, Gran cackled with pleasure.

It was the same conversation they had most days. Oz purposely went through Gran's checkout line just so he could put a smile on the woman's face.

Wanting to be alone to revive his sleep-deprived body, Oz scanned the cafeteria to find an empty table. He spotted several of his cardiac unit colleagues at a close-by table.

In particular, he saw Blair.

Pushing a short strand of her wispy dark hair behind her ear, she laughed at something the cardiac nurse manager she sat with said.

Blair.

He wasn't sure what it was about her that made him seek her out, but he always did. Perhaps he liked to see the pretty flush that rose in her cheeks when their eyes met. Or how she quickly looked away, her breath catching.

He liked Blair. Had from the first moment they'd met. She was a beautiful woman, inside and out. Oz had wanted her from the moment Dr T introduced them. But an affair was all he'd ever want from any woman. All he'd ever allow any woman to expect from him. He suspected, though, that Blair was the kind of woman who'd expect loads more than physical pleasure.

Which was why Oz might look, might tease Blair, but he'd never go further.

Based upon the way her feet kicked into high gear anytime he was near, she'd likely tell him where he could go if he ever did reveal how attracted to her he really was, anyway.

Maybe it was just as well.

With Dr T's failing health, the last thing Oz needed was to become distracted by a woman. His friend needed Oz to stay focused on the cardiac center and running Dr T's day-to-day life.

Passing by their table, Oz acknowledged the three nurses. "Hey, Kanesha, Blair, Becky."

"Dr Manning." Kanesha flashed her brilliant white teeth in a big smile. "Join us?"

"Please do." Becky scooted her tray over. "You can sit by me."

Not so long ago, Oz would have sat next to the blonde nurse, would likely have taken up the constant offer in her eyes. That was before Dr T had gotten sick.

Oz had decided to make his friend's life as good as possible under the circumstances. Currently, Oz spent all his spare time trying to make that happen, right down to moving hundreds of miles away from his home so he could be with Dr T and work in his place so the man could keep his health insurance. Oz didn't have time for dalliances with pretty nurses, particularly not ones who worked in the cardiac center.

He glanced longingly toward the empty table in the corner of the cafeteria.

"Come on, Dr Manning, we promise not to bite." Kanesha patted the empty chair next to her. "We're not taking no for an answer."

Reluctantly, he set his tray next to Kanesha's, across from Blair and Becky.

Kanesha took a sip of her iced tea. "How's Dr Talbot this morning?"

Why hadn't he told a corny joke or something before someone could bring up the subject of Dr T? Wherever he went, someone inevitably asked about Dr T. Wasn't that why he'd wanted to be alone? To not have to dwell on the fact he was losing the only person who'd ever really cared about him? That the man he loved was dying?

The older heart surgeon had been Oz's saving grace, the one constant good in his life. He had been more than a professor, more than a mentor. He'd been like a father. Much more so than the bastard who'd biologically fathered him.

Oz twisted the lid off his bottled water. "I spoke with Dr T's nurse after they got home from his chemotherapy. The treatment went okay, but he's had a rough day."

He wished his friend would let him go with him to the appointments. Dr T wouldn't. Not Oz. Not Blair. Not even Stephanie, Dr T's lady friend.

Blair glanced up, but quickly returned her attention to her food. She'd grown quiet the moment he'd stepped up to the table. Although he'd never figured out why, she didn't much care for him. Her earlier praise to Mr Duke had caught him off guard, had swelled his chest with pride and made him feel a little light-headed.

Praise from Blair didn't come easily. He'd found himself wanting more, to have her look at him with admiration, with attraction matching what he felt for her.

Just as well that Mr Duke's comment about Blair being a "keeper" had reminded him that he and Blair were nothing alike.

"I talked with him this morning before they left. He sounded so down." Blair still didn't directly look at him. "Did something happen?"

"He couldn't sleep. I sat up with him most of the night."

With a long, intricately designed fingernail, Kanesha gently scratched the base of a tightly wound hair braid. "I thought he had a private duty nurse around the clock?"

Although Dr T had complained about the cost, Oz had hired the private duty nurse, paying for the care himself when Dr T's insurance had refused. Normally a nurse stayed around the clock from Sunday night through Friday evening. Usually Oz covered the weekends, with Blair and Stephanie's help.

"Angie had something come up with her grandson around ten and had to leave."

Unfortunately after Angie had left, Dr T had awakened in pain and dry-heaving. He hadn't been able to return to sleep and had wanted company. Despite the long day Oz had put in at the hospital, he'd sat up with him.

"She'll be staying tonight, though?" Blair's concerned eyes met his.

Oz's breath hitched in his chest. Damn, but she had beautiful eyes. The most vivid green he'd ever seen. Her makeup-free face and natural beauty quite often had him staring at her, trying to figure out what it was that made him wish she were different, that she didn't expect the things from a man he knew she'd expect.

Not to mention Blair's daughter. Although he adored the little girl, Addy was enough reason to leave Blair alone.

He never became involved with women who had children. Never. Too complicated.

He nodded. "As far as I know, Angie will be there. She was back this morning prior to Stephanie arriving with Dr T's breakfast."

"I can sit with him tonight so you can get some sleep."

As if he'd sleep, knowing Blair was under the same roof.

"Me, too." Becky gave Oz a flirty smile.

"Thanks, but sitting up with Dr T isn't a problem." Oz

cherished the time with his friend. How many more opportunities would he have to chat with him? How long
before he'd never again look into his friend's caring eyes?

Seeing the once vibrant man so feeble was wearing
on Oz, but he'd never admit that to anyone.

Especially not Blair.

"No, but you can only sit up so many nights in a row
before doing so takes its toll on you," Blair pointed out,
staring at him closely.

Her concern pricked a sore spot deep in Oz's chest.
Other than Dr T, had anyone ever expressed concern
over his well-being? His mother on occasion when he'd
been young, but she'd sent him away to private school
about the time he hit puberty. He'd never returned *home*.

"You look tired. Dr Talbot needs you taking care of his
patients, not getting sick." Blair's reprimand put him in
his place. "If you get rundown and can't work, he'll worry
about the cardiac unit. He doesn't need that right now."

He should have known her real concern was for Dr
T, not him. She'd always shot him down at every opportunity during his visits. Or avoided him altogether. That
wasn't so easy this time.

"If Angie has to take off, I'll call, Blair." He shot an
apologetic look toward Becky. "Dr T is picky about who
he'll let stay overnight, but you're welcome to visit him."

"Thanks." Becky didn't attempt to hide her disappointment.

Kanesha chuckled.

Blair toyed with her fork, dragging the tines across
her mashed potatoes.

"What would you do about Addy?" He adored the
imp who, with the exception of her pale blond hair,

looked just like her mother. Only Addy's green eyes lit with delight when she looked at Oz.

"I'll bring her with me. She thinks the mermaid room is hers anyway." Although her plate was still half-full, Blair pushed back from the table, smiled at no one in particular. "I'm heading back to the cardiology unit to get our first patient for the afternoon started. I'll see you all there." She paused, glanced toward Oz. "Seriously, call if Dr Talbot needs me. I'm working with Stephanie on the fund-raiser tonight, but I can reschedule if needed."

Actually, unless Dr T's nurse got called away, Oz was helping Stephanie tonight, too, but he didn't tell Blair that, just nodded.

Becky began chatting, but Oz only half listened. Taking a big bite of his lunch, he watched the curvy brunette crossing the cafeteria.

Something besides hunger stirred deep in Oz's gut. Something he didn't know how to label or deal with, except that the only time he felt the stirring was when Blair Pendergrass was involved.

When Becky broke for breath, Kanesha, who'd observed their conversation, gave Oz a speculative look. "Dr Talbot is lucky to have you and Blair to take care of him."

"Luck has nothing to do with it." Oz forced his gaze away from where Blair emptied her tray. "Dr T earned my loyalty. There's nothing I wouldn't do for him."

"No, I imagine there isn't." Kanesha's gaze bounced to where Blair had stopped to say hi to friends at another table. "Blair's the same way. She had a fit when the hospital began searching for a replacement, threatening to stop Dr T's medical insurance. If you hadn't stepped

in to take his place until he could return, she would
have battled the entire board to keep his job open."
Kanesha sighed, her dark face somber. "Even if he beats
his cancer, and I pray he does, he'll never work in
surgery again. We all know that, but are grateful for
what you're doing."

Oz stuffed his mouth full of green peas. He wasn't
ready to discuss the fact that he'd never walk into a
surgery suite and see his friend issuing orders like a
mighty general and everyone hopping to do his
bidding.

What was Oz doing at the Madison Heart Association?
Blair seethed. Wasn't having to see him at the hospital
more than enough torture?

She punched in a phone number from the list of businesses she and Stephanie had put together to contact.

After swinging by her house to pick up Addy from the
neighbor who watched her each afternoon, Blair had gone
straight to Madison Heart Association's small office.

Ear to phone, Blair glanced around the small room
that housed three desks and was lined with dozens of
bookshelves loaded with educational material about
heart disease. Taking a break from her Oz worshipping,
Addy sat at a desk, playing a video game where she
cared for her favorite virtual pet, a chocolate lab she'd
named Boo-boo-too in honor of Dr Talbot's dog.
Wearing jeans and a Mayo Clinic T-shirt, Oz stood near
the largest desk, one cluttered with papers, books, mail
and a plastic replica of a human heart.

The man did wonders for a pair of jeans.

"You okay over there?" Stephanie called. In her

fifties, the vibrant woman was the director of the Madison Heart Association.

Blair and the woman she co-coordinated the fund-raiser with had become friends long ago. Over the years, they'd spent a lot of time together at Dr Talbot's. She often wondered if there was something between the couple. Both denied that there was. Stephanie's denial had been a bit misty-eyed, though.

"Fine."

Just fine, if only she could keep her mind off Oz. What was wrong with her? Usually she didn't have this much trouble focusing on her work rather than on the man who annoyed her so much. But the more she was forced to spend time with him, the more she watched him care for Dr T, interact with Addy, the more Oz got inside her head.

"Good." Stephanie smiled and returned her attention to the paper Oz held, outlining their plans for the fund-raiser in just a few short weeks. Stephanie had handed over the catering of the event to Oz. Blair only hoped they didn't live to regret the decision.

Like all females, Stephanie adored Oz and didn't bother to mask her adoration. The older woman giggled like a schoolgirl at something he'd said.

As if sensing her attention, he glanced up, caught Blair ogling him. He pinned her beneath his blue stare, defied her to look away.

Her heart pitter-pattered like a roller coaster making its highest climb, only to plunge to wicked depths and sharp turns. Her careening pulse was just from the em-barrassment of being caught eyeballing him. Surely. The effect he had on her irritated her all the same.

"Hello? Hello, is anyone there?" a voice asked from the phone receiver Blair gripped.

She'd forgotten all about her call. How many hellos had she missed?

She cleared her throat and gave her spiel about the fund-raiser, all too aware Oz's gaze remained on her. Her words came out jumbled, but to her relief, the florist on the other end of the phone pledged a hundred dollars and floral arrangements for the event.

The unexpected generosity to her garbled request pulled her back to the job she'd come to the charity to perform rather than on the man who always seemed to steal the show. She wrote down the information, then hung up the phone, a smile on her face.

"I take it you got a yes?" Oz asked.

She nodded, aware that Stephanie's attention was now focused on her, too.

"Great job." The older woman's dark gaze darted back and forth between Blair and Oz. "I was afraid you'd insist on addressing envelopes and stuffing them with the mailer."

Blair hated making cold calls, but someone had to do them. Stephanie had taken on a great deal of the work, but Blair wanted to do her part. Dr Talbot was worth making thousands of calls.

"As exciting as addressing and stuffing envelopes sounds—" Blair smiled "—I'll stick with calls. I know how important it is that we get the donations lined up as quickly as possible." She glanced at the stapled pages of names and businesses to be called. "Although I don't think I'll make it through the rest of these tonight."

"Do what you can, but no worries. You've already amazed me at how many local businesses have donated."

"I can stuff 'lopes, Mommy," Addy piped up from where she sat, her big green eyes eager.

"Addy, honey, Mommy needs you to be close in case I need your help." Addy was a darling and usually well-behaved, but like any child, she had her moments.

"But I'm a really good helper," her daughter insisted, wearing a pleading expression.

"Yes, you're a good helper," she began, but was interrupted by Oz going to Addy and taking her small fingers into his much larger ones. His strong fingers clasped Addy's fragile ones, twisting Blair's heart with a reminder of the one thing she could never give her daughter—a father's love and affection.

Appearing totally serious, Oz thoroughly examined her daughter's hands.

"I don't know, Stephanie," he contemplated, scratching his head. "What do you think? Do these look like good helper hands to you? Kind of look like pipsqueak hands to me."

Knowing a sucker when she saw him, Addy batted her lashes at Oz. From the moment they'd met, Addy and Oz had hit it off. Probably because he acted as much like a kid as Addy did and he showered her with his attention. Addy thought Oz walked on water.

But seriously, how could Blair expect a five-year-old to resist his charms when grown women couldn't?

"Mommy, tell Dr Oz what a good helper I am." Addy's bright eyes shifted to Blair, then to Oz. No puppy had ever given a more appealing look than the one her daughter bestowed upon her quarry.

Despite her melancholy, Blair bit back a smile. Oz had met his match in Addison Pendergrass.

"You're the best helper, Addy." Blair tried to be diplomatic in case Stephanie preferred Addy to stay near Blair. "But I'm sure the lady stuffing envelopes has things under control."

"Actually, she could use help." Stephanie earned a pleased look from Addy. "If that's okay with you, Blair?"

Blair silently mouthed *thank you*. "As long as she's not in the way."

"She won't be," Stephanie assured, smiling her acknowledgement. "Oz will help keep an eye on her."

Blair's gaze shifted to Oz.

His brow arched.

"Thank you."

"You're welcome." His gaze lingered, searched hers, and something flickered in his eyes, unreadable and disturbing. Surprisingly, for once, he looked away first. Turning to Addy, he poured on his own lethal brand of charm, bowing reverently.

"So, Pipsqueak, looks like you're in charge." He straightened, grinned, held out his hands palm-up. "I'm a good helper, too. Can I be your envelope stuffer helper?"

Taking his outstretched hands, examining them as closely as he'd done hers, Addy pretended to consider.

"Hey!" Oz teased when she dragged out the examination longer than he deemed necessary. "It's not like I have cooties."

"You can be my helper." Addy giggled, slapping her thigh at her joke. "Since you don't have cooties."

"No cooties here," he promised. "Let me finish going over this form with Stephanie while you save your game, okay? Then we'll show the world how envelopes are supposed to be addressed and stuffed."

Two hours later, Blair had procured donations of several more items for the event. She reached up to massage her contracted neck muscles. Man, it had been a long day.

"Tired?"

Startled, she glanced toward where Oz stood in the doorway, watching her. Her fingers paused mid-knead.

"A little." *How long had he been standing there?* "I sat too long without stretching."

She rotated her stiff neck.

When Oz moved behind her, she knew what he was going to do even before she felt his fingers. She wanted to stop him, opened her mouth to do so, but her breath caught, held, burned in her chest.

He touched her tense flesh.

Shards of electricity pulsated through her, lighting fires where he touched and radiating out to the tips of her fingers and toes.

Blair's insides turned to goop.

This was bad. Very bad.

But oh, my, did bad feel good.

Way too good to find her voice and make him stop.

It was just a quick therapeutic massage. Nothing more.

For therapy. That was all. Really.

Blair's hands dropped to her lap.

He stroked her tight muscles with a feathery touch. His fingers traced across the curve of her neck. So lightly she could almost think she imagined the burn of his fingertips through the short strands of her hair.

But she wasn't imagining his touch.

Or her reaction.

Every nerve cell zinged to life, jumped, flipped inside out.

Sighing, she closed her eyes.

His pressure increased.

Standing behind her chair, he worked on her neck and upper shoulders, dispensing every knot, leaving sensitized chaos in his wake.

Every breath echoed across endless time.

Every heartbeat thundered through endless space.

His fingers were magic that massaged away every reason she should tell him to stop, magic that made her forget she didn't like him.

His hand moved around her neck, stroked over her shoulders, her clavicle.

"Mmm." She angled to give him easier access, the back of her head brushing against his flat abdomen.

Oh, my.

His fingers skimmed back and forth, slow, teasing, caressing the column of her throat, her chin. He gently traced her mouth. Her tongue darted out to moisten her suddenly dry lips. His fingers paused.

Blair's breath caught and held.

Butterflies danced in her belly, sending up a fluttery rainbow of sensations that brought her black-and-white world into Technicolor. Sensations that made her acutely aware that she was a woman.

It had been a long time since she'd felt that awareness.

She turned, looked up at him, saw the desire reflected in his eyes.

He reached for her, taking her hand, pulling her to her feet, their bodies so close they practically touched.

In a daze, Blair breathed in his spicy scent, felt his palm cup her face, felt his body heat lure her closer, for her to close the small gap between them.

Although she knew she had to stop him, that she couldn't kiss Oz when she had no room for him in her life, when he'd only end up hurting her if she let her guard down, she touched his face, running her finger over the cleft in his chin, fighting the strongest desire to do the same with her lips. She loved that indentation, that impression on his flawless face.

"Blair, I—"

"How's it going, you two?" Stephanie stepped into the room.

Blair jerked away from Oz.

Oh, God.

What had she been doing? Thinking?

Addy could have walked in, seen.

Mortified, Blair couldn't look at Stephanie. How could she when she'd just been caught with Oz?

A man she didn't even like!

Dear, sweet heavens. She should have stopped him the moment he'd touched her.

She should have stopped him before her body throbbed from his touch, before she wanted to find out what all the hype about Oz Manning was really about.

A quickie massage didn't mean anything to Oz. but darn it, she didn't do this. Physical acts meant something to her, meant a lot to her, but…she should have stopped him. She wasn't one of his groupies. How could she have behaved no better than any of his other conquests? Hadn't she learned anything from her experience with Chris?

"Oh, sorry," Stephanie began, a little red-faced and flustered, too.

No way could she not suspect what Blair and Oz had been about to do.

They'd almost kissed. Oh…oh…oh, darn!

This was insane.

Insane. That was exactly right. Temporary insanity.

Because that was what Oz had done. Driven her insane with his playboy ways and his tenderness toward Dr Talbot and Addy. How could he be such a cad with women and yet so appealing with her daughter and dearest friend? With his patients?

"Did you need something?" Oz's eyes flashed with annoyance and perhaps relief, too, at Stephanie's interruption.

"What's going on?" Her gaze dropped to where his hand burned into Blair's lower back like a hot poker. Her thin cotton shirt was no barrier to the sear of his touch.

Needing to put as much space between them as she could, Blair stepped forward.

Oz's hand fell to his side. "Blair had a crick in her neck."

Stephanie's brow quirked. "And you offered to help out?"

"You know me. Always willing to lend a helping hand."

Blair refused to look at him. She didn't want to know if he wore a serious expression or if he'd waggled those thick blond brows, making light of the situation. She only wanted to rush to the bathroom and splash cold water on her face in the hope of waking herself and finding this was all a nightmare.

Seeming to have recovered from her initial shock,

Stephanie smirked at Oz's comment. "Especially when a female is involved?"

"Blair is certainly female."

Blair thought she might die of mortification.

At least then she wouldn't have to face the reality that she'd let Oz Manning touch her. Not just touch her, but *touch* her.

He might have started out just massaging her neck, but when Stephanie had walked in he'd been about to kiss her.

The worst part was that she'd let him touch her. As much as she wanted to believe she would have stopped him, she wasn't so sure that she would have. If Stephanie hadn't interrupted, she'd be swapping spit with the worst playboy she'd ever encountered.

With Addy in the next room.

Had she completely lost her mind?

"I came to tell you Dorothy is leaving in just a few. Addy is helping her finish the last of the mailers."

Drawing upon all her strength, Blair kept her shoulders high and walked around the desk. She checked her watch. Almost eight on a school night.

"I need to go, too, but I'm off duty on Saturday. Would that be an okay time for Addy and I to come back?"

Stephanie's curious eyes lit with gratitude. "That would be wonderful. Addy was a great help with the envelopes."

"I'll take the list home with me and finish making the calls while I'm at lunch tomorrow or Friday. Perhaps even at Dr Talbot's tomorrow night if he naps. Maybe I can get the rest marked off between now and Saturday."

"I'll be here on Saturday, too. I'll bring Dr T with me if he's up to it. He needs to get out of the house." Oz moved behind Blair, not so close that he was touching her, but enough that his scent enveloped her, taking her back to the moments before Stephanie had walked into the room. No. No. No. She did not wish she'd kissed Oz.

"We'll go over what we have covered for the fund-raiser," Oz continued, oblivious to the effect he was having on Blair. "Hire out what we don't, grab some lunch, then spend the rest of the day with Dr T."

"Thanks." Stephanie smiled knowingly at them, a pleased smile, making Blair even more self-conscious. "I'll just go tell Dorothy goodbye and leave you two alone so Oz can go back to…um…helping."

Great.

The moment Stephanie was gone, Blair spun toward Oz. "What do you think you're doing?"

"Don't go all defensive," he warned, giving her a frustrated look that said perhaps he wasn't as calm as he'd pretended. That maybe he had been aware of the effect his nearness was having on her and that he'd been just as affected.

"I'm not being defensive," she spat back, determined not to go soft on him again.

"Yes, you are. I understand." The blasted man stroked his knuckles across her face. "We should go somewhere and talk."

Talk? Yeah, right. Oz wasn't known for talking to women.

Glaring at him, Blair pulled back. He couldn't touch her. She couldn't let him. He was dangerous. Too dangerous.

Just look what had happened the last time she'd let a man get close to her. She'd ended up pregnant and alone, mourning the death of a man she hadn't known had been married to someone else, much less that he'd had other "girlfriends."

Now, she had a great life that she'd worked long and hard to forge. She wouldn't let a man destroy her a second time.

"We have nothing to say to each other."

"We need to talk about what just happened." Was he staring at her lips?

Dear Lord, he was.

She swallowed. Hard.

She'd known he hadn't really wanted to talk. Did he think she was a fool? That he could just almost kiss her and she'd fall at his feet?

"Nothing happened, Dr Manning," she snapped coolly. "Even if Stephanie hadn't walked in, nothing would have happened. I don't like you, and I certainly didn't want you to touch me or kiss me." The words ground out between gritted teeth. "I prefer for you to stay away from me and my daughter. Got it?"

Oz had wanted to kiss Blair more than he recalled ever wanting to kiss any woman.

He'd wanted to kiss her so much he ached with need from the ends of his hair to the tips of his toes and all in between.

He'd especially ached in between.

Now he just wanted to strangle her lying throat.

He wasn't some inexperienced schoolboy. He knew when a woman wanted him. Blair had wanted him to kiss her. Perhaps not as much as he'd wanted to kiss her, but she'd wanted his mouth on hers.

But she was right. He shouldn't have touched her.

Hadn't he always known not to touch Blair? That touching her wouldn't be nearly enough? Hadn't he subconsciously appreciated that she avoided him because it made doing the right thing easier? Hadn't he always made a point to keep a physical distance between them?

Why had he crossed that line tonight?

She was a complicated woman with a child. She was white picket fences and promises of forever. He was his father's son and liked women. Lots of women. He didn't do commitment, didn't do long-term relationships.

Yet, even now, with her staring at him as if he were the devil incarnate, he wanted to pull her to him and assure her that their touching had felt more right than anything he'd experienced in a long time. Maybe ever.

Which made no sense.

Likely the strain of caring for Dr T, of seeing his friend suffer, was getting to him and explained his weakness with Blair.

"I need to get Addy." She turned, picked up her purse from where she'd set the leather bag after they'd arrived, then moved to where Addy had left her satchel of goodies to keep her entertained.

"I'll walk you to your car." He should just let her go. Should take a leaf from her book and pretend nothing had happened. Surely that would be for the best?

So, why couldn't he? Why did he want to kiss her until she admitted that she'd been as affected as he had?

Blair slid the pink hand-held video game player into Addy's bag. "There's no need."

"I'll walk you to your car," he repeated, irritated that she insisted upon pushing him away at every turn. "This neighborhood isn't the best at night."

This time Blair nodded without looking at him.

When she said it was time to go, Addy proudly pointed to the box filled with stuffed envelopes.

"See what I did, Mommy? Miss Stephanie says I'm a great 'lope stuffer and she hopes I'll come back." Addy looked at Stephanie for reassurance and the director nodded. "Can I, Mommy?"

"We'll see."

Oz wondered if he was the only one who noticed the break in Blair's voice, the tremble of her hand, the way she looked anywhere in the room but at him.

"Dr Oz said I was a good helper, too, didn't you, Dr Oz?" Addy bestowed him with the smile of an angel.

"I did, Pipsqueak." Giving her an indulgent look, Oz touched Addy's curly blond ponytail, letting a ringlet wrap around his finger.

Tight-lipped, Blair reached for Addy's hand, effectively moving the girl away from him. He let her, hating how his rib cage crushed his internal organs to the point he could barely breathe.

Blair had told him to stay away from her and Addy.

Hell, no! The thought rushed through his heart. But if that was what Blair wanted, he'd honor her wishes. At least as much as he could, given their circumstances.

"Thanks for letting her help." Blair hugged Stephanie. She smiled down at her daughter, who'd taken her Hello Kitty bag and slung it over her tiny shoulders. "Let's go check on Aunt Reesee to see if she got lots of studying done."

"Aunt Reesee?" Oz followed them out of the building. Dr T had mentioned Blair's younger sister lived with her and Addy. Despite the twice-a-year trips

Oz made to the Gulf, he knew very little about Blair outside of what Dr T had volunteered. He'd purposely never asked questions.

"My nineteen-year-old sister." Blair kept her gaze locked on Addy, kept her tone even, probably for her daughter's sake, because he suspected she'd like to lash out at him. "She's in school at University of Alabama in Birmingham, but is taking several of her general study classes online to cut down on commuting and to help with Addy."

"Aunt Reesee is cool," Addy piped up, bouncing along beside them. "She lets me watch *SpongeBob* and drink soda pop after dark."

Blair's brow lifted. "Oh, really?"

Realizing her mistake, Addy faked a yawn and skipped ahead to Blair's mid-size four-door sedan. When Blair punched the remote entry, unlocking the door, Addy climbed in and began buckling herself into a child safety seat.

"Blair, about earlier," he began, speaking quietly in deference to the little girl who'd taken her video game out of her bag and chatted to her virtual pet.

Blair stepped back, not looking at him. "It was no big deal. Forget it happened."

Despite having just told himself the same thing, he didn't like Blair's quick denial. She was treating him as if he were a lecherous creep and her disdain annoyed him.

"Wasn't it?" he challenged.

Her teeth sank into her lower lip. "We both know you're an incurable flirt. What happened didn't mean a thing. Like I said, no big deal." She glanced toward where Addy played her game. "I need to go."

An incurable flirt? Blair's words stung. She made it sound as if he were diseased and condemned. Maybe he was. After all, wasn't that exactly how his mother had thought of his father? *Like father, like son.* Wasn't that what she always said?

"Fine," he bit out, "I'll see you tomorrow."

"Not if I see you first," she muttered under her breath.

She moved to Addy and checked to make sure the seat's safety catches were properly latched.

"Bye, Dr Oz." Addy waved, fighting back a yawn.

Oz's diseased and condemned heart squeezed. "Bye, Pipsqueak."

Blair closed the door, climbed into her car and drove away.

He raked his fingers through his hair, watching the taillights disappear into the night.

If he lived to a hundred, he wouldn't forget the feel of Blair's warm skin beneath his fingers, wouldn't forget the softness, the fullness, the way she'd stared into his eyes while he'd cupped her face.

Deep down he'd always wondered what touching Blair would feel like.

Now he knew and wished like hell he didn't.

CHAPTER THREE

"TELL me again that I'm imagining something between you and Dr Manning," Kanesha insisted the next morning. "Because I was at lunch yesterday and saw how you two looked at each other. The way you two always look at each other."

"You're imagining that there's something between Dr Manning and me." Blair didn't glance up at the cardiac unit's nursing director. Why should she when Kanesha might see guilt in her eyes?

"Yes, I am." Kanesha fanned her face. "And my thoughts are hot, hot, hot. You go, girl."

"There's nothing between us except a mutual love for Dr Talbot." Her friend was going to think what she wanted, regardless of anything Blair said. There wasn't anything between her and Oz. An almost kiss from the night before most certainly didn't count.

Kenesha glanced down the hallway. "Speaking of hot."

Don't look up. Don't look up.

Blair looked up.

And clashed gazes with Oz.

Her heart pounded against her rib cage. Why was

he looking at her like that? That almost kiss hadn't meant anything.

"Uh-huh. It's all in my imagination," Kanesha snorted. "Nothing at all going on between the two of you. That's why he's looking at you like you're the sweetest lollipop he's ever seen and he wants to see how many licks it takes to get to the center of Blair Pendergrass."

"Shh." Cheeks blazing at the images Kanesha's words elicited, Blair frowned at the nursing director. It wasn't as if she needed her friend putting ideas in her head. Hadn't her own dreams betrayed her the night before? Filling her sleep with images of Oz? Of his magical fingers? Of that almost kiss? Thank God Stephanie had interrupted. Too bad her alarm clock hadn't followed suit. "He'll hear you."

"Hear what?" Oz asked, stepping up to the nurses' station, his gaze still locked onto Blair.

Kanesha's dark eyes glittered. "That Blair is hoping you'll change your mind about being in the auction so she can bid on you."

Along with her stomach, Blair's jaw dropped. "I didn't say that."

"Didn't have to." Snickering, Kanesha walked off while mumbling something about checking the patient schedule and leaving them alone.

Why was everyone purposely leaving them alone? She didn't want to be alone with Oz.

"I didn't say that," she repeated, fighting to catch her breath. Did she sound like a broken record? No matter. *I did not say I wanted to bid on you.*

"I didn't think you did." Oz gave her a thoughtful look. "You're still short on bachelors?"

"Nothing's changed since last night," she snapped,

then realized she was being rude. Regardless of what had happened, regardless of the personal distance she wanted between them, they worked together.

Forcing herself to relax, she started over. "Latham Duke's son agreed to the auction. We need one more to even out the numbers between bachelors and bachelorettes," she said in an even tone, glad to focus on something other than the man standing so close to her.

"I'm the prime candidate?" Oz stepped closer to her, so close she could feel his body heat, was swamped with the fresh scent of his soap and spicy aftershave.

She gulped. "I didn't say that."

His gaze bored into her. "But initially, you signed me up to do the auction. If I had been agreeable you wouldn't be short a bachelor?"

"True, but…" She took a step back, surprised to realize she didn't want him in the auction, didn't want to watch women haggling over him. When had that happened? She'd been the one to initially put his name on the list and hadn't thought twice about doing so.

"I'll think about it."

"You will?" Blair blinked in surprise. He'd been so adamant about not being auctioned off, had seemed upset that she'd added him onto the list. What had changed his mind? Surely he hadn't believed Kanesha? Even if he had, so what? It wasn't as if Oz wanted her to bid on his date.

Did he?

"Why not?" He shrugged. "It's for Dr T. Like I said, I'll think about it."

Relief filled her. His reconsidering had nothing to do with the night before, had only to do with his love for

Dr Talbot. "How is he this morning? I called, but Stephanie said the physical therapist came early to work with him."

"Grouchy—the therapist came early."

Blair smiled. That was her Dr T. "Did he sleep okay?"

"Like a baby." Oz leaned against the nurses' station desk. "He only woke once during the night."

"Thank goodness."

Silence loomed between them for several torturous seconds.

"Mr Duke has an appointment this morning, doesn't he?"

Grateful for the subject change, Blair nodded. "I put him in room one. He plans to proceed with the mitral valve repair."

"Good," Oz said. "We'll get him on the schedule. What else do we have this morning?"

"Several consults and follow-up appointments. The lady Dr Majors spoke with you about yesterday is also here. He asked if you'd call him to let him know how you plan to proceed with Georgia Donelson's care. He had a few questions about his being auctioned off, too." Blair drew her brows into a vee. "He did really say yes, right?"

Oz laughed. "Why? Did you think I coerced him into volunteering?"

"He just sounded a little flustered when he asked me about the auction. I wondered why he'd agreed." Blair picked up her stethoscope from the nurses' desk and followed Oz toward the patient rooms. "It's no secret that he's involved with the nurse practitioner from his office."

"When I mentioned you needed more bachelors for the auction, Will volunteered. Maybe he just wants to help Dr T. Or maybe he's hoping Leslie will bid on him." Oz turned, gave Blair an intense look. "Maybe that's why I'm thinking about agreeing, too."

Blair's heart skipped a beat. "So Will's girlfriend can bid on you?"

"So *you* can bid on me." Oz's eyes twinkled with mischief. "You would bid me if I volunteered, right?"

"I wouldn't hold my breath if I were you."

Oz watched Blair review what Mr Duke would need for his pre-surgical workup. She moved in precise, skilled movements, just as she always did. But she was distracted, aware of him watching her.

Why had he said he'd think about agreeing to the auction? That he wanted Blair to bid on him?

Hadn't he decided the night before that the best thing to do was to forget about that massage?

If only he could.

Except for following Kanesha's joke, Blair had purposely kept her gaze averted from Oz's, sending a strong message. She really planned to pretend nothing had happened between them. Damn it. Why wasn't he grateful that she wasn't demanding more of him? That she wasn't asking what right he'd had to touch her?

In his dreams last night he'd done much more. He'd made love to Blair, over and over, until their bodies had been slick with sweat and he could no longer tell where he ended and she began.

He bit back a groan.

After Blair finished going over needed pre-surgical tests, Mr Duke turned to her. "My son is a little nervous about the auction. He asked me to find out if his date plans were okay or if he needed to come up with something more elaborate."

"His date package sounds fine to me." Blair stepped back so Oz could examine him. "Just so long as he's a skilled pilot."

"He is," Mr Duke assured in the proud tone he used when discussing his son. "He's been flying since he was a small boy. The Cessna is mine, but he takes her up more than I do these days."

"You should make time in the future." Oz placed the stethoscope diaphragm against Mr Duke's hairy chest. "Enjoy life more rather than spending all your time at the bank."

"From your mouth to God's ears." The man gave a self-derisive smile. "Actually, my wife is pushing me to retire so I can do just that."

"Good for her," Oz praised and meant it. Life was short. Each moment should be lived to the fullest. Something else he'd figured out since Dr T had gotten so ill.

His gaze went to Blair. She bit her lower lip, staring at him with a confused look.

Life was short. Too short.

More than anything, in that moment Oz wanted to touch her face, to feel her heartbeat next to his. He very quickly denied the unfamiliar emotion and buried it deep.

When he saw his next patient for the morning, he was the one ignoring Blair.

Oz listened to Georgia Donelson's heart. He didn't like what he heard any better than he'd liked her test results.

"I reviewed your echocardiogram, the ultrasound of your heart that Dr Majors ordered. Like he explained, two of your heart's valves aren't properly closing."

"Can you fix them?" The gray-haired woman laced her hands in her lap, possibly in a silent prayer.

"Yes, but not easily. I can repair the pulmonic valve by cutting away the portion that isn't sealing and suturing a new flap. But the mitral valve will have to be replaced. I need to schedule you for surgery as soon as possible. Preferably within a week or two at most."

Looking stunned, she shook her head. "I'm not sure I can put this on my daughter right now."

"Caden is doing better. Lacey is stronger than you think. She'll want what's best for you." Blair reached out, placed her hand over the woman's and gave a reassuring squeeze.

Oz hadn't initially made the connection, but everyone in the hospital knew of Georgia's grandson, who had been seriously injured in a motor vehicle accident.

"If we don't repair your heart, and soon, it'll likely kill you." He'd learned long ago there was a time for sugar coating and a time to lay it all out there. Georgia needed to make the right choice. The choice that would save her life.

She looked to Blair for confirmation. Blair nodded, her eyes a bit glassy from unshed tears.

Oz couldn't pull his gaze away. How did she do that? Be so connected to her patients? Blair treated each and every person she came into contact with as if they were a cherished family member.

Georgia's head hung low. "I need to talk to Lacey first. Then I'll schedule for whenever you think."

Oz explained what she should expect, then leaving Blair to make arrangements, he checked on another patient. On his way to lunch, he bumped into Blair.

"Going to lunch?"

She shook her head. "I'm skipping lunch. I need to make the calls on Stephanie's list," she reminded him. "I won't have time to do both."

Oz couldn't stand the thought of her going hungry.

"Sure you have time. We'll eat in the hospital cafeteria. When we're finished, I'll help you make the calls."

"That's not a good idea." She ran her fingers along her stethoscope, fiddling with the diaphragm. "People will think…" Her voice trailed off.

"That we're discussing the auction? Trying to make the fund-raiser as successful as possible for the man we both care about?" he filled in.

His gaze skimmed over her solid maroon scrubs. She shouldn't be skipping lunch. She was perfect just as she was. Generous breasts, nipped-in waist, curvy hips, but his gaze always came back to her wide eyes. Her gorgeous green eyes that sucked him right in.

Too bad Blair would want commitment. Too bad that was something he could never give her. Something he'd never want to give any woman.

"That is what we'll be doing, Blair. Nothing more, if that's what you're concerned about."

"No, I…" She wavered, looking uncertain. "You're right. We need to do this. For Dr Talbot. And I am hungry." Closing her eyes, she took a deep breath, then forced a smile, one that said she'd rather have a bikini wax than lunch with him. "I do need to hear about your arrangements for the catering."

"And to talk me into filling your last bachelor spot?" He wasn't sure why he'd said it. No, that wasn't true. He did know. He'd mentioned the auction because he knew Blair wanted him to agree to the auction, and like some schoolboy, he wanted to please her. Even if he couldn't have her.

Oz blinked. What the hell was he doing? Apparently his sanity had snapped.

"True, I do need to fill the last spot," she admitted, eyeing him suspiciously. No wonder with his odd behavior. "I still can't believe you don't want to be auctioned."

"You shouldn't be so quick to assume things about me." Hadn't that been how he and Dr T had gotten close? Because others assumed false things about Oz, but Dr T had taken a closer look, had seen someone worthy of taking under his wing.

When it came down to it, Blair was just like everyone else.

Her eyes darkened to a deep green. "I owe you an apology about last night."

Oz quirked a brow in surprise.

"I shouldn't have said what I did. About you staying away from Addy. She wouldn't understand and would be quite heartbroken if you avoided her. I'm sorry."

He hadn't expected her apology. Before he could respond, his cell phone rang.

He glanced at the number, silently cursed as he answered the call. A myocardial infarction had come into the emergency room and the E.R. physician had asked for him to be paged. He took the specifics, gave orders and promised to be there in less than two minutes.

When he snapped his phone shut, he met Blair's gaze. He started to apologize at running out on her after promising to help make the calls.

"No need to say anything. I heard." She waved him away. "Go. Save a life."

Wishing he had time to say more, that he had time for lunch, Oz reached for her hand. "I'll see you in the cardiac unit later."

Their fingers briefly touched.

Hurrying toward the E.R., Oz's mind raced. Why had he grabbed Blair's hand? Why had he felt the need to touch her?

Because of the night before? Because of the sweet softness of her skin? Because in his dreams he'd touched every inch of her?

Worse, how had the simple skin-to-skin contact made him feel better, yet more confused than ever?

That evening, hand in hand with Addy, Blair climbed the steps to Dr Talbot's beach-style home's front stoop.

Could she do this? How could she not?

Visiting her friend hadn't been so stressful prior to Oz moving in with him. The living arrangement made sense. Dr Talbot didn't need to be alone. Oz needed a place to live while he filled in for the heart surgeon.

But visiting with her beloved friend meant routinely seeing Oz outside of work.

Seeing him at work was bad enough.

Seeing Oz laugh and joke with the man she loved, seeing their close relationship, how Oz took care of Dr Talbot—well, it tugged at places inside her she'd rather not have tugged on, thank you very much.

Especially after last night. This afternoon.

She wouldn't even go into what watching him play with Addy did to her.

She preferred thinking of Oz as a playboy woman-izer. It was much easier to compartmentalize him as totally undateable.

He was undateable. Under normal circumstances he'd have a different woman every weekend. It was only Dr Talbot's illness curbing his sexual appetite, making him act out of character in ways that made Blair think she might have been wrong about him.

She knew all this.

But why had he touched her hand this afternoon?

"Can I push the bell, Mommy?" Addy asked, bouncing up and down at Blair's side on the small front porch. "Can I, please?"

Nodding, Blair braced herself. Would Oz be in jeans? Shorts? Please, not shorts. The sight of his hairy, muscular legs about did her in the last time she'd visited Dr Talbot. He'd been out running on the beach and—jeans.

He was wearing jeans.

"Hi, Dr Oz," Addy greeted him with a toothy smile. She'd lost her first tooth while at school that day and wanted the world to know she'd entered the world of being grown-up. At least that was how her five-year-old mind viewed getting a "grown-up" tooth. Blair pre-ferred not to think about her baby growing up anytime soon. It seemed as if Addy had only been getting her first tooth not so long ago.

Dear Lord, was she prattling to distract herself from the man standing in the doorway?

"Hey, Pipsqueak." Oz flashed a killer smile Addy's way, did their usual high-five hand greeting. Her daughter ate up the male attention, batting her lashes and smiling pretty as you please. Oz motioned for Blair and Addy to step inside the house. "You're looking beautiful today."

Standing in the hardwood foyer with its white spindled staircase, Addy giggled, eyelashes still fluttering. "What about Mommy? Is she looking beautiful?"

Blair grimaced. Out of the mouth of babes.

Oz's gaze shifted, ran over her from head to toe.

Oh, my. How did he reduce her to mush with one look? One *scorching* look, but still, just one look.

"Your mommy looks beautiful, too." His voice was low. "She always does."

Blair swallowed, refusing to look at him although she knew he still looked at her, sensed that he wanted her to look at him, that he wanted a response to his heated look, to his words. How could she respond when she didn't understand what was happening? When she was sure, whatever it was, she didn't like or want it?

"It's because I did her hair when she got out of the shower after work." Addy beamed at Blair's short bob that she'd blow-dried into a fluffy style. Much fluffier than Blair's usual cut that slanted in to frame her face. Addy had been so proud of her efforts Blair hadn't had the heart to comb out the teased locks.

"She even let me put in mousse." Addy wiggled her fingers back and forth as if they still had sticky mousse on them. "I like mousse."

Rocking back on his bare feet, Oz arched an eyebrow. "Mousse? That explains why she looks so sexy."

Addy giggled at his use of the word *sexy*. Blair melted, wishing she could recapture some of her usual cynicism when it came to compliments from Oz.

What was it about him that made her feel sexy?

Six years and she hadn't felt sexy, hadn't even wanted to feel sexy. Now, in front of her impressionable five-year-old daughter, she wanted to throw herself at Oz. She wouldn't, of course. But she couldn't shut off the images in her head. Images of Oz.

Blair bit the inside of her cheek.

What had that massage done to her? Surely, one little massage couldn't warp a woman's brain so intensely? And that touch of her hand, it might have rattled her, but surely it hadn't kidnapped her common sense?

"Mommy, why are your eyes closed?"

Because she might die of humiliation if Oz saw the truth in her eyes. She hadn't experienced passion since Chris.

Chris. Was that why she was attracted to Oz? He shared similar features with Addy's father. Blond hair, blue eyes, tall, pin-up calendar body, playboy personality.

Although a similarity to Chris should have a negative effect, it had to be why she felt so vulnerable around Oz. What else could explain her emotional weakness?

Only no matter how she tried to categorize him as being like Chris, she couldn't make the comparison work. Chris had been too self-centered to ever put his life on hold the way Oz had.

"Mommy?" Addy tugged on her hand. "What's wrong with you? Your face is squishy."

Blair opened her eyes, but she didn't know what to say. She didn't lie to her daughter. But she sure couldn't tell her the truth.

"I didn't know you did hair, Pipsqueak." Oz came to the rescue. He gave a look of being duly impressed by Addy's styling efforts. "I'll keep your skill with the mousse in mind the next time I'm in the mood for a new do."

Giving Blair one last confused look, Addy turned her intent gaze to Oz and studied him. "I like your hair, Dr Oz."

With a curious glance that said he wanted to know what Blair had been thinking while her eyes were closed, Oz tugged on one of Addy's pigtails. "You like my hair, Pipsqueak?"

Addy nodded. "Your hair is kind of spiky. In a good way."

Oz laughed. "Is there a bad way?"

"Oh, yes." Addy's blond head bobbed, her curly pigtails bouncing back and forth. "Scott Richards in my class at school has bad spiky hair." She made a thoroughly disgusted face. "He looks like an alien, doesn't he, Mommy?"

Blair gave her daughter a warning look. "Remember what I told you about saying things that aren't nice, Addy."

Her daughter blinked. "But Scott's not here, Mommy. How am I going to hurt his feelings if he's not here?"

How did a mother argue with a five-year-old's logic?

"Sometimes people overhear things we don't intend for them to hear, and it hurts their feelings. Scott is your friend. You'd never want to hurt his feelings."

"No." Addy considered her for a moment, then stage-whispered in all seriousness, "But he does look like an alien."

"Is that Addy I hear?" a gruff voice called from the living room before Blair could correct her daughter.

"Dr Talbot!" Addy shrieked, looking up at her mother for permission to go find the man she treated as a beloved grandfather. He was the closest thing Addy had to a grandfather since Chris's family had refused to acknowledge her existence when Blair had told them of her pregnancy. Their loss.

Blair nodded permission, and Addy took off at a run toward where she knew she'd find her favorite person, leaving Blair alone with Oz.

"She has a future in hairdressing." Oz gave Blair's hair another once-over. Her body, too. Hooking his thumbs through his belt loops, he slid his fingers into his front pockets. "You look great, like you just crawled out of bed."

What was she supposed to say to that?

Oz looked great in his jeans and royal blue T-shirt, too. She loved his hands, loved knowing what they were capable of in the surgery suite. But my, oh, my, his bare feet twisted her mind with unwanted thoughts.

Blair shook her head, unwilling to let that image go further. Ignoring his compliment, she focused on her daughter. "Addy still has a few lessons to learn in diplomacy and learning to censor what she says."

Must take after her mother, who certainly struggled with censoring her thoughts.

"She'll learn." Unabashed desire shone in his eyes. "You really do look great."

Blair swallowed. She didn't need this. Not while dealing with way too many things to consider becoming involved with a man notorious for flings and his commitment-phobia.

Not that she was looking for commitment.

She wasn't looking at all.

Not for a relationship. Not for a fling.

So why couldn't she drag her gaze away from Oz's tempting smile?

CHAPTER FOUR

OZ ROCKED back on his heels, watching displeasure furrow Blair's brow. What was she thinking? Feeling?

She was digesting what he'd said. He was sure of it. Had he crossed the line yet again? Hell, he didn't seem capable of not crossing it where she was concerned.

"If she doesn't learn diplomacy," he ventured, drawing Blair's gaze back to him, "she's so cute no one will care."

Her expression hardened. "That's a lesson my daughter has learned all too well. If she bats her lashes and looks cute, adults tend to do her bidding. I do my best not to give in since I don't want to encourage behaviors that are so reminiscent of—"

She stopped abruptly, but Oz could fill in the blanks. She'd been referring to Addy's father, had implied that he'd used his looks to manipulate those around him to do his bidding. He'd never heard Blair mention him before.

The reminder that there had once been a man in her life who she had cared for, a man who had fathered her child, did strange things to Oz's insides.

Like making him nauseated.

"She looks just like you."

Her scowl deepened. "Yeah, right. She looks more like you than she does me."

Her eyes widened. Her face paled. Interesting. Did that mean he looked like Addy's father? Why did that thought make him want to grab a few antacids?

"Addy's facial expressions are yours made over," he insisted, wanting her to think about anything other than the other man. "The way she smiles, the way her eyebrow quirks when she thinks I'm trying to pull a fast one on her, the intelligence in her eyes. That's pure you, Blair."

True, but perhaps he'd said so to wipe away the memory that Blair hadn't conceived Addy all on her lonesome. The thought of her with another man left him feeling as if someone had chopped him in the throat.

"Maybe." She stared at him, as if trying to see inside his head.

Good thing she couldn't because Oz didn't know what she might see. Lately, he didn't know what had come over him.

Just that he couldn't stop thinking about the woman who was now frowning at him.

Giggles filled the house. Pure in spirit giggles that lightened Oz's insides and made him smile.

"Come on. We'll call a truce for now." He held out his hand. "The old coot's been waiting for you to get here since I got home."

She didn't take his hand. Instead, she walked past him into the den. Oz sighed.

The "old coot" had Addy's arms wrapped around his

neck. Giggling, she placed sloppy kisses on his cheek while he told her something Oz couldn't make out.

"I missed you, Dr Talbot."

Anger sucker-punched Oz in the gut at the vision of the withered man Dr Talbot had become. A thin, frail skeleton had replaced the vibrant man Dr Ted Talbot had once been.

Still, his eyes shone brightly at Addy's enthusiastic affection. Blair, Addy and Stephanie's constant attention kept the older man going. It was what made him want to get out of bed each morning, what he most looked forward to each day.

"I missed you, too, darlin'." Dr T gave Addy another hug. He glanced up, spotted Blair and smiled. "Addy was telling me she styled your hair with mousse." He studied her for a moment. "Mousse becomes you."

"Dr Oz says Mommy looks sexy," Addy volunteered helpfully.

Leave it to Addy to repeat that particular compliment. After Stephanie's news from the night before, no doubt Dr T would be asking more questions about Oz's relationship with Blair.

"Oh?" A frown furrowed Dr T's pale face.

Embarrassment brightened Blair's cheeks to a pretty shade of pink.

Damn, she did look sexy. Her feet were nestled in white sandals that revealed pink toenails. She wore a sunny yellow top and white capri pants that covered more than they revealed, but left Oz's imagination running wild. Blair was the kind of sexy that reached out and caught a man unawares and left him panting to uncover every delectable morsel of her flesh.

Oz panted.

Not liking his thoughts, he shrugged. "I call things as I see them."

Oz thought she was sexy.

Flustered by his admission, Blair walked to where Dr Talbot sat on the brown leather sofa with a white cotton blanket covering his lower half. The pillow at the end of the sofa had a fresh head imprint, suggesting he'd been resting when he'd heard their voices. She kissed his cheek, which was still wet from Addy's kisses. Her daughter squirmed next to him.

Bony fingers grasped Blair's hand, held her until she looked at him. "Oz said you were sexy?"

"Dr Manning thinks every woman is sexy," she countered flippantly. Oz's words hadn't meant a thing. Just like that almost kiss hadn't meant a thing. Hadn't Dr Talbot been the one to tell her of Oz's many escapades with women? How he changed women every few weeks, none able to hold his interest for long? Hadn't she seen with her own eyes that he'd brought a different bombshell every visit he'd made to the Gulf?

"Blair?" Dr Talbot's body might be frail, but his pale blue gaze was strong, piercing.

"Addy asked what he thought about my hair. That's all." Blair smiled brightly. "I'll warn you, she's already offered to do Dr Manning's hair. Be careful what you say or she'll be offering to style yours as well."

Her little ears not missing a thing, Addy's eyes lit. She looked at Dr Talbot's shiny head, covered by only a few stray strands of white now that his once thick hair had fallen victim to his chemotherapy. She frowned.

"He doesn't have hair, Mommy." Apparently recalling their conversation in the hallway about hurting feelings, Addy's mouth rounded with an uh-oh.

"Did you tell Dr T about Scott Richards's spiky hair?" Oz yet again came to a Pendergrass female's rescue. Perhaps, instead of jeans, he should be wearing armor and riding a white horse. Nah, more like a black horse and dressed in some heinous villain garb.

Oz was no white knight. Blair would do well to remember that.

He sat down in a recliner where he'd apparently been watching a baseball game with Dr Talbot prior to their arrival. The television's wide flat-screen picture still played, but the volume had been muted. Probably by Dr Talbot when they'd been in the foyer discussing Blair's hair.

Avoiding looking toward Oz, Blair sat on the sofa near Dr Talbot, her hand still ensconced in his bony one. She refused to look at him, too, knowing he knew her too well not to see how Oz affected her.

Fortunately, Addy launched into a tale about her schoolmate's hair, running through a gamut of subjects, including her lost tooth, which she proudly pointed out, openmouthed, before glancing around the den. "Where is Boo-boo?"

Boo-boo, the inspiration for Addy's virtual pet, was the stray puppy Dr Talbot had taken in when it had shown up on his doorstep half-starved and flea ridden. After several years of Dr Talbot's care, Boo-boo flourished and adored visits from Addy almost as much as Addy loved playing with the rambunctious mutt that appeared part Labrador, part who knew what.

"He's in the backyard, Pipsqueak," Oz assured, looking restless. "You wanna go out and see if he'll play fetch with us? I'll go with you so your mom and Dr T can visit. If that's okay with your mom?"

Blair cringed. She'd been wrong to try to throw Addy into their disagreement last night. She'd apologized, but Oz's hesitation hit hard.

Addy squealed her delight. "Can I, Mommy? I like playing Boo-boo ball with Dr Oz."

Playing Boo-boo ball was Addy and Oz's thing and yet another reason Addy adored him. He never seemed to mind spending one-on-one time with her.

"You're sure you don't mind?" Surely his duties as Dr Talbot's house guest didn't include resident babysitter? Yet, each time they visited, Oz took Addy out to play with Boo-boo or to walk the dog so Blair could visit with Dr Talbot in private for at least a few minutes.

A man she'd judged as self-centered, his thoughtfulness never failed to surprise her. But she didn't allow herself to consider it too closely. If she did, Oz might climb out of the neat box she'd stuffed him into. If she ever allowed him to, she was in trouble.

After that massage, that touch at the hospital, the way he kept looking at her, she was in trouble enough.

"She gets cuter every time I see her," Dr Talbot praised.

Addy took Oz's hand and led him out of the den. She skipped with excitement and talked a mile a minute.

"You know she's going to be a total heartbreaker when she's older."

It was a conversation they had each time Blair and Addy visited.

"I know." Blair gave his hand an emotional

squeeze. "Good thing I'll have you around to help me fight off the boys."

Dr Talbot's pale blue eyes lowered. "Not so sure about that, girl."

"Has something changed?" Panic seized Blair. "What is the oncologist saying? Have you talked to the Mayo Clinic again? Are you a candidate for the experimental chemotherapy?"

"My oncologist is saying the chemotherapy has done all it's going to. The metastatic lesions on my liver and pancreas aren't shrinking. My blood counts are too low." Dr Talbot's hand tightened around Blair's, trembling slightly. "There's nothing more that can be done."

Unacceptable. She wouldn't let him die. Not if there was any possibility of treating his cancer.

"But the Xabartan is still an option?" Although U.S. trials were limited, the experimental drug was showing great success in China. Side effects were horrendous, but when one had nothing to lose, bad side effects didn't seem so daunting. "You'll do the treatments if you're approved as a candidate?"

She'd talk to Oz again, beg him to use his connections in Rochester to get Dr Talbot approved for treatment.

Dr Talbot gave a tired sigh. "I've done chemo, Blair. Radiation and surgery, too. The cancer is still growing. I've lost my hair, my dignity." He hadn't taken well to the colostomy bag after his descending colon had been resected. "Enough is enough."

She waved her hand in front of his face. "Hello. Where is the man who was going to fight this to the end? You can't quit now."

"Do I really want my last days to be spent battling not

only my cancer, but the ill effects of a medicine that's going to make me sicker?" He gave a weary sigh. "I want to die at home, Blair. In the comfort of my own home."

This was not her Dr Talbot speaking. He was a fighter. To the end. He had to be. She needed him to be.

Tears trickled down her cheeks. "I'm not ready to lose you from my and Addy's lives."

At Blair's anguished cry, he squeezed her hand again. "There's no need for tears, Blair. I had a good life and have no regrets. Selma's been gone a long time. Maybe it's time for me to join her."

Blair refused to believe that. Dr Talbot had a lot of life left to live. Had a lot of lives left to save. Had a lot of love left to receive.

Hers. Addy's. Stephanie's. Oz's. They all loved him.

"What does Dr Manning say about this new attitude of yours?" Blair sucked in a deep breath, steadied her frayed nerves and put on a brave face. She had to be strong. She was strong. She'd always had to be.

"Oz will support whatever I decide," Dr Talbot surprised Blair by saying. "I deserve to die in peace, in the comfort of my home rather than an out-of-state hospital if that's what I choose. It's what I gave Selma." Dr Talbot had practically bankrupted himself providing expensive private medical care twenty-four hours a day for his wife so she could stay at home, could die at home as she'd wished. "It's what I want, too."

"Oz is agreeable to you not pursuing every avenue?" She didn't believe it. Why would Oz not want Dr Talbot to try everything? "Why is he helping put the benefit together to raise money to help cover the cost of your treatments?"

"Because I won't take money from him." Dr Talbot sounded tired. "He's making the choice mine."

"Oz offered to pay for your treatments?" She'd wondered. Dr Talbot had once said Oz's family was old money, but she wasn't sure if that equated into Oz having part of that wealth. Apparently so. Handsome, a skilled surgeon, compassionate toward his friend, great with kids and rich to boot. Did the man have any flaws?

Oh, yeah, he did. He was a womanizing playboy. She needed to remember that. Just because there was a hiatus while he was taking care of Dr Talbot didn't mean he'd really changed.

"He's repeatedly offered, just as he did during Selma's illness, but I won't take handouts from the boy. He has better things to spend his money on than a lost cause." Dr Talbot's pale blue eyes bored into her, asking a thousand questions Blair didn't know the answers to, but likely wouldn't have answered even if she had.

"You are anything but a lost cause."

She couldn't bear the thought of losing him. Nor could she allow herself to give in to the sorrow plaguing her soul. Be strong. Be brave.

"Enough of this depressing subject." She pasted a smile onto her face. "Tell me about our favorite soap opera. Did Barbara discover that Nathanial is really still alive?"

Since his illness, Dr Talbot had spent a lot of time watching television simply because he'd been too sick to do anything more. Blair and Reesee had been fans of *Dare to Love* since they'd watched the show with their mother. Now Dr Talbot kept Blair up-to-date on the show's happenings. Blair mostly asked because the show gave him something to look forward to each day.

But her friend's pale eyes lit as he pinned her beneath his knowing gaze. "Why don't you tell me about your real-life soap opera instead?"

CHAPTER FIVE

"WHAT real life soap opera?" Blair pretended to have no clue what he referred to. Darn Oz for massaging her neck last night, for saying she was sexy. For so many reasons, darn him. "I lead a dull life."

"Dull?" Dr Talbot picked at a loose thread on the white blanket covering his legs. "That's not how I hear it."

Stephanie had told him. Blair sighed. Of course the woman had told Dr Talbot what she'd seen.

"I'm not sure what you heard, but I assure you my love life is quite dull."

"Did I mention your love life?" Dr Talbot's thin brows lifted.

She'd walked right into that one.

"Besides, if your *love* life is dull, it's because you choose for it to be." Dr Talbot's lips pursed in disapproval. "You should date. If I had my way, you'd be up for auction at my benefit just so you'd get out and meet a nice guy."

"A nice guy wouldn't necessarily bid on my date." Not at any point had she considered being one of the bachelorettes. She'd be busy enough helping oversee the night's events without being auctioned. "Besides, I don't have time for dating. Addy and Reesee are my priorities. Not searching for some elusive Mr Right."

They'd had this argument before. Dr Talbot didn't understand why she refused to date. Then again, he didn't know how badly she'd hurt after Chris. How betrayed she'd felt when she'd discovered the truth.

No wonder they'd bonded so intently when she'd come to work at Madison Memorial. Dr Talbot had been grieving for his dying wife and Blair had been grieving for Chris, her mother and so many of her dreams of a happily-ever-after.

"What about Oz?"

Oz wasn't her Mr Right. No way.

Blair blinked, knowing she didn't quite pull off as innocent a look as she wished. "What about him?"

"My cancer may have left me a feeble old man, but I'm not daft," her friend admonished. "Neither is Stephanie. What's going on between you and Oz?"

Hadn't she dealt with this question this morning at work? Dealing with Kanesha had been much easier than meeting Dr Talbot's expectant gaze.

"I'm tolerating Oz's company until you get well enough to come back to work."

Dr Talbot gave her a try again look. "You like him, don't you?"

No, she didn't.

"I like you and want you to get well so he can go back to whatever cave he crawled out of. He's a total Neanderthal. I have no clue how the two of you became such good friends."

"You're protesting too much, Blair. He gets to you." Dr Talbot chuckled. "Selma always said Oz was a killer when it came to the ladies. Why, I remember a whole slew of nurses with broken hearts when he finished his residency with me."

"Good for him," she huffed. A whole slew of broken hearts. No surprise there. Oz was a heartbreaker and would break her heart if she let him. She had no intention of letting him. "But I'm not interested in hearing about Dr Manning's love life."

"You sure?"

"Oz is arrogant and self-centered. I only tolerate him because he's your friend and because I work with him. Really," she added at his curious look.

"Oz isn't so bad," Dr Talbot said, once again surprising her. In the past she'd gotten the distinct impression he'd steered her away from any interest in Oz, that he'd encouraged her avoidance of his former star student.

"Actually," he continued, "I'd be hard pressed to name a better man or one I'd trust more. Don't write Oz off without taking a closer look."

Hadn't Oz said something similar? Accused her of making unfair assumptions about him?

Addy's muffled cries had both of their heads turning toward the French windows leading out onto the patio.

Adrenaline gripped Blair's heart in a tight fist. She jumped from the sofa. Before she'd crossed the room, Oz burst in, holding Addy close to his chest.

Blood covered her left leg, her hands, Oz's hands.

Tears ran down Addy's cheeks. Her lower lip trembling, she reached for Blair. "I want—Mommy."

She didn't need to be a nurse to register that her daughter was holding her bleeding knee and fighting sniffles in an effort to be brave.

Blair took Addy, hugging the little girl's shaking body.

"Shh, sweetheart, let Mommy see what happened," she soothed, trying to visualize from where the blood oozed. "What happened to your knee?"

"God, I'm sorry, Blair," Oz apologized, more repentant than she'd ever seen him. "We were playing with Boo-boo. She turned just as he jumped on her, and she fell."

Blair repositioned Addy to where she could see the gash. Blood gushed, making it difficult to see exactly how deep the cut was. She wrapped her hand around Addy's knee, pushing her palm tightly against the bleed, hoping the pressure would slow the blood flow.

"Get some antiseptic and a clean towel to apply pressure so we can stop the bleeding," she ordered a pale Oz. He didn't move, didn't seem to register that she'd spoken. "Dr Manning—" she spoke louder "—get something for me to clean Addy's cut with and a pressure bandage. Now."

"There's stuff in my medicine cabinet." Having tossed his blanket aside, Dr Talbot gripped his walker with both hands and strained to pull himself to his feet.

With one last glance toward Addy, Oz left the room.

"Baby girl, are you okay?" Dr Talbot peered toward Addy. He'd managed to stand and was making his way toward them.

Her lower lip quivering, Addy shook her head. "My leg hurts."

"It's just a cut, but she's bleeding steadily." Blair lifted her hand long enough to assess the wound. Not that she could tell much with the blood seeping from beneath her hand. "She's going to need a few stitches.

I'll call her pediatrician and see if he'll meet us at his office or if he wants us to go to the emergency room."

Both hands tightly fastened to his walker, Dr Talbot shook his head. "No need to take her anywhere. I have sutures in my doctor's bag." At Blair's surprised look, the old man shrugged. "Hearts aren't the only thing I can sew up."

"Okay." Her friend appeared too weak to stand, much less to sew up her daughter's injury. But Blair would not be a naysayer. Not when he seemed so determined. She hoped the incident would remind him just how much he had to offer the world still.

Addy's sniffles had almost stopped, but her tiny arms clung to Blair.

Oz came back into the room, his hands full of items and a big fluffy towel. Blair sat down on the sofa, angling her position to where Addy's hurt leg dangled, giving easier access to the cut.

"Get some pressure on Addy's knee." Dr Talbot tottered back to the sofa, weakness obviously overtaking him.

Blair kissed the top of her daughter's head, her gaze going to Oz.

His skin had grown sweaty.

Surely a cocky top-notch heart surgeon wasn't afraid of a little girl's bloody knee?

Oz had never gotten sick during any surgical procedure. Not even during early medical school when some fourth-year residents had tried to gross out the new guy.

He never broke a sweat while performing the most complex of cardiac surgeries. Not unless it was from the lights.

But a sheen of sweat covered him.

That was Addy's blood.

Although he knew it was just a cut knee, he'd felt real anguish the moment he'd realized what was going to happen when Boo-boo had bounded toward the little girl. He'd called to the dog, but it had been too late. Boo-boo's exuberant leap had knocked Addy off her feet. She'd taken a tumble forward, landing on something sharp, probably a rock.

A vise had locked around his heart as Addy's face had crumpled and she'd bravely tried to contain her cries. He'd rushed to her and seen the blood oozing from her sliced open knee.

He glanced down at his bloodstained hands. Similar to Blair, he'd tried to stop the bleeding by putting pressure with his bare hands. Not a smart thing to do in this day and age of blood-borne diseases. All he'd been able to think was that he'd let Blair's daughter get hurt. That Addy was bleeding because he hadn't watched her closely enough. That somehow he'd failed Addy, hadn't protected her. That he'd failed Blair.

That she'd been right to tell him to stay away.

Oz's gaze dropped to Addy's knee. The blood flow had slowed, was forming a clot. But the gash was jagged enough, wide enough that she needed stitches for the area to properly heal. What was he doing standing there?

He was a heart surgeon. Used to having lives in his hands. This was only a scraped knee. No big deal. What was his problem?

Straightening his shoulders, he knelt and examined Addy's knee.

"Pipsqueak, I need you to hold still." He kept his voice gentle.

Blair began to whisper soft words to her daughter. Oz couldn't make them out, couldn't tell what she was saying, but her voice sounded musical, calming, even to him.

Addy remained perfectly still in her whispering mother's arms. Blair maneuvered her daughter to face Oz, then wrapped her arms around her, pinning Addy's arms in a hug. With her thighs, she captured Addy's injured leg to where the girl could squirm but not make any big movements. Soothing with her soft words during the entire maneuver, Blair had effectively stilled her daughter without alarming her.

"Pipsqueak, love, I'm going to look at your knee. I'll be as gentle as I can."

Tossing the towel onto the tiled floor beneath Addy's knee, he poured antiseptic over the wound, dabbing at the excess to keep as much as possible from spilling onto the towel. He poured more disinfectant over some gauze he'd found in the medicine cabinet. As gently as possible, he cleaned Addy's wound, wincing at the jagged tear.

"She needs stitches," Dr Talbot said from behind him. "I have suture supplies in my doctor's bag. It's in my office. Go get my bag, and I'll sew her up."

Pressing the antiseptic-soaked gauze to Addy's leg, then covering it with a piece of paper tape to maintain pressure, Oz went and found the old-fashioned black medicine bag.

When he came back, he glanced toward Dr T's drooping shoulders. Sadly, the effort of standing without assistance had drained the man's energy.

"If it's all the same, I'll suture her." Waiting for Dr T's nod, Oz drew up some Lidocaine and prepared to squirt the numbing agent into the gash. "She's not allergic to anything?"

"No." Blair shook her head.

"Not a shot." Addy's eyes filled with tears again when she saw what Oz held. She squirmed to no avail in Blair's arms. "I don't want a shot."

This was his fault. If he'd been watching her closer, none of this would have happened. If he'd called the dog away from her sooner, before he'd leaped…

"This will make your knee stop hurting." Blair hugged Addy tightly.

Oz squirted the numbing preparation into the open wound. Then, injecting through the desensitized gash itself, he deadened the area so Addy wouldn't feel him suture her.

While waiting for the area to deaden, he prepared the needle-nosed suture holders and ethilon thread.

His gaze met Blair's, seeking reassurance that she was ready. She nodded for him to proceed.

With Addy studying his every move and Dr Talbot giving advice over his shoulder the entire time, Oz stitched Addy's knee, closing her gaping flesh.

"Beautiful," Dr Talbot praised from where he'd watched Oz make every suture.

"Thank you," Blair said, hugging Addy close, kissing the top of the little girl's head every few seconds and whispering comforting words.

"That's not beautiful." Addy's puffy eyes stared woefully at her knee. "Mommy's hair is beautiful. Not my boo-boo."

"No, Boo-boo is in trouble for doing this to you," Dr Talbot said gruffly.

"Boo-boo didn't hurt me. A rock did."

Oz would do anything if he could take away the pain in Addy's eyes. Tears streaked her cherub face. Although her cut was still numb from the anesthetic, when the sensation returned, she would be sore. Guilt like none he'd ever known blindsided him.

Blair would never forgive him for allowing Addy to get hurt.

He couldn't blame her.

Words his mother had used to scream at his father echoed through Oz's head. Words that said Manning men shouldn't be allowed to father children, shouldn't be allowed to be responsible for another person's heart because all they were good for was cheating and lying.

Like father, like son.

Oz steeled himself for the pressure in his chest that always followed those memories and wasn't disappointed in anything other than his own shortcomings.

The following day, while keeping a watchful eye on the monitoring devices, Blair studied Oz. He manipulated the catheter through their patient's ascending aorta and into his heart.

Great concentration shone on his face.

"Damn," he muttered under his breath, his skin pulling tight over his face.

Usually so relaxed, Oz's tension permeated the room. He'd placed three stents in the right bundle branch. Each time he did, the artery collapsed distal to the correction, once again blocking blood flow.

"Pulse is fifty-two," Blair said, although from experience she knew Oz was as aware of Buster Anderson's vital statistics as she was. Oz absorbed everything about his patients.

"Buster—" Oz addressed the man "—I'm afraid this isn't working. I'm going to try one more thing, a newer technique, but if it doesn't work I'm going to have to open you up."

The man swallowed. "Then let's hope it works."

Not only did the procedure not work, but the man threw a clot, cutting off blood flow in a vital artery.

"Double damn," Oz cursed, starting CPR when the man's heart stopped.

Blair called a code, administered epinephrine at Oz's order.

With life-saving speed, they had Mr Anderson in the operating room, intubated and hooked up to a heart-lung machine that would oxygenate and circulate his blood, keeping his organs viable while they worked on his heart.

While Blair cleaned Mr Anderson's chest with antiseptic solution, another nurse did an instrument check. A nurse anesthetist monitored him from the head of the operating table.

Oz made the incision into his chest, through his sternum, exposing his heart.

Oz opened up the blocked artery. The second surgical team removed the bypass vein from Mr Anderson's leg. Oz used the vein to reroute Mr Anderson's blood flow while the other team closed the leg wound.

With clockwork precision Blair performed her job duties, anticipating Oz's every need prior to his asking.

They worked well together. They had from the start.

Blair was only beginning to realize just how in sync they really were.

"You were amazing in there," she praised his efforts much later when they were removing their surgical gear. "Mr Anderson owes his life to your quick actions."

Oz raked his fingers through his blond hair, which was flattened from his surgical cap. "Hell, as soon as I saw that blockage, I should have sent him straight to the operating room instead of attempting to stent him."

"There was no way for you to know he was going to throw a clot. That he did wasn't through any fault of yours," she reminded him. For all his jokes, Oz took his patient care seriously. He thought he should be able to predict every patient's outcome. No doctor could.

"Some coincidence that he threw the clot while I was catheterizing him."

"Lucky for him," Blair insisted.

"Lucky." Oz paused outside the cardiac operating room, gave a quick smile of appreciation. "Thanks for your help. He owes his life as much to you as he does to me. You were fantastic when he coded."

Blair nodded. She hadn't done anything beyond what any trained nurse would do. Oz had been the miracle worker.

"What's next on tap?" he asked, his demeanor returning to normal.

"Two more arteriograms and a stress test," she reminded him. "Why don't you take a few minutes' break while I get the next patient set up?"

The next two arteriograms were uneventful.

Blair hooked monitoring equipment to Ralph Constance's chest, preparing him for his stress test. Due to the man's diabetic neuropathy and arthritis in his lower extremities, he was unable to do the stress test on the treadmill. A chemically induced test was being performed instead.

When they'd finished with the last patient for the day, Blair stepped into the hallway and let out a long sigh. She rubbed the back of her neck, massaging the tension twisting her muscles.

Why did her neck ache since Oz had massaged her?

What was wrong with her? Each day that passed seemed to leave her thinking about Oz more and more.

Each day that passed made her feel a little more susceptible to his charms.

A little? Now that was a joke. Her susceptibility was growing by leaps and bounds. Oz was climbing out of that box she'd stuffed him into. She needed him crammed back in there. Pronto.

Because, even if her brain knew Oz was really the womanizing playboy she'd painted him, the Oz of late had her heart thinking perhaps he wasn't so bad. Perhaps he'd changed and wasn't really like Chris.

Leaning her forehead against the empty back hallway of the cardiac cath lab, she dug her fingers deeper into her tense flesh.

Moist heat blew against the back of her neck, prickling every hair, electrifying every cell in her body. She didn't have to look to know who stood behind her. Instinctively she knew, her body recognizing Oz's presence.

Ready to tell him to stop, that she was becoming too weak to fight him, she spun.

And toppled right into his arms.

He caught her, but didn't let go.

God, he felt good. Smelled good.

His eyes twinkled and a smile curved his lips. "Really, Blair, can't you wait until the night of the auction before you throw yourself at me?"

The night of the auction? Did that mean he was agreeing? That he really wanted her to bid on him?

What was she thinking?

This was Oz. He was teasing her.

She needed to get a grip.

And not on Oz's shoulders to keep herself from falling.

Her throat tightened and the knots in her neck twisted so tight they threatened to snap. A strangled sound escaped from her open mouth.

But for the life of her, she couldn't speak, couldn't pull loose from his hold, couldn't let go of him.

His eyes darkened. His smile faded. Oz drew her close. So close she could feel his breath against her cheek. "Are you okay?"

She wasn't.

She felt light-headed. Dizzy. Breathless.

This was Oz. Why was she going into sensory overload? Why did the moist heat of his breath goose-bump her flesh? Why did she want to stretch onto her tiptoes and touch her lips to his?

His hand slid behind her, cradling the back of her neck. He held her close, his mouth centimeters from hers. "Blair?"

A hot flush drenched her skin. Her gaze dropped to his mouth.

What would it feel like to have Oz's mouth against hers? To have him kiss her with the passion for life that coursed through his veins? Would his lips be gentle? Demanding? Warm? Cool? Would his tongue slip into her mouth? Would—

She had to stop. She didn't want Oz. Not really. She couldn't deal with all the emotional pain that followed being involved with a man like Oz. She couldn't. Wouldn't.

She placed her palms against his chest, planning to push him away. Her fingers stilled. She flattened her hand over his heart.

His *racing* heart.

Her pulse jumped from eighty to a few thousand beats per second.

She lifted her gaze to his.

He wanted to kiss her. Surely that was why his heart beat so fast.

Dear sweet heaven, Oz wanted to kiss her, and his heart beat as crazily as her own.

It shouldn't matter that he was as physically affected as she was by the strange chemistry between them.

Unfortunately, it did and left her powerless against the desire erupting inside her body.

"Blair." Oz's lips brushed against hers. His mouth tasted hers. Soft. Gentle. Reverent.

Yet hungry.

Desperately hungry.

Starved.

She pressed against him, wanting closer, wanting as much contact as possible. Deep in her mind she registered stress had likely caused her weakness. Probably, stress had caused Oz's reaction to her, too. But she couldn't pull away, didn't even want to try.

Her fingers slipped into his hair. Soft. His hair was so soft. So were his lips. Soft, yet hard.

His whole body was hard.

He pressed her against the concrete hospital wall, pushed against her, groaned. "I swore I wasn't going to do this. I know I started it, but we have to stop. We're in the hallway."

He was right. If caught, she'd forever be labeled as the woman who had been making out in the back cardiac hallway with the seductive Dr Oz Manning. Eventually, he'd leave Madison, but she had no plans to leave. She'd be the one left facing the consequences of a few stolen moments of pleasure.

Nothing new there.

"I shouldn't have kissed you, Blair."

Rattled by his kiss and by how much she'd wanted him to keep kissing her forever, she frowned. "Why not?"

"I'd never want to hurt you or Addy." He drew in a deep breath, raked his fingers through his hair. "A relationship between us would never work. We're too different, want different things from life. We can't be more than friends."

"If we were more than friends you'd hurt me?" She knew it was true even before he answered. Hadn't she always known? Wasn't that really why she'd avoided him all those years? Because she'd known Oz had the power to hurt her? Perhaps even more so than Chris had?

"It's what I do." He took her hand in his and lifted it to his lips. "What I don't want to do to you, Blair. I don't do commitment, you don't do flings. This is new to me, but I really would like us to be friends."

Blair let his words sink in, searched his eyes for some

sign he was kidding. For some sign he wanted her to say yes, she'd love to have a fling with him. Because, in the insanity of the moment, that was exactly what she wanted to scream at the top of her lungs. Sure, she recognized that her insanity was temporary, that she'd regret saying anything of the sort. But in the heady aftermath of Oz's kiss, she didn't want sanity, didn't want logical. For once she just wanted to feel.

"I want to be friends, Blair. Say yes."

God, he was serious. He wanted to be her friend. "Why? For Dr Talbot's sake?"

"If Dr T is the only reason you can find, then yes, for Dr Talbot's sake. But also because I like you, respect you and enjoy spending time with you."

Blair considered him, admitting to herself that there was something different about Oz, that he really didn't fit the mold she'd created for him so long ago. But that didn't mean there could ever be anything between them.

Because he was right. He would only hurt her. Possibly Addy, too.

She forced a smile onto her numb face. "Friends it is. For Dr Talbot's sake."

She wasn't looking for a man in her life, but one could never have too many friends, could one?

Or was she fooling herself that they could ignore the sparks between them and just be friends?

CHAPTER SIX

Oz Manning might be completely undateable, but he was turning out to be a better friend than Blair would have thought.

That night they sat on Dr Talbot's back porch, enjoying the gentle breeze blowing off the Gulf, bringing the scent of the sea with it. The sliding glass door leading into the house was open so they could hear anyone who awakened.

Addy had played with Boo-boo until they'd both run out of energy, talked Dr Talbot's ear off until the man dozed and, when she'd finally sat still, had fallen asleep curled next to him. Stephanie had gone home shortly thereafter, leaving Blair and Oz virtually alone.

They'd been talking for hours.

"I owe so much to Dr Talbot," she told Oz. "When I first came to Madison Memorial, I worked wherever they needed me. My long-term goal was to work in the cardiac unit, but I was so nervous my first day there. I'd heard horror stories about what a bear Dr Talbot was and, of course, I'd been assigned to work directly with him."

Blair smiled at the memory.

"Instead of being a grizzly, he taught me more about

cardiac nursing in a week than the entire time I was in school." She'd soaked up every tidbit, every drop of knowledge. "Thanks to his request that I be his personal nurse, I worked hands-on with him from almost the time I graduated from nursing school."

"He's a brilliant teacher." Oz stared into the dark backyard. "The best."

"He insisted I have formal cardiac training." She might have gotten a certificate from the school, but the class hadn't taught her anything Dr Talbot hadn't already shown her. "Whoever permanently takes his place—God, I hate the thought of him never returning to the hospital—I'll be qualified to work with them."

"You won't have problems keeping up with any heart surgeon, Blair. You're an excellent cardiac nurse."

Warmth spread through her at his praise.

"Thanks. If anything new comes up, I'll learn." She looked up at the stars. Why did it feel so easy to tell Oz all these things when just the night before, she had still been professing not to like him? Why was she telling him about herself? Why did doing so feel so right?

Did the label of "friend" really make that much of a difference? Or had this ease been there all along but masked by the barriers thrown between them in order to protect her heart?

"You enjoyed school?"

She nodded. "I love learning. Had it not been for Reesee and Addy, I'd have gone further with my education. Perhaps obtaining a master's or a doctorate degree in acute care. I still may go back at some point."

"Dr T mentioned that you raised your sister."

"In many ways, we raised each other." Blair stared

at a tiny plane's light moving across the sky. "My mother died when I was nineteen. I moved out of my dorm, got an apartment and convinced a judge to give me custody of Reesee. She was thirteen at the time."

"There wasn't anyone else to take her in?"

"If you mean, was her father around, the answer is no. He wasn't. My mother was a good woman and a good mother, but she had a tendency to become involved with men who didn't stick around." Just like Blair. "The state was going to put Reesee into foster care. I couldn't bear that. Besides, I wanted her with me. We've always been close."

"You've been a blessing to her."

"As she's been to me." Feeling his gaze on her, she elaborated. "Less than a year after I got custody of Reesee, I gave birth to Addy. Without Reesee's support and unconditional love, I don't know where I'd be."

"You'd be fine, Blair, because you're strong, a survivor."

Yes, that was what she'd often told herself. But she rested her head against Oz's shoulder, just to see how it would feel to lean on someone. A *friend*.

Silence enveloped them. Blair felt no need to speak, and instead soaked in the sounds around them. Insects. The sea. A car off in the distance. She soaked in Oz's strength rather than feign any false sense of bravado.

She wasn't strong, wasn't brave. She'd simply done what had needed to be done. She'd promised to take care of her sister, and she had. Just as she'd taken care of Addy from the moment she'd discovered the precious life growing inside her body.

Chris had never been a part of Addy's life, had never shared any of Blair's joy or fears. How could he when he'd died mere weeks before Blair had discovered her pregnancy?

Why was she bothering with the past? A total waste of her time. She needed to focus on the future. On getting Reesee through college and making sure Addy had a healthy, normal start in life.

Whatever normal was.

Probably not a household of three females and an adopted grandfather figure who was fighting for his life.

Then there was Oz.

Where did he fit into the picture?

As her new friend?

His kiss had felt more than friendly. Way more. Yet she agreed that a relationship between them would never work. She didn't have time for a relationship. Particularly not with a man who had no plans to stick around. That would be asking to get hurt and wasn't that Oz's reputation with women anyway? To leave them broken-hearted?

They were better off as friends. Besides, being his friend was nice.

She rubbed her cheek against the soft cotton of his T-shirt, breathed in his spicy scent, liked that his arm went around her, cradling her against him, his hand resting low on her back.

Lately, everything came back to Oz in one way or another.

She couldn't escape him at work. She couldn't escape him at home as Addy chatted about him incessantly. She couldn't escape him at Dr Talbot's.

Maybe they could just be friends.

And, if they couldn't, Lord, protect her heart.

* * *

"I'm glad you came to visit tonight."

They stood next to Blair's car with Oz holding a sleeping Addy in his arms. Dr Talbot had stirred, and they'd gone into the house so Blair could bid him good-night. Addy had still been asleep curled next to him and hadn't wakened when Oz scooped her up to take her to the car for Blair.

"I enjoyed tonight, too." Blair glanced up at the sky, at the brilliant stars sparkling down at her. She marveled at the world around her. At how tiny she was in the grand scheme of the universe. Yet, in that moment, standing so near Oz with her daughter safely tucked into his arms, she could believe the world evolved around this moment. That they were meant to be. That Oz was the missing link to connect the broken lines of her heart and make her whole.

She'd obviously lost her mind.

"Dr T enjoyed seeing you." Oz smiled down at her. "He always perks up when you and Addy visit."

"We love him," Blair answered simply, wondering if she was imagining that Oz was procrastinating saying good-night. Did friends do that?

"I'll see you in the morning? At the Heart Association center to help Stephanie?" He shifted Addy's sleeping body in his arms.

"We'll be there by nine."

"I'll bring coffee and donuts."

"Sounds good, but better add orange juice for Addy. She has enough energy without coffee."

"Right." Grinning, Oz's gaze dropped to the little girl he held. "She's something else, isn't she? You're blessed, Blair. Addy is a special little girl. Just like her mother."

Why did his compliment settle in her belly and

blossom outward, spreading warmth throughout her entire being?

"Thank you." Blair stared at him in the starlight.

Silence stretched.

"I guess you should put her in her seat so I can take her home."

"Yes."

Blair turned, opened her car door and moved aside to let him deposit her sleeping daughter into the car. The interior light shone bright and the open door dinged. Addy stirred, looked at Blair with bleary eyes, then dozed off again while Oz struggled to get the safety straps properly latched.

"Let me." She stepped close and popped the pieces together with the ease of having done so a thousand times.

"Right," Oz said self-derisively at how easily she'd done what he'd struggled with.

She shut the car door, but made no move to go around to the driver's side. She and Oz stood close. Close enough to feel his body heat. Close enough that she fought filling her lungs with his wonderfully male scent.

Friends, she reminded herself again. They were going to be friends.

"I should go."

"You should." He cupped her face, tracing his thumb along her cheek.

Her pulse tapped against her throat. *Yes, yes, yes*, it shouted.

"Addy," she whispered, not quite sure what else to say, but knowing she needed a reminder of why she should go, of why she and Oz could only be friends, because her body had completely forgotten.

"Right." He let go of her chin and rammed his hands into his pockets. "Good night, Blair. I'll see you in the morning."

Oz balanced the bag of donuts, the tray of coffee cups and juice, and opened the door to the Heart Association with his shoulder.

He'd already pushed Dr Talbot in his wheelchair into the building. Stephanie and Blair had made a fuss, taking over the moment the older man was inside the building. Oz had gone back for their breakfast and to park his SUV.

Stepping inside the building, he took in the scene before him. Addy leaned in, whispering something to Dr T, eliciting a smile from him as only the little girl could. Stephanie watched with longing in her eyes—longing that bespoke of feelings much deeper than friendship. Blair was looking at Oz, but quickly glanced away when their gazes met, pretending she hadn't been watching him.

He'd wanted to kiss her last night. Badly.

But he'd been serious when he told Blair they should only be friends.

If he got involved with Blair, he'd hurt her and then where would that leave them?

No matter how much he wanted Blair Pendergrass—and he did want her—he couldn't have her. Blair was a white picket fences and PTA meetings kind of woman, a mother. He might not be the playboy he had once been, but he was no saint. He didn't plan to commit to a woman. Ever. Manning men shouldn't commit.

They couldn't commit even when they'd vowed to do so.

As long as Oz lived, he'd never do to a woman what his father had done to his mother. Oh, yeah, if he and Blair became involved he'd hurt her, hurt Addy. He suspected he wouldn't forgive himself easily for those transgressions.

"Here, let me take some of that." Stephanie reached for the tray of drinks. "Oz, this coffee smells heavenly. I swear you're an angel."

An angel? He wanted to laugh at the absurdity of it. He was no angel. Far from it.

His gaze met Blair's. Fire burned low in his gut.

Hellfire.

No, he wasn't a saint or an angel.

Far, far from it.

"Please, Mommy, can we go to the beach?"

They'd finished hammering out the fine details of the fund-raiser. Dr T had grown tired. Oz had loaded him into his SUV. The girls had followed them to Dr T's house.

After having been indoors all morning, they sat outside on the back patio. The sun shone. A soft breeze blew in from the sea. It was a gorgeous day.

"The beach?"

"Please." Addy danced around, exhibiting so much barely contained energy Blair didn't have the heart to say no. After all, Addy had been wonderful all morning.

"I'll stay with Ted. You three run along and have fun." Stephanie motioned for Oz to go too.

"Sounds good." Standing, Oz stretched his arms above his head.

Oz and Blair walked the block over to the beach. A well-sunscreened Addy skipped hand-in-hand between them. Once at the beach, they strolled along the edge of the water, picking up shells and checking out anything that happened to wash up along the surf. Mostly seaweed and unfortunate jellyfish.

Addy wiggled her toes in the sand and let the waves wash up around her feet. But she stared at the gently swelling waves longing to plunge straight in—longing Blair wouldn't give in to. Not today, with Oz with them. He saw things others failed to and might see how Addy being in the water turned Blair into a basket case.

She did her best to hide her fear of the sea, to never let that fear bleed over onto her daughter. That didn't mean Blair didn't struggle any time Addy was more than toe deep in the water. Luckily, they hadn't brought suits with them, limiting their excursion to the shallows and saving Blair from having to make explanations.

"Look, Dr Oz." Stooping for a closer look, Addy pointed to a blue jellyfish with short tentacles stretched out along the wet sand.

"Remember not to touch," Blair warned.

"It's breathing." Addy excitedly motioned at the jellyfish.

Sure enough, the sea creature moved.

Eyes huge, Addy tugged on Oz's hand. "We have to save him. We have to."

Oz looked to Blair for help.

"Addy, honey." She moved close to her daughter. "Once he's washed up on the beach like this, there's not a way to save him. He'd die even if we put him back into the water."

"But we have to try," Addy pleaded. She gave Oz her most appealing expression. "We just have to."

Oz wrapped around Addy's little finger right before Blair's eyes.

"Okay, Pipsqueak, let's see what we can find to rescue this guy with because we aren't touching him. You know why not, right?"

Addy nodded. "Because he stings."

They searched the beach for something they could safely move the jellyfish into the water with. A boy about the same age as Addy was building a sand castle several meters away. Running to him, Addy worked her big green-eyed magic. Blair wasn't surprised when he offered his bright orange plastic shovel and pail. Grinning, Addy turned to Oz, proudly showing him her wares, and introduced her new friend.

"This is Pete. He's going to help save the jelly."

Blair smiled at the boy.

"Okay, Addy, Pete, let's see what we have here." Oz examined the plastic shovel and pail. The jellyfish's body would easily fit in the pail, but the tentacles would be problematic if they weren't careful.

"What do you think? Should we shovel him up and carry him to the water, or do we put him in the pail?"

Addy and Pete studied the situation. "The pail," they said in unison, then giggled at their timing.

"I get to save him since it was my idea," Addy pointed out in a very grown-up voice to her new friend.

Standing close, Oz handed Addy the shovel.

Bottom lip tucked between her teeth, she concentrated on using the shovel to carefully scoop up the jellyfish. By going beneath the sand, she managed to maneuver it onto the shovel. But when it came to lifting her cargo, she looked perplexed, trying to figure out how she was going to transfer the jellyfish into the pail without burying the creature in sand.

"Maybe I could carry the shovel directly into the water," Oz suggested, looking relieved at the prospect of taking the shovel from Addy.

Addy and Pete looked at each other in question, then nodded. Oz tossed his cell phone, wallet and keys to Blair. With care, he took the shovel from Addy.

The keys held Oz's warmth, as did the worn leather wallet and phone. Blair slid all three into her shoulder bag, only letting her fingers linger a moment on the items still warm from his body heat, knowing she was sad and pathetic that her fingers had lingered at all.

When the two kids went to follow Oz into the water, Blair held out her hand, restraining them. "Sorry, guys, but Oz has to go into the water alone. The jelly won't mean to, but if you're in the water, he might accidentally sting you."

Addy and Pete sighed their disappointment at not being able to go farther into the water with Oz, but didn't argue. Neither liked the prospect of being stung.

Hands on hips, Addy murmured to her new friend, "He wouldn't really sting us 'cause we saved him and he knows we're his friends."

Pete agreed.

Watching for the right moment to avoid an incoming wave, Oz walked as far into the water as he could without completely soaking his shorts.

Blair could see him contemplating how he was going to put the jelly into the water without the creature washing back toward the shore, possibly stinging him in the process, but most definitely disappointing the two little rescuers. Finally, a larger incoming wave decided for him. Not having time to spare, Oz held the shovel as far away from him as possible and lowered the jellyfish into the water.

The moment the jellyfish was free Oz leaped toward the shore, the wave crashing in around his legs, soaking the hem of his shorts and splattering him completely.

"Dr Oz, you didn't check to make sure he swam away." Addy frowned, hands fisted on her slim little hips. "You need to swim and check on him."

"Oz can't swim out to check on the jelly." Just watching that wave come in around him had closed Blair's throat. She'd known the water wouldn't do more than crash around his legs, but in her mind she'd seen the water grabbing hold and dragging Oz out to sea, claiming him.

"Dr Oz can't swim?" Addy looked disappointed, her lower lip pouty. "Didn't his mommy put him in lessons, too?"

"I can swim, Pipsqueak." Oz took his cell phone, keys and wallet back from Blair's outstretched hands. "I just don't have a suit."

"Addy, the jelly is long gone by now." At least, Blair hoped so. The kids would be upset if their rescuee washed ashore.

Shaking away loose water droplets, Oz grinned at the two expectant children staring up at him with their arms crossed. "Who wants to build a sand castle?"

"I have a sand castle," Pete reminded them. Addy's gaze had shifted to the water, searching for a sign of the jellyfish. Fortunately, the creature hadn't washed back up on shore. Likely he would, though.

Building a sand castle sounded like the perfect distraction.

"I do," Blair said, reaching for Addy's hand. "We love sand castles, don't we, Addy?"

With one last lingering look at the water, Addy turned to her new friend. "Do you want to make another castle with us? I'm a good sand castle maker."

For the next hour they worked on building the world's greatest sand castle.

"I wish I had my camera," Blair mused, surveying their efforts. With the kids' help Oz had dug a moat around the castle and connected it to the neighboring castle Pete's parents had built that was also complete with an outlining moat.

"Yeah," Oz agreed. "Today is one of those memories you want to lock away to pull out on a rainy day."

That summed up her feelings perfectly.

Because Blair knew she'd cherish this day long into her future. That she'd savor the memory long after Oz had gone back to his real life.

Surprising her, Oz pulled out his fancy-looking cell phone and snapped a photo of where she sat next to Addy.

Blair's hands went to her face. "I meant that I wanted a picture of all of you. Not me."

"You should have said so. Too late now." He looked totally unrepentant. His blue eyes met hers, glittered as brightly as the sea. "You want to take my picture with Addy?"

Addy jumped up, sending a spray of sand in every direction. "I want to take a picture, Dr Oz."

"You don't want to be in the picture, Pipsqueak?"

She shook her head, reaching for his phone. "I want

to take the picture. Mommy lets me take pictures, don't you, Mommy?"

Before Blair could explain, Oz was showing Addy which button to push and how to focus his phone camera. "What do you want to take a picture of, Pipsqueak?"

"You and Mommy."

Uh-oh. Blair's gaze met Oz's. He just shrugged, sat down in the sand next to her, wrapped his arm around her waist and grinned.

Right then and there Blair decided she'd been in the sun too long. Had to be. Why else would she be having a heatstroke? Her insides had definitely caught fire.

"Smile, Mommy." Addy's lips twisted with great concentration. "Say cheeseburger."

Blair started to force a smile, but Oz's fingers trailed across her ribs, tickling her and eliciting a real laugh at the exact moment Addy snapped the button.

"Oh, that's a good one." Addy stared at the photo she'd taken, then held the phone out for Oz and Blair to see.

Oz looked handsome as ever with a mischievous grin on his face. The photo had captured a lightness in Blair's expression she didn't recall having seen in a long time. The photo made her look young, carefree, really happy. Her gaze had cut to Oz and laughter spilt from her mouth while she squirmed away from him.

They looked like a couple.

"Definitely a keeper," Oz agreed with Addy's assessment, saving the photo to his phone before allowing her to snap a photo of Pete and the sand castles.

Oz's conversation with Latham Duke popped into Blair's head. A keeper. And Oz was a catch-and-release man.

Their gazes met, held. Was he remembering too? Was that why his expression had turned serious?

Looking away, he tweaked Addy's nose. "I'll have the pictures printed for you, Pipsqueak."

Somewhere down the beach someone was cooking out and the scent of hamburgers drifted on the breeze.

Blair's stomach growled.

Oz looked at where she sat and grinned. "Hungry?"

Had her belly really just growled that loud? Blair burst out laughing. "A little."

Standing, she brushed the sand from her shorts.

"I am a lot." He reached for Blair, letting her pull him to his feet. His hand lingered on hers, his thumb tracing over her flesh. His gaze danced mischievously, his lips twitched, but his hand fell away.

Dozens of emotions roared to life inside her, growling in protest much louder than her stomach had. Unfortunately, the emotion she recognized most was loss at Oz's hand no longer touching hers. Also, sadness that nothing could ever happen between them. They were too different. Not only that but, sooner or later, Oz would leave to go back to Rochester and his playboy life.

And they were friends.

"Come on, Pipsqueak." He tugged on Addy's pigtail. "It's time for us to feed your mom."

Addy hated to say goodbye to her new friend, but she finally waved to Pete and his parents.

When they arrived back at Dr Talbot's, Oz popped turkey burgers onto the grill. Stephanie, Addy and Blair worked in the kitchen putting together whatever they could find to go with burgers.

When the burgers finished cooking, Oz placed the platter on the picnic table.

"Come and get 'em," he called with a cowboy twang, despite the fact they all stood within a few feet of him.

Addy giggled at the goofy way he'd said it. Blair just rolled her eyes.

Stephanie filled a plate for Dr Talbot, but he picked at his food more than he ate. Stephanie coddled him, fussing over him with great ado, even offering to cut up his food and feed him. He gave her a dirty look. Otherwise, he smiled and seemed to enjoy the evening, although fatigue was written all over his face.

Other than for doctor appointments, he rarely left his house these days. With the trip to the Heart Association this morning, spending the afternoon with Stephanie, and now their cookout, he'd had a long day.

Oz stepped onto the back porch and sat down in the lawn swing with Blair. He'd been playing with Addy and Boo-boo, but the dog now rested at Dr Talbot's feet.

"What were you so serious about when I came over here?"

"I was thinking about Dr Talbot."

Oz's gaze settled where Dr Talbot sat with Addy curled in the crook of his arm, reading him a story more from memory than ability to interpret all the words. "He's a grown man, Blair. Whatever he decides, we'll support him. It's his decision to make, not ours."

"But—"

"I don't want him to die any more than you do."

Blair flinched at the anger in his voice, but he didn't seem to notice.

"There's no guarantee the Xabartan would work.

Don't you think I'd have him in Rochester if there was? But there isn't. There's no way of knowing if he'd have complications and die sooner." Seeming to realize he'd lost his cool, Oz inhaled deeply, sent her an apologetic look. "Whether or not we ever find out is his decision. Not ours. Let up on him, Blair."

"There's no guarantee the Xabartan wouldn't work. He should try." He had so many reasons to want to live, so many people who wanted him as part of their lives. "He has to try, Oz. He has to."

His expression softening, Oz reached for her hand and gave a comforting squeeze. "You can't put pressure on him to do what you want, rather than what he wants. We have to honor his wishes."

Blair's gaze dropped to where Oz held her hand. Part of her wanted to pull away, to make sure no one noticed. She didn't want to answer awkward questions. Did friends hold hands like this? But Dr Talbot and Stephanie didn't have to see her and Oz holding hands to know something had changed between them.

Something had changed.

From the moment he'd kissed her in the hospital hallway, the moment they'd declared themselves friends, the way Blair looked at Oz had changed.

Or maybe it hadn't.

Maybe she'd just quit fighting the inevitable.

She was attracted to Oz.

Not that she was crazy enough to act on it.

She wasn't. She'd worked too long and too hard putting together a good life for her family to risk it on a man like Oz.

Only, since coming to Alabama this trip, Oz hadn't

seemed nearly as bad as she'd painted him and she kept forgetting he wasn't a man to trust with her heart.

Amidst a bevy of laughter, Addy chased a revived Boo-boo around the backyard. Blair caught her daughter in her arms, sweeping her little body off the ground and tickling her until Addy begged for mercy.

His eyes never straying far from Blair, Oz moved a lawn chair near Dr T's wheelchair. "Stephanie's still inside," he told his friend. "She had a few phone calls to make."

"Are you sleeping with Blair?" His friend's gaze didn't waver. Dr T had never beaten around the bush. Getting straight to the heart of a matter was one of the things Oz admired about his friend. Usually.

"No."

Dr T eyed him for a minute, then rephrased his question. "Have you had sex with Blair?"

Oz grinned. He couldn't help himself. Dr T in the role of overbearing father seemed inappropriate when the man had once patted Oz's back for his sexual prowess. Perhaps that had been for an outraged Selma's benefit. Dr T had loved to tease his wife. Selma had threatened that someday Oz's womanizing ways would catch up with him and he'd meet a nice girl and settle down.

Oz's gaze shifted to Blair. Selma had been right about one thing. He had met a "nice girl," but he had no plans to settle down. Ever. Why would he do that to someone he liked?

He liked Blair. A lot. Too much.

"No. Nor do we have any plans to have sex. We're friends."

That was all they would ever be. Unfortunately.

"Blair's not like the women you date."

"She's not," Oz conceded. "Which explains why we're not dating."

Blair was different. Better. Addictive. He wanted her more than any woman. Which scared him a little. Blair's lack of experience made her no match for him. He could have her if he wanted her. He knew that. But she'd regret it afterwards. So would he.

He couldn't—wouldn't—do that to her.

"You're the first man she's let close since Chris."

Addy's father. God, he was curious about the man who'd once held Blair's heart. He was tempted to ask Dr T what he knew, but he held his tongue. Being Blair's friend didn't give him the right to pry into her past.

"Women like Blair aren't the type to play the field. Addy's father hurt her deeply. Now, she's put her whole heart into loving that little girl." Dr Talbot's gaze went to where Blair played with Addy.

Blair knelt beside her daughter, petting the dog. As if sensing his gaze, she glanced up, smiled tentatively, vulnerability and something more shining in her eyes.

Something more that was meant for him.

Desire?

A tightness Oz couldn't label constricted his chest.

"Hurting Blair is the last thing I'd want," he choked out. "Which is why we're just friends and why we'll stay just friends."

CHAPTER SEVEN

THE following Friday morning, Oz stopped by the waiting room to check on Georgia Donelson's daughter prior to going in to the cardiac surgical suite to operate on her mother's heart.

The young woman sat in a chair, hunkered down as if she carried the weight of the world on her thin shoulders. She stared straight ahead, yet he doubted she saw anything.

Memories of sitting in a waiting room, waiting on news of his father, news that hadn't been good, washed over Oz. Only Dr T had been there for him during that difficult time. No one else had understood. No one else had cared to.

"Lacey?"

"Yes? Is my mother okay? Did something happen?" the tired-looking young woman gasped, knowing enough time hadn't passed for the surgery to be complete.

"She's being prepped for surgery as we speak."

"You're the surgeon?" Worry etched her face at the unexpected visit from him.

"Yes, I'm Dr Manning."

Lacey's already pale face blanched further. He hadn't come out here to increase her stress. Quite the opposite.

"Your mother is doing great. I expect a good outcome from her surgery. She's strong."

Lacey nodded, not looking convinced.

"If you want to wait in your son's hospital room, I'll call the moment I'm finished replacing the valve."

"You're sure?"

"Positive. It'll be several hours before I'll finish, but I will call you the moment I leave the surgical suite. There's no reason for you to sit here all day. Go wait in your son's room. You'll know something just as quickly there as you will if you wait here."

Lacey nodded. "Okay. If you're sure, I'd rather wait with Caden." Still looking hesitant, she bit her lower lip. "Just don't forget to call me the moment you know something."

"I won't."

Lacey stood and headed toward the door. That was when Oz noticed Blair. His breath caught in his throat. Wearing navy scrubs, she spoke to Lacey, gave the girl a hug, then turned to him. And smiled.

If he'd thought he couldn't breathe before, he was totally hypoxemic now.

"What are you doing here?" he asked, joining her.

"Apparently the same thing you are. Checking on Lacey."

"I didn't want her to sit here all day when she needs to be with her son."

Blair nodded. "That's exactly what I thought. I came to tell her I'd call the moment the surgery ended so she could come back to the cardiac unit then."

"Great minds think alike." Oz smiled.

"Apparently we do, too."

Natural and unguarded, her smile literally stole his breath.

"Are you implying we don't have great minds?" He placed his hand on her back to guide her toward the cardiac unit so they could scrub.

"You do, Dr Manning. There's no doubt about that. As for me—" she shrugged "—well, I get by."

Oz wanted to ask what she meant, but Kanesha stepped around the corner. A pencil-thin black brow arched high when she saw Oz's hand on Blair's back.

Not meeting the nursing director's amused gaze, Oz let his hand fall away in the hope of protecting Blair's reputation from gossip, and headed into surgery.

Georgia Donelson's pulmonic valve repair had gone without a hitch. The woman was now in ICU recovering. Oz at her side, Blair went to the pediatric floor and told Lacey the good news.

Although relieved the day had gone so well, Blair was nonetheless grateful when her shift came to an end and she stood in the break room, gathering her things.

"I just don't see how I can, Reesee," she said into her cell phone, glancing at her watch as she clocked out. "I'm supposed to sit with Dr Talbot tomorrow night so Oz can go out with friends. This is the first time in weeks that he's made any plans, so I hate to cancel on him." She'd been surprised when he'd asked her about sitting with Dr Talbot, had wondered if he'd wanted her to know of his social plans. Was he going on a date? she'd wanted to ask, but had bitten her tongue. She had no right to ask about his personal life. "Plus, I have Addy."

Reesee wasn't giving up easily. Her sister never did.

Blair sighed. "I know that it's not every day you come across second-row concert tickets, but it's just too short notice. I want to go. You know I want to go. But I can't."

"Stephanie is planning to visit with Dr T tomorrow night, too," Oz said from behind Blair, causing her to turn. "I'm sure she wouldn't mind staying with him until I return."

What was he doing in the break room? She'd figured he'd already left the hospital.

"I can watch Addy for you," he added, surprising Blair.

Oz babysit Addy? Her heart skipped a beat. She was so particular about whom she left her daughter with. There was Reesee, the neighbor lady who helped watch Addy prior to her starting school, a lady from church and Stephanie on the rare occasion, and that was it. She'd never left her daughter with anyone else other than schoolteachers.

Addy adored Oz, so that wouldn't be a problem. But to watch her late into the night? Why did the thought make Blair's stomach twist into knots?

"That is, if you trust me," he added, probably thinking of Addy's cut knee.

"It's not that." She put her hand over the phone's mouthpiece. "You don't have to watch her."

"I know, but like you said, it's not every day your sister gets offered second row tickets to see the concert of the year!" He grinned. "You should go. Addy will be fine."

Blair was torn. She wanted to say yes, but could she? Oz wouldn't ever intentionally hurt Addy, but what did he know about taking care of rambunctious five-year-olds? Plus, he'd asked her to sit with Dr T so he could have a rare free evening.

"I can't impose on your plans like that."

"My plans are nothing that Addy couldn't go to with me. Just an evening out with some friends."

So he wasn't going on a date. Why did that relieve the dull ache that had settled in her chest when he'd mentioned his plans?

"Blair, I can hear what he's saying," Reesee pointed out. "You have to go. Tell him yes right now," she demanded through the phone. "It's been forever since we had a night out together, just you and me. You love music. For once, just let loose and have some fun just for you. Say yes because I'm not taking no for an answer."

Her sister was right. She worked, cared for Dr T, worked on the fund-raiser and rarely did anything for the fun of it. Usually, when she did, that fun centered around Addy. How long had it been since she'd done something just for her? Just because it was what she wanted to do?

Blair eyed Oz, wishing her heart didn't jump so. "You're sure you don't mind watching her?"

A mischievous look twinkled in his eyes. "If you don't say yes, I'm going to ask your sister if I can go with her. For her personal virtue, you'd best tell her yes."

Having heard him, Reesee laughed. "I'd take him, too. Addy told me he's hot."

Blair's face heated. Addy had said that? Dear heavens, where had her daughter heard that expression? At school? Or from her aunt Reesee?

"Gee, you'd best count me in. I can't have Oz sullying your virtue."

But the way he was looking at her made Blair wonder if she wished he'd sully hers.

The smile on Blair's face made Oz's head spin. When she pressed the end button on her phone and slid it back into her scrub top pocket, she glowed.

"You enjoy the music that much?" he asked, unable to stop smiling in return.

Her green gaze widened. "Don't you?"

"As much as the next guy, I suppose." Oz leaned against the break room wall. God, she was beautiful. Sexy. Amazing. Intelligent. *Totally off-limits.* "I like his early stuff best."

"Anything he sings is phenomenal. He just has that raspy voice that pulls me right in." Blair grabbed her personal items. "Are you going to be at Dr Talbot's tonight?"

"Yep. Stephanie's coming by later, but it'll just be me and him for dinner. Unless you and Addy plan to stop by."

Why did he hope she'd say they would?

For that matter, why had he just agreed to babysit Blair's daughter? True that the little girl had him wrapped around her little finger, but offering to babysit crossed a line Oz didn't cross.

Ordinarily.

So why had he?

Hadn't he asked Stephanie to sit with Dr T and Addy so he could ask Blair to go out with him and his friends? So why had he offered to take Addy with him? Why had he changed his plans like that? To *babysit?* Him? Mr Playboy Confirmed Bachelor and happily so. Babysitting.

Why did he suspect he'd babysit a dozen nights just to see that smile on Blair's face?

"Of course we'll be by. I want to spend as much time with Dr Talbot as possible."

He understood. Dr T looked weaker and weaker each day. Oz suspected the older man wouldn't be with them much longer if something didn't give soon. He just hoped his friend lived long enough to attend the fundraiser, to see how many people turned out to show their love and support.

"Addy and I made a banana pudding last night." Dr T's favorite dessert. "Do you need me to bring anything else?"

"Nope. Where are you parked?" Oz followed Blair from the break room.

Blair's face pinched. "Actually, Reesee has my car today. Hers wouldn't start this morning and I let her take mine to Birmingham. I caught a taxi."

She'd taken a cab?

"You should have called me." He pushed the elevator down button. "I'd have picked you up this morning."

"It wasn't that big a deal."

"I'll drive you home."

He could tell she wanted to argue, but then she smiled. "Thanks. That's a friendly thing to do."

Friendly.

Yep, that was all he was feeling toward Blair.

Oz brought Blair to her apartment building, went with her to get Addy from her neighbor's and hung out while they got ready to go to Dr T's.

While Blair changed out of her uniform and took a quick shower, Addy showed him her schoolwork, read him a story and told him about her day.

Warning bells sounded in his head. Warning bells that said the scene was way too cozy, way too white picket fence and domestic for Oz Manning.

But Addy's adoring eyes as she snuggled in his arms had him ignoring the warnings, had him breathing in the scent of her shampoo and listening to her jump from one subject to the next with lightning speed.

Of course, focusing on Addy allowed him to ignore the fact that Blair was just down the hallway. Showering. Because he definitely needed to ignore what knowing that did to him.

Oz tugged on his collar, mentally giving himself a cold shower, and took the book Addy had just run off to collect for them to read together. Reading about a patchwork elephant sounded like just the thing to keep his thoughts off Blair.

Or at least distract him enough that he could pretend to.

When they were ready, he drove them to Dr Talbot's. Oz and Blair cooked dinner together while Addy entertained Dr T. While the pasta boiled, Oz chopped chicken breasts into strips. When done, he grilled the strips. Blair made a gallon of sweet tea, then spread garlic and butter on toast.

"Look out." Oz threw a noodle against the side of the cabinet, purposely missing Blair by inches.

She jumped back, laughing. "What's that for?"

"Don't you watch the cooking networks?" Stirring the ladle in the boiling pasta, he grinned.

"Um…no," Blair denied, eyeing him oddly. "Do you?"

"I've watched all kinds of television since moving in with Dr T. Whatever catches his eye, I watch." Oz sighed melodramatically. "He likes the cooking network. Lucky me."

"You learned to throw noodles at the cabinets from

the cooking network?" Her brow arched suspiciously. "Sounds to me like something a little boy would make up to cover for being naughty."

He raised his fingers in a scout's salute and winked. "On my honor. See." He pointed to where the noodle stuck to the cabinet. "When the noodle sticks, it's done."

"Heart surgeon. Babysitter. Noodle thrower," Blair teased. Her eyes raked over him, then returned to his, searching, asking for answers to who he really was, looking as if she'd like to peel away the layers to see the man beneath. To see the man he never let anyone see. "What other secret talents are you hiding, Dr Manning?"

Oz got the strangest urge to show Blair. To demonstrate every talent he had to the fullest of his capabilities.

Which was crazy.

Wasn't he just like his father? Didn't he forever bore with women and move on to the next? He didn't want commitment or to have a person's happiness depend upon him. He would never do to a woman what his father had done to his mother. Especially not Blair. She deserved better than a man like him.

"Oz?" Lips parted, she smiled tentatively up at him, her gaze dropping to his mouth.

She wanted him to kiss her.

If only he could without her paying the price.

"Here." He shoved the Alfredo sauce bowl at her. "Mix this."

She looked at the bowl. Looking confused, she reached for the sauce. Her fingers collided with his.

Tension sizzled back and forth.

Damn it. He didn't need this.

Oz pulled back, but only managed to slosh hot water,

splattering his finger. He wasn't sure if the burn was from the water or Blair's touch. Regardless, he yelped in pain.

"You burned yourself." She grabbed his hand and marched him the few steps to the sink to run cold water over his fingers.

Treating him like a child, she held his hand under the water for several silent minutes. Oz stared at the intent expression on her face, the concern in her eyes, absorbed the gentleness in her touch when she examined his fingers.

"It may sting for a bit, but it's only a first-degree burn. You'll be all right." She lifted his finger to her mouth and placed a kiss on the burn.

He swallowed. Hard. From the moment he'd met Blair he hadn't been all right. Not really. She'd always made him unsteady, a bit undeserving, perhaps even a tad rebellious. It was why he'd always brought a woman with him on his trips to visit Dr T. Because he'd been attracted to Blair, but had known that attraction was futile and wouldn't end well if he acted on it.

He still knew that.

That didn't keep his body from responding to her tender touch.

She dropped his hand, her gaze meeting his in embarrassment at what she'd done. "Sorry, I—"

Oz didn't plan his next move, would have denied that he was going to kiss her if someone had asked. But staring into Blair's eyes, seeing such vivid emotions flash in the green depths, seeing passion—for him—he couldn't resist, forgot all the reasons he was wrong for Blair. He lowered his head and kissed her full on the mouth, pressing her against the sink.

Damn, she tasted good.

Much better than pasta. Much better than the delicious banana pudding he'd snuck a bite of earlier.

He kissed her until he was breathless. Until she clung to him, kissing him with matching desperation. Until he knew he had to quit or he was going to lift her onto the counter and have her. Right then, right there.

Kissing Blair was one thing. Making love to her was something else altogether.

She brushed her finger over her swollen bottom lip. "A simple thank-you would have sufficed."

Oz didn't answer, just went back to their dinner.

Looked like they were having *blackened* chicken Alfredo.

Late the following night, Addy's little arms reached for Oz. "Night, Dr Oz." She stifled a yawn. "I love you."

With only the slightest hesitation, Oz bent and hugged Addy, accepting her kiss. "Night, Pipsqueak." He tucked the quilt in around her. "Sweet dreams."

Addy fell asleep almost immediately. No wonder. They'd had a great time out on his friend's sailboat. Addy had loved the sea, loved pretending they were pirates in search of treasure. She'd chattered nonstop from the time they'd gone out to the time she'd slipped on her pink pajamas from her overnight bag.

Sitting down on the edge of the bed, he stared at the sleeping little girl, battling another moment of nostalgia.

Not that he recalled ever being tucked into bed or having stories read to him. But spending the evening with Addy, feeling her genuine hug, was nice.

He'd taken her out to eat with friends, a few of whom

had ribbed him about robbing the cradle. Oz hadn't cared. He'd enjoyed his time with the little girl much more than if he'd taken a date.

Unless, perhaps, that date had been Addy's mother.

But he couldn't date Blair, he reminded himself for what seemed like the millionth time.

Not when he couldn't give her what she'd ultimately want.

He didn't do commitment.

Hadn't his father offered commitment to his mother? Just look at how pitifully that had turned out. They'd hurt each other over and over. They'd hated each other. When Oz's father had died, his mother hadn't even attended Oswald Manning's funeral.

Nor was she able to see her son without reminding him how like his father he was. In looks and personality.

Was that how he wanted Blair to view him? As an incurable playboy? Hell, she probably already thought of him in that way. In the name of friendship she'd opened up to him, treated him differently, and he liked her trust. Was he willing to compromise their relationship by pushing for more when he knew more would ultimately destroy everything?

Could he ignore their kiss?

He liked Blair, was attracted to her, and would like to pursue a relationship with her. Only, he wasn't sure how to define relationship.

In the past, his relationships consisted of his being totally upfront with the women he dated, telling them he wasn't interested in commitment or long-term. That they'd have fun for however long the attraction lasted and then they'd go their separate ways. No fuss, no mess. Crass, perhaps, but his honesty had worked and his conscience had never bothered him.

The thought of delivering Blair that same sex-without-strings spiel pricked his conscience.

She deserved better than a man only willing to have a good time today and leave her tomorrow.

His gaze dropped to Addy's innocent face.

Blair had already had a man do that to her once.

He reached out, pushed a lock of Addy's golden curls away from her cheek. She could be an angel dropped straight from heaven. No wonder Blair fought so hard to protect her from the world. With the fierce protectiveness that filled him, he could only imagine the lengths Blair would go to protect Addy.

He admired the great job she'd done raising the little girl, for providing a stable home for her sister, for being a friend a dying man could count on till his last breath. Blair Pendergrass was a woman who committed to those she cared about, no questions asked, no whining about what might have been.

Did he have any right to expect her to compromise her values to give a lost man like him a chance at redemption?

Midnight had come and long gone when Reesee and Blair returned from Birmingham. Despite the late hour, energized excitement flowed through Blair's veins. The concert had been fabulous. Their seats had been close enough to feel as if they could reach out and touch "The Boss."

They'd certainly given it their best shot.

Blair pulled out her cell phone to call Oz.

"She's fine," Reesee insisted before Blair had punched the first number. "Oz said to leave her with him rather than dragging her out in the middle of the night. Do it."

Blair shook her head. She'd never spent the night away from her daughter. Never.

"I don't want her to be a bother."

Her sister snorted. "Most likely she's been asleep for hours. You'll only wake her and Oz if you call. Besides, she's not a bother. Dr Talbot adores her and apparently Oz does, too." Reesee looked at her from the passenger seat. "What gives? You two an item?"

Careful to keep her eyes on the road, Blair shook her head. "We're just friends."

"Right," Reesee responded with a healthy dose of sisterly sarcasm. "Friends."

"We are."

"Uh-huh. Sure you are," Reesee teased. "Have you kissed him?"

Blair stared straight ahead.

Scooting forward in her seat as far as her safety belt would allow, Reesee squealed in glee. "Omigosh, you have. You've kissed Oz. That's wonderful."

"No," Blair denied, wanting to tell her sister everything and yet afraid to give voice to the burgeoning emotions threatening to burst her chest when she thought of Oz. "It isn't."

"Why not? You've been single too long and Oz seems like a nice enough guy."

"How can you say that? Before tonight, you'd never even met him."

"If you'd invite him over we could fix my not knowing him very well." Reesee twisted farther in her seat to stare at Blair. "You have to admit he's great with Dr Talbot, great with Addy, and it's obvious you like him."

Reesee was right. Blair did like him.

After all her huff and puff, she'd fallen for him.

Fallen in a not just friends way.

Which scared her.

If she was going to fall, Oz wasn't the kind of man she should fall for. A known heartbreaker. A man who women threw themselves at. A man who was a natural flirt. A man who'd be the first to admit he was commitment-phobic and enjoyed playing the field.

"There's nothing between us."

"Maybe you should remedy that, too, because there should be."

Blair shot her sister a scowl.

"It's been six years since Chris died. You've locked your heart away and I understand that. Sort of. But if you like Oz, why not give the guy a chance?"

"Oz isn't the kind of man who goes for relationships," Blair admitted, knowing she spoke the truth.

Her sister shrugged as if it were a no-brainer. "Then why not have a whatever he does go for?"

"Reesee Pendergrass!" Blair almost swerved the car off the road. "I can't believe you said that."

Her sister snickered. "Why? Because I'm still a child in your eyes? Sorry, sis, but nineteen is old enough to know you're lonely."

"I'm not lonely. I have you and Addy. And Dr Talbot."

"It's not the same as having a man in your life. You're young, Blair. Gorgeous, smart, witty. You're a fabulous mom to Addy, but it's okay for you to live a little, too."

"But…" Blair stopped.

She didn't want to give voice to what she'd been about to say.

But *she might get hurt*.

Was she so afraid of being hurt again that she'd locked her heart away? That she'd refused to acknowledge Oz as anything more than a friend despite knowing the electricity zapping between them was more than just friendly?

Was fear why she'd avoided him for years, telling herself she was avoiding him because she didn't like him, that he was like Chris?

If so, what did that say about her?

And just how far was she willing to go to confront that fear?

Blair dropped Reesee off at their apartment. Despite her sister's assurances that Addy was fine or Oz would have called, Blair insisted upon going to Dr Talbot's. Perhaps she was overly protective, but she couldn't bear the thought of not kissing Addy good-night. What if she woke during the night and Blair wasn't there?

She'd go to Dr Talbot's, check on Addy, then crawl into bed beside her daughter. Just the thought of curling up next to her warm little body, breathing in her baby shampoo scent, made Blair smile.

Going had nothing to do with Oz. Nothing to do with her realization that she'd been afraid of feeling the things he made her feel. Nothing.

Using the key Dr Talbot had given her months ago, Blair let herself into the beach house. Setting her bag onto the table in the hallway, she snuck up the stairs as quietly as she could.

Addy would be in what her daughter called the

"mermaid room." The mythically decorated room was where she and Blair always slept when they stayed over— something they'd not done since Oz had moved in.

The door stood open. Blair peeped inside. The ceramic mermaid on a rock lamp on the bedside table cast a soft glow on the pastel blue walls. On the bed, Oz lay on top of the covers with Addy beneath the covers, snoring softly and curled into the crook of his arm. She looked completely relaxed, at peace. Oz's chest rose and fell in even breaths.

Longing caught flame in Blair's belly, spreading warmth throughout her body, filling her with wants she'd long denied, wants that involved Addy having a father, someone to love her and care for her the way Blair did.

Chris had died before Blair had known of Addy's existence, but during her pregnancy she'd still dreamed of her daughter having a family. One that involved a mommy and a daddy.

She hadn't dreamed of that in years, had been content with the life they'd forged.

But she'd never witnessed her little girl tucked safely in a man's arms.

They looked…content.

As if they belonged together.

As if they belonged in Blair's dreams.

Her daughter had grown to care so much for Oz and the feeling was mutual.

Moisture pricked Blair's eyes, blurring her vision.

Reesee had been right. Addy was fine. Oz had taken good care of her. She should have trusted him, should have known he'd look out for her daughter, just as he looked out for Dr Talbot.

Despite what she'd thought she knew about him, Oz Manning was a good man.

One Dr Talbot trusted completely.

One Addy trusted completely.

One who deserved Blair's trust.

For the first time in years, Blair found herself wanting to give that trust and see if it might grow into something more.

Not wanting to disturb them, she flicked off the lamp light, turned the night-light on and pushed the door almost closed. She'd sleep on the sofa.

She'd barely made it back down the stairs before a heavy-eyed Oz appeared.

"I didn't know you were here." He sat close to her on the sofa, raking his fingers through his golden hair. "Or that you were planning to come here tonight." His gaze dropped to her concert T-shirt and he gave a sleepy grin. "How was the concert?"

Unable to suppress her pleasure at seeing him, Blair told him, enthusing over the performance and how she and Reesee had danced and sung along.

"Sounds like you had fun. I'm glad you went." He leaned his head back against the sofa, yawning. "Your daughter is something else, Blair."

"Yes, she is." Had she just slid closer to him? "She's the most precious part of my life. Did she give you any problems?"

"Only that she's smart as a whip and kept me on my toes. I swear nothing slips past her." Rubbing his hand over his face, he stretched and Blair slid another inch his way. "She soaked in every word, everything I said and did tonight."

Blair nodded. Addy was a sponge. "I'm amazed at how smart she is."

Hair ruffled, eyelids heavy with recent sleep, he grinned. "Not that you're biased."

"Just a little." His body heat lured her to curl into his arms the way her daughter had been. "I worry I'm somehow not giving her everything she needs and she's going to suffer for it. I try so hard to be all she needs."

Oz wrapped his arm around her and hugged her close. "You do a great job."

Oh, heaven. His arms felt so good. His solid chest beneath her cheek felt even better.

She snuggled closer, slipping her arm between the sofa and his lower back. She pressed her palm into the curve of his back, felt the coiled strength in his muscles. "I often wonder."

"Being a single parent can't be easy. Hell, being a parent period isn't easy, single or otherwise." His fingers traced over her free arm. "You shouldn't have to do this alone, Blair."

"Addy's father died before she was born." She gave the same answer she'd been giving for years, the same answer she gave to anyone who asked. Giving that answer to Oz seemed inadequate.

"What happened?"

Blair moistened her lips. She suspected Oz knew Addy's father had died. "Chris died about a month before I found out I was pregnant with Addy."

"How did he die?"

Blair's throat tightened. She didn't want to talk about Chris. Not with Oz. Not with anyone. She'd never spoken of what had happened. Not ever.

She wasn't sure she could.

Blair rubbed her cheek against the comfort she found in Oz's arms, praying she'd somehow absorb his strength. "He had an accident."

Oz's hold on Blair tightened. He hadn't a right to ask about Addy's father, but the question had slipped out. He blamed his slip on the dream he'd awakened from. A dream where he and Blair were a family with Addy. Where he'd been Addy's father. Blair had been his wife. He should look at the dream as a nightmare, but instead a warm, fuzzy nostalgia had turned his brain to cotton.

Probably he was still half-asleep, and in the light of the day he'd cringe, face life's realities.

He wasn't a permanent part of Blair's life. He had no right to know the intimate details of her past.

But he wanted to know.

He wanted to know everything about her. Every little detail that made her tick. Every little detail of the man whom she'd once loved so he could figure out what had made the guy worthy of her love, worthy of the precious little girl sleeping upstairs.

"He went sailing." Blair's voice was barely above a whisper.

Sailing? Foreboding filled Oz. He'd never heard how Chris had died, had never known any of the details.

Sailing?

Oh, hell.

He'd taken Addy sailing, had let her hold the wheel as they'd watched the sunset. She'd seemed thrilled by the trip. He hadn't seen any signs of grief or fear, but hell, what did he know about kids? Other than Addy, he hadn't spent time around anyone underage since he was underage.

Then again, her father had died before she was born.

"There were warnings of an incoming storm, but that never stopped Chris. He thought he was invincible." She drew in a deep breath, appeared torn with memories. "He responded to another ship's distress flare. He was trying to get the family moved over to his boat, but the two kids ended up in the water. The waves had gotten high. The wind was nasty. Even with their life jackets, they didn't stand a chance of making it back to the boat. Chris went in after them." She squeezed her eyes tightly shut, opened them and continued. "He managed to get one of the kids, a little boy, to his boat, where his parents were able to lift him to safety." She shuddered. "Chris and the girl didn't make it. There wasn't anything anyone could do."

He wrapped his arm tighter around her, kissed the top of her head. "I'm sorry, Blair."

Her pain was palpable.

The man had died saving a kid's life and trying to save another.

"He died a hero." No wonder Blair had loved him.

"A hero." Blair's lips pursed. "Yes, Chris died a hero."

The way she said the words made Oz think there was more to the story than what Blair was saying. But he wouldn't push. Not with her already looking so exposed, with her body trembling against him.

"He wasn't alone on his sailboat."

"Not alone?"

"He was with his wife," she confessed in a hoarse whisper.

Oz pulled back, staring at her in surprise. "His wife?"

"Yes."

"Addy's father was married?" Surely he'd somehow misunderstood? "You were having an affair with a married man?"

That didn't fit with his image of Blair. Didn't fit with the image she'd painted of Addy's father.

Tense against him, Blair nodded. "I know that makes me a bad person. I've never denied that. But I honestly believed he was divorced." She swallowed hard. "He wasn't. When he died, I was devastated. I'm not sure which hurt the most—that he was gone or that he'd been lying to me all along. I loved him so much I thought I wanted to die, too."

He held her, let her take her time before continuing.

"Like a fool, I went to his funeral. His wife publicly humiliated me in front of his friends and family. *His wife.*" She spat the words from her pursed lips. "She denied me the right to attend Chris's funeral. I only wanted to say goodbye. When I broke down, she..." Blair quit speaking, buried her face in her hands. "She had the right to send me away. I know she did, that she was hurting, and I shouldn't have gone. I understand that now."

Oz had no right to judge her. Addy's father was another story altogether. The man's dishonesty had put the women in his life in a horrible situation. His wife and Blair. "Of course you wanted to pay your last respects to his memory. That was only natural, Blair."

She wiped at her eyes. "Later, when I discovered my pregnancy, I told his parents. I'd never met them outside of that day at the funeral, but Chris was an only child. I thought they had a right to know." Raw pain bled from every word. "They told me they wanted nothing to do with me—" Blair's voice broke "—or my bastard child."

Oh, hell. Oz's fingers curled into a fist. How could anyone have been so cruel? Especially when they were talking about the child of their recently killed son? Their grandchild?

When they were talking about *Blair's* child?

"I think they were worried I planned to go after child support." Blair wiped at her eyes.

"They were idiots," Oz assured her. "Addy is a beautiful child, inside and out. Any man would be proud to call her his kid."

She looked up at him with red-rimmed eyes. "Would Chris have?"

Vulnerability bled from her soft question. Vulnerability that hinted at a need for validation, a need to know that she wasn't the bad person she'd been cast.

"He hadn't divorced his wife. He'd told me he was divorced, Oz, that he loved me. I was in love with him, and I was nothing more than a booty call."

"You can't know that."

"I do." Blair gave an embittered laugh. "If I'd been the only one, I might believe he loved me, that he'd have really filed for divorce when he discovered my pregnancy." She looked away, clearly embarrassed. "I wasn't. According to his wife, he had several women on the side, but they had enough class not to show up at his funeral." She sniffled. "I don't know how many, just that I wasn't anything special."

"He was an idiot." A complete and total idiot. How could a man have Blair's love and cheat on her? If Blair loved him, he'd… Hold up. What was he thinking?

He wouldn't do anything.

Because he didn't do love.

Didn't do commitment.

He also didn't deceive women the way Addy's father had deceived Blair.

"I'm sorry he hurt you."

"Me, too." She forced a smile to her face. "His betrayal destroyed my feelings for him, but no matter how hurt I was, I can't regret what happened. Without Chris, I wouldn't have Addy. She's worth everything."

Oz had the uncanny desire to pound his fist into Chris's face, into Chris's parents' faces. Into anyone's face who hurt Blair.

She was the most decent person he knew and that decency had been trampled on. She'd been through so much, yet, even now, she'd wiped away her tears and wore a smile on her lovely face. She saw the silver lining in her pain, cherished the little girl who must be a constant reminder of everything she'd been through.

"You're an amazing woman, Blair." Oz hugged her, kissed the top of her head. "Amazing."

"I've never told anyone." She looked at him in awe. Looked at him in a way that made him feel like puffing out his chest and strutting around like some crazy bird doing a mating ritual.

"Not even Reesee or Dr Talbot. They probably figured a lot of it out on their own, but I've never told anyone." She laughed a little self-consciously. "I thought admitting to what Chris had done would be hard, that I'd be embarrassed at how foolish I was to believe his lies." She placed her palm against Oz's face, stared at him with a sparkle in her eyes that made him feel like a bug under a magnifying glass.

A sparkle—he didn't know how else to describe the way she looked at him. Her eyes glittered like multifaceted emeralds.

"But I don't." She caressed his cheek. "Not with you."

Oz tried not to wince, wasn't sure he was successful.

More than anything, he didn't want to hurt Blair the way Addy's father had.

He'd rather end things now than add to the heavy burden her heart carried, thanks to the jerk she'd once fallen in love with.

The way she was looking at Oz as if she was falling for him. Had any woman ever looked at him like that?

He didn't think so. Fear and disbelief battled for pole position within him.

No matter what, Blair absolutely could not fall for him.

No way did he want to be responsible for another person's heart. He'd seen the power his father had wielded over his mother's heart, had seen the devastation that power wrought.

Blair's heart needed to stay far away from the likes of him.

In the end, he'd hurt her as Addy's father had. Not by lying to her, but by his inability to commit to one woman. His entire life, he'd never committed to anyone. What did that say about him?

Just what he'd known all along—that he was his father's son.

"I'm leaving as soon as Dr T is well enough to go back to work," he reminded her, feeling desperate to crawl out from under the magnifying glass.

"Do you think he'll be able to go back to work?" She

stared at him, the sparkle shimmering, enticing him to look closer. "Really?"

No, he didn't.

Neither did Dr T. They'd talked earlier in the evening and Oz would be working out a notice to give the hospital time to find a permanent replacement, spending all his time with Dr T until the end came, then he'd return to Rochester.

He'd return to his home with a gaping hole in his chest where his friend's love and respect had once resided.

Pain gurgled up his chest, burning the lining of his throat.

"Oz?"

He swallowed back the burn, lost himself in Blair's soft expression, in the way her lips curled around his name. Damn, his name sounded good on her lips. Soft, sexy, raspy.

"You don't think he's going to get better, do you?" Her lower lip disappeared between her teeth in a move he'd seen Addy do a dozen times during their sailing trip.

"Miracles happen every day." He sighed, unwilling to lie. "But no, I don't think he'll go into remission. The Xabartan is his only chance and he's not willing to undergo more chemo."

He couldn't bring himself to say that he thought their friend's days were coming to a swift end.

A strangled sound escaped her lips. "You're wrong. He will get better." She trembled. "He has to get better."

"I hope so, Blair. I really do hope so." Oz held her tight. The tears she'd been wiping away since she'd started telling him about Chris flooded unchecked down her cheeks. "Regardless, we'll be here for him and make sure each day is a good one."

As painful as he found watching his friend slowly die, he would stay until the end, would ensure that Dr T didn't want for a thing, that each day was as full as possible, that when Dr T's time came he'd die knowing he was loved.

Oz held Blair while she sobbed against him, held her while she buried her face into his chest, held her when her lips sought his, seeking comfort.

He had no right to give her that comfort. Not really. Not after what she'd revealed, not when he felt her pain and ached inside.

But nor could he deny her what she needed.

What he needed.

Oz kissed her back.

Desperately.

With all the hunger that had built inside him since the first time he'd laid eyes on Blair Pendergrass years ago.

He'd wanted her then, but had known better than to dally with the woman Dr T loved like a daughter, with a woman who had a daughter, and would expect more than dinner dates and hot sex.

Oz needed to stop, to remind Blair that even if they made love, nothing would change. He needed to remind her that for him, making love was just sex, that it wouldn't mean anything beyond the physical. That after he left Madison, there would be other women because that was who he was, who all the men in his family were, as if the trait was really some genetic flaw.

He needed to do all those things, but in her kisses Oz forgot that sex was just a physical act.

Because kissing Blair felt like so much more than physical.

When her hands slid under his shirt, over his abs, along his back, Oz didn't stop her. When she tugged on his T-shirt, pulling the hem over his head, he didn't remind her that he was the womanizing scoundrel she'd once accused him of being.

Instead, he pulled her into his lap, kissed the hell out of her, over and over until every breath he took was hers.

He stood, cradling her in his arms, inadequate in so many ways to be holding such a precious woman.

Her tender kiss against his throat, her sigh of pleasure almost toppled him back onto the sofa, his legs too wobbly to support them both.

He headed up the stairs, down the hallway, striding into his room with one purpose: to claim Blair. He gently laid her on the bed, paused to turn on the bedside lamp to take in the image of her lying on the bed, waiting for him.

For him.

Because Blair was his.

She inexplicably belonged to him.

He saw it in her eyes when she looked at him, felt it in the way she touched him.

He backtracked to the door, shut and locked it in case Addy or Dr T woke.

He turned, saw Blair had taken off her Springsteen T-shirt. Revealing the ample swell of her breasts above her silky blue bra, she bent forward and shucked her shorts down her hips, revealing matching high-cut panties that made her legs look impossibly long.

Damn. Oz instantly transformed into the big bad

wolf he remembered once seeing on a cartoon. His eyes bugged, his tongue lolled out the side of his mouth, and wolf whistles blared through his brain.

She was amazing, had his already fully aroused body hardening to painful proportions.

Under his stare, her cheeks brightened. "Sorry."

"Don't be." He had no clue what she could possibly be apologizing for. "You're beautiful, Blair. Perfect."

Her lips curved in a slow smile. "Apparently your hormones are running amok and affecting your eyesight. I'm not beautiful, Oz. But when you look at me like that, you make me feel as if I am. Thank you."

"My pleasure." Oz wasn't going to argue with her. Not when there were so many other things he wanted to be doing. With her. To her. In her.

Closing the distance between them, he reached for the snap to his uncomfortably restrictive shorts.

Shedding his clothes, Oz joined Blair, kissed her, ran his palms over her curves.

When he thrust inside her, he couldn't look away, couldn't help but lose himself in her eyes.

What he saw there scared him, made him think perhaps he should run like hell.

Lying back on the bed, both of them breathless, both of them staring at the ceiling, Oz wondered what he'd done.

He shouldn't have had sex with her.

No matter how much he'd wanted to.

She deserved better than what he'd given her.

He refused to treat her the way Chris had.

He might be like his father when it came to his lack of ability to commit, but he was a better man.

Yet, what more did he have to offer Blair? He wouldn't make false promises about the future. Not when they had no future.

But how was he supposed to ignore what he'd just shared with this incredible woman? How was he supposed to forget what being inside her felt like?

He doubted he'd ever forget, that the rest of his life would be measured by the past hour.

"About this…" he began, wishing he could find the right words to let her know how amazing she was, how good he'd felt holding her, kissing her, making love to her.

To let her know that, no matter how much he wanted her, it couldn't happen again.

Blair cringed. Here it came. The speech reminding her that sex was just sex to Oz. No matter that it had felt like so much more to her.

It had been more than sex to her.

Dear Lord, she'd spilled her guts to him, had revealed how Chris had hurt her. She'd practically thrown herself at Oz, had practically begged him to make love to her, and had definitely had the most amazing sex of her life with the playboy doctor.

What had she been thinking?

So she wasn't like the svelte blondes Oz notoriously brought with him on his visits. He had wanted her. He'd been as wrapped up in their lovemaking as she had.

Hadn't he?

Every insecurity she'd ever known blindsided her.

She pulled the sheet up over her, crossed her arms in front of her breasts.

"I can't do this, Blair." He rolled onto his side, looking at her.

"It's a little late for that, don't you think?" Still staring at the ceiling, Blair battled tears. She would not cry. She wouldn't. So she clung to her anger at herself for forgetting who he was—who he really was. "We already did do this."

Now that the urgency had been curtailed, had he realized she wasn't his usual fare? Was that the problem? Had her generous hips and bosom, the fine stretch marks that marred her lower abdomen from carrying Addy turned him off? Had her enthusiasm for his touch bothered him?

"It's not that I don't still want you, Blair. I do." He reached for her, but she pulled back.

She couldn't deal with him touching her. Not at the moment. Not when her body still sang from repeated orgasms. Not when she was so aware of every breath he took. Not when he was rejecting her and her pride freely bled.

What if he'd only had sex with her out of pity? If he hadn't had the heart to reject her after what she'd revealed about her past?

Darn it, she didn't want his pity.

"I don't want to ruin our friendship."

Their friendship? Surely he wasn't going to play the friendship card? If she'd been honest with herself, she would have admitted from the beginning that they couldn't be friends. She hadn't wanted to be honest because she'd wanted an excuse to be near Oz.

Because she'd been attracted to him for years, but it had only been this trip, seeing him take care of Dr

Talbot, that she'd realized Oz's depth, and the depth of her desire.

He raked his fingers through his hair, leaving the golden tufts ruffled. "I value you too much to take you to bed for cheap sex."

Blair tried to keep from wincing, but failed.

Cheap sex. That was all she'd been to him?

Just like Chris.

"That came out wrong," Oz recanted, scooting up in the bed. She forced her gaze not to rest on his bare chest, to ignore the scattering of hair that tapered to disappear beneath the sheet.

Even now, so soon after they'd made love—had cheap sex—desire stirred in the pit of her belly.

She hated herself for it.

Cheap sex.

Humiliation washed over her. She wasn't going to let anyone embarrass her again. Not the way Chris had.

She held up her hand. "Look, you really don't have to do this. We got caught up in the moment and forgot that we barely tolerate each other under normal circumstances. I was still high from watching Springsteen and just got carried away. I know what we did was nothing more than sex."

She couldn't bring herself to say *cheap* sex. She just couldn't. Not without bursting into tears.

There hadn't been anything cheap about the way she'd felt in Oz's arms. She suspected the price she'd pay would be quite high.

"I'm leaving, Blair." He stared at her, his eyes a steely-blue. "I don't know when, but I will leave. To pretend otherwise would be wrong."

"I didn't expect you to stay. Not because of this." She hated the guilty expression on his face. Hated that he felt he had to explain himself. It wasn't as if she thought he was madly in love with her. She knew he wasn't. After all, this was Oz. He didn't do love and commitment. He did "cheap sex."

So why did her heart protest? Why did her heart argue that Oz could love her? That she was lovable? That what they shared was so much more than cheap sex? Fool, didn't she ever learn?

"Blair."

She could hear the strain in his voice. She even knew why he was making sure she understood.

Oz loved Dr Talbot and didn't want anything to upset their friend, didn't want anything to mar his last days.

She knew exactly what she had to do. The only thing she could do.

She reached over the edge of the bed and retrieved her Springsteen T-shirt from the floor. She pulled it over her head, grateful for the barrier between them. The sheet just hadn't been enough. Not when she knew Oz's well-defined naked body lay beneath it, too.

"Look—" she began, trying to sound as if she did this kind of thing all the time, as if it hadn't been six years, as if her heart wasn't gasping like a fish out of water "—I don't need explanations. Not about this. It's late. We're both tired and we acted on physical needs. Let it go. I plan to." She forced a smile to her face. A *this is really no big deal* smile. "I'm going to go sleep with Addy."

Not moving from where he lay, Oz watched her dig under the covers for her underwear. She could feel his gaze boring into her. God, where were her panties?

"I don't want you to go. Not like this." He sounded tormented, which in some masochistic way vindicated what she was doing. Yet she knew his turmoil wasn't really regarding her, but Dr Talbot.

For the same reason—for her love of the older man—she'd follow suit and say what needed to be said.

"Don't make more of this than it was, Oz. That would unnecessarily complicate our lives." She clenched her fingers over the silky fabric of her underwear. Thank God. "It's no big deal."

She was lying. Lying though her teeth. But she knew it was what she needed to say, what Oz wanted to hear.

His sigh of relief confirmed her suspicions, shattered the remaining tatters of hope in her heart.

She didn't turn around, didn't look back.

Instead, she went into the room across the hallway, slipped beneath the covers next to her daughter, and willed sleep to heal her breaking heart.

CHAPTER EIGHT

THE following morning, Blair slept later than normal and, amazingly, so did Addy.

Despite the sick feeling in the pit of her stomach, the same sick feeling that had caused her to lie in bed for hours before finally drifting off to sleep, Blair thanked God for her blessings. Thanked God for the precious little girl peeping at her from the other side of the bed.

Everything would be okay.

Stretching, Blair smiled at her precious daughter. "Morning, sleepyhead."

Yawning, Addy grinned, her tongue pushing through the gap created by her missing top tooth. "I didn't know you were here."

"I missed you."

But oh, if she'd known what the night would bring perhaps she'd have stayed home with Reesee.

Facing Oz this morning wouldn't be easy. Thank God she hadn't admitted that her feelings were much more than physical.

How much more she wouldn't allow herself to contemplate.

She'd slept in her Springsteen T-shirt and underwear.

She hadn't brought extra clothing, so she put her shorts back on and slid into her sandals.

When she finished, Addy had dressed and stood with her brush and elastic bands. Blair brushed out Addy's golden locks and plaited her hair into a single French braid down the back of her head.

When they went downstairs, Stephanie was sitting at the kitchen table. As usual, she'd brought breakfast. Knowing Addy had stayed the night, she'd brought extra.

"Blair, honey—" the older woman said, giving the little girl a hug "—I didn't realize you were here or I'd have brought you a cinnamon streusel."

Blair's favorite. Just as well, she might throw up if she ate a thing.

She walked over to Dr Talbot and kissed his cheek. "How are you this morning?"

"I'm here." He shot an annoyed look toward Stephanie. "She's force-feeding me as usual."

"If you'd eat, I wouldn't have to force-feed you." Stephanie picked up a spoon and held it out to the older man, sitting in his wheelchair at the table. She nodded toward the box of muffins. "Help yourself, Blair. I brought extra for Addy and Oz, but he didn't eat."

Oh, Oz.

"He's gone?" Oh, no. She shouldn't have asked that. She busied herself by pouring a glass of orange juice for herself and Addy.

"He had Ted up, dressed and in the kitchen when I got here, but then he took off. He left a little over an hour ago."

When Blair turned, Dr Talbot and Stephanie were looking at her. Was what had happened written all over her face like a scarlet letter? Knowing she must look guilty, based on the growing concern in her friends' eyes, Blair searched through the box of muffins, but her mind raced.

Had Oz left to avoid seeing her this morning?

Of course he'd left to avoid seeing her.

Because he was sending the message that what had happened between them really was no big deal.

If he'd cared, wouldn't he have stuck around? Wanted to see her first thing this morning? Wanted to know how she was? How she felt?

Why did his doing exactly what she'd expected of him hurt so much?

But she knew. Deep in her heart she'd believed Oz cared about her. Cared more than his "cheap sex" comment let on. Cared about her as a person, as a woman, as his lover, and, yes, as his friend.

He didn't. The sooner she accepted that, the sooner she quit fantasizing about a man who admitted he didn't want a relationship that consisted of more than casual sex, the better.

"Was Dr Oz going sailing?" Addy pulled the paper wrapper off the chocolate chip bran muffin Stephanie had given her.

"Sailing?" Had Blair's voice squeaked? Her gaze cut to her daughter. Why would Addy think Oz might be sailing? Had he mentioned plans to go sailing? Why would he go sailing on the day after she'd told him about Chris? That was plain cruel.

"I love sailing." Addy didn't glance up from her muffin.

Blair's stomach plummeted. Her rib cage put a death grip on her lungs. "You do?"

Addy nodded. "Sailing is awesome. Dr Oz took me. He let me drive the boat!"

Legs weak, Blair plopped into a chair.

Addy had been out on a sailboat with Oz?

She'd driven the boat?

"We watched the sun disappear, and we saw dolphins," Addy continued, oblivious to the fact Blair's blood had all settled below her ankles.

"Oz took you sailing last night? In the dark?" Did her voice sound as breathless as she felt? As panicky as she felt?

"He wouldn't let me feed the dolphins," Addy complained, her lower lip momentarily pouty as she tore off a piece of her muffin.

"You went sailing with Oz?" Blair repeated, stunned, trying not to envision Addy leaning over the boat railing to feed fish.

"We sailed into the Gulf looking for treasure," Addy informed matter-of-factly. "I got to be a pirate and Dr Oz was my first mate." She giggled at some private memory. "I want to be a sailor when I grow up and sail around the whole world bilfering and blundering."

"Pilfering and plundering," Blair automatically corrected.

Oz had taken her daughter out in a sailboat without her permission. She'd trusted him with the most precious part of her life and he'd taken her out to sea, in the dark.

How could he have been so irresponsible?

How could he not have told her when she'd revealed how Chris had died? He'd had to know, yet he'd purposely not said anything. Then he'd had "cheap sex" with her. The bastard.

"Did Dr Oz go sailing without me?" Addy's forehead wrinkled in consternation. "He promised to take Mommy and me with him the next time he went, but he didn't."

"Oz didn't mention going sailing." Stephanie stared at Blair with concern. "Just that he was going for a run, but he might have jogged to the marina. He's been talking about buying a boat someone has for sale down there."

Boo-boo, scratching at the back door, wanting to be inside the house, saved Blair from saying what she thought about Oz buying a boat. Addy jumped down from her seat to let the dog in.

"Never much cared for sailing," Dr Talbot said from where he sat at the table, still eyeing Blair.

Stephanie placed her hand over Blair's. "Are you okay? I take it you didn't know Oz was taking her out on a boat?"

"No, I didn't." Blair tried to keep her voice calm for Addy's sake, but anger erupted inside her, blowing through her with volcanic force. "But Oz Manning is going to know about how angry I am that he took my daughter out on a boat without my permission."

Sweat covered Oz's brow, his body. He'd been jogging for nearly an hour. Usually nothing cleared his head like a good run. In Rochester, he ran a route from his condo to the park and back, a little over five miles total. In Madison, with the sea air filling his lungs, the breeze whipping at his skin, he felt as if he could go on and on.

Or maybe thinking about the night before was what had him so wired.

He'd made love with Blair.

He grinned, probably looking a fool to the older

couple walking along picking up shells. Not that he cared. He felt a fool.

A fool high on life.

Last night his eyes had been opened in many ways.

Ways he'd never dreamed of seeing clearly, but thanks to Blair, he saw.

When she'd hurried from his room, he'd sighed. At first he'd thought his sigh had been in relief. But as he'd lain there, analyzing everything Blair had told him, everything they'd shared physically and emotionally, he'd realized his sigh hadn't been in relief. Instead, he'd sighed at Blair's backtracking, trying to protect her heart.

He recognized the motions well.

He had a lifetime's experience.

He'd always compared himself to his father, but wasn't that taking the safe route? Because, if he wasn't like his father, that meant he must be like his mother, who had been devastated by Oz's cheating father. He'd watched his mother's heart crumble, watched her self-destructive path, and somewhere along the way he'd decided he was like his father as a safety mechanism.

Wasn't being the cad much easier than being the victim of a broken heart?

For years, he'd operated under that misguided notion. He'd never met anyone to make him question his belief, had never met anyone to make him risk being more than a self-proclaimed cad.

Not until Blair.

While lying in the bed they'd made love in, surrounded by the scent of her on his favorite Egyptian cotton sheets, on his pillow, he'd questioned…well…everything.

The fact that he'd done more than either of his

parents, that he had committed to medical school, to Dr T, that he'd met a woman he wanted to explore the possibilities with, a woman worth taking risks with.

Mostly, he'd questioned his feelings for Blair.

From the time he'd met her, he'd recognized something different about her, about the way he treated her, felt about her. He'd thought it secondary to Dr T. Now he knew his feelings went deeper.

He wouldn't go so far as to say he was in love with Blair, but he cared for her a great deal.

More than he'd ever cared for a woman.

Knowing that she'd been hurt by his silence, that she'd run because she thought that was what he wanted, Oz had snuck across the hallway to the "mermaid room."

He'd tapped on the door, but Blair hadn't answered. He'd pushed the door open to see her curled next to Addy, fast asleep.

He'd watched her and Addy sleep, wondering how he could care so much for the two sleeping beauties. How he couldn't have realized how important they were to him. That he'd used the guise of friendship to give himself permission to be close to Blair.

He'd gone back to his room, content they'd talk when they woke. He'd risen early, anxious to tell her everything, but not surprisingly, Blair had slept in.

Not breaking from his normal routine so as not to alert Dr T or Stephanie that anything had changed, not until he and Blair had a chance to talk first, Oz had taken off for his usual run. Which was likely for the best.

When he came face-to-face with Blair again, he was going to pull her into his arms and kiss her until she was breathless and no longer spouting garbage about why they'd ended up in bed together.

They'd ended up making love because it had been inevitable. From the day they met they'd been moving in that direction.

Just the memory of making love with her had him stirring beneath his gym shorts. Hell, he was going to have to run into the cold Gulf water if he didn't get his act together.

Only taking a dip would mean being away from Blair longer and surely she was awake by now? Surely when he got back to Dr T's he'd be able to look into Blair's eyes and she'd know he wanted her, cared about her, and that for the first time in his life he wanted to pursue a committed relationship.

Blair loaded the few dirty dishes into the dishwasher and started the load. Addy was in the living room with Dr T and Boo-boo. Stephanie sat at the table, still sipping on a cup of coffee.

"Do you want to talk about it?"

Blair glanced toward her friend. Did Stephanie know what had happened between her and Oz? "About what?"

"About why you looked so upset earlier."

"Oh. That." She almost sighed in relief. When her gaze met Stephanie's she realized her mistake.

"Is there another reason you might be upset?"

Blair shook her head. "No. There isn't."

"Just that Oz took Addy sailing?"

"Yes." She pulled out the chair next to Stephanie's. "Oz should have asked before taking her out. He shouldn't have assumed something like that would be okay."

"I'm sure he watched her closely. He adores Addy."

She nodded. "That doesn't give him the right to decide to take her out to sea without my permission."

"He's an experienced sailor. Apparently, his family had a boat that he took out a lot during his younger years. Plus, he's been out several times since he's moved in with Ted."

"It's not that." Blair sighed. "I know I'm paranoid in not wanting Addy out in a sailboat, but her father died in a sailing accident."

She couldn't believe she'd just said that out loud. Perhaps telling one person made telling another easier, though, because she didn't regret her admission.

"I'm sorry, Blair." Stephanie patted her hand. "I didn't know."

"It's not something I talk about."

"I understand." Stephanie gave her hand a reassuring squeeze. "Let's go sit with Ted."

Blair glanced at her watch and nodded. "I'll visit for a short while, then I'm going to go home, shower and work on odds and ends for the fund-raiser. Can you believe it's so close?"

She and Stephanie went into the den. Addy sat on the floor brushing Boo-boo's fur. Dr T's head dipped forward, his eyes shut, his shoulders slumped.

"Is he already napping?" Stephanie sounded disappointed. "He usually doesn't nap until around noon."

Taking in his gray color, his lack of movement, Blair realized Dr T wasn't napping.

Oh, God.

No, please, no.

She rushed to his side, kneeling next to his wheelchair.

"Dr Talbot?" She shook him, relief filling her when his eyelids fluttered open, when he gasped for a breath.

He attempted to focus on her, slurred a response, then closed his eyes.

"Dr Talbot?" she repeated, grabbing his wrist and taking his pulse. Thready and erratic. She glanced at Stephanie, who was shaking his shoulder and saying his name over and over. "Call 911. Now."

Oz heard the sirens long before he rounded the corner to Dr T's street. He'd sped up. Likely he was being paranoid, but he couldn't get rid of the urgency inside him that said he needed to get home ASAP. Something was wrong.

He'd been right.

The ambulance was parked in front of Dr T's house. The front door stood wide-open. Two uniformed men carried out a body on a stretcher.

Dr T? *No!*

Oz ran the distance between him and the driveway. His chest burned from the exertion, burned from fear his friend might no longer be with him, that he hadn't been there when his friend needed him, that maybe he could have done something. He didn't slow until he stood next to the ambulance.

"What's going on?" he asked no one in particular. The two paramedics had lifted Dr T into the truck. Stephanie stood with her arms around Addy on the front porch stoop. Both of them sobbed uncontrollably.

"What the hell is going on?" he demanded, preparing to climb into the back of the ambulance. "Somebody tell me what's going on!"

Saying something he couldn't quite make out to the

paramedics, Blair stepped out of the ambulance and the men closed the door.

Pale, Blair pulled him out of the way so the emergency vehicle could back up.

"Blair!" He grabbed her shoulders. "Is he alive? What's happened? Tell me."

"Alive. Weak, thready pulse. Incoherent. In and out of consciousness." Her gaze never left the truck, never blinked. The emergency vehicle sped down the road, sirens blasting. "We've got to get to the hospital."

Oz looked down at his sweat-drenched body and shorts. "Let me grab a shirt."

As if noticing for the first time that he wore only jogging shorts, Blair's gaze ran over him. Whatever her thoughts, she only nodded.

When he came back out, Blair and Addy were gone and only Stephanie waited.

"Where's Blair?"

"She's gone to the hospital. Her sister is meeting her to take Addy home."

"Fine," Oz bit out, trying not to read anything into the fact that she'd left him. "Let's go."

CHAPTER NINE

DR TALBOT had gone into renal failure due to hypovolemia, an electrolyte imbalance and severe anemia. With IV fluids and multiple blood transfusions, he was slowly coming around.

Oz sat next to his friend's hospital bed, along with Stephanie and Blair.

Blair hadn't said a single word to him. Had barely even acknowledged his presence. Instead, she clung to Stephanie. The two women had hugged, crying, while they waited on news of their friend. The emergency room doctor had acted quickly, got treatment started, then admitted Dr T to the ICU. His and Blair's employment with the hospital hadn't hurt, but only because of Dr T's status had the three of them been allowed to stay in the room.

Oz's gaze went from the hospital bed to the woman sitting across from him. She looked devastated. Tired.

She leaned forward, her head resting in her hands.

God, he wanted to go to her. He wanted to hold her.

But without words being spoken, he knew now wasn't the time to confront their feelings for each other.

He'd rubbed her back earlier, but she'd gotten up, paced the floor.

Damn, this was all so complicated. His gaze settled on Dr T. *So painful*.

Oz said a silent prayer for his friend—that he pull out of this, that the cancer would miraculously disappear.

What would Oz do if he lost his friend? How would he cope losing the man who meant so much?

"You should go home and spend some time with Addy." Stephanie reached over to touch Blair's arm. "We'll call if there's any change."

Blair glanced at her watch and nodded. Her gaze returned to the sleeping man with multiple wires and tubes hooked up to him. "I hate to leave him."

"The doctor says he'll sleep most of the evening, anyway. Go home and give Addy a hug for me." Stephanie's hands clenched together. "I hate that she had to witness everything this morning. I'm sure Reesee has smothered her in love, but you know she's anxious for you to return home."

Strained, Blair nodded, walked to the bed and kissed Dr T's cheek. "I love you and will see you in the morning. Please be better. *Please*."

The older man's eyelids fluttered, but he didn't speak.

Oz's eyes pricked with tears. All afternoon, he'd stayed strong, had tried to provide strength for Stephanie and Blair, but hell, his insides were raw with grief.

He stood, needing a moment to collect himself.

"I'll walk out with you." When Blair started to protest, he added, "I need to."

With only a glance his way at his brusqueness, Blair

hugged Stephanie goodbye, promising to call later to check on Dr Talbot.

Oz followed Blair from the ICU room. Silently, they walked to the elevator. Oz trying to pull himself together. Blair thinking Lord only knew what. She punched the down arrow.

When the door slid closed, locking them into the privacy of the car, Oz reached for her, needing to hold her, breathe in her goodness, to grieve with her just for a moment.

"What are you doing?"

"What I've wanted to do since I woke up this morning." He wrapped his arms around her, pulled her close and closed his eyes. Maybe if he held her just a minute the ache in his heart would ease. Maybe he wouldn't feel as if his friend were dying.

"No." She pushed away from him.

Confused, Oz blinked. "No?"

"Don't touch me."

"Huh?" God, he hoped she didn't see the tears in his eyes.

"Just because I've been civil does not mean that I'm speaking to you," she spat at him.

Reeling, Oz just stared at her. She hadn't said a lot, but he'd thought that was due to Dr T's condition. "You're not speaking to me?"

"No."

"Blair, about last night—" How did he tell her that he wanted a repeat? Lots of repeats? That he wanted her in his life?

"You mean when you took my daughter out on a sailboat without my permission?"

He frowned. "I thought you meant when we made love."

"Had cheap sex," she corrected. "You had no right to take Addy out in a sailboat. None whatsoever."

In everything that had happened since she'd told him about how Addy's father died, he'd forgotten about the sailing trip.

"We barely went out of Wolf Bay. She was never in any danger."

"I don't care how far out you went. You didn't have my permission to take her out in a boat. That's so irresponsible."

"Irresponsible? How is my spending time with Addy and teaching her to sail irresponsible?"

"Because you risked her safety."

"That's crazy, Blair." One hand holding the closed door button on the elevator, he cupped her face, forcing her to look at him. "At no point was Addy's safety in question. She was with me. I wouldn't let anything happen to her."

"Like when you were watching her play with Boo-boo and her knee had to be sewn up?"

Blair knew she'd delivered a low blow even before Oz's jaw clenched. He'd hurt her, had risked Addy's life, and a man she loved dearly lay dying. She wanted to lash out at the world. To lash out at Oz.

His hand fell away from her face. "That was an accident."

"Exactly. Which proves my point." She jabbed his chest with her finger. "You can't stop accidents from happening. Taking her out in a boat is tempting fate."

"Because of Chris?"

"Because sailing is dangerous."

"You know this because you've spent a lot of time on a boat?"

"I know this because…because…" Because Chris had died during a sailing accident.

"Addy loved being out in the boat. She's a natural-born sailor."

Blair lifted her chin defiantly. "No, she isn't."

"You're being unreasonable," he pointed out. "If Chris had died in a car accident, you wouldn't forbid Addy from riding in a car."

"He didn't die in a car accident."

He sighed. "I'm trying to make a point, Blair. Be logical."

"Be logical?" Was he kidding? Her whole world was turning upside down and he wanted her to be logical. Glaring, she told him where he could go and it wasn't anyplace nice.

She hit his wrist, hard, and, catching him unawares, knocked his finger away from the door closed button. The elevator door slid open.

Head held high, Blair stormed out of the elevator, ignoring the curious onlookers who'd been impatiently waiting.

Two weeks had passed since Dr Talbot's hospital admission. Having received timely treatment, Dr T was recovering quite nicely and was in better spirits than he'd been prior to his admission.

"What are you looking so gloomy about, boy?"

No wonder Dr T asked. Oz had been staring unseeingly out the hospital room window for Lord only knew how long.

"I'm going home today," Dr T reminded him, pushing up on his hospital bed pillow. "That's cause for celebration."

Dr T was right. His going home was cause for celebration. Actually, the man looked better than he had in weeks. Oz only hoped his improved health wasn't the calm before the storm.

Still, his friend's smile was enough to pull one out of Oz, too.

"You're right. Your going home is cause for celebration. Although Stephanie's wound tight about your fund-raiser tomorrow night, she'll still manage to pull together something to mark your coming home."

"Figured she would." The old man gave him an ominous look. "Blair and Addy going to be there tonight or are you two still avoiding each other?"

Blair was adamantly avoiding him. The first week, she'd taken leave from work to sit with Dr T. Canceling the surgeries on schedule could mean loss of lives. Oz hadn't been able to reconcile that with his conscience, so he'd continued to work, another nurse filling in for Blair. At night, instead of going home, he'd slept in Dr T's room. Which left him and Blair on alternating shifts. Scarcely speaking.

When she had returned to work this week, she'd only said the bare minimum to him.

He'd tried to talk to her, but she'd shut him down, telling him she'd made a horrible mistake thinking they could be friends and that things were better this way.

Better for who? Certainly not him.

He looked like hell. If he hadn't already known, Kanesha had kindly pointed out the fact to him, telling him to go home and get some sleep or he wasn't going to get a single bid at Dr T's auction. Like he cared. He'd match whatever the highest bid was and be done with it. He'd never wanted to be auctioned off in the first place and had only agreed because of Blair.

Dr T's hired nurse, Angie, would be at the house tonight to sit with him, but Oz doubted he'd sleep much for worrying about the older man's first night home. For worrying about how his friend would hold up to attend his fund-raiser. Both his oncologist and his primary care provider had okayed the excursion, but Oz worried it was too soon for him to be undertaking such an outing.

"Son?" Dr T prompted. "You ready to talk about what happened between you and Blair?"

"Not really." Oz sighed. He hadn't told Dr T that anything had happened between him and Blair. He doubted she had. But their friend was no fool. They'd gone from cozy to barely speaking. "She's upset with me."

"Noticed that, did you?" Dr T pressed the button on his hospital bed to raise him to a sitting position. "Question is, what did you do and what are you doing to make things better?"

"She's upset I took Addy out in my boat." He wouldn't go into all the other things Blair was upset about. Rightly so. He sighed. He should just leave her alone. He wasn't good for her and she didn't trust him. So why couldn't he just put her out of his mind? "I've tried talking to her twice since the night you were admitted, but she refuses to talk about it."

"Just twice?" Dr T looked disappointed. "Surely

you know women well enough to know that groveling twice isn't nearly enough when you committed that big a mistake."

"Taking Addy sailing wasn't a mistake." Perhaps he should have asked Blair first, but she should have trusted him.

"No?"

"Blair shouldn't put her fears on Addy. It isn't healthy."

Dr T's thin brow lifted. "She told you about Chris? About how he died?"

He nodded.

Dr T's forehead wrinkled in thought. "She's in love with you. That's what all of this is about."

"Blair doesn't love me." He'd thought so, but now he knew better. Otherwise, how could she have turned on him so quickly? How could she have kicked him when he was in just as much pain as she was? When they should have been helping each other through their pain, she'd turned her back on him.

But it had been her verbal attack that had left him cold. Listening to her curse him had opened old wounds of fights between his parents, reminded him that he'd had no business to think he could have a relationship with Blair.

After all, he was a Manning male, and wasn't that better than giving Blair the power to hurt him?

"Hogwash."

Oz's gaze cut to Dr T.

"If you really believe that, then you're a fool. Just like you're a fool if you think I don't know what goes on in my house. I may be dying, but I'm not dead yet."

Oz winced. Nope, his friend didn't mince words.

"She scares you, and you're doing what you do best. Playing the role you think you're supposed to."

Oz leaned back in the chair, propped his feet against the side railing of Dr T's hospital bed. "Blair doesn't scare me."

"You think not?" The older man's thin brow rose. "Then why aren't you fighting for her?"

Fighting for her? Not meeting Dr T's eyes, Oz crossed his arms over his chest. "She doesn't trust me."

"Do you trust her?"

Oz glanced up, stared into unrelenting pale blue eyes. "I'm not the one who threw a fit about my taking Addy out in my sailboat."

"If you trust her, why haven't you told her how you feel?" Dr T's pale eyes narrowed and as usual he cut right to the heart of the matter. "How you really feel about her?"

Why, indeed?

That evening, Blair and Addy helped Stephanie blow up balloons and hang a welcome home banner in Dr T's living room. Ever efficient, Stephanie had even had a cake made. When Oz had arrived with Dr T, they'd cheered, "Welcome home."

"You're looking at him again," Reesee whispered in Blair's ear.

Standing just inside the patio door, Blair sighed. Darn it. She wasn't. "I was looking at Addy."

"Who just happens to be sitting in Oz's lap."

True. Much to Blair's chagrin, Addy couldn't get enough of Oz. From the moment Oz had arrived, Addy clung to him, telling him in no uncertain terms that she'd missed him and demanding to know why he'd yet to take her sailing again.

"Personally, I agree with Addy. He's hot."

"Quit saying that." Blair frowned at her sister. "Whether or not he's hot doesn't matter. He's a jerk."

"A jerk who adores Dr T, adores your daughter and looks at you like he wants to rip your clothes off with his teeth." Reesee shrugged. "Whatever he did that upset you, get over it, Blair. Life's too short to stress the little things."

"The little things? You have no idea what you're talking about." Blair bit into her lower lip.

"Then perhaps you should tell me. Or better yet, why don't you tell him?"

"I don't want to talk about him or to him." She didn't. She didn't even want to think about Oz, yet her brain failed to take note and constantly dwelled on him. "I should go make more tea."

Before her sister could do more than shake her head, Blair ducked back into the house. Anything to escape her sister. To escape the vision of Addy cuddled in Oz's lap. Besides, Dr Talbot loved her sweet tea. She needed to make him a pitcher prior to going home.

And she would be going home soon. She couldn't take much more of Oz. Reesee was right. Oz had been looking at her like he wanted to rip off her clothes.

Why?

Did he want more "cheap sex"?

As if.

She might be a slow learner, but eventually even she got the message. She wouldn't be used by a man again.

She got the teapot out of the cabinet, filled it with

water, and placed it on the stove. Twisting the control knob to high, she leaned against a countertop.

"I'm sorry I took Addy out in my boat without your permission."

Blair spun toward the opposite end of the kitchen. Looking impossibly handsome in his jeans and American Heart Disease T-shirt, Oz stood in the doorway.

He searched her face, waited for her to respond. Did he expect her to leap with joy? To fall down on her knees in praise that he'd apologized for something he shouldn't have done to begin with?

"Fine."

"No, it's not fine." He advanced toward her, grasped her arms, forcing her to look at him. "Nothing has been fine since the morning I came back from my run and you started shutting me out of your life."

Wasn't that what he'd wanted? Or had he wanted to continue their little fling a while longer before he called it quits?

"Dr T was being rushed to the hospital. What did you expect? That I'd throw my arms around you?"

God, would he quit touching her? She couldn't think straight with him this near, with his skin against hers. The last time he'd touched her, they'd been in his room, in his bed.

Wincing at the unwanted memories, she averted her gaze. Unfortunately, she stared at the cabinet where Oz had tossed a noodle at her and it had stuck to the oak finish. Everywhere she looked, some memory of Oz lambasted her.

He inhaled a deep breath, brushed his palms over her bare arms. "I'd have preferred that to you giving me the cold shoulder during a time when we needed each other."

She pulled free of his hold. "I didn't need you."

"No?" His brow arched. "I needed you, Blair. Each and every night while I lay in that god-awful cot in Dr T's room, I needed you there with me."

Blair's heart raced. What was he saying? That they'd shared more than cheap sex?

No, that couldn't be what he was saying. He'd told her point-blank he was leaving. He'd been the one to pull away before his heart rate had even returned to normal.

"You need to find someone else to be your friend, Oz. I no longer want that job."

"Damn it, I'm not talking about being my friend, Blair. I'm talking about me and you, about what happened between us, about what is happening between us." He frowned. "Or was happening."

"Don't act like I'm the bad guy here, Oz Manning. You were the one who called what happened 'cheap sex'."

He shook his head. "You misunderstood, Blair. Making love to you could never be cheap sex."

Only it had been. With Chris. And that night with Oz. Afterward, he'd left her feeling cheap. Feeling that once again, she'd let her heart put her in a humiliating place, a place that would leave her raw and aching yet again.

"None of this matters." She just wanted away from him. Far away. Somewhere she wouldn't have to be constantly confronted by what she'd foolishly wanted. "So what, we had sex? It's not like either of us expected anything more."

"I expected more, Blair. Lots more."

He'd wanted to keep having sex with her? Okay, so

that soothed her hurt ego a little, but she couldn't handle an affair. Not with Oz. She cared too much for him. Addy cared too much for him. The best thing she could do was put as much distance between them as possible so when he left they wouldn't be devastated any more than they already would be.

"I don't want more." She wanted everything. All the things Oz would never give her. All the things she'd dreamed of prior to Chris breaking her heart. She wanted a happily-ever-after of her own. One where she loved and was loved. One where she had someone to share her life with. One where Addy had a father who cherished her. One where Blair had someone to share a pregnancy with, to have him caress her belly and love the growing life inside as much as she did. She wanted all that and more from Oz.

He wouldn't give her more. She wouldn't settle for less.

"The night we made love was the best night of my life, Blair." His words teased, made hope surge inside her. "I didn't want that night to end. I still don't. I want you in my life. I want to be a part of Addy's life."

Did he have any idea how difficult he was making this? It would be so easy just to say yes. To let Oz carry her upstairs and make love to her again and again. But then what? He'd leave and she'd be left to pick up the pieces of her and Addy's broken hearts. No, she wouldn't do it.

She'd focus on what had happened with Chris, on the horrible pain she'd felt, anything to protect her from allowing Oz to do the same.

Oz raked his fingers through his hair. This wasn't going as well as he'd hoped. Hell, when he'd followed

Blair into the kitchen, he hadn't had a plan. He'd just known that he'd been ignored long enough, that he wanted her in his life. All day, he'd been trying to figure out how he felt about Blair, what exactly it was he wanted from her.

A few cold, hard facts hit him. The main one being that he missed her. Her smile. The way her eyes sparkled like big green jewels. The expression she wore when deep in concentration. The feel of her lips against his. The taste of those lips. God, he missed how she tasted.

He reached for her. "I want you in my life. Quit shutting me out."

She shook her head in denial, backing away from him. "You took Addy out in a sailboat. A sailboat." She practically choked on the word. Her eyes searched his. "How could you?"

"I didn't know about Chris, Blair. But even if I had, I might still have taken her." The truth hit him, hard. Why hadn't he realized before? Probably because he'd been gutted by Dr T's collapse, gutted by Blair's refusal to have anything to do with him. "This isn't about my taking Addy out in the boat, is it?"

Her gaze narrowed. "What do you mean? Of course it's about you taking my daughter out to sea without my permission."

"I don't believe you."

"I don't care if you believe me or not." She rolled her eyes, snorted, turned to remove the whistling teapot from the stove. Ignoring him, she dropped a couple of tea bags into the boiling water. "Go away, Oz. I have nothing to say to you."

She wasn't going to make this easy. Had he really

expected her to? Was he laying everything on the line for nothing? Yet he had to tell her, had to know.

"Fine, then listen to me." He held up his finger, shushing her when she started to interrupt him. He'd been cut off by her one time too many over the past two weeks. Tonight, she was going to hear him out. "For the first time in my life, I want a relationship. With you. I understand you were hurt by what happened with Chris, but I'm not him." Did she have any idea how difficult this was for him? How it went against everything within him to make himself so vulnerable to her whims? "But we can't have a relationship without trust."

She opened her mouth again, but he rushed on. "You have to decide, Blair. Do you trust me? Do you really trust me and want to be a part of my life?"

CHAPTER TEN

THE following night, Blair sat in her car in the hotel parking garage. She closed her eyes.

She didn't want to go inside. Once she went into the hotel, the evening's events would move forward without her having any real control.

For so many reasons, she'd rather go home, to the safety of the nice little cocoon she'd made for herself over the past two weeks.

For the past six years.

From the passenger seat, Reesee patted Blair's arm. "No worries. You look great, sis."

"Like a princess," Addy piped up from the back.

Taking a deep breath, Blair nodded. "Thanks to you two."

She touched one of the rhinestone studded combs that Reesee had pulled her hair back with. When Reesee had asked what Blair planned to wear to the fund-raiser, her sister had thrown a fit and taken Blair shopping for a new dress, heels and handbag. She just hadn't had time for shopping. Not with worrying about Dr T, sitting with him at the hospital, spending time with Addy and fielding questions about why the little girl hadn't seen Dr Oz.

Blair had insisted Addy and Reesee have new outfits, too. Her treat. They'd had great fun dressing up and for a short while Blair had forgotten all the things weighing so heavily on her mind. Her sister and Addy had done Blair's makeup and hair, too.

Glancing in the mirror, she admitted that she didn't look bad. As a matter of fact, they all looked great, and she was ready to spread her wings and fly.

Okay, so maybe not really, but she still had to go inside. After all, she'd helped put the bash together.

Determined to be positive, even if it killed her, Blair winked at Addy in the rear-view mirror. "Come on, Princess Addy. The party can't get started without the Pendergrass princesses."

Addy giggled as Blair let her out of the car seat.

They left the parking garage and rode the elevator up to the ballroom level. Addy insisted upon pressing the buttons, of course.

Planning to help Stephanie with any last-minute items that came up, they'd arrived early. When Blair had spoken to her at Dr Talbot's the night before, Stephanie had assured her the night would be a success and that every detail had been covered.

Last night at Dr Talbot's.

Blair closed her eyes, took a deep breath, and stepped into the ballroom.

Immediately, she spotted Oz talking to one of the band members.

How appropriate that he'd be the first person she'd see.

How appropriate when just looking at him in his tux with its crisp bow tie tugged at her heart.

His gaze lifted, met hers. For several heartbeats neither of them moved.

"There's Dr Oz." Addy tugged on Blair's hand. "Mommy, come on. It's Dr Oz!"

Blair's gaze dropped to her daughter. Just because tension zapped between her and Oz didn't mean her daughter didn't still idolize the man.

"You can say hello with Aunt Reesee." She glanced at her sister for confirmation. "I'm going to see if Stephanie needs help."

Addy practically ran to Oz. Blair hated watching, but couldn't look away.

Oz scooped her up into his arms. Addy kissed his cheek and held up her wrist to show him the tiny pearl bracelet she'd gotten during their shopping excursion.

When Addy's exuberance paused for a breath, Oz spoke to Reesee. Her sister shook her head at whatever he said. His gaze shifted to Blair. Wishing she hadn't been caught watching, she lifted her chin and walked away in search of Stephanie.

Her friend was in a tizzy, trying to make sure every detail was attended to, but took the time to hug Blair.

"I love that dress," she praised, stepping back and letting her gaze sweep over Blair. "The color matches your eyes perfectly and makes them look huge."

"Thanks. You look great, too," she told her honestly. Stephanie wore a coppery dress that bespoke timeless elegance and class. "Mine is Reesee's doing."

Blair looked down at the simple green satin dress her sister had convinced her to buy. A rhinestone brooch nestled where the material veed at her breasts. In Blair's opinion there was way too much of her chest on display in that vee, but Reesee insisted she looked hot. She wore silver four-inch heeled sandals that would be killing her feet if she stood for more than fifteen minutes.

"You should let Reesee dress you all the time," Stephanie said, checking out Blair's hemline, which fell to just above her knees. "You look gorgeous."

"Thank you. Tell me where I can be the most help."

Something behind Blair caught Stephanie's attention and her brows drew together.

Stephanie gave a nod toward Dr Talbot. "Tonight is all about Ted. Go keep him company. If you'll just make sure he's taken care of, that he smiles often, I can handle the rest."

Frowning toward the band, Stephanie took off to redirect where they were setting up.

Blair took a deep breath, spotted Dr Talbot sitting at a table in his wheelchair. Wearing a tuxedo, he looked handsome despite his illness and Blair smiled in pride and love.

She went to the table and hugged him. Before long, Reesee and Addy joined them.

Addy immediately monopolized Dr Talbot's attention, recounting their shopping adventures.

Reesee leaned near Blair's ear. "Oz is crazy about you."

Her heart slamming against her rib cage, Blair snorted. "Yeah, right." If only. Oz wanted a fling while in Madison. She was convenient.

Blair ignored the tiny voice whispering that sex was always convenient for a man like Oz. Women bent over backward to get close to him.

He wanted her trust. Did one have to trust a fling? Where was that rule written? And if he had really wanted her trust he should have earned it instead of practically kicking her out of his bedroom.

"I'm serious." Reesee's expression said she was, but Blair wasn't buying it.

"Then why doesn't he come over here to see me?"

"He doesn't have to come over here to see you." Reesee waggled her penciled on brows. "Don't look now, but he's seeing you this very moment."

Blair looked.

"Hey." Frowning, Reesee poked her. "I told you not to look."

Oz was looking at her.

At least, he had been. Without acknowledging her, he turned toward the couple he stood with.

"He made his feelings clear last night." He'd made his feelings clear just then. Either she trusted him or he wasn't willing to have a relationship with her.

As if she'd asked him for a relationship. *Relationship.* She and Oz had very different definitions for that word.

Besides, had he forgotten that she was upset with him about taking Addy out in a boat?

Of course he hadn't. Her not trusting him to look out for Addy, to make decisions where her daughter was concerned, had been one of the trust issues he'd been referring to. Knowing he'd break her heart if she let him was another. She didn't intend to give him that opportunity.

"Are you sure you didn't misunderstand?" Reesee asked. Blair hadn't told her sister about Oz confronting her the night before, about his professing to having feelings for her and wanting a relationship with her.

"I just can't understand," Reesee continued, "because I know I didn't misinterpret his asking me how you were."

Oz had asked how she was?

"Nor did I misunderstand when he commented on how beautiful you looked. He couldn't take his eyes off you."

Okay, so he'd asked how she was and said she was beautiful.

"For Oz that's nothing more than polite conversation." Blair glanced to make sure Addy couldn't hear their conversation. Her gaze collided with Dr Talbot's.

He'd been eavesdropping and didn't look one bit ashamed. Nor did he look surprised by any of the things he'd just heard. He loved her and wouldn't want her hurt. Had he realized she'd fallen for Oz and intervened on her behalf? Did he know about what had happened the night she and Addy spent the night at his house? That she'd ended up in Oz's room? Was that what last night had been about?

Of course it was.

Oz hadn't told her he loved her.

His confronting her in the kitchen made sense now. He could even honestly tell Dr Talbot that he'd offered to have a relationship, but Blair had walked away.

She couldn't be angry at Dr Talbot for caring, for doing what he thought was best for her by encouraging Oz to have a relationship with her.

But she was angry at Oz.

Trust. Ha, she'd give him trust.

She had a good mind to walk up and tell him she'd decided she did trust him. Just to watch him try to squirm his way out of that one. But she wouldn't give him the satisfaction of rejecting her, of telling her that he'd been joking, that he'd only offered a relationship under duress.

No, she wouldn't ever give Oz Manning the opportunity to hurt her again.

* * *

An hour later the event was in full swing. A stage dominated the far end of the ballroom. The band played to the right. Buffet-style snack foods and tables occupied the opposite end of the room.

The event was sold out to the room's full capacity. Which was great for Dr Talbot. Horrible for Blair's stomach.

"You don't look like you're having a very good time," Dr Talbot mused from where he sat beside her. After the MC had introduced him to the crowd he'd been pushed in his wheelchair to the table closest to the stage. Seats had been reserved next to him in Blair, Reesee and Addy's name. They had a perfect view of the stage. Addy took every detail in with excitement, insisting on sampling the chocolate fountain and strawberries.

Reesee had volunteered to go with her as chocolate was involved.

Blair forced a smile to her face. "I feel like I should be doing something to help Stephanie, but she insists I stay with you, which I enjoy. But big shindigs like this aren't my usual cup of tea."

"Mine either," he agreed. "Who likes all this attention?"

But there was a light in his eyes she hadn't seen in weeks. A sparkle that said he was enjoying all the hoopla even if he implied otherwise.

For that alone, all the work they'd done had been worth it.

Blair followed Dr Talbot's gaze and smiled for real at what she found him watching.

"Stephanie really went all-out to make sure this was

a spectacular party, didn't she?" Blair leaned closer to him and placed her hand on his upper arm.

"Yes, she goes all-out in everything she does. Reminds me of Selma."

That was something she'd never heard him say before. "Stephanie reminds you of your late wife?"

Dr Talbot nodded. "In ways. In others they are as unique as night and day."

His ache infected Blair. How sad it must be to have loved someone so completely only to have to watch them die. To go on with life without the person you most loved.

Blair's eyes watered. "You miss her, don't you?"

"Selma?" His pale eyes took on a faraway gleam. "Every minute of every day."

"I can't imagine having a love like that."

"Can't you?" Dr Talbot's gaze shifted to her.

Despite her feelings for Oz, they were never meant to be. Eventually, he would have left her. Then she'd have been alone, nursing a broken heart; alone, trying to explain to Addy why Oz was no longer a part of their life. So she pretended to misunderstand.

"What I had with Chris was nothing like what you and Selma shared."

"I wasn't referring to Addy's father. I was referring to Oz." Dr Talbot placed his hand over hers, giving her a fatherly pat. "But you already knew that."

Her gaze shifted to where Oz stood with a group of women. All evening he'd gone from one group to another, working the crowd. He checked on Dr Talbot periodically, but otherwise he stayed away from their table.

"I don't love Oz." She plastered what she hoped was a convincing look on her face.

She wouldn't place the burden of her broken heart on their mutual friend. She wouldn't have him pushing Oz to say things he didn't mean in an effort to spare her. Oz didn't love her. If he did, he'd have told her last night.

"Are you sure about that?"

Absently rubbing her sternum, Blair nodded. "I'm sure. He's too much like Chris for me to ever take him seriously."

"Odd, from what little you've told me about Addy's father, I wouldn't have thought him and Oz had anything in common." Dr Talbot paused. "Except you and a love of sailing."

"I'd really rather not talk about Chris." At Dr Talbot's open mouth, she quickly added, "Or Oz. Or sailing."

She swallowed, trying to clear the wave of emotion tightening her throat. She could do this. She could be strong. Could keep her tears reined in for one night.

"Oz adores Addy. Just as he adores you." Dr Talbot gave her a pointed look. "You're in love with him, aren't you?"

Blair shook her head. "Oz is a persuasive man. I got caught up in his charms. That's all." She called upon acting skills she wasn't sure she had, but desperately needed. For that matter, Oz was a persuasive man and she had gotten caught up in his charms. Horribly caught up. But what had happened with Oz hadn't been all bad. For the first time in years, she'd felt like a woman. She'd felt desire and desirable.

"Actually, I'm grateful to him," she admitted. "I buried myself after what happened with Chris and had forgotten what it felt like to have a man's attention." A real smile lifted the corners of her lips. "Maybe I'll bid on a date tonight and meet someone."

Dr Talbot didn't comment, just stared at her long moments before nodding and returning his attention to the band. Blair let him, not wanting to peel away the pretty wrapping she'd just hidden her aching heart inside.

Soon it was time for the auction. The women were being auctioned off first.

A radio DJ was first. Loving the concept of being auctioned, she worked the crowd, winking and egging on higher bids. Blair was quite impressed with the upper four-digit sum the woman's date went for.

The next few dates passed in a blur. All of the women drew ridiculously high dollar amounts for an evening of their time. But it was for a great cause and Blair suspected this was a way for Dr Talbot's friends and colleagues to feel that they were doing their part to help him.

Prior to the auction for the men starting, Blair and Stephanie had a few announcements to make. They took the stage, gave their spiel about Dr Talbot and his lifelong generosity to those he came into contact with. Blair thanked the audience for their generosity and encouraged them to bid on the silent auction set up at the side of the room, encouraged them to make donations to one of the many collection bins set up around the room.

When she made her way back to her table, Dr Talbot reached up to hug her. "You were magnificent."

"I was too scared to move."

"Too scared to move worked brilliantly." A proud gleam in her eyes, Reesee hugged her, too. "I don't think there's a dry eye in the building."

"Mommy—" Addy jumped up and down, too excited to stay in her seat "—you looked beautiful up there!"

Magnificent. Brilliant. Beautiful. Blair laughed. "I stood there petrified. I hope my words came out clear." She smiled at Dr Talbot. "They were from the heart. We love you, don't we, Addy?"

Her big grin showing off her missing front tooth, Addy nodded and spread her arms as wide as they would stretch. "This much."

Dr Talbot's smile reached his glistening eyes. "I know you do. That's why I'm here. Why I'm getting on a plane for Rochester tomorrow afternoon."

Blair's stomach flip-flopped. "You were accepted for the Xabartan?"

"My hospital stay convinced me that I'm not quite ready to give up yet. Oz arranged everything. He's offered to let me stay at his place until I've completed my therapy. Hate to bum off the kid, but figure there's not much difference in living in his house here or living in his house there." He paused, then dropped another bombshell. "I'm going to ask Stephanie to go with me."

"Thank God." Blair wrapped her arms around his neck. "The treatments will work. I know they will." Then what he'd said about living in Oz's house hit her. "What do you mean, living in his house here? Oz is living with you."

"Technically." His gaze fell to his wrinkled hands on the table. "I sold my house to Oz prior to Selma dying. The banks wouldn't loan me any more money and I wouldn't take a handout. Oz paid off the mortgage on the house and paid me a hefty sum as well."

"But…" Dr Talbot had never said anything. Oz had

never said anything, but then he wouldn't, would he? To do so would be stripping away yet another layer of Dr Talbot's pride. Oz would never do that.

"I owed more than the house was worth, but he insisted I take the extra and I was desperate to allow Selma to spend her last days as she wished—at home."

"I'm sure Oz understood that." Sensing how embarrassed her friend was at his admission, she refocused on his good news. "I'm so pleased you're going to Rochester. If Oz made that happen, then I'm eternally grateful to him."

Blair hugged him again and sat back down. Addy climbed into her lap, kissing Blair's cheek and giving an excited clap although Blair was sure Addy didn't fully understand what she was excited about. Or perhaps her daughter was just excited about the entire glitz of the night.

Blair took a drink of her ice water. "I really do love you, you know."

"I know, Blair. It's one of the reasons why I'm going to Rochester."

A country music singer who'd just been auctioned off sang a song, putting the crowd back into an upbeat mood prior to the auction starting back. This time with the men.

The thing Blair had been dreading most was watching a bunch of women haggle over Oz, knowing one of them would buy his date, spend precious time with him on his cursed sailboat.

He'd be sailing off into the sunset with another woman and making waves. Well, she supposed that depended on who won Oz's date, but the man led a charmed life. Some gorgeous knockout would probably bid some insanely high bid on him, then rock his world.

After all, it was only a matter of time before he moved on to the next woman.

Just as well she hadn't made a fool of herself by throwing her arms around him last night and telling him everything in her heart.

She sucked in a deep breath and prayed the night would soon be over.

The bid prior to Oz's was his friend Will Majors from Madison Medical Center. A cute blonde in the second row of tables immediately piped up with a three-thousand-dollar bid.

"Are you okay?" Stephanie asked from Oz's side. "I've seen you look at Blair a dozen times. Why don't you just go and talk to her?"

"The ball is in her court. I told her what I wanted. Apparently, she doesn't want the same. Or, if she does, it's not enough."

Stephanie gave him a suspicious look. "You told her you were in love with her?"

"I'm not in love with her," he quickly denied. Far from it. He'd had sex with Blair—amazing sex—but the world kept turning. He wasn't his mother. He wouldn't shut down and turn to life's vices to deal with a broken heart. His heart wasn't broken. He was just fine, regardless of how Blair felt.

"Are you planning to bid on any of the bachelors?" he said, changing the subject.

"The only man I'm interested in isn't up for bid."

They both glanced toward Dr Talbot. He leaned toward Blair, laughing at something she said.

"Unfortunately, he refuses to let me tie myself to a dying man, says we'll only marry if he beats his cancer."

"Stubborn old fool. Guess that gives him one hell of an incentive to get better."

Stephanie shrugged. "I think he just uses the cancer as an excuse to keep from hurting my feelings. He's still in love with his wife."

"He'll always love Selma, but that doesn't mean he doesn't care about you."

"I know he cares," Stephanie agreed, sighing. "But caring isn't enough, is it? Just look at you and Blair."

Him and Blair?

"There's nothing between me and Blair."

"Exactly."

"I don't want her to get hurt, if that's what you mean." Or would he have been the one hurting?

Damn.

He was hurting.

"You think you didn't hurt her?"

He had.

He knew he had.

So what was his excuse?

He and Blair shared sexual chemistry. Nothing more.

He glanced toward her, saw her laugh at something Dr T said. His heart ached. Would she ever laugh like that for him again? Would he ever look into her eyes and see that sparkle?

That sparkle that he'd been sure had been love.

So sure he'd felt like a million bucks the next morning and had planned to whisk Blair off her feet.

Because he loved her.

Addy, too.

Whatever feelings Blair had for him, he'd killed when she'd walked away from his bed and he'd told her he just wanted to be friends.

Idiot.

And last night, what had he done? Pushed her to trust him when he hadn't trusted her.

He hadn't, not with his heart.

Stephanie cleared her throat, causing him to look at her. "Tell her, Oz. Tell her before it's too late."

Could he tell Blair how much he cared? To do that would give her the ultimate power over him. Would give her the power his father had held over his mother. Would cast him in the role of his mother if Blair didn't feel the same, if she couldn't trust him with her heart.

The MC motioned for Oz to take the stage.

Blair didn't have to prove anything by watching women bid on Oz.

"Can you keep an eye on Addy for a few minutes?"

Reesee nodded, giving Blair a sympathetic look. Her sister knew exactly why she was leaving the room.

"Mommy, you'll miss Dr Oz." Addy's big eyes looked at Blair as if she were insane to leave now. "We have to bid on him 'cause I miss him. And his date is sailing. And I love sailing."

Blair's mouth opened, but she didn't know what to tell her daughter. She looked at her sister, hoping for help, but Reesee only shrugged. "She loves sailing. Buy the kid a date with the man."

Like Blair could afford him, even if she wanted to bid on Oz, which she didn't.

"Addy, hon, we can't buy Oz's date."

"Why not?" Addy frowned at her mother. "I want to go on Dr Oz's boat again. I'm a good captain and we need to do more bilfering and blundering."

"Pilfering and plundering." Blair waited for the panic to set in. The panic that always hit her when she thought of sailing. The thought of Addy being on a boat would likely send her into ventricular tachycardia.

Only her heart kept beating normally.

Because Oz would never put Addy in harm's way. Never. He'd protect her with his life.

"Addy, I can't buy Oz's bid. I know you don't understand, but things are complicated."

"Don't you want to go sailing with Dr Oz?"

She couldn't lie to Addy. "I do want to spend time with him, but like I said, things are complicated. His date will go for a lot of money and I don't have a lot of money."

Addy's face squished with confusion. "But Mommy, we don't need lots of money. Dr Oz takes us places for free."

"I'm sorry, Addy, but I'm not bidding on Oz." She glanced at no one in particular. "Excuse me."

She left the table before anyone could try to convince her to stay.

Blair made it to the edge of the room and was on her way into the hallway in search of a bathroom when Stephanie caught up with her.

"Where are you going?"

"To the bathroom."

"Now? Oz is up for bid."

Did everyone think she was oblivious to that fact? If only.

"And Oz being up for bid matters to me how?"

Stephanie frowned at Blair's snappish question. "He matters to you a great deal. Don't pretend otherwise."

"Then you'll understand why I have no desire to watch women fight over him."

"Why aren't *you* fighting for him?"

Blair stared blankly at Stephanie.

"If you care about him, why did you let him walk away so easily? He told you he wanted a relationship and you walked away, Blair. Why?"

"I didn't understand why he said that last night. Not at first, but tonight I realized. He thinks our being involved would make Dr Talbot happy, that's why he said what he did. Because he loves Dr Talbot and would do anything to make him happy."

"Surely you don't believe that bunch of bull?"

Her eyes watering, Blair blinked at her friend. "He's going to leave, Stephanie. What then? Am I supposed to beg him to stay?"

Stephanie shrugged. "If that's what it takes. Loving a man like Oz isn't easy, but nothing worth having ever is. The real question is—do you love him enough to risk everything to be with him? Even knowing it might not last, even knowing you'd be devastated if it doesn't? Is the risk of pain worth the joy of loving?"

Blair stared at Stephanie, a woman in love with a man full of cancerous lesions, a man she'd likely lose to death sooner rather than later. "I do care about Oz."

"I'm not the one you should be telling. You need to tell him, right now."

"He's on stage."

Stephanie shrugged. "Life's too short to let something like that stop you. He wants you to buy his date."

"This is crazy, Stephanie. I can't bid on him." His date was sailing. "I won't bid on him."

Looking disappointed in her, Stephanie shrugged. "Oz wants you to trust him, Blair."

Damp heat flushed her skin, darkened her vision.

"Do you love him?"

Blair couldn't speak.

"Do you?" Stephanie demanded, shaking Blair's arm.

"Yes."

"Then perhaps it's time you showed him just how much."

CHAPTER ELEVEN

Oz scanned the crowd, but the stage lights prevented him from seeing beyond the first row of tables.

Blair hadn't returned to her seat. She'd caught his eye when he went onto the stage, but he hadn't been able to spot her since. Had she left?

She'd cared for him, but he'd been a fool and lost her.

Hell, he'd pushed her away.

He'd been right about one thing. He didn't deserve Blair.

But he wanted her.

With all his heart.

Prior to meeting Blair, Oz would have winked at the busty redhead bidding on him. He would have grinned at the leggy blonde raising the stakes. These days he only had eyes for one woman.

Because he was nothing like his father.

A curvy little brunette had captured his heart.

And she'd left.

Out of love for Dr T, he kept a smile pasted on his face, but his heart wasn't in the auction.

His heart was wherever Blair was.

Damn it. As soon as the auction was over, he was going to find her, make her listen, make her understand.

Then he was going to do what he should have done to begin with after they'd made love, what he should have said last night when he'd made such a mess of telling her how he felt.

He was going to ask Blair to marry him.

He'd win her heart.

Win her love.

Win her trust.

In the process he'd win his own happiness.

Because when he'd been with Blair he'd been happier than he recalled ever being.

His mother had warned him about being led astray by women. Oz had taken her advice to heart. He'd planned to learn from dear old Dad's mistakes.

But Blair wasn't a mistake.

Losing her, however, would be the biggest one of his life.

God, would this auction hurry and end? He had to go find Blair and beg her to forgive him. To marry him.

He'd never be like his father. He'd earn Blair's trust and cherish her love. He'd spend all his days glorying in the fact that she'd chosen him to love, chosen him to spend her life with.

He wouldn't consider the alternative.

Hands shaking, Blair motioned to the MC.

"Looks like we have a new bidder, ladies and gents."

Oz glanced in the direction the MC had looked, but Blair knew he couldn't see her. Still his gaze landed on where she stood and she couldn't help but wonder if he sensed her.

"We have a counter bid." The MC played to the crowd.

Blair nodded to the bid taker, who'd moved near where she stood.

The MC shouted in delight at Blair's bid, calling out for someone to go higher. Someone did.

Blair cringed. She'd have to sell her soul to come up with the cash to cover her bid if she went higher. Still, the money was going to Dr Talbot.

She bid higher.

But so did whomever she was bidding against.

Blair looked at the man onstage, noted that he was worth whatever it cost to make him hers. What guarantee did she have that he'd even give her a chance to tell him how she felt? To tell him how foolish she'd been?

None whatsoever if she didn't win this date.

She would win his date.

She would go out on his sailboat with him and while out there she'd show him how much she loved him. She'd give him her heart for all time.

Blair wasn't surprised when the MC glanced back in her direction for another bid. Fine, what was another five hundred dollars at this point? She motioned to the bid taker, who flashed in her bid.

"Going once, going twice."

Blair held her breath, praying she'd win Oz.

"Sold. To the cute little blonde in the front."

"What?" Blair demanded of the bid taker who'd taken her bid. "I bid. You saw me. You gave him my bid."

The poor volunteer shrugged in confusion. "I guess he didn't see me."

Oh, this would never do. She'd go onstage and demand the bid be opened back up, demand her bid be given fair opportunity. No cute little blonde in the front row was going sailing with Blair's man. Uh-huh. No way.

Determined to set things straight, she marched toward the stage.

"Mommy!" Addy exclaimed as Blair stormed past. When she didn't stop, Addy grabbed her dress. "Mommy, I have a surprise!"

Blair paused, glanced at her daughter. She didn't want to dampen Addy's excitement, but she was desperate to correct the MC's oversight. "Addy, honey, Mommy needs to talk to the MC a minute about Dr Oz's date."

"Isn't it wonderful?" Addy grinned, wiggling back and forth in her princess dress, then throwing her arms wide. "Surprise."

"Huh?"

"Aunt Reesee and I bought Oz for you. Dr Talbot and Stephanie helped, too."

They'd...

"Oh, Addy." Tears stung Blair's eyes. She'd been bidding against her daughter for a date with Oz. The absurdity of it caused laughter to bubble up her throat. She stooped down and hugged her cute little blonde. "You bought Oz for me?"

Grinning proudly, Addy nodded. "'Cos we love him, right?"

"We do, Addy. Mommy loves him so very much."

"But do you trust him?"

Blair spun toward Oz, her face pale as she realized he'd heard what she'd said. He hadn't meant to eavesdrop, but her words had made his hopes soar. Had she meant her claim? Did she love him?

God, he hoped so.

Blair stepped toward him, looked unsure of herself.

"How do you feel about me, Blair?" he asked, then realized he was taking the easy way out again. He held up his hand. "No, don't tell me. Listen, instead, to how I feel about you."

"I know how you feel about me. You told me last night."

"You know that I want to marry you?"

Her mouth dropped open.

"Say yes, Mommy," Addy encouraged from beside them. "Yes, Dr Oz, we will marry you."

Oz glanced toward Reesee, and she immediately retrieved her niece, who was unhappy about leaving.

"Because of Dr Talbot?" Blair's green gaze bored into him. "Is that why you want to get married? Because you know it'll make him happy?"

Oz digested what she'd said and put his heart on the line. "How about marrying me to make me happy?"

Blair blinked. "Why would you want to marry me?"

"For the same reason most men want to marry a woman."

"Which is?"

"I love you, Blair. I think I have from the moment I first met you, but I was too blind to see it." He took her hand in his. "My parents weren't happily married. Not at any point during any of their many marriages. I decided long ago that I wasn't going to venture into love or marriage. I didn't realize I wouldn't be given a choice."

"There's always a choice, Oz."

"Then I choose to love you, Blair, and want you to choose to love me."

Sincerity shone in his eyes. He was serious. He loved her.

Blair closed her eyes. "I'm afraid I'll lose you. I couldn't bear it."

"You won't lose me, Blair."

She shook her head. "You don't understand."

"I do." He cupped her face, stared into her eyes. "What happened with Chris was an accident."

Blair bit her lower lip. "What if another accident happens?"

"It won't."

"How can you be sure?"

"No one can ever be sure of something like that. I'll sell the boat, if that's what you want, Blair, but this isn't really about the boat, is it? It's about taking a chance on loving someone, on possibly getting hurt. It's about trust, so I have to ask again—do you trust me?"

He was right. It wasn't about the boat.

"Trust me, Blair."

"You'll catch me?"

He nodded. "Always."

"I trust you, Oz. With my heart, with Addy, with my future."

"I want you, Blair. Forever. I want you to be my wife, my partner, the mother of my children."

"I am yours. Probably from that first day Dr Talbot introduced us, but you scared me." She pressed her palm to his heart, stared into his eyes and smiled. "I'm not scared anymore, Oz. Not as long as I have you by my side. I'll marry you if that's what you want."

Tugging on his bow tie and pulling it free from his neck, Oz grinned, feeling as if he could take on the world and win. He took his bow tie, tied it around her wrist. "I don't have a ring, so for tonight, this shows the world that I belong to you."

"That you belong to me? Or vice versa?" Blair laughed.

"Both."

"I like the sound of that." Blair twined her arms around his neck, stared into his eyes. "I love you, Oz."

"Just so you know—" he pressed a kiss to her lips "—I'm going to hold you to that love every day for the rest of our lives."

ONE SUMMER IN SANTA FE

BY
MOLLY EVANS

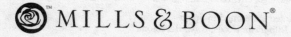
MILLS & BOON®

All the characters in this book have no existence outside the imagination of the author, and have no relation whatsoever to anyone bearing the same name or names. They are not even distantly inspired by any individual known or unknown to the author, and all the incidents are pure invention.

First published in Great Britain 2009
Paperback edition 2010
Harlequin Mills & Boon Limited,
Eton House, 18-24 Paradise Road, Richmond, Surrey TW9 1SR

© Brenda Schetnan 2009

ISBN: 978 0 263 87665 9

Harlequin Mills & Boon policy is to use papers that are natural, renewable and recyclable products and made from wood grown in sustainable forests. The logging and manufacturing process conform to the legal environmental regulations of the country of origin.

Printed and bound in Spain
by Litografia Rosés, S.A., Barcelona

Molly Evans has worked as a nurse from the age of nineteen. She's worked in small rural hospitals, the Indian Health Service, and large research facilities all over the United States. After spending eight years as a Traveling Nurse, she settled down to write in her favourite place: Albuquerque, New Mexico. In days she met her husband, and has been there ever since. With twenty-two years of nursing experience, she's got a lot of material to use in her writing. She lives in the high desert, with her family, three chameleons, two dogs and a passion for quilting in whatever spare time she has. Visit Molly at: www.mollyevans.com

Recent titles by the same author:

THE GREEK DOCTOR'S PROPOSAL
THE EMERGENCY DOCTOR'S CHOSEN WIFE

This book is dedicated to my husband.
I could not be where I am
without your love and support.
Whether you know it or not, you're my real-life hero.

CHAPTER ONE

Santa Fe, New Mexico, USA

"YOU want me to *what*?" Dr. Taylor Jenkins asked his sister. He'd do anything for her. Except this. This was impossible and entirely beyond his abilities. He was a physician, not a—

"Please, Taylor. I've never asked you for anything. After all the things we've been through together. I *need* this."

Caroline walked forward and placed her hand on his, her pale blue eyes begging. Pleading. Working on the guilt he strongly resisted. For so many years, guilt had ruled his life, and he had vowed long ago to elude its poison. No commitments, no guilt. It was that easy. He lived his life his own way, followed no one's rules but his own.

"I can't send him to Mom and Dad. You know that."

"What about—"

"José? No. His father is off on weekend military camp and could be deployed at any time." She waved that suggestion aside. "I can barely get him to take Alex one weekend a month. I couldn't comfortably leave Alex with him for that length of time."

"But…" Panic clawed up his throat and tried to

strangle the life out of him. He was a well-respected professional. He would figure a way to get out of this situation Caroline was presenting him with. There was no way he could—

"You can do this. I trust you completely. And it's only for six weeks, not forever. He's old enough to be by himself some. I have babysitter names for you, too, and his cousins will want to see him over the summer. Carmelita's been very helpful since I divorced José. She doesn't want her kids to lose touch with him, despite her brother's problems." She stepped closer and kept her gaze locked with his.

Damn. Somehow, she sensed he was caving in. Women had an extra sense about those things and used them to their advantage against the men of the world. Resistance *was* futile. He was going to be assimilated.

Taylor hauled out a long sigh and placed a hand over his face as his shoulders slumped. He just knew he was going to regret this. The idea that he could care for a child, his nephew, for weeks at a time was preposterous. He simply didn't have it in him to care for another living creature for longer than a few hours. He didn't even have a plant or a fish in his house.

"I knew you would do it! He's going to be so excited. Thank you, Taylor. Thank you. You don't know what this means to me." She hugged him and nearly bowled the two of them over. If he hadn't leaned against the desk, they'd both be on the floor.

"You promise you'll be back in six weeks, Caroline? Not a day longer?" Putting his life on hold for six weeks was about all he could cope with. By the end of it his tolerance would have run out.

"Yes, yes, yes. This is going to help me build a solid future for Alex and me. The company provides everything, so the only cost there is my food, but they absolutely refuse to allow children during the focus training session in California." She took a deep breath. "It's the only way I can do this. Believe me; I've thought of everything else."

Sadness crept into her eyes, and Taylor knew he was doing the right thing for his sister. Just didn't know if it was the right thing for him. His life was about freedom, about adrenaline, and physical challenges, testing himself, testing what he could accomplish after the next challenge was met. Would he have any time for his own life while he was caring for his nephew? If he'd wanted to be a parent, he could have been one by now.

"Anyway," she said, and playfully slapped him on the shoulder, "it's about time you got to know your nephew better."

"I resent that. I know my nephew." Didn't he?

Caroline snorted and flung a few tears away from her face. She never cried. "You know his name, his birthday, and stuff like that. But you really don't know the young man deep down inside him." Again, she touched him. "Alex needs you right now. His father has let him down so many times that I don't know if he'll ever recover. Kind of like you in that way with Dad."

"I know. I know." Taylor thought of the times when his father hadn't been there for him. Had been off doing something more important than getting to know his own son. Pushing those memories away, he focused on Caroline and gave a long, long sigh. "When do you leave?"

"Next Monday. Early."

"Bring him over Sunday afternoon, and we'll go through everything I need to know about being a parent for six weeks."

"Thank you so much, Taylor. Somehow, I'll make it up to you."

"Right." Was there anything that could truly make up for this lost time? Then again, was six weeks that much to sacrifice if he could help out his sister and nephew? He wasn't that selfish.

"Sure I will. When you have kids, I'll be the best auntie they'll ever have."

"Having kids of my own seems pretty farfetched at this point in my life." There were no guarantees that he'd be a better parent than his own and childhoods like theirs should be avoided at all costs.

That should be avoided at all costs. Caroline was certainly trying to give Alex a good home and a stable life despite the challenges of being a single parent. No, he'd be better off just living his life single and being a good uncle to his eleven-year-old nephew.

"If you ever stop jumping out of airplanes and climbing mountains by yourself, you might meet a woman that intrigues you enough to keep your feet on the ground." She patted his shoulder and gave him a look that made his stomach knot. "Then it will be easy."

"Yeah, yeah, yeah. Didn't we have this conversation when you tried to fix me up with that nurse friend of yours?" The memory of the disastrous arranged date made him shiver. Never going there again.

"We did, but repetition helps. Someday you'll get it."

Doubtful, Taylor ushered her out the door and returned to the ER where it was safe.

* * *

Nurse Piper Hawkins walked into the ER on the first day of her new travel assignment to pure chaos. Before introductions could even be made, she shoved her purse under the desk and dove into the fray. Adrenaline pumped through her system, and she was ready to tackle anything. At her best in the midst of an emergency, she just hoped the other staff would accept her help quickly. Every assignment was different, and she hoped this one would be a good one. First impressions were always important, and she was about to make one right now.

"I'm new here, but someone give me a job to do," she said at the first trauma room. With only one doctor and one patient present, Piper figured this was as good a place to start as any.

"You a nurse? Glove up. I'm going to have to intubate this guy and get him off to surgery." A tall man in green scrubs spoke to her from behind protective mask and goggles. Only his eyes were exposed, and they were intently focused on the trauma patient in front of him.

"Got it." Piper grabbed gloves from the box on the wall rack and put them on, then a pair of goggles from her pocket. Automatically, she looked at the monitor and assessed the patient's vital signs. Blood pressure was low, and the heart rate was erratic. "I'm Piper Hawkins, your new travel nurse," she said, and grabbed the suction setup and cleaned the patient's mouth.

"Taylor Jenkins, ER doc on today."

"Tell me what you need." While noise and movement went on all around them, Piper felt as if she and Dr. Jenkins were in a world all their own. Just the two of them focused entirely on the patient in front of them. This was why she was a nurse, stepping right into the chaos and knowing exactly what to do to save a life. This was what she had trained to do.

Dr. Jenkins nodded to a cupboard behind her as he struggled to keep the oxygen mask on the patient's face. "Intubation tray, in there."

"You okay with me helping on this?" Piper asked, knowing some physicians preferred to work with certain nurses, but in an emergency situation, that didn't always work.

"You qualified?" Taylor asked, and paused to shoot her an inquiring look.

"Absolutely," Piper promised confidently.

"Then I'm good. Open the tray."

Nerves still made her hands shake, and she almost dropped the tray on the floor, but managed to catch it and keep it sterile. "Oh, I'm sorry, I'm sorry." She was such a klutz sometimes and a blush lit up her cheeks and neck.

"It's okay. Just relax a little," Taylor said. "Take a deep breath."

The sound of his deep voice and the reassurance he was trying to give her did help. She gave a worried glance at him, but he was as calm and relaxed as he sounded and some of the tension left her shoulders. Some doctors would have just barked at her not to be clumsy, but Dr. Jenkins hadn't. He must have nerves of steel. That alone calmed her own nerves somewhat, and she connected with the cool energy that seemed to roll off him, trusting him immediately as they worked on the patient together. Confidence like that didn't come along every day. This wasn't the first day on the job she had envisioned, but it was the one she was receiving, and she was going to do her best to focus on the task at hand.

Piper tore open the sterile intubation tray and assisted Dr. Jenkins to place the breathing tube through the patient's mouth and into his lungs. The tube helped to control the airway and allowed the doctor or anesthetist to place the patient on a mechanical ventilator. After the airway was secure, they could deal with the rest of his injuries.

She looked down at the man, who appeared to be in his midfifties. He was unconscious, his face covered in lacerations that oozed blood. A hard plastic neck collar kept him immobilized to prevent injuries to his neck until he could be taken to Radiology for films. He was, in short, a mess. She bit her lip, knowing that he was in serious, if not critical condition. She hoped that their rescue attempt today was going to pull him through and that he had the stamina to survive. The snap of a memory tried to intrude, but she pushed back the unwanted thoughts. Now was not the time to relive the traumatic deaths of her parents. Focusing on the patient right in front of her was her priority.

"Can you keep the suction in his mouth? I'm ready for the tube." Keeping his gaze focused on the patient's airway, he held out a hand to Piper.

"Yes, Doctor." Piper gave him the needed item with one hand and kept the suction in place with the other. She stood beside Dr. Jenkins as he crouched over the patient's head and slid the tube into place. The tension between her shoulders released. Once the airway was secure, the first hurdle was over.

"That was the smoothest intubation I've ever seen,"

she said, and secured the tube into place, amazed that it had gone so well as they'd never worked together before.

"Thanks. I did consider a career in anesthesiology, but ER was more to my liking."

"Well, you certainly are good at it. If I ever need intubation, can I call you?" she asked with a quick laugh.

Dr. Jenkins laughed, too. "Sure."

She listened to the patient's lungs. "Good breath sounds, tube sounds like it's in place. His heart sounds are kind of muffled, though," she said as she listened to the rest of the man's chest. "Can you have a listen to be sure?"

Dr. Jenkins applied his stethoscope and listened, confirming her suspicions. "You're right. He's had blunt force chest trauma, so I'm sure we're not out of the woods yet." He glanced at the monitor and watched for a few seconds.

Piper wiped her forehead with her forearm when the procedure was over. "Where is everyone?"

"We had four traumas come in at once, so everyone's tied up."

"Wow. I didn't think this ER was going to be as busy as my last assignment." Now she understood why her company had offered such a hefty bonus for this job. She was going to be on her toes from the very start.

"We're the closest hospital to a major freeway system, so we have all the trauma you could ever want. Today was an unfortunate tragedy." His jaw clenched and he fell silent.

Though Piper didn't know this man, she sensed he was disturbed by the events that had taken place today. Those who cared the most often seemed to carry the weight of the world on their shoulders.

"Want to fill me in?" Offering to listen was one of the things she did best. Though she often couldn't change things, listening helped. Stress was an ever-present issue for healthcare workers. Venting could help.

"Head-on crash. Damn drunk driver going the wrong way on the highway access." He shook his head and reached for a suture kit.

"Oh, my." The nerves that had been rumbling inside her now shot to every corner of her mind and heart. A few seconds passed before she had control of the emotions that wanted to go wild. Her parents had been killed by a drunk driver when she'd been twenty years old, her sister twelve. An incident that had turned her instantly into the main carer of her young sister. Each time she dealt with the situation again, she had to keep her emotional distance to get the job done. Some wounds never healed completely and this was one of them.

Looking down at the patient between them, she stroked his hair back from his face with a hand that trembled. "In those sorts of crashes, everyone suffers, don't they?"

The cardiac alarm rang out, and Piper's gaze flashed to the monitor. Her heart rate accelerated along with the patient's. Something was going on that they hadn't picked up on yet. "He's having EKG changes."

"Sixty-cc syringe with a cardiac needle—now." Taylor moved out from the head of the stretcher to the patient's left side. "No time for niceties, just get it ready."

"Here." Piper placed the syringe into his open hand. Urgency hummed through her, and she hoped that Taylor's efforts could save the patient. Even in the right place at the right time with all of the best medical care available, people still didn't make it.

Without a word, Taylor placed the tip of the needle between two ribs below the man's left armpit and inserted it as far as it would go. Blood immediately flashed into the syringe and Taylor extracted excessive blood from the pericardial sac, which was causing pressure on the heart. This was why the heart sounds had been muffled.

"He's bleeding into the pericardium. We really need to get him to the OR."

"Are they expecting him?" The alarm continued to screech, and Piper reached up to silence it, the noise making her nerves jump more than they already were.

"Yes. We put them on alert when we got the call."

Glancing at the monitor, Piper was pleased to see the lethal rhythm resolving. The patient wasn't out of danger, but at least the immediate crisis was over. "Nice one, Doc."

"He had a chest contusion, so it was expected. Let's get this guy to the OR." Dr. Jenkins removed his goggles and mask.

Piper paused for a brief second, then continued to pack the patient's IV for transport. When she'd looked up at Taylor, a shock of electricity had shot through her. He was simply the most handsome man she'd ever seen. Even with a two-day growth of beard, the shape of his strong jaw was clearly visible. His full mouth curved up slightly as if he were reacting to some slight amusement. But it was his eyes that devastated her the most. Blue, crystal clear, and piercing, they were look-right-into-your-soul eyes.

She had to focus on the patient and not on the flutters that rolled in her stomach. She hadn't reacted this way when his face had been covered, so why should she now? He had been just another doctor she'd worked with, right? But unmasked? Oh, he was absolutely gorgeous.

"Piper? Are you ready?" Taylor asked, and shrugged into his lab jacket.

"Yes, Doctor. Just finishing." She clamped the transport monitor onto the rail of the stretcher.

"It's Taylor, please."

"Okay, thanks." She smiled at him and swallowed down the bubble of attraction that wanted to surface. "Ready to go, but you'll have to lead the way. I don't know where the OR is."

"Happy to." Taylor grabbed a rail on the stretcher and assisted Piper to push the patient down the hall where an OR team waited to put him back together again. Taylor gave his verbal report to the surgeon, and Piper gave hers to the anesthesiologist.

After handing the patient off, Taylor was ready for a break. The new nurse had certainly had her trial by fire and survived, so he was sure she could use a break, too.

"Ready for a cup of coffee?" he asked, and led the way back to the ER and to the staff lounge.

"I should really check in with the charge nurse and let her know I'm here."

They entered the staff lounge. Someone had brewed a fresh pot, as the bright fragrance of exotic coffee hung in the air. Piper sniffed appreciatively, and her eyes went soft. "Oh. I suppose one cup first won't hurt, will it?"

"Hardly." Taylor poured for them, and Piper fixed hers with milk and half a packet of sweetener. "It's not like you weren't working. Emily just didn't know it."

"Emily is the charge nurse, then?" Piper asked, and plopped down into a chair.

"Yes. She was with one of the other traumas that didn't survive." He hated that. Hated that he couldn't fix each and every patient that came through his doors no matter the cause.

"Oh. It's tough to lose patients that you work hard on, isn't it?" There was something in her eyes that was vulnerable, painful, but it wasn't any of his business.

"Yes, it is. Especially when the problems could be prevented." Taylor sat beside her and tried not to think of the two patients he'd lost that morning. Though the odds had been stacked against survival from the start, he still felt like a failure when patients under his care died right in front of him. He didn't like to lose.

His cellphone rang.

"Dr. Jenkins."

He listened for a moment with his eyes closed and a finger pinching the bridge of his nose. "And just *how* messy is it, Alex?"

Pause as he listened. "Can you clean it up by yourself?"

More listening. Bigger headache forming behind his eyes.

"I'll come home at lunch. Don't worry about the stain on the carpet. Or the walls. Or the couch. It's okay. See you at lunchtime."

Amusement fairly sparkled off Piper as he looked at her.

"What?" There was nothing amusing about his end of the conversation.

"Nothing." She sipped her coffee, but couldn't hide the gleam in her eyes. "Your son home alone?"

"Nephew. Staying with me for…" he looked at his digital watch "…five more weeks and six days."

"Not counting down the days, are you?" she asked.

"No, just the seconds." He showed his watch to her and the time counting down every second of that period.

"You're serious. You're really counting down the time like that?" Her blue eyes widened as she looked at him in surprise.

"I'm doing my sister a favor, and that's when the favor ends." Not one moment longer. He had a life to live, airplanes to jump out of and mountains to climb, all before the summer ended. Putting his life on hold was a temporary measure. Very temporary.

"I take it you aren't happy your nephew is with you?" she asked, then paused. "Not that it's any of my business, I realize."

"It's not that I'm not happy. It's just a completely different way of life than I'm used to. People here are taking bets on how long it will be before I drag my sister home from California to take Alex back." He leaned his head on the back of the couch and groaned. There were headaches and then there were headaches.

"Oh, that's so sad," she said, but laughed.

"No, what's sad is that he opened a grape soda on my couch, carpet and walls." Not that it was a huge deal, but it was going to be on the couch and carpet for a very long time. From his memory of being a kid, grape stains came out of nothing.

"They aren't white, are they?" Piper asked, and a sneaky little smile curved up the corners of her lips.

Was she psychic or something? "Not everything. Just the walls and beige carpet. Couch is light brown."

"Oh, dear." Her eyes widened abruptly. "You can't let that sit, or you'll never get it out. Call him back. Do you have any peroxide or seltzer water at the house?"

"Peroxide, I think." He was hardly there, so he really didn't know what might be in his cupboards. Hadn't he bought a bottle of peroxide about a year ago when he'd sliced open his hand on a piece of broken climbing rigging?

"Call him back and tell him to pour half the bottle on the carpet stain and half on the couch. The walls should be okay. At least you can paint over them."

"Why?"

"Getting purple stains out is like getting blood out of your clothing. Peroxide might take it out."

He opened his mouth to protest and then thought of how much more difficult it would be to argue. "I'll call him."

Piper stood. "And I'll check in with Emily. Thanks for the coffee."

CHAPTER TWO

PIPER had survived her first very long day at the hospital. The high desert capital city of New Mexico was lovely with its classic southwest architecture and way the city seemed built into the cliffs and hills rather than taking over the landscape. No highrises here. Living at 7000 feet was going to be a challenge for her, having come from sea level at her last assignment. The air was much thinner at elevation and would take some getting used to.

Piper sighed. Exploration would have to wait for another day as she was scheduled for three more days of work before her first weekend off. Some of the staff had given her information on must-see places and restaurants around the area, so she had a plan for when her time was free. Santa Fe was starting to look like a great assignment. Her travel nurse assignments satisfied her need to travel and explore exotic places that she wouldn't otherwise be able to visit. Most of the time she stayed close to her sister, but some assignments were too good to resist.

New Mexico so far seemed a spectacular mix of

cultures from the old-world Mexican and Native American that had blended over the years to form a new culture altogether, one unique to the area. No wonder people were drawn here, as she had been. There was magic in The Land of Enchantment, as the state motto claimed. She was thoroughly looking forward to getting to know this place before she moved on to her next assignment. If there was another assignment. Though she had hoped to find a place to settle down eventually, the lure of travel and another city to discover seemed firmly enmeshed in her blood. She loved the travel and had no reason to put down roots yet.

As she entered the ER the next day, a small case of nerves shot through her. This would be a quick assignment. Just six weeks, then she'd be off somewhere else. Eventually she'd have to find a place to settle down for good. She'd put her life on hold long enough. Her own needs had always taken a backseat to those of her sister. Now her sister wouldn't need her financial support any longer, and she could…have a life of her own. What a concept. She'd been so dedicated to supporting her sister and providing financial stability for Elizabeth that Piper hadn't really had her own life in a long time. Except for one disastrous relationship that still stung her ego, she had remained relatively free of entanglements. Even thinking of her ex-boyfriend made her clench her jaw and narrow her eyes.

She sighed, trying not to think too hard about him and his wandering ways. After this assignment her responsibility would be over. Then what? She tried to put the question out of her mind when voices from behind her interrupted her train of thought.

"I'm sorry you feel that way, Alex, but I have no choice today." Dr. Taylor Jenkins and a boy she assumed to be his nephew entered through the doors right behind her.

Turning, she took in the sight of the very tall man dressed in scrubs and the tousle-haired boy dragging his feet beside him. Once again, she noticed what an incredibly handsome man Taylor was. Part of being a nurse was paying attention to details, and she noticed every detail of him. Part of her wanted to allow her eyes to linger on his tall, lithe form, but another part of her shuddered. Finding a man attractive and *being attracted* to a man were two different things. She was too far into the being attracted to Taylor, and every red flag in her system was waving.

He was danger on a grand scale. Attraction was what had gotten her into trouble with her last failed relationship. Being attracted to Taylor was out of the question. She'd sworn to herself, never again. Unfortunately, it appeared that never had arrived.

Attraction needed to leave her alone, but she had a feeling that wasn't going to happen. Especially as that little flutter in her stomach grew wings.

"It's way early, Uncle T. I should be in bed, sleeping away my summer vacation, not hanging around a gross hospital all day."

"Be that as it may, this is where I work, and where you are going to spend the day. The babysitter wasn't available and, frankly, after yesterday's fiasco, you can't be trusted at home by yourself."

"But it was an accident, I *told* you that. I said I was sorry."

Clearing her throat, Piper caught their attention,

watching as the two males who couldn't have been much more different in physical appearance entered the lobby. "Hi, guys."

As if just noticing he was about to plow her over, Taylor stopped a few feet from her. "Oh, hello, Piper. Back for more?" he asked, but his eyes were distracted.

"Wild horses couldn't drag me away."

"They could drag *me* away. Pu-lease." Alex made a rude sound deep in his throat.

"Piper, this bundle of enthusiasm and joy is my nephew, Alex."

"Nice to meet you, Alex." The kid couldn't be more miserable looking. He didn't look at her and kicked at the floor. The backpack slung over one shoulder looked weighty. She supposed that he had every book for summer reading in there.

"Hi."

Hearing the tension in his voice, she fished into her purse and extracted a large mixed package of bubble gum and candy. "I was going to put this in the staffroom, but I'll bet you'd like some." Piper tore the bag open and offered it to him.

"Whoa, yeah. Awesome." Alex took two packs of gum and a few wrapped candies, and for the first time looked up into her face, his dark brown eyes intelligent and curious.

"What do you say?" Taylor prompted.

"Thanks." Ducking his head, he flushed and looked away.

"See you inside, Piper," Taylor said with a sigh.

"Okay." Piper followed a few paces behind.

As they walked away, Alex leaned closer to Taylor,

who bent over to hear what he had to say. "Wow. She's hot."

Taylor straightened with a look of amusement on his face and turned to Piper with an extremely male glance. "Yes, she is."

At that moment, Piper heard her name paged overhead. "Oh, gotta go." She dashed around the two and hoped that Taylor hadn't seen her flush. She colored ridiculously, and it was something she had tried to overcome, but couldn't.

Arriving at the nurses' station, she found Emily.

"Oh, you are here. I was hoping that we didn't scare you off yesterday with that wild start to your contract. Some nurses would have headed for the hills." She shook her head and her straight black hair bobbed around her shoulders.

"Not me. I'm tougher than that." She'd had to be. When her parents had been killed, she'd had little time to feel sorry for herself or grieve the loss. So she'd found strength that she hadn't known she'd had. Anything else, compared to that, well, just didn't compare.

"Well, good. I'd like to pair you up with one of the nurses for the orientation you were supposed to have yesterday, and then we'll go from there. After yesterday, I'm certain you won't have any problems."

Emily introduced her to her preceptor, and she spent the rest of the morning familiarizing herself with the ER.

At lunch, she entered the staff lounge to find a sullen-faced Alex sitting with a book on his lap.

"Hey, kiddo. What's wrong with you?" she asked, and took a seat beside him. He looked as if he was about to have a meltdown.

"I'm s-o-o-o bored." He snapped the book shut and

held it out to her to see. By the look of Alex, it certainly was going to be a long, hot summer. "Reading isn't part of my summer plans. Uncle T. gave me this. Said it was a good book, but I just don't get it."

"I don't think I got it when I was your age, either. Might have to be a little older to appreciate it. What grade are you going into?"

"Sixth." He folded his arms over his chest.

"What do you want to do instead of reading? Anything?"

"Yeah, I want to skydive, and climb mountains and ride a motorcycle really fast, just like Uncle T." For the first time today excitement shone in his eyes, and he came alive right in front of her.

"He does all that, does he?" She was beginning to see worship of Uncle Taylor, Super-Hero, in Alex's eyes.

"Yeah, and a whole lot more really cool stuff, like base jumping in Norway. He took videos and it was so awesome." Alex flopped back against the couch. "But I never get to do anything. I'm gonna be stuck inside all summer."

Taylor opened the door to the lounge to check on Alex, but stopped when he heard Piper's voice. It was soft and filled with compassion. Knowing he shouldn't listen, he seemed powerless to stop himself.

"Maybe there's a day camp you could go to. My younger sister used to go to one when I worked back in San Francisco," Piper said.

"Did she like it?" Doubt was heavy in the boy's voice.

"Sure did. Had to drag her out of there every day."

There was a momentary pause. "What kind of stuff did she do?"

"Biking, hiking, crafts, and maybe some sewing, I think."

"Those are *girl* things. I want to do *guy* stuff." The sigh that followed said it all.

"Why don't you talk to your uncle when he comes for lunch?"

Another pause. "I don't think he'll listen to me. He's kinda like my dad that way. He doesn't listen, either."

Taylor closed his eyes and allowed the door to shut silently. Caroline's parting words had been not to disappoint Alex as his father had done. What had he done so far with Alex? Total disappointment.

Determined to fix it right now, he coughed loudly and entered the staffroom.

"Hey, Alex. How's it going?" Taylor asked, and glanced between them.

"I'm sick," Alex said, and made a face, then clutched his abdomen.

"Sick?" Taylor frowned and grew concerned. The kid hadn't been feeling poorly that morning, just ornery because Taylor had dragged him out of bed at the crack of dawn. Maybe bringing him to the hospital had been a bad idea after all. Though he'd been here just a few hours, there were all sorts of bacteria in hospitals that he could easily pick up. "Sick how?"

"Sick of being here. Can I go back to your house if I promise not to spill anything again? I won't drink anything. Not even water, I promise," Alex said, his dark brown eyes beseeching in a way that cut right through Taylor. He ran a hand through his hair. He wasn't prepared for this. He couldn't work sixty hours a week and care for a child. That camp thing Piper mentioned might have potential, though. Dammit. He just didn't have it in him. The family he'd grown up in was no role model to draw from, either.

"You just can't sit at my house and play video games all summer, Alex." Taylor ran a hand through his hair, more than frustrated already and Alex had only been with him a few days.

"Why not?" he said, and gave Taylor a very adult look. "It's what I do, Uncle T."

"Didn't you just say you wanted to climb mountains and jump out of airplanes like your uncle?" Piper asked from her seat beside Alex.

"Piper," Alex whispered out of the corner of his mouth and cast her a conspiratorial glance. "He wasn't supposed to know."

"So how are you going to do any of this stuff if no one knows about it?" she asked, her manner totally at ease while talking to Alex. Taylor wished he could be that way, but his experience with kids was limited to birthdays and holidays and presents sent from far away.

Apparently, Alex had to think about that a moment because he didn't have his usual snappy comeback ready. Then he shrugged. "I don't know."

"Why don't we go get a burger and fries and talk about it?" Taylor asked. "I'm sure there's something we can fix you up with that we can both agree on."

With only a sullen expression on his face and a non-committal shrug, Alex tucked his belongings into a worn backpack. "Okay."

"Want to join us, Piper?" Taylor asked, hoping she would.

"I brought a sandwich."

"You can have that any day. Today is green chile cheese

fries day at the cafeteria." For whatever reason, he really wanted to have lunch with this woman. She'd offered him some hope in dealing with Alex and he'd...needed that.

"Sounds like death by french fry." But she stood and followed them from the room. "But I'm game."

Taylor slowed as Piper tugged on his sleeve and pulled him back.

"Just so you know, a *bored* kid is a *bad* kid. Especially the really smart ones." She nodded at Alex who continued down the hall in front of them.

"So, tell me about this camp business I overheard," Taylor said, and ushered Piper forward. "I ran wild on military bases as a kid, so I don't know anything about how they work."

Piper smiled up at him, and Taylor took a second look at her. Though not beautiful in the classic sense, her heart-shaped face and full lips were definitely attractive. But her warm blue eyes that sparkled with suppressed humor intrigued him more than anything. Straight caramel-colored hair in a shoulder-length bob swung enticingly as she moved. She was tall and trim, but curvy in the right places. Though he'd observed those things yesterday, he really hadn't *noticed* them. Too busy with patients and work as usual.

Something in his chest cramped as he watched her catch up with Alex. If he'd been too busy to notice a woman as lovely as Piper, there was something seriously wrong with him.

After lunch, Piper returned to the ER to relieve another nurse for her break. Emily, the charge nurse, called her aside to make the assignment. "By the way, I hope I'm not intruding here where I don't belong," she said, and chewed thoughtfully on her lip a moment. "But I think I need to give you a warning."

"A warning? What did I do?" Piper stared transfixed at Emily, unable to think of any infraction so far.

Emily touched Piper's arm in a friendly gesture and Piper relaxed somewhat. "No, not in your work. Sorry. But I happened to notice that you had lunch with Taylor."

Still not sure of what to make of this conversation, she said, "Is that against the rules or something?"

"No. But just to give you a heads up, Taylor's a player, got a reputation with the ladies, especially the nurses who come through here."

"I see."

"He's got CDD."

"You mean ADD? Attention Deficit Disorder?" Piper asked, puzzled at the mistake.

"No." Emily shook her head. "I mean CDD. *Commitment* deficit disorder. He hasn't stayed with one woman for more than a few weeks at a time." She patted Piper's arm. "He's a wonderful man and a great doctor, but he acts as if he's at a dating buffet. He keeps going back for more." She waved a hand. "Anyway, you're a grown woman, but before you proceeded any further with him, I wanted you to have that information. Take it or leave it, at least you have it."

"Thanks." Piper said, then tried to change the subject, certain she wasn't going to have to worry about Taylor getting too interested in her. He was just grateful and had bought her a burger. But Emily's warning was certainly something to consider.

CHAPTER THREE

"OKAY, so rock-climbing camp it is," Taylor said as he clicked the "send" button on the computer and registered Alex for the camp with before- and after-care programs, starting tomorrow. No more bored days spent at the hospital.

Alex raced through the living room at full speed. "Yeah! I'm going climbing!" He raced back to the office and nearly flung himself at Taylor. "Thanks, Uncle T. I'll never ever forget this."

Taylor caught the boy to him before he knocked them out of the office chair and stood Alex in front of him. "Whoa, there. It's okay, Alex." He gave Alex a pat on the shoulder, surprised at the amount of enthusiasm sparking off the boy.

"I'm serious. You have no idea how totally cool this is." He looked wide-eyed at Taylor. "Wait. You *do* know how cool this is, 'cause you already go rock climbing. *Duh*," Alex said, and slapped himself on the forehead.

"It's okay. I'm just lucky we got you in." When Taylor had been Alex's age, and living under the domineering thumb of his father, he had been lucky to get out of the house without an altercation of some sort. There had been no camps for Taylor. Climbing trees and rock formations had saved his sanity in his pre-teen years, challenging himself in ways that his father couldn't understand. After that, progressing to bigger and more dangerous excursions had seemed natural. Honing his muscles and growing into his height, his father had no longer been able to control him. That's when things had really changed between them, and they hadn't spoken for years. Thankfully, he'd had an uncle help him figure out how to get what he wanted out of life. He hoped to pass that gift on to Alex. Perhaps not medical school, but whatever the kid wanted to pursue in life.

"Let's finish this conversation another day. Time you're off for a shower. You don't want to smell like a polecat your first day at camp, do you?"

"No, I don't wanna smell like a polecat," he said, and frowned, staring up at Taylor. "I... I don't even know what a polecat is."

Taylor gave a laugh. "It's a kind of skunk. Hit the shower, kiddo, just to make sure," he said, and tousled Alex's hair.

"Okay."

Taylor laughed as Alex headed for the bathroom. Maybe this thing with Alex was going to turn out okay after all. Caroline was right. He didn't really know his nephew, and he should. Even though his life was a little on the wild side, Taylor was the only stable male influence in the boy's life. But now, spending so much time with Alex stirred up feelings that he thought he'd put to rest long ago. His relationship with his father was not much different than the one Alex had with his own father. More like they tolerated each other than liked each other's company. Whatever. Over and done with for him. Rising from the chair, he changed into jogging pants and his running shoes. The last two days he'd been off his exercise schedule and desperately needed the release it gave him. *Endorphins, here I come.* He knocked on the bathroom door.

"Alex, I'm going for a jog. I'll be back in an hour."

"Okay." Alex called through the door.

Once out into the evening air, Taylor drew in deep breaths and stretched a few minutes before walking to the park. Exercise and strength training had made him physically strong, and he needed that endorphin kick he'd been missing the last few days. Sometimes that was all that got him through some very long and intense days at work. Though he worked with a lot of very good nice people, he had few truly close friends. A few guys he climbed with, a few doctors like Ian McSorley, and a few women he'd had casual relationships with. Nothing serious. Nothing long-lasting and that was how he needed it. At least at this point in his life.

In minutes he reached the nature park, filled with desert flora and fauna native to the high desert of New Mexico. Breathing in the cooling evening air, he relaxed into his pace and sought the zone that had been his salvation for many years.

Piper watched as Taylor loped around the sand-filled track. She'd never catch up with him with the pace he set, so she just walked along behind him, enchanted with the plant life and terrain that was so different from any place she'd ever been. Now she understood what was meant by high desert. Muted browns and greens covered most of the ground, but here and there were fabulously colored blooms, usually attached to thorny cacti. There was beauty here, you just had to look for it. Up ahead, a jackrabbit zigzagged in a crazy move to dash away and hide beneath a bush. Unaccustomed to the 7000-foot elevation of Santa Fe, Piper was winded after a few minutes, so she found a large rock to rest on, took in the nature scene and caught her breath.

She kept her eye on the lone jogger working his way up and down the hills through the park. There were no trees to speak of, just clumps of large bushes, so she could see him as he moved around the park. Numerous other people walked and ran past her on the trail, but no one captured her attention as Taylor did.

The man was intense. As intense as any doctor she'd ever worked with, and her heart noticed every time she'd been close enough to smell his spicy cologne. She wondered how he was going to cope the entire summer with his nephew at his side, but she was not willing to take a bet as the other staff had done. Men like Taylor valued their freedom and independence more than anything. That had been her ex-boyfriend exactly. Another physician. Another assignment. Another town, miles away. Another heartbreak she was not going to repeat. She'd never been enough for him. He'd made that clear from the start. She'd never be enough for a man like Taylor, either.

Taylor dropped behind a hill, and Piper lost sight of him, then he reappeared on the next rise, closer to where she was. The man in motion was definitely a wondrous sight.

Eventually, he jogged right up to her. "Hey, Doc."

"What?" He looked at her then. "Oh, hey, Piper." He

stopped and bent over to catch his breath. "What are you doing out here?"

She caught herself looking at his lean, muscled legs, bared by almost indecently short jogging shorts, and the way his chest pumped with each breath he dragged in and pushed out. "Er, just reviewing my anatomy."

"What?" He tilted his head up to look at her, a frown on his face.

"Nothing. Don't let me interrupt your exercise. I just wanted to say hi." Embarrassment flooded her. She hoped he hadn't caught her looking at his legs or that magnificent chest. Working with someone and finding them physically attractive could be a snag. Not that she couldn't be professional about it, but it could certainly make her assignment, uh, interesting. A perk she hadn't thought of. Working with a handsome man could never be termed a hardship.

"No problem." He waved away her concern. "I was just about through anyway, ready to cool down."

"Did you find a camp for Alex?" Distraction. That's what she needed to keep her mind off of Taylor's gorgeous body revealed by those shorts and tight T-shirt.

"Yep. Got him all signed up, and he starts tomorrow morning. Thanks again for that suggestion. I don't know what I'd have done otherwise."

"I'm sure he's thrilled." A warm feeling pulsed through her that he'd taken her advice. Though it had been a little thing for her to make the suggestion, she had been glad to do it.

"Yeah. He about hugged me to death." A frown briefly crossed Taylor's brow, and he looked away.

"Hugs bother you?" she asked, watching him closely.

Many men weren't comfortable with affection. They wanted sex, sure, but real affection was another thing. Intimacy? Forget about that, too. She'd found that out with her doctor ex-boyfriend. Sex equated intimacy, then you rolled over and went to sleep. Right. While your partner stared at the ceiling for a few hours.

"Not usually. Just not used to them." He placed a foot up on the rock beside her and stretched out his leg, then switched to the other side. "I'm not very demonstrative by nature."

"There's a theory out there that we need four therapeutic hugs a day for survival, eight a day for maintenance and twelve for growth," she said. "I read that somewhere. Stimulates the immune system and fosters well-being."

"That's a lot of hugs in a day." He trained piercing eyes on her and raised his brows.

"I kind of like it. And there are documented benefits of therapeutic touch."

"There's a lot of that stuff going on in Santa Fe, but not much in the traditional settings. More in the outpatient setting, though I think there could be benefits for inpatients, as well."

Piper nodded. "I took a few courses on healing touch and have used it successfully for pain control when nothing else works." The touch was a form of meditation and self-healing that some people responded to.

"Really? There is a school for healing touch here, and I think it's mostly for nurse-type people if you're interested."

"I'll think about that, but as I'm only going to be here a few weeks, I probably won't have the time." She'd witnessed too many incidents of success with the technique to doubt it. "Works for me when I need it." Boy had she needed the human touch over the years. Raising her sister, losing her parents at a young age. That had been a brutal loss to her and her sister. That single event had changed her life. She'd been forced to grow up overnight.

The loving hands of her aunt Ida had sustained her when she'd needed it. Those loving touches were a thing she missed now. Unfortunately, the current ache in her life couldn't be filled by the simple touch of family. She was beginning to suspect that she craved a satisfying relationship, that she just hadn't found and wasn't willing to stick her neck out for. Maybe loneliness was something she'd just have to get used to, like an ache that would never go away. By now, it was certainly her constant companion. Sure, she had friends and people to do things with, but she always went home alone. That hollow ache could be dulled, but never seemed to go away completely. Looking at Taylor, she knew he'd never be able to fill that void. She wasn't what someone like him craved.

He took a step closer, but then stopped, recalling his conversation with Alex about personal hygiene. "I'm hot and sweaty now, but I'd be willing to give the hug thing a try another time." His gaze dropped to her mouth and lower and the breath that had returned to him after his run was somehow stuck in his throat.

Hugs, huh? He'd have never thought that hugs were beneficial, just some sort of activity that made people think they felt better. Denial was powerful, especially during emotional situations, which was why he tried to avoid them. But standing here looking at Piper and how attractive she was, the hint of a flush on her face and neck, he'd be willing to consider testing her theory at some point. Her full lips curving up at the corners nearly made him reconsider. It had been way too long since he'd been in a relationship, considered having another one. Not that he'd do that with Piper. She was a coworker and a temporary staff member. As he glanced over her figure again, he reflected she was a fine-looking staff member.

"So, I know you're a traveler, but what brings you to Santa Fe? Family, boyfriend?" This wasn't like him, he thought, and frowned at that. He wasn't this interested in people and generally didn't make polite conversation. Something about Piper made him want to know more.

Before answering, she tucked her hair behind one ear and shot a quick glance at him. "Oh, I'm not really sure. I've been a lot of places, but not New Mexico. This short assignment seemed like a quick way to see the area and grab a bonus, too. And you?"

"I started out in Albuquerque at the university there and migrated up to Santa Fe. My sister lives here, too." Piper's answer just generated more questions in his head. "I was wondering how you know so much about children. Do you have any?"

"No. I don't have my own children, but I've had to pretty much raise my little sister since our parents were killed years ago."

"I see. That must have been tough."

She gave a small, sad smile. "More brutal than you'll ever know." Unable to look away from the intensity of him, she met his gaze and held on, seeing how far it took them.

The heat of attraction poured off Taylor as he stared

at her mouth, and her heart skipped a beat just imagining long, slow body contact with him. She swallowed, a hint of desire crawling along her spine in reaction to him.

Attractions between nurses and doctors happened. The intensity of their work lives pushed the attraction to higher levels. Unable to look away, she stared at Taylor, and he held her gaze, seeming unafraid of the connection forming between them. But then, according to Alex, he wasn't afraid of anything. Someone like her wasn't going to scare him one bit.

In the distance, the faint yip-yip of a coyote signaled the fall of night. Desert nights were a sight to behold, especially, when she was out in one with Taylor in front of her.

She blinked as the persistent yip penetrated the web of attraction between them. Oh, God. She was simply staring at him. And he was…staring back. She licked her lips, and pushed her hair behind her ear as her mouth went dry, feeling much like the desert around her. This wasn't good.

Then Piper sat up and listened, not sure what she had heard. "Did you hear that?" Whew. Anything to provide a distraction, divert Taylor's attention from her and hers from him. Taylor seemed to break free of the hypnotic spell between them, took a step back from her and huffed out a quick breath. The tension stretching between them snapped.

"Oh. Hear what?" Taylor asked, running his hands through his hair as he turned away. "I don't hear anything."

"Kind of sounded like the noise I heard earlier. I was thinking it sounded like a coyote, but I'm not sure."

Sudden cries for help echoed through the park.

"Now I hear something." He paused a second, listening, and cries for help carried through the park. "Let's see what's going on."

They raced to the top of a small hill and found an elderly gentleman sitting on the ground, a pile of blood-covered fur at his feet.

"Oh, dear," Piper said.

"What happened?" Taylor said as they approached the distressed man. Piper knelt beside him.

"Coyote. Attacked my dog," he said between wheezing gasps.

Piper checked his pulse, then pressed her hand to his cheek. His coloring was a startling red. "Sir, do you have any medical conditions?"

"Please. Just help. My dog," he said, and tears flowed down his rounded cheeks.

Piper looked up at Taylor, her blue eyes full of inquiry. He knew the question in her gaze, and when he looked down at the animal, he knew it was already too late and shook his head.

"Let's see what we can do about you first." Her calm voice and soft tone was designed to comfort the man beside her.

"Oh, no! Is Muffin dead?" he asked, and clasped her arm.

Piper took his hand and drew his attention away from the site. "I don't know. We'll help Muffin all we can, but I think you need some help, too."

The man responded to Piper and nodded. "Okay. Okay." He fumbled in his pocket and withdrew an inhaler. Piper held his trembling hand to his mouth as he took two puffs of the medication that would assist his breathing. Tears still trickled down his face. "I'm short...of breath."

"Were you bitten, too?" Taylor asked, and knelt beside them. The dog was past any help they could give it. A small dog was no match against a coyote that was probably rabid. The kind of behavior the man described was unusual for the normally reclusive coyote. They would have to report it after the man was seen to.

"No. It just tore out of the brush and attacked poor Muffin." He wiped his tears with his hands, which were covered in scratches. "I tried to pull it off."

Taylor assessed the man's condition. Without medical equipment, he was limited as to what he could do. Basic first aid was about it. "That was a very brave thing to do, but it appears that the coyote got a piece of you, too."

"What?"

Taylor pointed to the puncture wounds on the man's hands and forearms. "It bit you, too."

"Oh, no." The man looked at his arms, apparently seeing the wounds for the first time. With wide eyes, he looked from Piper to Taylor and fainted.

Piper tried to catch him, but landed in a heap with the unconscious man. Reaching forward, Taylor lifted the man so Piper could scoot out from under him.

"Are you okay?" he asked, and eased the man to a prone position.

"Yes. Do you think he's just passed out?" she asked, and checked his pulse again. "His pulse is okay, but his color is ghastly."

"I think he's simply overcome with emotion. Some people react badly when they see their own blood. I'm going to call 911 and have him checked out. He'll need treatment for the bite in any case, especially if the animal was rabid." Taylor pulled his cell phone from his pocket and gave the necessary information. "They should be here in a few."

"I feel so sorry for the guy," she said, and looked at the mess that had once been the beloved Muffin. "Yuck. Do you think it's really a rabid coyote or just a dog attack?"

"He was probably right. We have coyote attacks a few times a year here, and they are always rabid. Fish and Game Department keeps close tabs on rabies cases and want people to report it if they find suspicious animals." He hoped that Piper was going to be okay and not frightened of being out in the desert. This was definitely an unexpected event at the park.

Piper looked around them as the night deepened, casting shadows where there had been none moments ago. "We aren't in danger, are we? I mean, you don't think it'll come back, do you?"

Taylor glanced around. The coyote was probably long gone. "Don't know. But keeping an eye out for a coyote heading toward us with bared teeth is probably a good idea."

"Taylor!" She laughed despite the tense situation. "That's awful." But she glanced around anyway.

"Made you laugh, though." And that was a wonderful sound.

"You certainly did."

The man on the ground between them moaned and raised a hand to his head.

"Don't try to move, sir," Taylor said, and pressed a hand to his shoulder to keep him down. "An ambulance is on the way."

"What for?" he asked, his voice sounding weaker than it had moments ago.

"Piper, can you go to the entrance and lead them over here?" Taylor asked, now not so sure the man was as stable as he appeared.

"Yes. I'll be right back." She stood. "I see the lights."

In minutes she returned with the crew, carrying medical equipment. They hooked the man to the monitors, checked his blood pressure and watched his heart rhythm bounce across the screen.

"I'm Piper and this is Dr. Jenkins. What's your name?" Piper asked, and patted his arm gently, her voice a soothing tone that even Taylor was responding to.

"Jesse. Jesse Farmer."

"BP's low," a paramedic said.

Taylor watched the heart monitor, interpreting the rhythm. "Looks like he's in third-degree heart block, too. No wonder he fainted." Potentially not good. "Jesse, have you ever been told you have a heart condition?" He spoke to Jesse, but kept his eyes on the monitor.

"Once. But it went away."

"Heart conditions don't generally go away," he said, knowing that many patients resisted the idea of their bodies failing. He would, too, he supposed. But ignoring medical advice and symptoms only led to disaster.

"My cardiologist said I need a pacemaker, but I didn't like that idea." Another paramedic placed an oxygen mask over Jesse's face.

"Well, this incident tonight proves that you definitely need one. That means immediately. Boys, take him in. Have the external pacemaker on him and ready in case he loses his rhythm during transport."

Taylor helped them lift the stretcher while Piper reassured Jesse.

"What about Muffin?" Jesse cried, and gripped Piper's arm.

"We'll take care of Muffin," Piper said, and patted Jesse on the arm. "You need to call your family as soon as you get to the hospital so someone can come be with you. You shouldn't be alone right now."

"Okay. Okay." He lay back on the stretcher as exhaustion overcame him.

Taylor stood beside Piper as the ambulance pulled away. "So how do you think we should deal with Muffin?" he asked.

"I have some supplies in my car and can put him in a hazardous materials bag. If it's been killed by a rabid coyote, isn't someone going to want to know about it?"

"Wildlife Department. Let's collect the remains, and then I'll call them." He looked at his watch and noticed the timer continued counting down the seconds of his commitment to Alex. "It's probably too late for them to come get it. They'll tell us what to do, though."

Fifteen minutes later they had trekked to Piper's car, collected Muffin's body and placed it in Piper's trunk. "That ought to do it," she said, and squirted hand sanitizer in her palm and offered some to Taylor. "Just in case."

"You come prepared, don't you?" he asked, and rubbed the solution into his hands.

"Girl Scout of long ago and a home-care nurse sometimes." She held up three fingers of her right hand and crossed her thumb over her pinky in the Girl Scout salute.

Full darkness had fallen and streetlights flickered on.

"Damn. I almost forgot about Alex." Taylor looked

at his watch, near to panic. "I was only supposed to be gone an hour and it's been nearly two." He was such a failure at being responsible.

"He would have called you if something was wrong, right?"

"Probably. Just the same, I'd better get home." If something happened to the kid, he'd never forgive himself. He'd not only disappoint Alex, he'd disappoint his sister, too.

"Why don't I drive you? It'll be faster." She placed her hand on his arm in a small gesture of reassurance.

"Thanks. It's not far." Relief poured over Taylor. He'd known Piper about two days, and she'd already been incredibly helpful to him. Somehow he was going to pay her back.

"With wild coyotes out there, you shouldn't take any chances, right?"

"Right." He grinned as Piper climbed into the little sedan he barely fit into.

CHAPTER FOUR

WITHIN minutes, Piper had delivered Taylor to his house.

"Come in a minute while I check on Alex, and then I'll call the Wildlife Department. Let me at least offer you a glass of water or something."

Piper followed him through the garage, the kitchen and into the living room where Alex sat on the couch in his pajamas, listening to a headset and reading a book.

Startled at their abrupt presence in front of him, he jumped slightly and ripped the headset off. "What?"

"Are you okay?" Taylor asked. He stepped closer and ran a hand through his hair. "I was gone a lot longer than I told you." He'd promised to take care of Alex. He just didn't know how he was going to accomplish that by himself. Being thrust out of airplanes was a lot easier than being thrust into fatherhood. Or unclehood, or whatever you wanted to call it. The domain of the responsible adult male. A place he'd purposefully avoided and here he was standing knee-deep in it.

"You were?" Alex shrugged, his eyes wide and just a bit too innocent. "I didn't notice." He patted the book in front of him.

"What are you reading?" Piper asked, and stepped closer to the boy.

"Uh," Alex said, and looked down.

Piper followed his glance and tried to hide the smirk that wanted to erupt onto her face. Reaching for the book, she turned it right side up and returned it to his lap. "You might want to try reading it this way. It's a lot easier."

Beneath his tawny skin, Alex flushed to the roots of his hair. "Busted," he said under his breath, his lips barely moving.

"Busted is right," Taylor said with a frown. "I thought you said you were going to read."

"I was. I mean, I really wanted to, but I got so excited about tomorrow that I had to play some video games to calm down." He leaped from the couch to reveal a horrific large stain on the fabric that the peroxide obviously hadn't conquered. "Piper, Uncle T. signed me up for rock-climbing camp tomorrow. Thanks!" He gave her an exuberant hug and then raced to Taylor. After a brief hug, he pulled back. "Oh, gross. You're sweaty."

Taylor's face revealed momentary shock before he laughed. "I am, man. Sorry."

Alex backed away and walked toward the hall to the bedrooms. "Well, at least now I know what a polecat smells like. 'Night."

"'Night, Alex." Piper stood and redirected her attention to Taylor. "What was that about a polecat?" she asked.

"A previous discussion on personal hygiene," Taylor said without elaborating. The light sparkling from her eyes intrigued him. He'd been around plenty of women who climbed mountains, jumped from planes and raced bicycles. The intensity flowing off Piper was a different sort of energy. One he'd not been around much before. One that was comforting and settling. Completely foreign to him. "Yes, well. I'll call Wildlife and see what we need to do with the dog."

Minutes later, Taylor hung up the phone. "It's too late to send someone over tonight from their office, so Animal Control is coming over. We're not supposed to touch it any more than necessary and to wash well."

"Sounds good." She sighed. "I feel so bad for the poor thing. But at least, from the sound of it, it was quick."

They noticed a young presence at the door and turned. "Can I see it?" Alex asked.

"No," they said in unison.

"Aw, c'mon." He scuffed a bare foot on the tile floor.

"You're supposed to be in bed." Taylor stood and turned Alex by the shoulders and nudged him back to his temporary bedroom.

"I needed a drink, and I heard you talking about the rabid coyote."

"*Suspected* rabid coyote," Taylor corrected. Piper was right, this kid was smart. Smarter than he'd realized. Caroline was right and that saddened him, too. He didn't know his nephew. Somehow he was going to make up for not being there for his nephew. In six weeks.

"Uncle T., even *I* know enough about coyotes to know it was rabid. They just don't act like that."

"You're right. But it's long gone now, and it's bedtime for you."

"It's summer, can't I stay up longer?"

"You have your first day at camp tomorrow, so I'd suggest getting a good night's sleep. When I'm going on a climbing expedition, even I go to bed a little early." For him that was midnight, usually. Sleep was a luxury he didn't always have or take advantage of when he had it.

"Okay." Ducking his head down, Alex shuffled his way down the hall. A large yawn interrupted his goodnight, and he disappeared from sight.

"I think I'll head home, too." Piper raised her brows, her inquisitive gaze holding on Taylor's for just a lingering second, and a hint of that sizzle between them returned. "It's been a lot more interesting evening than I had anticipated. From a walk in the park to a medical rescue to a rabid coyote. Wow."

"No kidding. Got more than you bargained for." Taylor walked her outside, retrieved the animal carcass from her trunk and placed it on the sidewalk by the front door. Animal Control should be arriving soon.

"See you tomorrow," Piper said, and drove away.

In silence, Taylor watched until the small car faded from view. What was it about Piper that had captured his attention? The blue eyes, the sensual mouth that looked like it needed a long, hot kiss? Or the curves his hands itched to try out.

Taylor entered the house and flopped down on the couch, pressing his hands against his face. Though the enormous stains on the carpet and couch were glaring in their contrast to the fibers, Piper hadn't said anything. She was certainly polite, intuitive when it came to children, a good nurse. But none of those things were what had intrigued him. Maybe it was the spark of laughter in her gorgeous eyes or the sizzle of attraction that had unexpectedly flared between them. Kissing her would be—

His thoughts came to a screeching halt. He had no business thinking of a coworker this way, no matter how attractive he found her. He knew well enough that he was a poor candidate for a relationship, and she had long term written all over her, something he was incapable of giving a relationship. Knowing that about himself had kept him away from entanglements. That settled it for him. He was no longer going to be attracted to Piper.

With the echo of his father's rage and his mother's tears ringing in his head, he hit the shower and stayed there for a very long time. Memories weren't that easy to wash away.

After a hot shower and dressing in a light nightshirt, Piper pulled her laptop computer from its case and settled it onto her lap in bed. A cup of tea beside her, and she was ready to tackle some e-mails.

Right now, her sister was about to enter cooking school in Phoenix, Arizona, a short flight from Santa Fe. As she waited for the computer to boot, she realized this was the first time Elizabeth would truly be on her own. Away from Ida. Away from her. She hoped that Elizabeth would do well on her own. A sudden pang hit Piper's heart as she wondered how she was going to do when Elizabeth didn't need her.

Thoughts of her evening adventure with Taylor pushed aside thoughts of responsibility and cooking school. A man like that made her want to abandon all restraint and the goals she had set for herself and just dive right into him. He would certainly be a joy to behold in the bedroom. Of that she was certain and her stomach clenched just at the thought of him. Strong, commanding, a man who knew his way around a woman's body.

Piper shivered and sipped her tea. Those kinds of thoughts weren't going to be conducive to sleep.

A little icon raced across the computer screen, alerting her to new e-mail.

That was the ticket. Distraction. Keep her mind off Taylor. Distraction. Keep her mind on the e-mails. Distraction, she thought as her mind recalled the long, lean strength of his muscled legs. Yes, Taylor was nothing but distraction. But, oh, what an exceptional distraction he was.

Could she consider this a hardship assignment?

CHAPTER FIVE

JUST after she arrived home from work the next day, Piper's phone rang and she groaned, hoping it wasn't the night nurse calling about something she'd forgotten.

"Hello?"

"Hi, Piper. This is Alex, Dr. Jenkins's nephew. Remember me?"

Pleasure filled her at the sound of the young voice on the phone. "Well, sure, I remember you. How could I forget?"

"Anyway, Uncle T. and I are going climbing on Saturday, and I want you to come with us. Can you come?"

Hesitation filled her. Although she'd love to go, she wasn't sure about climbing. Her feet rarely left the ground and when they did for airplane transportation, sedation was usually involved. "Does Taylor know you're calling me?"

"Yeah. I told him. I mean, I asked him if I could invite you."

She smiled at that. "And what did he say? It was okay?"

"He really wants you to come, too," Alex said.

At that, a bubble of pleasure burst over Piper and the fatigue from the workday evaporated. Although she doubted Alex's sentiment was completely accurate, the idea of it still pleased her. What else did she have to do on a beautiful summer Saturday except watch two men risk their lives climbing a big dangerous rock? "Is he there? Can I talk to him a minute?"

"Hold on."

Seconds later, Taylor's voice came through the phone into her ear. "Piper?"

Heat suffused her at the sound of her name, and she shivered involuntarily. The phone lent an intimacy that wasn't real, but Piper clutched the phone to her ear as if it were. Intimacy had been almost forgotten in her life, and the sound of his voice breathed a memory of it through her.

"Hi. Alex tells me you're going climbing, and he wants me to go along. Are you okay with that?" she asked, hoping that he was. For some unknown reason, she wanted to be with him, even if it was on such an expedition.

"Absolutely. We can take a picnic or something, make a day of it."

"You're not going to the Alps, are you?"

The sound of his deep laugh sent a thrill of pleasure through her. "No. No Alps this weekend."

"Okay, then. I'll come." Whether she was going to regret this or not, she didn't know, but she was going to go climbing for the first time in her life.

"Are you kidding?" Piper exclaimed. "I'm not climbing that." She pointed to the huge rock formation they stood in front of. She looked up and up and up at the giant craggy brown rock and felt her stomach slide all the way to her feet.

"It's not that big," Taylor said, and laughed at her reaction. "Besides, we're not climbing that one." He pointed to a much smaller rock nestled up against the larger one. "We're going on that one."

"Uncle T.! That's only ten feet high. I climb higher than that at camp," Alex said, protest in every syllable.

"I'm not taking you up 500 feet the first time out. You gotta show me what you got first, kiddo. Learn to trust each other as a team, and we go from there."

Alex nodded, bounced around lightly on his feet and shadow-boxed. "I'll show you what I got. Just you wait and see."

"Alex, are you sure you want to do this?" Piper swallowed, trying not to be intimidated by a rock. It was just a rock. Right? A really big one.

"It's okay, Piper. I'll climb up first and show you how it's done," Alex said, cinching on his gear.

Taylor checked Alex's rigging and gave it a firm tug, then pulled his gear from a bag. "I hadn't had this stuff out for a year, so I checked everything last night." He looked at Piper and the serious doubt etched on her face. "Look, you can stay down here and watch us. Might be pretty boring, though."

"I'll take my chances," she said, sarcasm heavy in her voice, then she smiled. "It's okay. I would rather watch with my feet planted on the ground."

"Well, if you're climbing, your feet are planted on the ground, it's just vertical."

"Your logic eludes me, Taylor. Go. I'll stay here and guard the picnic basket or something." The way things were going she wasn't going to have an appetite for a picnic. Just watching them made her anxious, and they were still beside her. Every spark in her that was an ER nurse went on full alert. This was a disaster waiting to happen, and she just knew she was going to watch them splatter themselves on the ground below.

"Okay. Promise you'll catch me if I fall?" he asked, his eyes full of mischief as he buckled on a helmet.

"You aren't going to fall, are you?" she asked, her heart racing at the thought.

"No."

"Then I won't have to worry about catching you, will I?" She stepped back from them and found a seat on the ledge. "I'd rather catch some sun and watch you two." Yep. Staying right there on solid ground. Of course, watching Taylor was pretty easy on the eyes.

Smiling at her response, he finished rigging while an impatient Alex danced beside him. "Gloves and helmet on, kiddo," Taylor said, and applied his own, which covered most of his hands, but left half the fingers exposed. The gloves were of worn and scarred leather and had seen better days.

"But—"

"No buts. No safety, no climbing." On this, for Taylor, there were no compromises. "Safety equipment has saved my life more than once over the years. I'll never, ever sacrifice safety for fun. Especially when I'm responsible for another person."

"Aw, man," Alex said, but complied. "That's what they say in camp, too."

"I'll go up first," Taylor said as he fastened Alex's harness to him.

"What's that for?" Alex asked.

"If you slip, I can stop you with it."

"Okay. I guess we haven't gotten that far in camp yet."

From the ground, Piper watched as the two inched their way up the side of the rock. Now that she knew she wasn't going to be climbing up its rough surface, she didn't think it was as big as she had imagined at first. It didn't mean she wanted to be up there with them, but her fears were forgotten as she remained safely on the ground.

A profound measure of serenity folded itself around Taylor as he focused on each precise movement. He loved climbing. Sharing that love with his nephew, teaching him a sport that they could share together, somehow made it that much more important to him. The protection of the secluded canyon placed the three of them in a quiet bubble away from the city, crowds and the stress of the job. A warm desert breeze lifted their hair.

Taylor lived for times like this and allowed himself to sink deeper into that place where he could just think and live in the moment. There was nothing as important as the next handhold, the next foothold, the next move up.

"Uncle T.?" Alex asked, his breath panting just a little.

"Yeah?"

"How high are we going to go?"

"I don't know—why? Are you tired already?" He grinned down at the boy who gave him a look of disgust.

"No. We're only ten feet up. I just want to tell my class I climbed a thousand feet high."

With a laugh, Taylor dispelled that notion. "The big rock's only 500 feet high. This one's about fifty. We'll go 'til we're tired, then come down, okay?"

"Okay."

"We'll figure out the height later." Taylor moved up

again and waited for Alex to catch up. He gave instructions and alerted him which handholds to use and which to avoid. After half an hour of climb and wait, climb and wait, Taylor thought that Alex had probably had enough. The sun was warm on his back and he reached into his waist pack for a water bottle. "Stop and have a drink of water. Your muscles probably need it about now."

Alex stopped, panted. "Okay." Alex sipped his water and then returned it to his pack. "Let's go."

"Let's just rest a minute, then we'll head back down."

"I want to go to the top," he said, his dark eyes imploring Taylor.

"Sorry. I think we're high enough, and going down is a whole different skill set to work on. Your muscles will be too tired if we go any more."

Nodding, Alex looked down for his first foothold and reached for it. Taylor moved down in sync with Alex. As he watched, he noticed Alex's leg trembling as he held his weight.

"Are you okay?" Concern flooded him. Now was not the time to have a muscle spasm, but it often happened to inexperienced climbers who pressed themselves beyond their abilities. Taylor would have to take extra care to get the boy down safely.

"I'm okay, I'm okay," Alex said, and Taylor could hear the false bravado in his voice.

"Alex," Taylor said, his voice firm, but calm, and Alex looked up.

His face was too red and his breathing was too fast. The exertion was getting to him.

"Piper!" Taylor yelled for her. If anything happened, he wanted her to be on the alert.

She rose to her feet and shaded her eyes as she looked up. "I'm here. How's it going? You look great up there."

"Alex is tiring."

"I am not!"

"I'm going to lower him with the rope, and I want you to help guide him to the ground." If anything went wrong, he'd never forgive himself.

"Okay. Will do."

"Uncle T.! I can do it."

"No arguments right now."

As Taylor readied the extra rope and rigging, the canyon winds stirred, tugging at his clothing and pulling at his hair. What had started out as a soft breeze had turned ugly. Gusting canyon winds were going to make this more difficult, but there was no help for it. Summer storms whipped up unexpected winds, even when the weather looked calm. Clenching his jaw, he hurried with the rope and climbed down closer to Alex.

"I'm going to tie this to your harness so I can lower you down."

"This is so embarrassing," he said in a hot whisper.

"Why, because it's safe?"

"Because it's like I'm a baby."

Taylor heard the shame in Alex's voice, and he was sorry he'd put it there. "Alex, you're no baby. This is safety, pure and simple. If you were any other climbing partner who was fatigued, I'd do the same thing, as they would do for me. We're still fifty feet up and your muscles are too tired to continue as we were." Taylor shook his head in disgust at himself. "I'm sorry." He should never have taken Alex so far up, should have watched him closer. After climbing at camp all week, his muscles needed a break to recover.

He knew better. But he'd allowed Alex to talk him into something he shouldn't have. He'd also wanted to climb, get a little exercise and leave the city behind for a few hours. And he had been looking forward to spending more time with Piper, if he was honest with himself.

Piper watched from below, her heart racing as she watched Taylor move down to Alex and make adjustments to his harness. Anxiety shot through her, reinforcing her decision to stay on the ground. "Everything okay?"

"He's coming now," Taylor shouted over the wind that seemed to have a mind to force them into the rock.

Taylor braced himself and even from the ground Piper could see the muscles in his arms and legs straining against Alex's weight. Her own heart racing and muscles tense, Piper waited helplessly from the ground below. Watching. Waiting. Praying.

"I'll help you, Alex. Don't worry." Taylor would see him safely down. She knew that. But, still, she worried that any number of things could go wrong with the wind crashing around them.

The rope slipped through Taylor's hands as he eased the boy down. Five, ten, fifteen feet, twenty to go. The strain was getting to him and in the next instant ten feet of rope sizzled through his hands before he could stop it. "Alex!"

Looking down, he watched as Alex slid roughly down the rock before catching a foothold. "I'm okay. I'm okay."

"Taylor!" Piper's voice cried over the wind, and he watched as she hurried forward, arms raised, as if to catch Alex.

Damn. This was all his fault. He clenched his teeth, cursing himself silently. If anything happened to either one of them, he'd never forgive himself. Trying to control the fear that shot through him, he took a deep breath and pushed down the voice of his father that tried to berate him. Now was not the time to listen to that voice. Now was the time to keep his nephew safe.

"Piper, can you climb up to the ledge?" he shouted down. If she could get to the ledge just a few feet off the ground, there was a better chance of Alex getting down unscathed.

"Yes. I'll do it." He watched a moment as she scrambled up and then waved at him. "Go ahead."

Wind whipped at them, increasing in its intensity with every passing moment. Each time he lowered Alex, he became a pendulum on a string, succumbing to the fate of the canyon winds trying to crush him against the rock. Muscles screaming, Taylor focused on lowering Alex one inch at a time. He was just a few feet from the security of Piper's arms. Relief shot through Taylor. Safety was just a few feet away.

The rigging snapped.

Piper's scream echoed in his mind as Alex plunged the last few feet.

Powerless, helpless, Taylor could only watch as the two tumbled from the ledge down to the bottom of the cliff face. Without hesitation, he released the rest of the rigging and climbed the rest of the way down.

In minutes that passed like hours, he dropped the last few feet to the ledge and leaped down beside them, his muscles screaming from the exertion.

"Are you okay?" He reached for Alex who sat up and

rubbed his face. Overcome with emotions he couldn't name, Taylor grabbed his nephew and folded him into a hug. "Are you hurt, are you okay?" he asked, and pulled back, running his hands over Alex's neck and shoulders.

Scratches and a few bumps were all he found.

"I'm okay, Uncle T. That was awesome. Did you see Piper? She caught me."

Taylor turned his attention to Piper, who had taken the brunt of the fall.

"Piper, are you hurt?" he asked as she sat on the ground, slow to get up. He ran his hands over her arms and legs. Nothing broken there.

"My back is gonna feel this tomorrow," she said, and sat up with Taylor's assistance. Moving gingerly, she took in a few deep breaths. "Everything feels okay, except..." She moved a hand to the back of her head. "Ow." She pulled her hand back and grimaced at the blood on her fingers. "Guess I hit my head harder than I thought."

"Let me see." Taylor turned her away from him and pressed his fingers into her hair. Moving it aside, he felt the lump and inspected it, but it appeared to be a small laceration. "It looks okay. Maybe needs an ice pack, but doesn't look like you need stitches."

Piper turned. "Good. Is Alex okay? He looked like he might have got some scrapes on that last bit."

Trembling, Taylor looked away from her. "He's remarkably okay."

"Uncle T., I'm thirsty." Alex shook his water bottle. "I'm out."

"Here, you can have mine till we get back to the car," Piper said, and gave Alex her water bottle as she watched

Taylor walk a few paces away. Crouching beside Alex, she inspected the scrapes on his legs, arms, and face, but he appeared no worse for wear. "You okay?"

"Yeah! I can't wait to do it again," Alex said, and guzzled her water.

Piper grinned. Kids were so much more resilient than adults. She pulled a few energy bars from her pack and handed them to Alex. "You're going to need these, too. I'm going to check on your uncle."

With caution, she approached Taylor. He stared off into the canyon, his thoughts a mystery, but she could well guess the internal litany of curses he was hurling at himself. "Taylor?" She spoke softly. "Are you okay?"

"I'm fine," he said, his voice flat, and he didn't look at her.

She watched while he removed his gloves and noticed an abundance of deeper abrasions on his arms and legs. Removing his helmet, he tossed it onto the ground beside him. "You don't look okay."

Angry eyes turned on her, and she almost stepped back from the intensity pouring out of him, but he didn't scare her. He was hurting and blaming himself for something he wasn't responsible for. Strong men often hurt the most. Intentionally invading his space, she stepped closer and closer until she almost touched him. The heat, the energy, the power he exuded washed over her like the canyon winds. Everything about him spoke of anger, but she knew beneath that anger was an all-consuming fear he didn't know how to deal with. Strong men also didn't know how to deal with fear.

"I'm ready for my hug now," she said, raised her arms and placed her hands on his shoulders.

"What?" Incredulous, Taylor blinked. She wasn't serious, was she? A hug? Now?

"At the park the other night you said you'd give me a hug. I'm ready to collect on it now."

"Piper, now really isn't the time," he said, and swore under his breath, looking away from her. He'd nearly killed his nephew and almost maimed her.

"Now is the perfect time," she replied, her voice husky with emotion. Without his consent, she put her arms around his shoulders and drew him closer to her.

Surprised by her audacity, Taylor's arms automatically went around her and fit her body against his. The tension that had fired every muscle in his body paused. The feel of Piper against him, the way her lithe body fit against his, and the anxiety of the climb conspired to rob him of his good sense. He should step away from her, and he tried to, but when his hands touched her hips to push her away, something shifted in him, something needy broke free, and he pulled her tightly against him. Burying his face in the side of her neck, he closed his eyes and drew in a ragged breath, savoring the feel and the sweet scent of her. God. She was right. Now was the perfect time.

"I'm sorry, Piper," he whispered. "I'm so sorry. I didn't mean for any of this to happen." The women he'd taken climbing in the past had been experienced climbers, and he hadn't had to worry about them. Today had been a disaster that he never wanted to repeat. Of all the stupid things he'd done in his life, this was one of the worst.

"It's not your fault. And no one was seriously hurt." She squeezed her arms tighter around his shoulders and held him. The feel of her lush breasts against his chest, her hips pressed against him inspired a new kind of tension in him, and he pulled back to look into her lovely face. His gaze dropped to her parted lips and a wild hunger for her raged through him.

Without thinking, he took her mouth with his and poured out all his fear and frustration into the embrace. Desire, hot and urgent, swept through him, matching the ferocity of the canyon winds surrounding them. Her mouth parted beneath his and the sweet thrill of her tongue gliding against his made him hunger for more. In a flash, he knew he wanted to take her home and explore every inch of her. Tunneling his fingers into her hair, he held on to her head and deepened the kiss as a dam of emotions broke free in him.

Piper jumped and pulled back. "Ow," she said, and raised her hand to her head.

"I'm sorry. I got your bump, didn't I?" he said, stepping away from her and the intensity of shocking desire that surged between them. A few deep breaths did nothing to calm his heart or the needs raging in him.

"Yes, you did, but it's okay." She smiled and touched his arm. "I liked everything else."

That brought a slight smile to him, and he trailed a knuckle over her cheek. "Me, too. Probably more than I should have."

"This wasn't your fault, Taylor. The winds weren't something you could have planned for." Her eyes were serious, trying to convince him, but he knew better.

"I brought Alex here. I'm responsible—"

"Stop beating yourself up," she said, and gave him

a quick smack on the arm. "It was an accident and we're okay."

"But—"

"Shh. Shh." Piper hugged him to her, then stepped back. "I suppose we ought to collect Alex and head back."

For a second longer, Taylor stared at her and absorbed the effect his kiss had had on her. Blue eyes limpid with desire, lips red from his kiss, cheeks filled with color. Desire looked good on her. And it was dangerously compelling. Better to give that a wide berth right now.

"Okay. Let's go." He took her hand and turned, but stopped. Alex was gone.

CHAPTER SIX

"ALEX!" Taylor cried, and turned to Piper. "Where is he?"

"He was right there by the packs," she said, and pointed a few feet from them.

"Then where is he? Maybe he was more seriously injured than I thought." Taylor cupped his hands around his mouth. "Alex! Where are you?"

"Coming! I'm coming."

Turning, Taylor huffed out a sigh of relief as Alex came running out from behind a clump of cedar trees and straightened his clothing.

"What were you doing?" Taylor asked.

"I had to…you know," he said, and turned a vibrant shade of red. "I drank a lot of water."

Relief shot through Taylor, and he placed a hand over his face, wiping away the lingering fear. Suddenly, the day had ceased to be enjoyable. "Why don't we head home now? I don't think I'm in the mood for a picnic," he said. Without another word, he gathered the fallen equipment and began placing it into the packs.

Alex looked at Piper with tears in his eyes that he tried to control. "Am I in trouble?" he whispered.

"No, you're not." Piper reached out to hug the boy

against her side. "I think your uncle was just really worried about you."

"I just had to go to the bathroom," he said, and wiped his face on his arm and pulled away.

"I know. Sometimes we adults don't say the right things at the right times." She patted his shoulder and cast a glance at Taylor, who continued his task. "He'll be okay. Don't worry."

Nodding, Alex kept his gaze downward and pulled away from Piper, apparently not convinced by her words of reassurance.

Taylor picked up the stuffed packs and looked their way. "Ready?"

Without a word, the three returned to the vehicle. The drive back was solemn and tension vibrated in the air. Attempts to draw Taylor into conversation failed, and Piper settled down to watch the scenery.

When they returned to Taylor's house, Alex climbed out of the vehicle and raced through the garage into the house. As Taylor and Piper entered a bit more slowly, the slam of a bedroom door echoed through the house.

"You really hurt his feelings," Piper said, and carried the untouched picnic lunch into the kitchen.

"I hurt his feelings? He scared the devil out of me," Taylor said, and tossed the packs onto the floor.

"And you yelled at him for it. Why don't you go talk to him?" she said, and picked up the picnic basket and set it on the counter.

Taylor stared at Piper. "What the hell am I supposed to say?"

"'I'm sorry' for starters."

"About what? Being cautious? Being safe? For being scared out of my mind?"

Starting to feel as upset as Alex, Piper frowned at him. "For being a stubborn, pigheaded uncle who doesn't know how to say he's sorry when he was scared and not angry. He thinks you're mad at him, that he did something wrong."

Taken aback at that, Taylor looked at Piper. She was completely serious. "When I was his age..." He stopped. When he had been Alex's age, he'd been hospitalized twice by his father for supposed injuries sustained in falls from rocks.

"What is it?" Piper approached him and placed her arm on his, her anger forgotten and her gentleness moving out to him.

Taylor sat down abruptly on one of the kitchen chairs and shook. She knelt in front of him and placed her hand on his face, raising it until his eyes met hers. "What's wrong? You can tell me, Taylor."

"Caroline is going to have to come back. I can't do this anymore, Piper. I just can't do it."

"You have to. Your sister is depending on you, and Alex...needs you. I think more than you know."

"There's so much you don't know about me, about why this was an impossible task to begin with." Taylor raised his hands to cup her face. "Caroline should never have asked me. Being alone and on my own is the way I live my life. I don't have it in me to care for a child."

"You do, Taylor. You just have to dig deep inside yourself to find it. I know what it's like to have the responsibility of a child thrust on you. But it's something we do for family, right? Why don't you go talk to Alex? He'll understand. You just have to talk to him."

Looking into her clear blue eyes, Taylor wanted to reach out to her, wanted to erase the events of the day and lose himself in her soft touch, in the honey sweetness of her woman's body. But that was out of the question. He wouldn't use her that way. No matter how upset he was right now, he wouldn't do it.

Heaving out a long sigh, he nodded. "You're right. I'll go talk to him."

Piper stood, but stiffness was in every movement, and she groaned. "Yikes. Guess I'm going to be hurting tonight." She placed a hand on her hip.

Concerned, Taylor stood, too. "Your back?"

"Yeah."

Though she tried to hide the frown of pain, he saw it. "Let me see. You fell flat onto your back, didn't you?" he said, trying to recall the sequence of events when he had released Alex into Piper's waiting arms. He clenched his jaw as the memory of the day came back to him. He should have done more to protect both of them. It was his fault that they were both hurting, and he had come away with just a few scratches that would be gone by tomorrow.

"I did. I'm sure it's nothing that some ibuprofen and a hot shower won't fix." She tried to wave away his concern.

"Still, let me see." Determined to examine her back, he turned her round and eased her shirt up. Clenching his teeth against the anger that wanted to surface again, he turned her into the light and pulled her shirt higher. "Why didn't you say something sooner?"

"It really didn't start to hurt in earnest until just a little while ago. What is it?" Twisting, she tried to see her back.

"Abrasions, embedded gravel, and you're going to have a hell of a bruise on your right flank." All because of him. And he was going to fix it right now.

"Well, no wonder it hurts." She gave a quick laugh and patted his hand. "It's okay. I'll live."

He dropped her shirt. "I'm going to have to pick out some of that gravel. Why don't you take a shower here to see if that takes care of some of it, then I'll remove the rest?" Offering her a shower and cleaning up her back was the least he could do.

"Oh, no, Taylor. I'm sure it's going to be fine."

He looked down at her, gave her his best unblinking stare that he usually reserved for stubborn patients who didn't want to listen to him. "That really wasn't a request." He took her by the shoulders and walked her to the door to his private bathroom, knowing she didn't want to trouble him, but he was insistent. He needed to do this to make amends, despite what she had said. "Take a shower. Help yourself to anything in there."

"Okay, okay. I'm going." Piper entered the large bathroom and closed the door. She removed her clothing and looked in the mirror at her back. "Ew." No wonder he was concerned. It was much worse than she had first thought. Tiny grains of dirt peppered the lower half of her back, and she had abrasions on her shoulder blades. Taylor was right, she was going to have a doozy of a bruise. At the time it hadn't felt like much, but the adrenaline must have been pumping and had masked the pain. She pulled a large fluffy towel out of the linen closet and started the water. As she entered the glass enclosure, she tried not to think of Taylor standing there naked every day.

She really tried, but thoughts of him leaning with one hand against the tile wall as the water sluiced down over his shoulders and back and lower refused to leave her brain. An image of herself stepping into the shower with him flashed into her mind and the fever of desire hit her hard. She'd never considered herself a really passionate person, more content to stay at home on a Saturday night than hook up with nameless men in nameless bars. Around Taylor, the dormant needs of her body seemed to have shed their husks and were blooming to life.

Turning her face into the blast of water, she closed her eyes and tried to think of other things. The scent of his masculine soap filled her senses with thoughts of Taylor that weren't going away. And, Lord, the man could kiss. Her body tingling from the memory of his mouth on hers, Piper reached up and cooled the water a bit. She was no lover of icy showers, but something had to take her thoughts off Taylor.

The water stung her skin, but she bore the discomfort in order to cleanse out the wounds. A little sting now was better than a raging infection later. After tolerating the water as long as she could, she dried off and put her shorts on. If she put her shirt on, she'd just add dust and dirt to the scrapes she'd just cleaned. Not sure what to do, she wrapped the towel around her torso, trying to keep it from sticking to her back.

Steam billowed out of the bathroom in puffy white clouds when Piper opened the door. She returned to the kitchen and hesitated in the doorway, Taylor stood at the sink, staring out the window. Maybe the smell of soap or something alerted him to her presence, but he turned and stilled. Piper's mouth went dry as that intense gaze of his rolled over her from her bare feet up over her legs, and lingered the longest on the towel. Then his eyes met hers and there was no doubt that he found the sight of her to his liking. If she were brazen enough, brave enough, bold enough, she'd drop the towel. Unfortunately, she wasn't that brave or brazen and there was a boy in the house. But if things had been different, brazen would have been her middle name. She tried to swallow down that flutter of anticipation winging its way up from her stomach.

"How was the shower?" Taylor asked, his gaze following her as she entered the kitchen.

"Great." *Just trying not to imagine you naked in it,* she thought.

"Sit down and straddle the chair while I'll look at your back." Taylor flipped a chair around at the table and adjusted one behind it so he could sit while he worked.

With just a nod, she sat as instructed and swallowed. This was going to be harder than she'd thought. No man had seen her naked, or even half-naked, in a very long time and the thought of Taylor's touch aroused her beyond any memory of past lovers. With a sigh, she tried to control her swirling senses and rested her forehead on the back of the chair.

Seeing her wrapped in his towel almost snapped whatever control Taylor had left today. For her sake, he needed to control himself. Standing in the doorway of the kitchen all damp and fresh from the shower made him forget about not being attracted to her. His body had instantly hardened and tensed, ready for action it hadn't seen in way too long. If the circumstances had been different, he would have been hard-pressed to stay away from her at that moment. Seduction and innocence wafted off her, and he wanted to take a bite out of the tempting fruit she unknowingly offered. She wasn't the kind of fruit he normally indulged in, but lately it had soured him. Allowing himself to look her over had probably been a mistake and hadn't cooled his interest or desire one bit. She adjusted the towel to cover her front, and he parted the ends to reveal her back. The first sight of the long expanse of her curved back and flare of her hips made him want to reach out to stroke the silky skin and cup his hands around those luscious curves she covered so well.

Concentrating on the task at hand, Taylor pulled a surgical kit from his first-aid supplies and picked out the tiny bits of gravel left behind. Brushing her hair aside, he applied an antibiotic ointment to the abrasions, covered them with light gauze, and added soothing balm to the bruise that had begun to turn ugly. "There." He'd gotten through that without unleashing the demon of desire struggling to get out of him.

"Thank you." She looked away for a second, then looked up at him, her eyes filled with hesitation. "I don't want to put my shirt back on."

"By all means." Taylor grinned and the tension between them burst.

"Taylor!" She laughed and colored brightly. "I meant because it's filthy, not because I've turned into an exhibitionist. Could I borrow one of yours until I get home for a clean one?"

"Certainly." He returned shortly with a clean T-shirt and handed it to her. "In case you change your mind, the other option is open anytime. Just watch it around Alex, though, he's very impressionable."

She gave him a drab smile. "I'll be back in a minute."

As Piper closed the bathroom door behind her, Alex opened his bedroom door and entered the kitchen. Eyes red and puffy, he approached Taylor. "I'm sorry, Uncle Taylor."

"I'm sorry, too," he said, and reached out to fold his nephew into a hug. "I didn't mean to be upset, and you didn't do anything wrong. It was all my fault. I over-reacted when things got tense, and I didn't make them any better." The boy's arms closed around Taylor's neck and his thin body shook. Taylor squeezed him tight and thought that Piper might be right after all. Hugs were good for a body. Especially those that came from a child.

Piper didn't mean to eavesdrop, but she heard part of the conversation when she left the bathroom. Clearing her throat, she entered the kitchen with a bright smile. "Hi, guys."

"Hey, Piper." Alex pulled away from Taylor. "Wanna see the new video game that Uncle T. got me? It's really cool."

She laughed at his abrupt change in disposition. Evidently, the talk with Taylor had been a good one. "Sure."

Alex shot out of the room. "I'll set it up."

"Everything okay?" she asked. "I know it's none of my business, but he looks a lot better."

"It's okay. He does look a lot better and, frankly, I feel better, too." He raked a hand through his hair, not ashamed to admit that to her. Though they hadn't known each other very long, he had shared more with her than he had with just about anyone else in his life. At least, for a long time. And it felt good, it felt right. Like the way things were supposed to be. But for her sake, he knew he needed to not depend on her so much. Giving her the wrong impression was a bad idea. "It's been an odd day, hasn't it?"

"It has."

"Piper, I'm ready," Alex called from the living room.

"I'll go see the game for a few minutes and then head home myself."

Taylor only nodded and watched her walk away, wondering why he'd become so enamored with Piper so quickly and how he was going to get through the next five weeks without depending on her so much.

CHAPTER SEVEN

PIPER greeted the next morning with a groan. Every muscle in her body ached. Even her hair seemed to hurt. Glaring at the cheerful sun streaming in through her window, she pulled a spare pillow over her face and contemplated how long she could stay in bed without moving.

The phone rang and solved the problem for her. Moving as little as possible, she reached out for the noisy thing and dragged the receiver under the pillow to her ear.

"Hello?"

"Piper, it's Taylor. How are you this morning?"

The sound of his deep voice in her ear while she was still in her bed put intimate thoughts in her mind. "I'm okay."

"Sore?"

"Brutally." There was no use lying about it, he'd know the truth anyway.

"I'm sorry."

"It's not a problem, Taylor. Just need to get moving, loosen up my muscles, and I'm sure I'll be fine." Acetaminophen, ibuprofen, and maybe some hemlock would help. Was it bad form to have wine with breakfast? The problem would be choosing red or white.

"Yes, well. Alex's cousins invited him over for the day, so I'm by myself and...wanted to make up for yesterday."

"Taylor, that's very sweet of you, but there's no—"

"I mean, we didn't get to our picnic, so how about brunch on me?"

Now *that* idea appealed greatly. No climbing involved and she didn't have to cook. "Don't you want to do something else with your day since Alex is occupied? Jump off a cliff or leap out of a plane or something equally daring?" She didn't want to intrude in that time if he needed to be by himself. "I don't want to be a wet blanket on your day."

He gave a quick laugh. "I had no other plans. Maybe a run in the park again tonight, but that's all."

"Then I'll gladly take you up on the invitation." She rolled over and stifled a groan.

"Be ready in an hour, and I'll pick you up."

After he rang off, Piper threw the covers back and tried to leap from bed, but only managed to crawl pathetically to her feet with a groan. Half a piece of toast, some ibuprofen, and a shower saw her ready to meet the day.

Taylor arrived, looking handsome and fresh in khaki pants, loafers and a navy polo shirt. With hair still damp from his shower, he smelled like the soap she remembered and her mouth watered. She swallowed, remembering her time in that same place. She really ought to stop thinking of him that way, considering he was just the type of man to put a kink in her heart.

His gaze roamed over her from her red peep-toe heels, smooth bare legs and the linen skirt that fell just below her knees. His bold gaze crawled up over her hips and breasts and she felt her nipples tingle in response.

Then his eyes met hers, and he smiled, releasing her from the spell of his thorough inspection.

"Ready?" he asked, and even held out an arm for her.

With a smile, Piper took his arm and allowed him to escort her to the convertible. "Where are we going?" she asked, and buckled in, glad she had pulled her hair into a sleek ponytail.

"There's a place by the Opera House that serves a great Sunday brunch." He put the vehicle in gear, and they were off. "All the New Mexican food and Mimosa you can handle."

"Opera House? I didn't realize that Santa Fe had one."

"One of the most unusual in the world. An open stage nestled into the hillside with acoustics like you've never heard. World class. You like opera?" he asked, casting her a quick glance. "I wouldn't have thought."

"*Some* opera. Some makes my eyes go crossed and my ears want to crawl inside my head."

Taylor laughed. "Mine, too."

"I guess it's like art. I know what I like, whether it's considered good or not."

"I hear you. Santa Fe is a haven for artists of all kinds. Some I get, some I don't. You'll have to check out the Indian Market at the end of August. They have the biggest, best art exhibits from every Indian pueblo and Indian nation of the Southwest. It's great."

"Oh, that sounds fabulous. Elizabeth's birthday is in September, and I can use that as an excuse to get her a present." She rubbed her hands together. "I love it when I can rationalize like that. I also send my aunt Ida a gift from every assignment I go to. Keeps her in the loop that way."

"Indian Market only comes once a year, so you do

have to go while it's here." Though he'd lived here for years, he'd only managed to take in half of what the city's culture had to offer. It was shameful not to take advantage of it. Perhaps walking through the city would be better than flying over it sometimes.

"Good to know, thanks. By the way, here's your shirt back." She pulled it out from her purse and placed it on the seat beside her. "Thanks for letting me use it."

"Anytime."

A short time later they were seated in a one-story adobe restaurant that offered an incredible view of the surrounding valley and mountains to the north. Ceiling fans overhead stirred the air just enough, and classical Spanish guitar played quietly on a hidden speaker system around them. If Piper hadn't seen the cars in the parking lot, she could have believed she'd opened the door to time and been thrown back to the era of the Spanish land barons. At times, atmosphere was everything.

Silence filled the air between them, and Piper's gaze skittered away from his, the smile she offered a nervous one. Adjusting her position more comfortably in the carved wooden chair, she reached for the salsa and chips on the table.

"Don't get shy on me," Taylor said, and reached for her hand.

"Who me? Shy?" Her gaze fluttered away from the intensity of his. She'd been right the first time. He had eyes that saw right through a person, right into their very soul. Right now her soul was transparent.

"Yes, you." He raised her hand and kissed her knuckles. "Today it's just you and me." He lowered her hand, but didn't release it and tugged once. "When Alex is around you relax, but with just me there's tension between us."

"I'm sorry. I don't mean for there to be." She sighed, knowing the tension in her came from trying to resist a raging case of sexual attraction. They were coworkers and anything between them would be temporary at best. "You make me a little nervous sometimes. I'm sure I'm not the kind of woman you normally spend time with, am I?" Looking up at him, she swallowed. He was so handsome, so confident and masculine. He was a powerful man. She was just someone trying to get through life. He challenged it at every step. Beside him, she felt small and insignificant.

"No, you're not. I have to admit that. But there's no reason to limit myself, is there?"

"I guess I just don't understand what your interest in me is. Aside from being grateful I gave you some suggestions for Alex." Men of his caliber never noticed her, so having Taylor spend his time and attention on her was an exciting, but puzzling, experience. "I don't want you to feel indebted to me for that." Her hand wrapped inside his warmed her fingers, and she wanted to reach out to him, pull his face down to hers, see if his kiss was as enticing as she remembered and not just the heat of the moment.

"It's not that, although I am very grateful for your help with Alex. There's something going on between us, isn't there?" he asked, his face serious, his gaze pinning her to her chair.

"What do you mean?" Playing dumb wasn't her way, but she didn't want to make assumptions about Taylor, either. Though she found him wildly attractive, she knew he wasn't the kind of man who would be into the kind of long-term relationship she now realized she wanted. She'd heard the gossip at the hospital, been warned by a nurse or two to watch it around him, that he was dangerous to a woman's heart and libido. But the vibes she was getting from him were so compelling, they were very hard to resist. She swallowed, her heart skipped a beat, she couldn't look away from him.

Without answering, Taylor leaned forward. Cupping a hand around the back of her neck, he drew her forward and pressed his mouth to hers. Surprised, Piper tipped her face up and met his kiss. As if he had read her mind, he leisurely explored her mouth with his lips and tongue, testing, teasing a response from her, and her heart fluttered in reaction. Hot and wild. That's what Taylor was and that was the reaction going on in her body.

He withdrew, but reached for her hand again. "*That's* what I mean."

"I see." Piper reached for the glass of ice water and took a quick sip, wanting to dump the whole thing over her head to cool off. "I'd have to agree with your assessment, Doctor."

"Just making sure I wasn't imagining things."

"Oh, no." She raised her brows and blew out a quick breath, grateful when the waitress came and took their orders for brunch. Piper stood, her mouth suddenly dry. "Shall we? I'm ready for that Mimosa about now."

"Me, too." Taylor followed her to the brunch tables.

Wanting to make her as comfortable as possible, he drew her into conversation. Work was a safe topic, and he suggested some places of interest for her to see. They relaxed, they touched, and the electricity hummed between them. Plates empty and appetites sated for the moment, Piper leaned back in her chair and sipped her Mimosa. "So, tell me what it's like to jump out of an airplane."

"Exhilarating." Pushing his plate back, Taylor reached for his coffee, seeming to settle into a memory. "It's like nothing you've ever experienced." He looked at her, considering. "Have you ever ridden a roller-coaster that made your stomach do flips?"

Piper's eyes widened. "Oh, yeah, sure. And then I threw up."

Taylor laughed. "Well, jumping out of an airplane is like that multiplied tenfold."

Piper pressed a hand to her stomach, not liking the image of that after such a full meal. "I think I'll stay on the ground. Getting me into an airplane usually requires sedation."

"For me, every second's a thrill. One that I'll never want to give up. I'll be jumping out of planes when I'm eighty years old." He shook his head and gave a self-indulgent smile, as if he were chastising himself mentally but knew he could never give it up.

"How long have you been jumping?"

"Had my first jump when I was sixteen. My uncle took me. Been hooked ever since."

"I know I'll sound like Alex, but is there anything you don't do well?" Everything she'd seen so far had been on the mark.

Taylor snorted. "Lots of things, but I try to stay away from them. It interferes with my self-confidence and charm."

Laughing, Piper stood when Taylor pulled out her

chair for her. Stiffness had set in again and a quiet groan escaped her throat.

"Still sore?" he asked, and placed his hand on her shoulder.

"Yes. I know it will go away in a few days but, man, it hurts when I move the wrong way sometimes." Maybe a long soak in the hot tub at her apartment complex would help, followed by an indulgent afternoon nap, including fantasies of Taylor to entertain her.

They left the building and approached Taylor's car. "Stand still a minute."

Puzzled, Piper remained still as Taylor moved around behind her. His hands touched her shoulders, and he pressed his thumbs into the tender space between her shoulder blades on either side of her spine.

Crying out, Piper cringed and pulled away. "I'm sorry, Taylor. Massage normally feels good, but seems I'm too tender right now."

Stepping away from her, he opened the door for her. "Let's go to my house, and I'll do a manipulation on your back. I think you might have something out of place in your spine that won't resolve on its own."

"Manipulation?"

"Yes. An adjustment to your spine. I'm also a trained D.O., Doctor of Osteopathy, and we do manipulations, or adjustments, to bring the body back into normal alignment." He shrugged. "Treating a condition that can be managed by a simple manipulation before resorting to medications is a good first step. It's a great supplement to the standard medical practice."

When they returned to Taylor's house, he led her to the living room. "There's more room here to maneuver."

Positioning himself behind her, Taylor gave her instructions. "No matter what I do, just relax. If you tense up, I could hurt you, and the point of this is to take that away."

"Okay. I'm ready." Piper's heart raced when Taylor pulled her back to rest against him, his entire body fitting her length. He pressed her head back against his left shoulder and swayed her back and forth a few times, settling her into position. A shiver of desire tried to overwhelm her, but she resisted. Taylor said to relax, not get tense, but the intimacy of him holding her led her mind to think of other things.

"Now, place your arms across your chest, hands on your shoulders."

Piper complied, but jumped when Taylor's arms went around her. Desire sparked between them. "Are you sure this isn't just a ploy to get me into your arms?" she asked, her breath wispy, not at all opposed to the therapy, seeing its side benefits, as well.

"No." His chuckle rumbled through his chest, and Piper felt it in her back. "It's legit. Now, relax against me again, breathe in and then out all the way, fast. I'm going to lift you up by your arms."

Needing the deep breath, Piper pulled in as much as she could, then exhaled hard. The instant her breath was out, Taylor encased her arms with his, hugged her tight against him and bent her backward with a small shake. Her back snapped and the crunch reverberated through her. "Ugh," she said when her feet were back on the floor.

"How does that feel?"

Piper moved a bit to the left, then the right, testing her back. Remarkably, there was little discomfort now.

A tweak in her back muscles, but nothing like before, and her surprised gaze flew to Taylor's face. "Wow. I'm amazed. You have the magic touch, Doctor. Thank you."

"You're welcome. The other thing you ought to consider is hydrotherapy." He pushed her hair to the side with one hand and rested a hand on her hip.

"Like a bath or shower?" she asked as her brain immediately recalled in graphic detail her image of him in the shower. Unable to muster the motivation to move away from him, she stayed where she was, leaning against him, liking the stirring of her senses as he held her, the stroke of his hand on her hip, wondering how far she should let this exploration of the senses go. Too much time had passed since she'd allowed a man to hold her. Oh, being around Taylor was going to be so bad for her. One touch and she wanted to toss caution to the wind and reach out for what he offered, even if it was for just one moment in time.

"Like a soak in my jacuzzi."

His voice had turned to a husky whisper and the heat of it in her ear created shivers that crawled along her skin. Even his voice was magic, entwining its way into her mind. The thought of the two of them in his tub made her mouth go dry and she dragged in a ragged breath. A decision was on the line. One that could take her to heaven or to the depths of pain.

"Really?"

"Really."

"I don't have a swimsuit." Like that was going to stop her from such an experience.

"That's not a problem for me. I don't usually wear one," he said, his hands roaming from her thighs to her hips and holding her against him. His breathing had changed, and so had hers.

"Will you be in the tub with me?"

His lips moved across the outer curve of her ear. "Do you want me in the tub with you?"

Oh, God, did she ever. Was that going to be the best decision of her life? Probably not, but if she didn't take the chance, was she going to regret it? Probably so. Opportunities, chances, came so infrequently in her life that she sometimes didn't recognize them when confronted with one. Now, with this glaring opportunity in front of her, she recognized it for what it was. A chance to be with Taylor, no strings attached. For two healthy, sexual adults to share an experience together. Beyond that, they would simply return to being coworkers. She could accept that, couldn't she? For one day, she could live for herself and savor the experience with Taylor. This attraction between them was heavier than anything she'd ever experienced. They wanted each other. It was that simple.

Nodding, she turned her head to the side, allowing him more access to the sensitive flesh of her neck. Hot and wet, his mouth opened and teased her skin, hitting all her erogenous zones and tugging at them, drawing away any resistance she might have had. Desire that she'd tried to deny blossomed inside her. Alone with Taylor, resting in his arms, she could find no urge to resist him or herself. The voice of reason was a distant echo that soon faded away. Living in the moment was Taylor's way. A way that she had longed for, but had never reached out to grab. Her life had been so controlled and molded that she hadn't embraced many of life's experiences. Now she wanted to clutch Taylor to her and let the rest of the world fade away from them.

She turned in his arms and looped her arms around his shoulders. His eyes were glowing with desire she knew was for her, and the thought that this powerful man wanted her made her body moist in anticipation. Shoving the past back where it belonged, she reached out to boldly embrace the moment and take what Taylor was offering her, even if it was just for a moment.

"Then I'm going to need that shirt back."

CHAPTER EIGHT

TAYLOR moved back from her and gave her lush curves a wistful look. "If you insist on covering yourself."

"I do." At least the trembling in her heart did.

He left her for a moment and returned with the T-shirt she had borrowed.

"I'll be right back." She fled to the bathroom to change, any lingering stiffness in her back remarkably absent. Minutes later, she entered the back yard to the hot-tub deck, nicely shaded by enormous cottonwood trees from too much sun or any prying eyes. High fences surrounding the yard ensured no one could peek in.

Taylor was already in the water up to his chest and leaning his head back against the cushioned bumper, his clothing in a rumpled pile on the deck. Piper eased her legs into the steaming water just as Taylor opened his eyes.

Petals of desire blossomed free in Piper as she entered the water. Stiff muscles forgotten as she looked at Taylor, she submerged all the way to her neck and leaned back, allowing the jets of water to pound her muscles and dissolve her bones. "Oh, this was a fabulous idea. I think I'm going to melt."

Relaxing was out of the question, though. As Taylor slid

closer to her, a different kind of tension pulsed through her, and she opened her eyes to slits to observe him.

"Remember, you're only supposed to stay about ten to fifteen minutes beneath the water, and then you have to come out for a while." Taking both hands, he ran his wet fingers through his hair and pushed it away from his face, looking much like an ad for the ultimate aphrodisiac. Who needed drugs when a wet, naked man would do the job?

"Okay." Piper swallowed, her tongue feeling thick in her mouth as he neared. Did he have a suit on or was he as naked as he suggested that she get? Heart fluttering wildly, she didn't know if it was from the heat of the water or the heat of Taylor so close to her.

"Your face is flushed. Are you okay?"

"I'm sure it's just the heat of the tub making my blood vessels dilate." Yeah, right. That was a great excuse, so flimsy he could see right through it.

Taylor grinned. "I'm sure." He reached for her hand and tugged until she semi-floated across the tub closer to him. "I'd better check your pulse." With his fingers on her wrist, and his gaze locked on hers, he smiled knowingly. "Heart is fast, too. Are you sure it's the water?"

"No. I could be having a reaction to something."

"Like what?" He drew her closer until she stood in front of him, no longer up to her neck in the water. "It's certainly not an adverse reaction. You look very healthy to me."

Taylor's gaze dropped and her nipples tingled as if he had touched them. The sodden white T-shirt clung to every curve and nuance of skin, revealing everything to his hungry gaze that she had sought to hide beneath the water. "I'm not sure. Mimosa maybe?" Probably a reaction to too much Taylor. Too close, too fierce, too hot.

"You only had one."

As he spoke, Taylor's hands drifted from her hips upward, dangerously close to her throbbing breasts.

"Yes, but—"

"I think it's something else."

Raising his gaze to hers, Taylor's eyes flamed with desire that made her heart rate more erratic than it already was. Piper licked her lips and dropped her gaze to his mouth. With nothing but hot water and a flimsy sodden shirt between them, Piper wanted to reach out to him, to take what he offered with his body. That sweet release she hadn't known in a very long time urged her boldly forward. One step closer and his thumbs stroked her peaked nipples. They were already hard and pressed against the shirt.

"I think you're right." Was admitting that bad? Giving him more power over her than he already had? She didn't know, but seemed powerless to stop herself. She wanted this. She needed his touch, more than she had known even moments ago. So much of her life went to giving to others. Wasn't it time she allowed herself to take a little, to please herself just a bit? That wasn't being selfish, that was experiencing life and everything it had to offer. For too long she'd sat on the sidelines, watching while life raced by her.

"I'd also like to say that the shirt looks better on you than it ever has on me. I think I'll have it bronzed later."

Piper took a deep breath and inched herself closer, her gaze locked on him as something inside her broke free. Her arms crept out to his shoulders, and her hands rested on the slick skin. Oh, how she wanted this man.

This adventurer, who had begun to creep into her mind, her dreams, and her heart, pushed aside the past, pushed aside the memories of hurt, until there was nothing except him in front of her. With him there would always be excitement, but would she be enough for him? Could she be enough? Be bold enough, brazen enough, passionate enough? There was only one way to find out. The past had no place here. The now was filled with Taylor in her arms.

"Do you want it back?" She pressed forward until her breasts met the solid wall of his chest, and she tipped her face up, her mouth inches from his. Every sense she had was focused on him. Standing between his parted legs, she let herself drift forward.

"Yes," he whispered, and cupped the back of her head.

"Then I think you should take it." Desire made her speak. Boldness urged her forward. Temptation made her close the gap between them.

With a groan, Taylor moved. His arm around her waist pulled her against him and the hand behind her head guided her mouth to his. Parting her lips, Piper surrendered to the need and the desire raging within her. It wasn't the heat of the tub or the effects of one Mimosa that made her want Taylor. It was everything he was, and he was everything she wanted.

The kiss he'd first given her paled to the heat of his mouth now. Lips moving over hers, his tongue probed deeply, eagerly stroking against hers. As he kissed her, Taylor drew her knees to either side of his hips so that she straddled his lap, providing her with proof that he wore no suit. Groaning deep in her chest, she pressed herself against Taylor, against the muscle and the heat of him.

Hands roaming over the curves of her hips, Taylor raised her up until her breasts reached the level of his mouth. Holding her above him, he opened his mouth over a nipple and teased. The tremors of her arms clutching his shoulders let him know how much he affected her. Moving to her other breast, he rolled his tongue around the nipple through the wet shirt that clung to her. The sight of her in his shirt stirred him deeply, as if in the wearing it had marked her as his.

Easing her down, he pulled her tight into his lap and stood, his breath coming hard and fast. "I think our ten minutes is about up."

Nodding, she clung to him as he climbed over the edge of the tub and lay down with her on the wooden deck. Mindful of her back, he rolled with her until she lay on top of him, and he fit her comfortably to his body. Panting, Taylor sought her sensitive neck with his mouth while his hands held her hips pressed to his.

"Taylor, someone's going to see us." She tried to pull back, but he held on to her.

"No, they won't. That's why I built very high fences."

Raising herself up to verify his statement, she exposed her front. Ever one to take advantage of a situation, he scooped a nipple into his mouth and pulled until her attention refocused on him.

Overcome by Taylor's touch, the heat of him and the needs of her body, Piper lowered herself closer to Taylor, unable to stifle the groan of pure sensation in her throat. She pressed her hips forward, touching her delicate femininity against the heat and bold hardness of him. Ultimate aphrodisiac indeed.

Hands trembling with need, Taylor cupped her face

and ravished her lips, then pulled back, resting his forehead against hers, his breath harsh in his throat. "Piper, I want to make love to you. Right now. Right here." He panted. "I need to make love to you. Now." He cupped his hands around her face, pulling her as close as possible, spreading kisses all over her skin.

"Yes." For her, there was no other answer. Ever since she'd met Taylor, she'd felt as if she were moving to this place and time with him. There was no wrong or right, there just was.

"Are you on birth control?" God, he hoped so, because he didn't want to move from this delicious spot with her weight pressing on him making him feel more alive than he'd felt in a long time. She was beautiful and funny, and he wanted her with everything in him.

"Yes. The five-year implant." Nodding eagerly, she pulled his mouth back to hers. Seconds later, Taylor had divested her of her panties and his hands were firm on her hips. "I have to tell you I don't do this often. I'm not promiscuous."

"You may have heard otherwise, but neither am I. I'm clean. Look at me," he said, and paused until Piper raised her face.

With his eyes firmly locked on hers, he pulled Piper's body down over his erection. As every part of him joined with her, her moist flesh encased him, and her eyes closed. She was delicate and firm around him, and he eased gently inside her until he could go no further. Every inch forward was a sweet torture.

"Oh," she whispered, and clutched his arms. "Oh, my. Taylor." Every word she breathed against his skin urged him on, and the beat of his heart raced. She wasn't someone who made love often as evidenced by the feel of her body against his. Something inside Taylor popped, something in his chest opened up. Something he hadn't realized had been closed off from his emotions until now. Being with Piper freed him.

The feel of Piper surrounding him released the chains that had held his heart closed for too long. With his hands on her hips, he began to move, urging her hips forward and back until she cried for release. She clung to him, her voice soft in his ears, and he quickened the pace between them.

Every move Taylor made took Piper closer to the edge of paradise. He was strong and commanding, his body hard and masculine beneath her. Hands tender on her skin, he sought to please her, and she gasped as the feelings surging within her built to a crescendo. Release was a second away, and she dug her fingers into Taylor's shoulders as instinct took over, and she gave her body free rein. With another powerful move from Taylor, Piper's body rocked. She cried out, helpless in Taylor's arms as pulses of pleasure shot through her, and her body tightened around Taylor's flesh.

Control was something he never lost, but at that moment he saw no need for it. The strong pulses of Piper's body took Taylor over the edge, and he bucked beneath her, losing himself to the sweet pleasure of her, clutching her body to his.

Piper collapsed on top of him, and he wrapped her in his embrace as he regained his breath. After a long slow kiss, he pulled back to look into her face. She was all soft and well-loved looking, and it looked good on her. He didn't want to let go of her just yet, but he checked his watch to see how much time was left to them.

"Do you have to go?" she asked, and sat upright, still joined with him.

"Not yet. Alex won't be back for two more hours." Stroking his hands down her arms, he marveled at the softness of her skin, wanting to explore it further. "Want to come inside for a while?" he asked.

"I'd love to," she said, and he dragged her down for another kiss.

Piper stood in the shower later that evening and reluctantly washed away the fragrances of the delightful afternoon spent with Taylor. It had been such an indulgence, being with him. An indulgence that made her want to stay put for a while and give up the traveling for good. She could if she wanted to. Anytime. Having an affair wasn't something she took on lightly, but with Taylor, excitement would always be part of the relationship, for sure. Hadn't she earned a little excitement in her life? After so many years of commitments, of doing for others, hadn't she earned a little time to do something just for herself?

She sighed and allowed the steaming water to flow over her. Muscles she hadn't used in a long, long time now made their presence known. The back injury from yesterday was certainly resolved after the manipulation. The rest of her had benefited from his touch, as well.

As she turned the showerhead to massage, she allowed her mind to roam free and unbidden thoughts of her last relationship intruded.

Derek Winsome, an MD in Los Angeles, two years

ago. Gifted with such talent and charm that no patient or female he set his sights on had been able to escape. She'd been just as susceptible as anyone else. Having fallen for his charm and ended up in his bed, she had allowed herself to want more from him than he had been able to give her. Or that he had been willing to give her alone.

Unfortunately, she had been just one in a long line of women parading through Derek's life. She wasn't special, not by a long shot, and after she had popped in on him unexpectedly at home, he'd made that very clear. So had the woman beside him, warming his bed.

Regret started to slide over Piper as she scrubbed and shampooed. Was this thing, this attraction to Taylor, going to end up the same way, with her being made a fool of and hurting for what he couldn't give? She'd allowed herself to be vulnerable and care about Derek and nothing good had come of it. Other than a valuable learning experience. Was anything good going to come of having an affair with Taylor?

Probably not. He wasn't the type to settle down to home and hearth. After having to deal with the responsibility of her sister for so long, she wasn't sure if she was, either. The long-ago dream of a husband, home and family of her own had been dangling by a thread for so long, she wasn't sure it was something she wanted any longer. Once, she would have wanted it. But after so many years alone, she couldn't really imagine her life any other way. Sure, if she had met the right man, the dream would have returned in Technicolor. But now it was still in black and white, just another unfulfilled fantasy.

She turned the water off and left the shower, dried and dressed for bed. Unable to chase away the dark memories that wanted to intrude on her precious time with Taylor, Piper checked her e-mails, hoping for a message from Elizabeth. But there was nothing. E-mails from friends and other travel nurses occupied her for a while, but thoughts of Taylor and Derek battled for the upper hand in her mind.

Was she going to regret her time with Taylor? Should she continue to see him outside a professional relationship? What the hell was she going to do when it was time to seek a new assignment in a few weeks? San Francisco had been home for the first twenty years of her life, but it hadn't been home for so long, she doubted that she'd want to go there again on a permanent basis. Though her aunt still lived there, Elizabeth was in Phoenix and who knew where she'd end up after school? Santa Fe was a wonderful place with a diverse culture that called to Piper. She could live here if she wanted. Most hospitals were happy to hire travelers on a permanent basis.

Pulling up her company's Web site, she searched their database for other assignments. She'd been just about everywhere she wanted to go, so there weren't too many places of interest left, and she didn't need to take assignments for money anymore. She had the option of taking a job she loved in a place she wanted to be.

The images on the Web site were designed to be exciting. People who were skiing, at the beach, climbing mountains or fishing in a lake. Those were all things that had enticed her into travel nursing, but after eight years of it, she was ready to settle down. Somewhere. She sighed and left the Web site. Her restless feet had calmed over the years and so many assignments. Now she just wasn't in a big hurry to go anywhere. She had time.

Now that Elizabeth was going to be living her own life, Piper could live her own, too, couldn't she? Too much of the last eight years had been spent on other people, and it was time Piper spent some time on herself.

Cruising over to another Web site, she indulged in one of her favorite pastimes that she could take anywhere: shopping.

Taylor pulled into his driveway just as Alex's cousins returned with him. He'd taken Piper home and lingered in the doorway with her almost too long. The feel, the smell, the look of her made him want to touch her, to kiss her, and to take her down the hall and show her once again how much he desired her. They were both mature adults, right? They could enjoy each other without strings tangling things up. At least that's how he'd always played it and he didn't see a need to change that philosophy now.

"Uncle T.!" Alex yelled from the other car and bounded across the driveway with his backpack bouncing along behind him. "Where were you?"

"I just took Piper home."

"Oh, man. Did you go climbing without me?" he asked, obviously disappointed.

"No, no. We just went out to eat since we missed the picnic yesterday."

"Oh. Well, that's okay, then. I didn't want you to go climbing again without me. I'm your new partner now, right?"

"I'd never think of it, Alex." He held out his hand and Alex slapped him some palm. Even though the thought of taking Alex climbing again made him shudder. "Why don't you say goodbye, and we'll go inside?"

Alex collected his belongings from the car and waved. "I'll see you on Friday," he said.

"What's Friday?" Taylor asked.

"They want me to come for a sleepover. It's Elliot's birthday. Is that okay?"

Taylor thought. "Sure. I don't see why not. Does your mom let you sleep over?"

Alex shrugged. "Sure. Sometimes they come to our house, too."

"Then I don't see any problem." As they walked into the house, he thought of Piper. Might be the perfect time to take her on a proper date, too. He'd have to check and see what the Opera House had going on that night.

CHAPTER NINE

THE next week of Piper's assignment flew swiftly by as Piper and Taylor immersed themselves in their work. There was little time for much else at the moment—work came first for both of them.

E-mails continued to come in from Piper's sister, but they were vague, leaving Piper feeling strangely disconnected. She felt their bond as sisters slipping and wished that it was different between them. But as Elizabeth found her way in the world, Piper knew that she would have to let go of her sister the way she should. She just hadn't realized how difficult it was going to be. They had been through some rough times together and their relationship was closer than that of most sisters. Piper sometimes felt as if she was losing her best friend.

Resisting the urge to call every day under the guise of checking in became harder and harder. Piper had been thrust into the deep end of life at age twenty. There had been no choices, no options except to take on the responsibility of her sister. Handing her sister over to the state to raise had been unthinkable. It had been a responsibility that she had sometimes endured, sometimes relished, sometimes wondered why, oh, why, their lives had been changed so dramatically. Though she had missed out on some of life's challenges and learning about herself in her early twenties, she'd grown up hard and fast with the death of her parents. Her relationship with her sister was one that she had always loved, even through the changing seasons of Elizabeth's life. Now that relationship was changing once again and slipping away from her.

Piper was just sitting down to an unappealing-looking sandwich when Taylor entered the employee lounge. She paused and took a look at him as her heart raced at the surprise of seeing him there. Even in scrubs, there was no mistaking he was a man of power. He didn't need a suit for that. Masculinity and energy flowed off him in the simple scrubs, and Piper tingled as if it reached her from across the room, making her promptly forget about the e-mail from her sister. And her lunch.

"It's Wednesday," Taylor said with expectation in his eyes.

She thought a second, as if that was supposed to mean something to her, and she tried to make her suddenly dry mouth work right. "Okay. Did I miss something about Wednesday?"

"Put down the sandwich, and no one gets hurt. It's green chile cheese fries day."

"Right. I forgot." She put her sandwich down as her mouth watered in anticipation. Before coming to New Mexico she'd never eaten green chile, and now she craved it like some life-sustaining substance. "You're going for some, I take it?"

"Yep. Wanna come?" he asked, and took a step forward, the light in his eyes mischievous.

"You look like you're up to something. You've ruined me for all other fries, you know. Nothing even compares." Probably ruined her for all other men, too. No comparison there, either.

"It happens."

"I supposed you planned that." She wrapped her nothing lunch back up and tossed it in the garbage can. No comparison.

"Let's go."

After settling with a steaming pile of French fries, covered in green chile sauce liberally sprinkled with shredded Cheddar cheese, Taylor finally relaxed. There was something about green chile, it didn't matter in what form, that kept him going. Maybe it was more symbolic of home than anything else in his life. Something he somehow needed and had not realized.

Small talk related to work and cases they had shared in the ER. Then the awkward silence that he'd hoped to avoid ensued. "So how's your sister doing in school?" he asked.

"Fine, I think." Piper frowned and chomped a fry in half.

"What's wrong?"

"I'm sure it's nothing, and she's just engaged in school, but her e-mails are short and don't say much. Totally unlike her. She usually runs off at the fingers." She shrugged and picked up another fry. "I think I'm feeling a little left out of her life now that's she's old enough to have one." She gave half a laugh and shook her head.

"Don't worry. I'm sure she'd just caught up in school. First semesters can be overwhelming, especially if she isn't used to being away from home."

Piper nodded and looked at him. The questions in her

eyes reflected the same questions he felt inside. What was going on between them now that they had made love? Usually, the women he became involved with wanted nothing more from him than the use of his body on a temporary basis. That suited him just fine, too. No strings was how he led his life, with the exception of his work. But now that he and Piper had connected, he was starting to re-evaluate that philosophy. Thoughts of her had intruded his life for days now, and he wasn't sure how to handle it. Being attached to a woman for more than the short term had never happened to him. But, hey, he was all about taking chances. Why not take one more? If things didn't work between Piper and himself, he could always revert to the way things had been before she'd shown up. Either way it was win-win for both of them. He leaned forward a little and spoke softly to her. "What are you doing Friday night?"

She thought for a second. "Nothing. Why?"

"I'd like you to go out with me," he said. And he did. Surprising himself at how strongly he wanted her to say yes. She was only going to be in Santa Fe for a few weeks, so he had to pursue her now if he was going to. They could have a great time together, then she'd be off again. No complications for him, so it was perfect. "Get dressed up. A real date."

Hesitation flared up inside Piper. Wasn't this just like her former boyfriend? Swept her up with fancy dinners and mysterious dates, only to dump her at the last minute? Taylor was just substituting green chile for French cuisine. But the sincerity in Taylor's eyes made her pause. If she mistrusted every man, she'd be stuck in the past, and she definitely didn't want to live there again.

The first time around hadn't been that great and definitely wasn't worth repeating. Lesson learned. Move on.

"I'd like that. Where do you want to go?" Despite her reservations, anticipation hummed through her. This was going to be fun. Something that had been sorely lacking in her life for a long time. Why not reach out and take the fun, the short term, the inspirational that Taylor offered? Just because it wasn't her norm, it didn't mean that she couldn't have some fun.

"It's a surprise, but dress up. It's going to be snazzy."

The corners of her lips curved upward as if she liked the idea of a surprise, and if they hadn't been in the middle of the cafeteria, he'd have pulled her to him and explored those lips thoroughly. Oh, yes. Friday night was going to be good for both of them. Time to spend together, time to explore each other afterward. Though having Alex around as a buffer between them sometimes was a good thing, sometimes being alone with a woman had its benefits, too.

"Sounds great. What time?"

"I'll pick you up at six, we'll have dinner, then go."

Just then the paging system overhead called him back to the ER, and Piper didn't see him the rest of the day.

When she arrived home on Friday night, she raced to the shower, peeling her scrubs off as she went. Dashing by the phone, she noticed a message flashing on the answering-machine, but decided to get ready before checking it.

As she scrubbed the day off her skin, she stopped as the water dripped over her face. What if that had been Taylor calling, canceling their date? Just like Derek. She didn't want to get dressed up if he'd had to cancel. Just like Derek. Damn. Memories of the past tried to squeeze in, and she pushed them back where they belonged. Just like Derek. She grabbed a towel and ran out to the answering-machine, pushed the button and listened. It was from Elizabeth, who wanted to talk. *Later.* She ran back to the shower to finish getting ready, relieved that it hadn't been Taylor canceling. She'd been looking forward to this night more than she'd wanted to admit.

She had just patted her hair into place and slipped into black heels when the doorbell rang. Heart thrumming in anticipation, she opened the door.

Her mouth about dropped open and the breath in her throat froze. Taylor stood there in a black suit, holding a single rose. Warmth rose up within her and tears nearly flooded her eyes at the sweet gesture. "Oh. Hello." Breathe in. Breathe out. Don't faint.

He stepped forward, nearly overwhelming her in the small confines of the apartment. He'd never looked so good and heat pulsed in small waves from somewhere behind her heart. He was doing no good for her resolve to keep it casual between them.

"Hello, yourself." He held out a hand, and she took it. With a quick move of his arm, he spun her around. "You look fabulous, Piper," he said as his gaze devoured her.

Smoothing the luxurious satin fabric down over her hips, she smiled her thanks and blushed at the compliment. She did feel fabulous. More indulgence she hadn't allowed herself. "So do you."

"Let's go."

"Are you going to tell me where?" she asked as he escorted her to the car.

"Dinner first, then the surprise."

"Okay. I'm yours."

Taylor picked up her hand and kissed her knuckles, his eyes full of silken secrets and passionate promises. "Alex is at a sleepover tonight."

A tingle of desire swept over her at the thought of having Taylor to herself for an entire night. Her mouth went dry and she licked her lips. "That sounds fun. The cousins again?" she asked.

"Yes."

"They certainly come in handy now and then."

After a fabulous dinner of New Mexican cuisine, Taylor drove to a familiar-looking place. With the summer twilight as a backdrop, Piper recognized the lights up ahead.

"We're going to the opera?" she asked, and sat straight up in her seat, her eyes wide, bubbles of surprise shooting through her like champagne.

"We're going to the opera. I promise it won't cross your eyes, though."

"What is it? What is it?" she asked, eager as a child, and patted him on the arm.

"*Mama Mia.*"

"Oh!" She flopped back against her seat.

"What's wrong? Don't you like that? I know it's a musical, not an opera, but—"

"Oh, yes. I've been wanting to see that for ages, but I've never been in the right city at the right time."

"Then I'm glad I picked this show." He found a parking place, then turned to face her.

"Thank you, Taylor." She stroked his cheek and tried not to be too overwhelmed that he had chosen this evening for her. No one had so gone out of their way to treat her in such a very long time. What a sweet gesture. She gave a mental sigh as she looked at Taylor. Wasn't it time she did something, took some time, for herself? Putting her life on hold for eight years was long enough.

He popped a quick kiss on her cheek. "You're welcome." Although going out of his way to take someone on such a special night wasn't something he usually did, this seemed the right thing for Piper. And surprising himself, Taylor wanted to do it. They might not have much time together as her contract lasted only six weeks, they could have a good time while she was here and then say their goodbyes. There was no harm in that. They were adults, they could deal with it.

After the show, on the way home, Piper's cell phone rang. After a few seconds, she gripped it in her hand. "What?" She sat upright in the seat, intently focused on the conversation. "No, no, no. You can't do that, Elizabeth. I won't allow it."

A horrified gasp sprang from her throat. "What do you mean, 'I don't have the right'? I have the right because I'm your sister, and I'm paying for your school and—"

Piper snapped the phone shut and stared straight ahead, trying to collect her thoughts and settle her breathing, embarrassed that Taylor had witnessed the exchange.

"You hung up on her?" Taylor asked.

"Uh, no. Other way around."

"Something you want to share?" he asked.

The sound of his voice was so gentle that tears tried to prick her eyes, but she resisted the urge to play the delicate female. She was tougher than that, and she'd figure this out. Somehow. "I can't believe she's doing this." Piper tucked her phone into her purse and clutched it in her lap. "She's ruining everything I worked for."

"How?"

"She's leaving school for a man! She's only twenty years old. How can she do that?" Piper covered her face in her hands, the joy of the evening gone in an instant.

Taylor turned the car into her apartment complex and parked in front of her building. "I'm sorry. Do you want to talk about it?" He let the question hang. "This was rather unexpected, I take it."

"Yes, it is." Piper unbuckled her seat belt, but didn't get out of the car. "Why don't you come up, and I'll make some coffee?"

Taylor followed her into the apartment and watched as she puttered around the kitchen in her evening gown. This fretful woman wasn't the Piper he knew, but he wanted to help her. Even if it just meant listening. Something new for him, but he was game to try. Too many times he'd bolted at the first sign of feminine emotions. He didn't need them, didn't want them, and he damned sure wasn't going to play games. But this time was different. He couldn't just walk away from her. Piper had helped him out when he'd needed it. He could help her out a little tonight without giving himself a hernia. "Why don't you go change, and then we'll have coffee?" He nudged her away from the sink to finish the job himself.

"But…"

Wide blue eyes filled with distress, worry, and something else, maybe relief. He turned her and gave her a little push toward her bedroom. "Go. I know my way around a coffeepot." But not his way around a woman's tears. Those unnerved him in an instant. He'd rather have an ER full of hostile patients than one upset woman on his hands. That was enough to make any determined bachelor run for the hills.

"You're still in your suit." Piper's eyes were bruised looking and defeated. "You probably ought to go home. I'm not good company in any case. I'm sorry. This was a bad idea."

"It's okay. I always carry spare sweats in my car. I'll change, too, then we'll talk."

Minutes later, both back in casual attire, Piper poured large steaming mugs of coffee for both of them. Curling herself into a corner of the couch and tucking her bare feet beneath her, she waited for Taylor to join her. "This wasn't the ending of the night I had hoped for."

"Me, either. But at least your eyes didn't go crossed tonight, right?" he asked, trying to tease a smile out of her.

It worked, and her lips curved upward, but the movement evaporated quickly. "You're right. I just wish that phone call had come a day later."

Taylor could imagine. He'd rather have had Piper in his arms all night long while they discovered pleasurable moments. One afternoon of intimacy with her wasn't going to be enough. She had invaded his day, as well as his night dreams, and he'd woken up in a sweat more than once in the last week. She'd had a more profound effect on him than any other woman he'd been with. Normally, he would have escaped that sort of entanglement quickly, but for now it worked.

"So tell me why she's leaving school for a man." He sipped and watched.

Piper heaved out a sigh and focused on the rim of her

cup. "She met this guy, Eduardo something-or-another the first day there. He's got big dreams of having his own restaurant, apparently comes from a family with their own, so he thinks he knows it all already. He's also abandoned school to jump in with both feet. She must really be smitten to go this far overboard." Piper covered her face with her hand. "It wasn't what they wanted."

Confused, Taylor frowned. "What who wanted?"

"Our parents." Piper sighed and looked up at him. "I made a promise when they died that I would see Elizabeth through school and set her up where she can be independent, where she'll have an education and won't be living in the gutter."

"You made a promise or they made you promise?"

"I made the promise. They were already dead by then." She shivered at the power of the memory.

"What happened?" Taylor reached over and placed a hand on her leg in silent support.

"They were killed in a car accident. Eight years ago on the way back from their second honeymoon." Piper's lower lip trembled a second as she spoke, then seemed to gain control of herself again.

"I'm so sorry, Piper." He moved closer to her and placed an arm around her shoulders. She leaned into him for a moment, seeming to draw strength from the connection with his body, then straightened.

"So am I." The pain in her whisper said it all.

"You've been the strong one your entire adult life, haven't you?"

"I've had to be. There was just the two of us, three including Aunt Ida."

"It's made you stronger than I think you know."

"Our lives would have been completely different if they hadn't died then."

"You've been raising your sister this whole time?" That amazed Taylor. Piper couldn't have been more than a child herself, and then to have that responsibility thrust on her, as well as losing her parents. His respect for Piper jumped several notches. She was one tough woman. Taylor looked at his watch that still ticked down the minutes and seconds of his time with Alex. "I can barely deal with my nephew for six weeks and you've had the responsibility of actually raising your sister for, what, eight years now?"

"Me and Aunt Ida. My mom's sister. We lived with her while Elizabeth was in high school, and I was off on assignments earning money to keep her there and pay the mortgage. My parents didn't have a guardianship set up, so when they died it fell to me by default as her closest living relative. I was of legal age. Just graduated from nursing school. There was no way I could just hand my sister over to the state, so for me there was no choice in the matter. Any plans I might have had came to a screeching halt." All the fears she'd harbored over the years now came flooding back to her. She was older than Elizabeth, she was responsible. She'd had to make something of herself instantly so that her sister could, too. They had only each other as Aunt Ida was aging and would need care herself one day. More responsibility to come. She pulled her knees up and wrapped her arms around her legs, hugging them to her chest. "Maybe I need to go find her, talk to her."

"Maybe you need to let her cool down and call her tomorrow."

"How can you say that?" Piper demanded. "She could be endangering herself or trusting the wrong person! I don't know anything about this man, and she's going to take off with him to God knows where."

Taylor tugged at one of her hands until she let him take it. "Piper. She's over the age of consent. There's nothing you can do about it legally right now."

"I have to. I have to try." She flung away a tear with her other hand. "I have to convince her to stay and not throw her life away."

"Why? Why is it up to you to live Elizabeth's life for her? Why can't she live her own life, have her own adventures like her big sister?"

She tried to snatch her hand away, but he held it fast. "What are you talking about? I never ran off with a man, or abandoned my obligations. I did what I was supposed to do. I had no choice at all."

"And you resent her for having opportunities to be young and free that you never did?" he asked.

"Taylor! How can you say such a thing? I love my sister—"

"But you don't want her to have the fun that you were denied at this age?"

"That's simply not true." Wasn't it? A flush of anger pulsed within her, replacing that warm, fuzzy feeling she'd had earlier. So much for the good vibes running between them. "Here she is with opportunities staring her in the face once she finishes school, but she's going to abandon everything we've worked so hard for."

"Okay, look at it from where she's sitting. Big sister Piper the breadwinner, the one who's off on adventures all over the country while she's left at home with

Aunt Ida. How do you think that looks to an impressionable teenager? She's had stars in her eyes for years thanks to you."

Piper opened her mouth as she stared at Taylor. "But...but..." As a teenager she had been eager to be out on her own, traveling, learning new things, going places she'd dreamed of for years, something that her parents had encouraged. The memory of that forgotten anticipation washed over her as she looked into Taylor's face. Her sister had apparently worshiped her the same way that Alex worshiped Taylor. She just hadn't seen it that way. And she didn't like it. Alex was a child. Elizabeth certainly wasn't.

"She wants her own adventures, and may not be as patient as you want her to be for that. How old were you when you graduated nursing school?"

"Nearly twenty-one. But I faced my responsibilities, I didn't drop everyone and everybody to go do what I wanted." A sigh huffed out of her. "I did what I had to do because I had no choice in the matter. Putting Elizabeth in the care of another was never a choice."

"Maybe you'd like to have her nice and safe, learning her trade, but she's got other ideas, other dreams. Probably always had them, but didn't share them with you, her superstar sister." Taylor's hand snuck over to her neck and began to knead the muscles there.

Tears glistened in her eyes as pressure flooded her chest, the pain enormous. "Then I've failed my parents."

"No, you haven't. I know a few things about failures and you're not one of them."

"How can you know anything about failure, Mister I-Jump-Out-Of-Airplanes? Everything you do is magic."

Taylor gave a harsh laugh. "It didn't used to be." He sighed, not wanting to relive his past, but it seemed he was going to right now. This conversation was supposed to make Piper feel better, but maybe sharing some bit of himself would help her to put things into perspective. "I had an abusive father and a mother who could never stand up to him. There were no arguments. He was military and his word was law. I was never good enough for him. Nothing I ever did was right."

Taylor took a breath as the past washed over him. "I was really scrawny as a teenager and had little in the way of co-ordination skills, so my father believed I was weak in mind, as well as body. I was continually told I was inadequate, a failure in his eyes, and for a time I believed it, too. It wasn't until I went to college that I saw things clearly. I wasn't the one with the problem, my father was." He paused at the memory. "My uncle was the one who helped me more than anyone. He never had kids, but he was a great uncle, a sounding board when I needed one, helped me do all those things my father should have been doing." During those teen years, he'd sure needed it.

"That's terrible, Taylor." She touched him on the arm, some of her floundering compassion resurfacing for a desperate gasp of air. "Children shouldn't be treated that way. No one should be."

"No, they shouldn't. It's not something I think about every day, but it is something that happened to me— shaped me, I guess. Gives me a lot more sympathy for people in the same boat."

"Your sister, too?" she asked.

"Yeah. Caroline had a different kind of experience.

Cooking, cleaning, sort of a child-sized servant. Married young to escape, but that turned out to be a mistake. Except for the Alex part. That was the best part of her marriage."

"She must be a very strong person, too."

"She is. We kind of banded together to survive."

"That's why you're so close, isn't it?"

"Yes."

Settling into her thoughts, Piper sipped her coffee and tried to make sense of what was happening, why she felt so out of control, why she needed such control over her sister's life. Didn't she have enough on her plate to worry about? "I put myself into the role of parent when I could have been a sister, a friend, to Elizabeth. I insisted on having things my way. She went to the schools I chose, we vacationed where I thought was right." Piper snorted at a memory. "She wanted to go to Jamaica when she graduated from high school, I took her to Disneyland."

"Those are the small details. Right now, your sister needs your support."

"How am I supposed to give her my support if I don't know what she's doing and the things I do know she's doing sound outrageous?"

"To you, but not to her. Where is this restaurant going to be opened?"

"I'm not sure. She's in Phoenix, Arizona. I think Eduardo was from that area, too, so probably there."

"Why don't you take a weekend and go spend it with her, see what she's up to? Might do you some good to be with her a while. Get to know her as an adult, not the teenager who has grown up on you." Taylor pressed a kiss to her temple, then rose, pulling her to her feet. "I'll go home and let you do what you need to do."

"I'm sorry, Taylor," Piper said, and escorted him to the door. "This wasn't the night I had…hoped for."

"Me, either, but I'll survive." He gave a quick smile and a kiss on her nose. "Weather's supposed to be good, so I think I'll go jump out of an airplane."

Piper laughed at his go-with-the-flow attitude, wishing she could be more that way. "Just don't forget to open the chute," Piper said, feeling somewhat better having talked to Taylor.

"I won't."

"Thank you for listening. I needed it." She pulled him down for a hug, warmed when his arms wrapped her up for a squeeze and went no further. He was becoming a friend, more important to her than she had anticipated. And that…surprised her, scared her, and made her wonder if there could be anything else between them. As she watched Taylor from the doorway, she wondered if she was deluding herself. A man like Taylor didn't settle for women like her. Men like him needed more excitement than she was capable of offering. Maybe cooling things between them would be better for both of them, rather than looking for opportunities to heat things up.

Though her time here in Santa Fe was limited, it wasn't out of the question for her to extend her contract or even take a permanent job in Santa Fe. There were definite possibilities, but she didn't want to set herself up for heartbreak. Was she asking too much of an affair with Taylor? Could she just take what he had to offer and leave it at that?

Someday she wanted a family. Someday she wanted a relationship that would stand the test of time. Someday she wanted to stay in one place and put down the roots that she hadn't been able to.

Closing the door, she sighed. Someday was getting closer every day.

CHAPTER TEN

PIPER returned to work on Monday morning exhausted. She'd spend Saturday and most of Sunday with her sister in Phoenix, returning to Santa Fe late Sunday evening. They'd fought, they'd yelled, they'd cried, they'd made up. She'd let go. Elizabeth was on her own, standing tall beside a man she professed to love, who seemed to adore her, as well. That was more than Piper had in her own life, something she'd put off in order to see Elizabeth cared for. A small thorn of jealousy stuck in her side for the trip back to Santa Fe.

Although she knew that Elizabeth was diving head-first into dangerous waters, Piper finally realized that she had to let her, couldn't stop her anyway. She wasn't Elizabeth's mother or guardian anymore, and as Taylor had said, Elizabeth was of age to make her own decisions, good or bad. She was the one who had to live with the consequences, not Piper. Sighing, Piper had resigned herself to being there to pick up the pieces when Elizabeth's world came crashing down around her. Maybe after the restaurant venture failed, she'd go back to culinary school the way she was supposed to have done in the first place.

Thirty seconds into Piper's shift, a cardiac arrest, a car crash victim and a woman in late labor all arrived in a car, an ambulance and a taxi.

"I'll take the crash," Taylor said, steering away from the pregnant woman. "Piper, you're with me."

Relieved, she followed Taylor into the trauma room where she forgot everything else except the patient and her work, and the symmetry with which she and Taylor moved together. She removed the ambulance crew's monitoring equipment and hooked the patient up to the room's equipment.

Though her hands trembled slightly with the unexpected intensity of the situation, this anxiety was familiar and something she could deal with. Much better than personal trauma any day.

Taylor listened to the man's lungs, then immediately palpated the man's throat. "He's got a deviated trach."

"Chest tube set-up?" Piper spun around without waiting for Taylor to answer and extracted a large procedure tray from the cupboard, opening it as she turned back.

Taylor whipped off his lab coat and thrust goggles over his face at the same time. As soon as Piper opened the sterile gloves, he shoved his hands into them. "Betadine," he said, and held out a wad of gauze.

"Yes, Doctor." Piper squeezed the skin prep solution onto the gauze, then cast a glance at the monitor. "BP and oxygen saturation are okay, but his heart rate is creeping up."

Arturo, the respiratory therapist, stood at the head of the bed, pumping oxygen into the man's lungs. "He's getting a little harder to ventilate, too. Not good, man, not good." He shook his head as if he knew something was going to happen.

Sweat broke out between Piper's shoulder blades. A deviated trach indicated tension pneumothorax. If not corrected immediately, it could lead to further life-threatening problems. As she looked at Taylor, her pulse evened out and her breathing no longer seemed tight. Though he moved quickly, every move had purpose and was extremely efficient. He exuded confidence and absolute certainty in what he was doing. Just watching him calmed Piper. Taylor knew what he was doing, and he was going to save this patient's life. There was no doubt in her mind.

"Once we get the pressure off his heart, that should improve." Taylor finished scrubbing the skin on the outside of the patient's left ribs and tossed the gauze away. Keeping his eyes on the chest, he palpated the ribs with his left hand and held out his right to Piper. "Blade first, then the tube with stylette."

Piper placed the items into his hands and watched as Taylor nicked the skin with the scalpel blade, then placed the tip of the chest tube in the small opening. With his strong right forearm, he forced the tube through the patient's ribs and into the pleural sac over the lungs. Piper held her breath as she watched Taylor's focused motions, knowing this was a painful procedure for the unconscious patient, but a lifesaving one.

As soon as the tube reached its destination, Piper's breath burst from her lungs. She connected the external end to the chest tube set-up filled with sterile water. "Bubbles. We have bubbles, Doctor." Piper gave a small smile. The procedure was a success.

"Good." Taylor nodded and wiped his forearm on his forehead. "Always makes me sweat getting those tubes in."

"A little sweat saves a life. No problem." Standing on her toes, she mopped his forehead. Their eyes connected for a brief second and a flash of heat consumed her. Piper moved away, then handed him the suture kit to secure the tube to the patient's skin. If the tube became displaced, the patient would be back to critical in seconds.

Taylor palpated the man's throat again and nodded. "Looks like that did the trick. Everything's back where it should be."

"I'm always amazed at what air in the chest cavity can do."

"Air where it doesn't belong causes all sorts of problems. Air where it belongs is just fine." Taylor took the dressing that Piper handed him and applied it to the chest tube site. "Go ahead and call Radiology. We need a head CT, spinal films, probably chest and abdomen, too."

"Got it." Piper reached for the phone.

Taylor walked to the sink to scrub and removed his goggles as he listened to Piper's brisk voice. She knew her stuff, he had to admit that. Casting a glance her way, he wondered how her weekend had gone with her sister. Shrugging, he turned back to the sink. If she wanted to talk, she would. It wasn't any of his business unless she wanted to make it that way.

Despite his attraction to her, he really needed to cool things off between them. She was such a responsible, conservative person, she didn't need him in her life. Not that he was irresponsible. He simply didn't want any romantic entanglements at this point in his life.

Sure, he liked her, she'd helped him with Alex, was beautiful, more fun than any woman he'd dated for ages, and… Was he trying to talk himself out of being attracted to Piper? With a frown, he scrubbed at the sink, and tried to keep his mind focused on the work in front of him. They were getting along great right now, but sooner or later their friendship was going to head south. Always did with him. Relationships never lasted more than a few months with him. Somehow, he always found a reason to move on.

Hours later, Piper handed the patient over to the ICU nurse and gave report. Chest trauma and lacerations were his biggest problems. "Head CT, spinal and abdominal films all negative. Got a pneumo on the left. Chest tube placement confirmed by X-ray."

She glanced at the man who was now rousing in the bed with his concerned family hovering around him. "He's darned lucky."

"Yeah. We don't see many drunk-driving accidents early Monday mornings. They're usually the Friday- and Saturday-night types," the ICU nurse said as they finished report.

Piper returned to the ER and for the rest of the day dealt with the mundane complaints more usual for a Monday. As she wearily slung her bag over her shoulder and headed out the door, she could think of nothing better than filling her tub and her wineglass to the top and diving into both. Which made her think of the hot tub at Taylor's house and she flushed with the memory. Since he'd adjusted her back, she'd had no stiffness and the cuts and scrapes had healed nicely. Not even on the flight to or back from Phoenix. Though they had been only hour-long flights, seats on commercial flights weren't known for their great comfort.

Guess the man with the magic hands knew what he was doing there, too.

It seemed that her thoughts conjured him as Taylor walked into her peripheral vision.

"Hi, Piper. Heading out?"

"Yep. Been a long day. You?" She heaved a heavy sigh.

"Yep. Alex stayed after camp for a birthday party, so I'll pick him up, then head home."

"How much longer until your sister returns?"

Taylor consulted his watch. "A few weeks."

"Fabulous. Then what will you do with your free time back?"

They strolled to the parking lot together as staff hurried by on their way home, too.

"Climb mountains, jump out of airplanes and various other super-hero stuff."

Piper laughed. The sensation felt good in her chest. It seemed that Taylor knew just what to say and when to say it to draw her out of her doldrums. That, she appreciated more than he knew. He was so out there sometimes. She needed her feet firmly on the ground. In that they were polar opposites, but they had somehow made a connection that she was reluctant to see end. After his sister returned, he probably wouldn't need her help with Alex any longer and then where would they be? The boy had been somewhat of a buffer between them, serving as common ground, something they could talk about if things got uncomfortable between them. Would things be the same between them when life returned to normal?

Or would her greatest fears be realized? Her world was so normal and Taylor's as big as the sky. She had to make a decision.

"So, did you go skydiving over the weekend?" she asked.

"Hang gliding."

"You lead a dangerous life, Doctor." Piper shook her head. What an adrenaline junkie he was. Trauma patients, hang gliding, parachuting and helping to raise his nephew. Couldn't get more dangerous than that.

"It's not as wild as it seems," he said, and shifted his position. "At least, not most of the time."

"Ri-ght." They arrived at her car, and she leaned against it.

"How'd it go with your sister?" Though he'd told himself to wait, he apparently wasn't listening to himself.

"Well." Piper curved her hair around one ear, something he was recognizing as a nervous gesture, something he found endearing. "She's determined to go through with her plans with Eduardo." Shaking her head, she looked away from the intensity of Taylor's eyes. "I met him. They took me to the place they're opening. They have big plans."

"How are you doing with all that?" he asked, and took a step closer to her.

"Oh, well, that's going to take some getting used to." She finally met Taylor's gaze. "They certainly think they're in love and are going to be successful together."

"They could be."

"And they could fail miserably."

"They could. But together they might accomplish more than either of them alone."

Piper paused a second, staring at Taylor, surprise in her eyes. "That's exactly what they said."

"Then maybe they're smarter than you're giving them credit for."

Piper sighed, then stuffed her belongings into her car. "You look tired."

"It was a long weekend, then a long day today. I work the next two days, so I don't think I'll be catching up on rest until then."

Taylor started to reach out to her, then clenched a fist and resisted the temptation. She wasn't his to fix or comfort or anything like that. She was just a nurse he worked with. Just a woman he'd had the most incredible sex with. Just someone who was getting under his skin in a way he didn't understand and wasn't comfortable with. Just someone he was starting to think of as a friend. And more. And he didn't like it. His idea of a long-term relationship was a four-day weekend at a ski resort when the skiing was bad. Something about Piper was changing that perspective and he resisted, though part of him wanted to embrace what she offered. Something about her resounded inside him, silently melding with the torn and hurt parts buried deep inside him, healing the things he hadn't even known were broken.

"I'm working those days, too, so I'll probably see you."

"I'll be there for green chile cheese fry day on Wednesday." Piper gave a small smile. "You've got me hooked now. I may have to stay in Santa Fe forever because of those darned fries."

Taylor smiled. "Good. Green chile is good for all that ails you."

"Wouldn't it be nice if that were true?" she said with a tired smile.

As she climbed into her car, he squatted down beside the door as she rolled down the window. "I know you're too tired tonight, but maybe Wednesday after work we can meet up at the park for a run." Taylor told himself he wasn't pursuing her, just wanting some company for some exercise. Give himself something to look forward to over the next couple of days. That's all.

"Just no coyotes, okay?"

"Okay." He grinned, then stood, and he watched her drive away.

The woman intrigued him. He knew she was all about long term, commitment and loyalty. Those were things that he had taken great pains to avoid in his life, but now they weren't looking so bad. Maybe he was changing. Maybe being around Piper had changed him. Maybe he'd had a long day and his defenses were down, and he didn't know what the hell he was thinking. Maybe a drink with some friends would relieve the loneliness that lived inside him.

Loyalty and commitment were starting to look more appealing than they ever had.

CHAPTER ELEVEN

NOT having made any firm plans with Taylor for the park on Wednesday, Piper drifted toward the place after work. Changing into her walking shoes was about all the energy she had left after three grueling days at the hospital. Twelve-hour shifts weren't for sissies. Every cell she had seemed to have had gone on strike. Even her eyelashes hurt. But she supposed that a little exercise and fresh air was going to do her good. She certainly couldn't feel any worse than she did now.

Summer evenings were longer now, but remained somehow cool, though July was nearly on them. She supposed that was one of the perks of living at high elevation in the desert. Warm days and cool nights were just about perfect to her. She stretched her muscles while waiting for Taylor, but he didn't show. So she started her first lap around the track, continuing the warm-up without him. Somewhat disappointed that he hadn't come, deep down she'd known that he was going to revert to his normal life at some point and leave her behind. Seemed like that was the story of her life. She was just a side dish in life's buffet, something to keep a man from starving but not enough to sustain him.

Though disappointment churned in her stomach, she kept going. That's always what she did, she just kept going forward no matter what.

The quick footsteps of a runner behind her made her move over to let the person by.

"Hi, Piper!" Alex said as he jogged in place beside her. He was red-faced and sweaty, but he looked like he was enjoying himself.

"Hey, kiddo. What are you doing here?" Where Alex was, Taylor was sure to be close by. Anticipation hummed in her belly and some of her fatigue mysteriously evaporated, as did the disappointment and her somber mood.

"Uncle T. tortured me until I came." He grinned, jogging backward so he could see her.

"Tortured you? With what, a book?" She laughed.

"Oh, man, you guessed. It was either read or come to the park. At least this way I might see a rabid coyote."

"Not if you're going backward," she pointed out with a laugh.

"Oh, yeah." He turned around, glancing at the path ahead of them.

Piper laughed, suddenly glad that she'd pushed herself a little and come. Glad for the company of a child who didn't expect too much from her and had a way of looking at things that was totally foreign to her. Alex was a great kid. When she had children, if she had children, she hoped they would be as nice as this one.

"So where is he?" She glanced ahead on the trail, but didn't see the familiar form.

"Right behind you," Taylor said.

Piper jumped. Her nerves shot to full alert, but she

congratulated herself on maintaining a calm facade. "There you are. I thought I beat you here. I had decided you weren't coming, so I started without you. Then when Alex caught up with me, I realized that you'd started without me."

"I am a man of my word. I never break it," Taylor said, and slowed his pace to match theirs.

Piper cast a doubtful glance his way as they rounded a sharp curve in the trail covered with riverbed rocks. "Really?"

"Really."

"He's right, Piper. Uncle T. never breaks his word. And sometimes that's not good." He gave her a serious look.

"What do you mean?" she asked.

"If he says I get punished for something, he means it." Alex's eyes went wide. "He never forgets."

Laughing, Piper put her pace into high gear, but the boys easily caught up with her. "That's good to know in case I ever need punishing."

"I hope that never happens to you, 'cause he'll never forget. Ever." Alex pointed off the side of the trail. "Jackrabbit. I called it."

Piper watched as the animal skittered away from them in a crazy pattern and disappeared in the brush. "Why are you calling jackrabbits?"

"We're playing a game. Whoever sees the most wildlife wins and the loser has to do the dishes," Taylor said.

"Did either of you catch that raven sitting on the fencepost over there?" she asked, and pointed to the large black bird watching them with dark, dark eyes.

"It's mine!" Alex yelled.

"Mine."

Piper laughed at their banter and the remainder of their walk raced by until they could no longer see the trail in front of them.

The evening ended with three happily exhausted people who went to Taylor's house and ordered pizza. The dishes were forgotten as were the stains on the couch. And the carpet. And the wall.

Taylor sat on the floor with the other two and stretched his legs out in front of him, oddly content. Relaxing at home in front of the TV was something he rarely did. Too much energy boiled within him to have downtime very often. But this was nice, this was comfortable, and something he could get used to in the right circumstances. He took one last bite of the pizza crust and tossed it into the nearly empty box. Piper sat cross-legged on a pillow beside Alex and watched as he showed her the ropes of his latest video game. He enjoyed watching the two of them and listening to their conversation.

"You killed me!" she cried, and gave Alex a playful shove with her elbow.

"You were just standing there, so I had to take advantage of the shot."

"Oh, I give up. I'm no match for you. I'll just watch, okay?"

"Okay. Is there any pizza left?"

"I'll check." She turned back to Taylor and her breath refused to go in or out of her lungs. He was simply the most devastating-looking man she'd ever known. Sitting with his legs extended and crossed at the ankles, leaning toward her on one elbow, it made her want to crawl up every inch of him and have her way with him. Then his eyes darkened and a seductive smile curved his lips up at one corner.

"Your mouth is hanging open, Piper."

She clamped it shut and redirected her gaze to the pizza box. "Alex wants something."

"What?"

"What do you mean, what?" She blinked, trying to bring her brain into focus. She was supposed to do something, wasn't she? Think, woman, think.

"You said Alex wanted something. What was it?"

Dammit, did she have to lose her mind right then? "Another slice of pizza." She reached for it, but he moved swiftly and caught her wrist, and she gasped.

"What do you want, Piper?" His voice was low and hypnotic, and she had to look up at him, look into those piercing blue eyes. And she was lost. She was falling for Taylor, right here, right now. This was so not good, but she was helpless to avoid that impulse deep within her that longed to be free, longed to reach out and take something, even if it wasn't right for her. She had a right to be happy, didn't she?

"If Alex weren't sitting right beside us, I'd show you." That hadn't just come out of her mouth, had it? She never spoke like that, was never so bold. The memory of their time in the jacuzzi flashed through her, and she bit her bottom lip, desire throbbing low in her belly. His gaze dropped to her mouth and she licked her lips.

"If Alex weren't sitting right beside us, I'd let you."

"Pizza?" Alex asked, without taking his attention from the game.

"There's one slice left." She picked it up and was

forced to drop her gaze from Taylor as she slid the slice onto Alex's plate.

With his hand still a band on her wrist, Taylor tugged her closer. "Come here," he whispered.

"Taylor." Unable to resist, she allowed him to draw her closer, closer, until she was just inches from him.

Electricity hummed between them. "Can you stay tonight?"

Reluctance heavy in her sigh, she shook her head and indicated Alex. "I can't." Her body came alive at Taylor's touch, and she wanted to re-experience their shared passion. It was a seductive lure that she was highly susceptible to. She doubted she'd ever develop a resistance to Taylor. Every night she went to bed with her body aching for his, for the heat and the hardness that made her body come alive as it never had before. The way she wanted it to again. Cooling things between them was going to be the best solution for both of them. They couldn't go on this way. They each had different goals, different objectives in life that were poles apart. Her mind knew that, but the thought didn't stop her body from responding to Taylor's touch.

With one hand, he cupped his hand behind her neck and drew her forward. Nuzzling her ear, his voice was hot and warm, sending shivers across her skin. "I want to make love to you, Piper. We're good together, and I don't just mean in bed."

Closing her eyes, Piper let his voice, his words swirl through her. Those cherished words raced through her and nearly had her on her knees. No man had ever said those words to her, so why would Taylor? She was so close to falling for him that it wouldn't take much to send her over the edge and into the abyss of heartbreak. She knew it. She had to resist the thought that he could be her forever man. The man she'd spend the rest of her days with. As her mind took an imaginary leap forward, there was no other man she wanted to stand beside, only Taylor. Maybe it was already too late for her, and she'd fallen and not known it.

Pulling back a little, she looked into his eyes and that was a mistake. When they'd first met, she'd thought he had eyes that saw right through a person. Now, watching him, looking deep into those depths, she knew it was true.

The phone rang, breaking the spell of desire between them.

Alex jumped up and raced to the kitchen. "It's probably Mom."

Piper watched Alex go, then let out a surprised little scream that was quickly silenced by Taylor's hot mouth on hers. He pulled her onto his lap and then rolled, pinning her beneath him.

His mouth was hot and urgent against hers, and she let him take her deeply. The pressure of his body against hers made her want to reconsider staying with him. He could take her to heaven, she knew that. The crash back to earth was going to be painful, she knew that, too. Easing back from the kiss, she tried to cool the passion raging between them. He was like one giant overdose of chocolate. Just because she wanted him, it didn't make him good for her.

"What's wrong?" he asked, and sat up. "I can feel you pulling away."

Piper sat and curved her hair around one ear and avoided his gaze. "I'm just not comfortable with Alex in the other room."

Taylor stared at her, his eyes hard and assessing. "I'm not convinced. Something else is going on. Is it Elizabeth again?"

"Taylor, what are we doing together? You know I'm not the type of woman you usually go for."

"So what? I happen to like being with you."

"And that surprises you, doesn't it?"

"Again, so what? I'm willing to go with the flow a while longer, see where we get to."

"And that's where we differ."

"Are you saying you want to know my intentions toward you?"

"No. I'm saying I already know your intentions, and they won't coexist with mine. We have some things in common, but in the long run you'll be moving on, and I'll be left holding my heart in pieces. I've done it before. I don't want to do it again." She stood and walked toward the door just as Alex entered the living room.

"She wants to talk to you," he said, and held the phone out to Taylor.

"Piper, wait. Just a minute," Taylor said, and took the phone.

Though his gaze remained on hers, he spoke to Caroline.

Without knowing what else to do while he was on the phone, Piper started to empty the dishwasher. She hadn't gotten far when Taylor's hand on her arm stopped her. "Don't. This isn't why I want you here."

"It's okay."

"No, it's not." He pulled her away and shut the dishwasher. "We need to talk."

The hairs on the back of her neck stood up when she

heard that phrase. It was always the beginning of bad news, the end times were near. Protective instincts jumped into high gear as her heart raced and her breathing came too fast. "Taylor, it's okay. Really. I understand." Did she ever. This was the part where he said he didn't need her any longer, thanks for a good time, now have a nice life, and I'll get back to mine. Echoes of the past bombarded her. Just like her ex. She extricated her arm from his grip as bursts of anxiety jumped across her skin. "I'm sure you have things to do, and it's been a long week for me. So I'll just get going." Before I humiliate myself more.

"Caroline's coming back. A week early."

"Is everything okay?" She moved away from him and leaned against the counter while she caught her breath.

"Yes. The company feels she's ready to start at this point, and she's flying into Albuquerque the end of next week." He glanced away and ran a hand through his hair, his gesture of nerves.

Forcing a smile, Piper tried to keep her emotions from her face, but the telltale blush crawling up her neck betrayed her. "That's great news. I'm sure Alex will be thrilled to have his mom back."

"Yeah. I'm sure." Taylor stuffed his hands into his pockets and turned away from her, not sure how he was going to feel about Alex going back with Caroline. It was certainly the right thing to do, for them to be a family again, but, damn, he was going to miss the kid, miss that feeling of family that he had wanted but never had when he'd been a kid. "It will be good to have my life back again. Back to my usual routines. The way it used to be."

He looked at his watch, still ticking down the last few days. May as well shut it off now. No point in—

"Taylor?"

Distracted, without finishing the small task, he turned back to Piper. She stood by the door, looking like she was ready to bolt. Regret had replaced desire in her eyes, and he didn't like it one bit. This thing between them was more heated than his past relationships, and something he didn't want to let go of yet. Despite her reservations, he really liked her company and didn't want to stop seeing her now. This relationship hadn't imploded the way so many others had. The why of it he didn't explore too deeply at the moment. "You're going to go, aren't you?"

"Yes. You're obviously capable of handling Alex without my help, so I think it's for the best. You don't need me." She curved her hair behind her ear and moistened her lips, avoided his gaze.

"Best for you or me?" Anger snapped inside of him. This wasn't what he wanted, wasn't how he wanted to end things between them. Hell, he didn't see any reason to end anything between them at all. They were adults, and if it worked, then so be it.

"For both of us. Taylor, you know I'm not what you need, even though there's a healthy dose of passion between us. We had a beautiful experience together, and I'll cherish that. But I think all you want is a temporary lover, and I've been there, done that before. The same story only ends in heartbreak for me, so I'm not really interested in going there again."

"Coward."

Shocked, Piper stared at him. "What?"

"Yes. You're a coward. You're afraid to experience your life. You've been so busy trying to manage Elizabeth's life, and worrying about what's going to happen to your aunt, that you've forgotten to live your own. Don't do that, Piper. Don't let go of something before you even know what you have." He stepped closer, the light in his eyes dark, intense, and a little frightening. Leaning over, he pinned her between his hands braced on the counter behind her. "Don't be afraid of me."

Tears pricked her eyes. Though her chin trembled, she didn't break down. "I'm not afraid to experience life. I'm afraid to have my heart trampled all over again. My last serious boyfriend was someone just like you. I was never enough for him. In his head he had ended our relationship, but only when I walked in on him in bed with another woman was it over for me. By hanging on too long I was humiliated and it's not something I'm likely to forget." She dropped her head and wiped her eyes with her fingertips. "I know I'll never be enough for you, either, so it's best if I walk away now, before we both get hurt."

"Piper, you're convicting me based on another man's idiotic behavior. I don't accept that." His eyes turned cold, his lips pressed tight together and a muscle in his jaw twitched.

"Life lessons, Taylor. Hard ones. I don't need another round in the classroom to know this isn't going to work. I've graduated and don't need a refresher course." Piper broke out of the small trap of his arms, unable to bear the close intensity of him. "I just need to go. There's no point in any of this."

"No point? Piper—"

"No! I'll just go my way, you'll go your way, and find someone else suitable to your lifestyle, and we'll both be fine. I've put my life on hold long enough."

"Piper—" Anger hissed through him. This was *not* what he wanted at all. Was there bitter truth in her words? Probably, but he didn't want to hear it, didn't want to think about it, didn't want to accept it. Until he acted the fool, he didn't want to be condemned as one.

"No. I can't." She held up her hand to prevent him from speaking. "Taylor. What in the world do you want *me* for? You've had seriously better offers, I'm sure. I've heard the gossip at the hospital, how you are a whirlwind of affairs, and I don't want that. I can't take it. I let myself take what you had to offer for a time, but I know it was just a fantasy, not real life. I want more than that. I need more than what I think you're willing to give to a relationship. Really, Taylor, our lifestyles are so not suited for each other, it's not funny."

Taylor remained silent, but his eyes smoldered with anger.

"See? You can't deny it." She took a backward step toward the door and pulled out her car keys. "I think I need to go now. It's better for both of us this way, Taylor." She shook her head. "I'm sorry. Really."

"Aren't you going to say goodbye to Alex?" he asked as he turned away from her.

"'Bye, Alex!" she called.

"See you later," he called back.

"That's not what I meant. You need to tell him you're not coming back."

Opening her mouth to protest, she knew he was

right. It wouldn't be fair to Alex otherwise. "Fine." She strode past him into the living area where Alex was playing his game.

Taylor watched as she stooped down beside him. By the shocked expression on Alex's face, she was indeed saying goodbye, to both of them.

"But I don't want you to go," Alex said.

"I'm sorry, Alex. I have to. Your mom's coming back and you won't need me anymore."

"But—"

"I'm sorry." She reached out and pulled him into a fierce embrace, leaving both of them with tears on their faces, and the knife that had twisted in Taylor's heart shoved deeper.

This wasn't what he wanted. Wasn't what Alex wanted, obviously. Telling himself that he *hadn't* used her to help him with Alex, he took a step forward, then stopped. Dammit, he hadn't used her, but she'd been seriously helpful to him with Alex. He scrubbed his hand over his face, trying not to think too hard, but that was impossible right now. He wasn't about to reach out to her again when she'd made up her mind. He watched as she ran out the door.

Alex rushed over to him. "She said she's leaving."

"Yeah, I know." He gripped his jaw shut.

"Did you have a fight? Mom and Dad fight sometimes." He looked down.

"No. Sometimes things just don't work out between adults, Alex."

"I like her."

"Me, too."

"I'm gonna miss her."

Pain squeezed his chest as he reached out to Alex's shoulder, needing that connection with family. "Me, too."

Piper drove away from Taylor's house, then pulled over to a side street and stopped the car under a lamppost. Covering her face with her hands, she cried. Over and over she'd told herself, Taylor wasn't right for her, wasn't the one she would be able to have a long-term relationship with. Unfortunately, her heart hadn't listened.

She plucked several tissues from a box sitting on the passenger seat and covered her face with them. The pain behind her eyes was so sharp that she thought she'd faint from it.

"Dammit," she cursed aloud. Once again, she'd done it. Set aside her own life to help someone else in need. Taylor had needed help, and she'd served herself up on a silver platter. Was she the ultimate enabler or what? Maybe she needed a counselor to figure out why she did things like this. Was he right? Was she afraid to live life, to reach out and really take what life had to offer, the consequences be damned? No. She couldn't do it. The responsibility gene was deeply rooted inside her, and she couldn't just let it go.

She sighed, then took a few deep breaths. She liked people, she liked helping them through difficult times, whether that was an illness, an injury, or a personal crisis. All kinds of people needed all kinds of help. And it helped keep her from thinking of how much help she needed in her own life.

Drying her tears, she leaned her head back and closed her eyes until the pain in her head subsided enough for her to drive home. Oh, God, oh, God, oh, God. She was so stupid! Taylor and Alex were something that she craved so desperately. Or at least what they represented. She wanted a family, needed to belong, wanted all the complications that having a family required, and would cherish every minute of being a wife and a mother. Good times and bad. That's what families were for, right?

Alex's mother was going to come back, so he wasn't going to need Piper. Taylor was going to move on to another woman, so he obviously wasn't going to need her, either.

Couldn't she live without being needed? Must she have some sort of earth-shattering chaos in her life to be happy?

Without fail, on every assignment, someone voiced envy for her lifestyle, the adventures, the travel. Sure, she was a traveler and moved around a lot, but all she needed was one good excuse to stay put somewhere. One good reason was all it would take, and she would stay.

One good man to ask her.

Now she knew staying in Santa Fe was pointless. As soon as she got home, she was calling her company to end her contract early. Since Taylor wasn't officially in her life, there was no reason to include him in the decision. No reason at all.

This wasn't going to be her last assignment after all. Wiping her face again, she checked her mirrors and pulled onto the road.

Staying now would only be more pain than she could handle.

CHAPTER TWELVE

DAYS passed with Taylor in a foul mood. He hadn't seen Piper at work for most of the week, not even in passing. She was on a rotation of night shifts while he remained on days. He'd heard from his colleagues that this was her last week at the hospital. She'd obviously decided to cut short her assignment. He supposed that was for the best but, damn, it just didn't feel right leaving things this way. He wanted to see her, even if it was at work. That didn't sit well with him, either. He didn't need anyone. He lived a single life and liked it that way. At least he had until Alex and Piper had burst into his life. The quiet that had once seemed therapeutic now created the opposite effect in him.

Restlessness as he'd never known plagued him night and day. The evening runs at the park weren't enough to put his black mood to rest, even when he pushed himself harder than ever. Dreams of soft sighs and softer kisses haunted him.

He needed some action. Caroline would be returning in two days, so he could get back to his usual routine and perhaps that would be the answer he needed. He reached for the phone and called Santa Fe Jumpers. He hung up after a disappointing call. Full. Every damned day for the next two weeks. Tourists filling up the dockets. So he'd put in a reservation for weeks away, but that wasn't going to ease the emptiness in him. He needed action, and he needed it now.

He knocked on Alex's door on Saturday morning. "Hey, sport. Let's get out of here and go do something."

Alex opened the door. "Like what?"

"How about mountain biking? Or we can to go Tetilla Peak. I need to get out of here and go do something physical—how about you? Exercise your muscles a bit and get some fresh air. Shake off the cobwebs."

With a vague shrug, Alex said, "I guess."

"A little enthusiasm would be nice," Taylor said with a sideways smile.

"I'll get my hiking boots."

"I'll get the rest."

No sooner had they set foot on the trail than a summer storm struck, soaking them to the skin in minutes. They raced back to the car and climbed in.

"How about Plan B?" Taylor asked, and wiped his wet face with a hand. Normally, the rain wouldn't bother him, he'd faced worse weather over the years. But with Alex along, he couldn't take the chance of him getting sick when his mother was due to return in two days. He was in the home stretch and didn't want to screw anything up now.

"What's that?"

"Dry clothes. Pizza. Movie and arcade." What almost-teenager wouldn't jump at that?

"Awesome, especially the dry part." Alex shook his head like a wet dog and sprayed them both with water.

Taylor laughed at the kid's antics. He was going to miss him. The laughter dropped right out of him and the smile faded from his face.

This was what Piper had been talking about.

This is what he had resisted for so long and now, right here, slapping him in the face, was his own admission that he was going to miss it, miss Alex. He glanced at Alex as he started the car. How had this happened? He was a confirmed bachelor. How had he succumbed to the lure of home and hearth? Piper, that's how. Alex, that's how. He'd never opened his eyes to the possibilities until they had overtaken his life, and he'd allowed them to without much in the way of resistance. Maybe subconsciously he'd wanted it and not known it? Psych 101, here we go. Self-analysis. Closing his eyes, a pang of remorse shook him. He just couldn't be what Piper needed. Maybe he was broken inside and was unable to have a normal relationship, to see it through to what it could be. The word *commitment* apparently wasn't a part of his vocabulary.

Now, he knew, it was best to let her go as she wanted. When you cared for someone you didn't ride roughshod over them, or try to change their minds about something they were quite certain of, did you? Who was he trying to kid? In the end, they would probably go their separate way anyway. Piper had been right, he just hadn't wanted to admit it.

But, dammit, he missed her. He blew out a sigh and turned on the wipers, then put the car in gear, but kept his foot on the brake. The windows fogged up on the inside, and he used the flat of his hand to wipe away the condensation. Having a car crash and ending up at his own ER was not going to be a way to spice up the weekend.

"Are we going, or what?" Alex asked.

"Yeah, we're going."

So they spent their afternoon a different way than anticipated and both of them loosened up, waiting for Caroline to return home.

"This is almost your last night with me," Taylor said as they drove home, a pang of surprising longing spiking through his chest. What had begun as a nuisance and a favor to his sister had turned into a surprisingly good experience for him. For Alex, too, he hoped.

"Yeah. I kinda liked hanging with you, Uncle T." Alex gave a quick glance at him.

"I liked hanging with you, too. I'll have to make arrangements with your mom to have visitation weekends or something," he said with a smile, reaching over and ruffling Alex's hair. "I know I'm not your dad, but maybe you could spare me some time now and then."

"My dad doesn't really like me, I don't think." Alex shrugged and looked away.

A pang shot through Taylor as memories of his own father sprang to life. The man had taken the loyalty and commitment thing to the nth degree and had soured Taylor on life ever since. "Why do you think that?"

Alex fiddled with the hem of his shorts. "I don't know. He kinda yells a lot, and when I'm at his house we don't do anything. Just watch sports on TV."

"Does your mom know?" Not that his own mother had been able to do anything to ease relations with his father. But Caroline would want to know, if she didn't already.

"Yeah. She can't do anything, though. The judge said I have to go."

Taylor wondered if *he* could do something about it.

If he could have a talk with Alex's father. He snorted. He'd never liked the bastard, so he doubted that would go over well. If José didn't want the kid, then he should give up his parental rights to Alex. That would be better than a parent who didn't want his child and treated him like garbage. With his gut churning, he fought the urge to stick a fist up the guy's nose and perform a lobotomy the hard way. Alex was a great kid and needed a better dad than the one he had. Taylor had survived because his uncle had helped him. He wanted to do the same for Alex. "Well, you can come to my house anytime you want to, okay? I'll make sure you have a set of keys of your own." This was a commitment he could make, one he vowed to never fail at.

"Okay." Alex remained silent for a few minutes as they returned to town. "Can we have a party for Mom? I mean, like a welcome-home kinda party?"

"Sure. Got any ideas?"

"Cake for sure."

"What kind?"

"Are you kidding? It has to be chocolate."

Taylor laughed and let the tension of his past fade back to where it belonged. "Chocolate it is."

They worked out plans for the next evening. They shopped and bought party favors, even a cake that Alex was sure she would like. Caroline was scheduled to have a late-afternoon flight into Albuquerque, then rent a car for the sixty-mile drive home to Santa Fe, declining Taylor's offer to pick her up.

As they waited for her to arrive, Alex danced around in anticipation, unable to settle down for more than a second at a time. "Where is she? Can I call her cellphone?"

"Go ahead. Maybe she ran into traffic or something. There's always construction in the summer."

As Alex called his mother, Taylor's cellphone rang. "Maybe that's her now."

"Hello?"

"Taylor? It's Piper."

His heart paused a beat as her voice filled his mind. "Hi. How are you?" Maybe she'd changed her mind, and he gripped the phone tighter, anticipation thrumming through him. Maybe she'd decided to stay on. Wasn't this going to be her last night on assignment? Maybe she was calling to say goodbye or even say she'd extended her stay a while. What he wouldn't give to spend another night with her. Another day. Another—

"I'm in the ER, and we just had a bad trauma come in."

Immediately, his anticipatory mood deflated. Business. Nothing personal. "Isn't there enough staff on?" He only got called when they were swamped, but right now he just didn't want to go in. He wanted to have a nice evening with Alex and Caroline. The "Welcome Home" banner they had made hung precariously from the archway, and he reached up to secure it better.

"There is, but... God, Taylor. It's Caroline!"

"What?" The happiness that had been inside him turned to a rock of dread.

"It's her. She's suffering multiple trauma and a possible head injury. We're on the way to Radiology. You need to come now."

Without another word, he snapped the phone shut and grabbed his keys from the counter, then stopped in midstride. Damn. What the hell was he going to tell Alex?

"She didn't answer, so I left her a message." Alex

returned to the room and looked up at Taylor, stopping at the look on Taylor's face. "What's wrong?"

"It's your mother."

"She called? Is she almost here?"

"No, Piper called."

"Can she come to the party, too?"

Choked by emotions, he took Alex by the shoulder and led him to a chair. Taylor needed to sit down, as well. God, how was he going to say this with his throat closing off? "She's been in a car accident, and she's at the hospital now."

"Wh-what happened?" Alex began to tremble, and his wide eyes filled with tears. "Is she okay?"

"I don't know. Piper's taking care of her, and we need to go see her now." Thank God Piper was taking care of her. At least that was one small consolation. He trusted Piper as no other.

"Okay." Alex nodded, in obvious shock, his breathing quick. "Okay."

"Let's go." Taylor kept his hand on Alex's shoulder and led him to the car. Ten minutes later they raced through the ER doors and found Piper waiting for them.

"Come on, she's over here," Piper said, leading them to the first trauma room. Before she opened the curtain, she needed to prepare them. Somehow. She looked at Taylor, but couldn't speak for a moment. How was she going to tell him? Tight-lipped, he gave a curt nod and stepped behind the curtain. In that brief visual exchange between them, he knew it was bad.

Piper knelt and hugged Alex, trying to offer some comfort to his trembling little body. "Your mom's been in a bad car accident, and she's not awake yet. She has some tubes and things hooked up to her to help her breathe and give her medicine, so it's going to be a little scary when you first see her. I've checked everything myself and it's all okay." Nothing had been as difficult as telling this little boy his mom was near death. "I'll go in with you so you won't be scared."

He sniffed and pulled back from her, obviously trying to be brave. "Okay. I'm ready."

From experience, Piper knew that no child was ready to see their parent laid out on an ER stretcher hooked up to life support. She'd been twenty when it had happened to her, and sometimes she felt she still hadn't recovered from the shock of seeing both her parents that way. "I'll be with you, and Taylor's here, too."

Pale and silent, he only nodded, and Piper led him into the room.

Grim faced, Taylor stood on the opposite side of the room in deep conference with his coworker, Dr. Tony Santiago, who had stabilized Caroline. Piper spared them a glance, then concentrated on leading Alex forward.

Caroline was still unconscious, both eyes swollen shut, her nose broken and multiple lacerations on her face, neck, arms and hands. "She's not awake right now and will have to go to surgery to fix her broken leg."

"Why won't she wake up?" he asked, and hung back, staying close to Piper, his voice thin with fright. "Tell her to wake up."

"I can't, darling. Sometimes after an accident, people kind of faint, from being jolted around. I think that's what happened to her. You need to come over and talk to her a minute so she knows you're here."

"But she can't hear me if she's not awake." Tears overflowed Alex's eyes, and he seemed unaware of them.

Tears dampened her eyes as she spoke. "She hears you. She needs to hear your voice and know you're with her. She'll know. Mothers always know." Piper looked up at the monitor. Vital signs were stable, so Caroline was probably okay to undergo surgery now. She sent up a quick prayer that Caroline could feel Alex beside her and know she was loved.

"Mom? It's me. Alex," he said, and his voice cracked.

"You can touch her hand." Piper took Alex's hand and placed it over Caroline's, careful to avoid the IV site.

"Mom? Uncle T. took me rock climbing, and I'm in camp and everything," he said.

The monitor showed that Caroline's heart rate skipped a beat, then raced for a few before settling down again. "I think she hears you. Good work, Alex."

Piper looked up at Taylor, and her breath lodged in her throat. Longing, such as she'd never seen in him, was etched on his face. She rose from her knees beside Alex. "Keep talking to her," she whispered in his ear. She approached Taylor and placed a hand on his arm. "Taylor? Are you okay?"

Turning his attention to her, he nodded, then shook his head, then gathered her against him. Piper held his trembling body tight to her, hoping to instill some of the comfort she'd shared with Alex. It wouldn't be enough. It was never enough, but perhaps it helped just a little.

She pulled back and touched her hand to his face. "Can I get you some coffee? Some juice for Alex?"

He nodded and released her. "I want to talk to the

surgeon and see what they have planned, see if I can scrub in with him."

"Oh, Taylor. That's not a good idea. He probably wouldn't let you anyway." Piper bit her lower lip, knowing Taylor was desperate to do something, but this wasn't it. He couldn't sit idly by while someone else fixed his sister. Sitting on the sidelines wasn't going to satisfy him.

"I know, dammit," he said in a low growl. "But I have to do something. I just can't sit here and wait." Sitting and waiting weren't what he did. It wasn't his way. His way was to charge forward, take control of a situation and make it right. Frustration rocked through him, and he clenched his jaw.

"Let me get those drinks, get Alex settled a little, and we'll talk." She turned away from him, allowing her hand to linger on his chest for a second, needing that moment of contact with him. "Alex, come with me." She held out her hand to the boy. "We need to go get your Uncle T. some coffee."

Without hesitation, Alex launched himself at her, hugging her around the hips. His small body shook, and she held him tight. Then she felt the touch of Taylor's hand on her shoulder. He knelt beside them, embracing them both. Tears clouded her eyes and pressure built in her chest. Here was the family she had longed for.

And it wasn't hers.

With a sniff, she pulled away before she broke down in front of them. Now she had to be the strong one for both of them. "Come on, Alex."

She led the boy away, and Taylor watched them go,

feeling like a piece of him was leaving with them. Cursing, he shoved to his feet and grabbed the room phone and called the orthopod. A friend of his, Dr. Ian McSorley, was a man he could talk to. They'd climbed and base jumped together, and he trusted Ian like a brother. A curt conversation that ended the way Piper had said it would didn't put him in any better frame of mind.

As he paced outside the trauma room, Piper returned with the drinks as promised. At least she had something to do. He reached for the cup. Taking a deep breath, he sipped the steaming brew, savoring the taste. Just the way he drank it. How had she remembered that? Taking a look at her, as if seeing her for the first time, he stared. She was a gem in so many ways, and he hadn't seen it. He was such a bastard.

"Maybe I should have gotten you decaf," she said, her sharp gaze assessing, wondering.

"No, this is fine. Thanks." He pulled back. He had to or he was going to allow his emotions to overtake him and that couldn't happen. He allowed his gaze to fall to Alex and the heat of emotion sliced right through him. The kid's face was a little pale and his eyes were red, but both were normal under these stressful circumstances. "I talked to Ortho, and they'll take her to the OR in a few. Ian won't let me scrub in." A muscle twitched in his jaw. Dammit.

"It's really for the best."

He ran a hand over his face and tried to shake off the anger that burned in his gut. "I'm glad her abdomen is stable. It's her head that worries me more than anything."

"Radiology didn't see anything significant, so it's probably just a concussion, and now we're sedating her a little, too."

She touched his arm, the gesture sympathetic, but he couldn't respond to it right now. He couldn't reach out or he would break. "I'm sure you're right."

"What's all that stuff mean?" Alex looked up at him, his brown eyes dark and filled with questions.

Taylor looked at Piper, and she nodded. It was his place to explain. The words stuck in his throat. How was he going to explain this to Alex? The kid would likely read through anything he said. Helplessly, he appealed to Piper, needing her now more than he ever had and hating himself for it. "The words won't come," he said, his voice rough.

Piper looked at Alex, her gaze soft and filled with compassion for the boy. "Your mom has to have surgery on her leg to fix it, so Taylor's friend Ian is going to do that tonight. She doesn't have any brain damage, even though she's still not awake. She had some X-rays of her head and everything's okay."

"But her eyes are shut, and she has cuts all over her and she won't wake up." His chest heaved with anxiety.

"I know. Right now her body is trying to heal and that takes a lot of energy, so she can't spare the extra energy it would take to wake up just yet." She sighed and looked at Taylor for confirmation. He looked as if he was getting his feet under him again. That was good. He was going to need to be the stable one for Alex for a lot longer than he'd anticipated. Caroline's injuries weren't going to heal overnight.

Piper explained the process of going to the OR, then to ICU until she woke up. Alex seemed to take it all in, but he was still a child and fears still clung to him.

"Piper?" one of the secretaries approached. "OR's ready for bed one."

"Thanks." She spoke to Alex. "I'm going to get your mom ready to go to the operating room, and you can go with us up there, but just to the big doors, then other nurses will take over for us."

"Okay." He nodded.

Minutes later, they had Caroline ready and wheeled the stretcher down the back hallway. The neon lights overhead were too harsh, too bold, and revealed too much. Taylor saw everything with surreal vision, one color bleeding into the next. Nothing seemed real right now. Everything about him was exposed and raw in the awful lighting, leaving him stripped bare.

After handing Caroline off to the OR team, Taylor took Piper aside. "Is your shift almost over now?"

"Yes. Do you want me to stay over?" She would. For him, she would stay forever and beat herself up later for being such a marshmallow. Now he needed help. Should she tell him it was her last one? He was going to find out sooner or later.

"No." He fished out his keys and removed one. "This is to the back door. Can you go to my house and take down the party stuff?"

"Party stuff?"

"Yeah." He blew out a harsh breath and shoved a hand back through his hair. "We had a welcome-home party planned for Caroline. I don't want Alex to see it."

Oh, God. "That's a good idea." The key he gave her was warm from his pocket and she closed her fist over it. "I'll do it. Do you want me to call when I'm done or what?"

"I don't know, yeah, maybe. I'm going to want to stay here the rest of the night. I know it's a huge impo- sition, but maybe you could take Alex home for me in a little while. He should go home, but he can't go by himself. Someone needs to be with him." Looking into Piper's face, he knew she would do whatever he asked of her. She was loyal to a fault, and her compassion overwhelmed him right now. Unable to name the emotions filling him, he pulled her close for a quick hug and pressed a hard kiss to her temple. "Thank you." It was as close as admitting to her and himself that he needed her once again. He needed her more than he could admit to either one of them.

Nodding, she pulled away. "I'll be back." She said goodbye to Alex and left them alone in the waiting room.

CHAPTER THIRTEEN

PIPER let herself into Taylor's home. The lights were on and the video game still shot bullets at empty targets. They'd obviously left in a hurry. She turned off the TV and most of the lights, leaving one lamp burning by the couch. The atmosphere certainly would have been festive if the circumstances had been different. She carefully removed the banner and folded it, hoping that maybe they could use it if...when Caroline came home from the hospital. The festive paper plates, napkins and cups she put into a paper bag with the banner and set it on the bottom of the pantry. The cake was going to be a problem, though. It was too big to hide easily and wouldn't fit in the freezer, so she just put it in the oven until she could ask Taylor what to do with it. Maybe she could scrape the icing off it and take it to the ER for the staff rather than just tossing it out. She hated to waste cake, especially chocolate.

By the time she returned to the hospital to pick up Alex, it was very late, and he was asleep on the couch in the surgery waiting room.

"She's still in surgery. The leg's a mess, so it's taking longer, but so far she's tolerating it okay."

"How are you tolerating it?" Piper asked.

"Tolerating what?" he asked, his face closed off and emotionless, the look in his eyes flat.

"I see. Back to your old self again. You can't think through this one, Taylor. You can't use your super-hero talents here."

"What are you talking about?" Glaring down at her, he tried to push her away. "This isn't what I need right now, Piper."

"I think it's exactly what you need right now." Whether he knew it or not.

"You can't force me into some psycho-babble therapy session that's going to make me spill my guts and be all warm and fuzzy."

"I agree. If you can't open yourself just a little when your sister's in the OR, then what will it take?" She crossed her arms, feeling the disconnection between them growing. Tonight was the last night of her contract. Though she was staying on in Santa Fe for a week or so while deciding what she was going to do next, she probably wasn't ever going to see him again. She might as well say what she had to say. No one else was going to tell him. "You can't plow through this situation, Taylor. This isn't a mountain to conquer or a plane to jump out of or anything like that. You have to feel it. Don't push people, especially Alex, away. For better or worse, you need to stop and feel it, to understand what it is to care about someone much more than you care about yourself." She took a deep breath and blew it out fast as her past and emotions nearly swamped her. "Why don't you take Alex home? He needs you more than me right now. I can stay until Caroline's in the ICU later. Do you trust me?"

"I trust you. You know I trust you." Taylor looked at his nephew, covered with a white patient blanket, asleep on the couch he knew had to be as lumpy as hell. His mouth parted with his breathing and a frown marred his brows, even in sleep. Running a hand through his hair again, he looked at Piper. "I know he needs me, but I have to stay here until she's in the ICU. I have to." He paused and looked down at her guarded eyes. The disappointment he didn't want to see was right there. He placed his hands on her shoulders and squeezed. "I know I don't have the right to ask you and it's a huge imposition, but I'm going to ask anyway. Could you take him home for me and stay until I'm sure she's really stable?" The trembling in his arms made its way to his hands and to Piper's shoulders. "I...I need you, Piper." More than ever, he admitted only to himself.

"Taylor, it's you he needs, not me."

"Please."

Looking into his eyes, she seemed to come to a decision and glanced over at Alex. "I'll take him. Just come as soon as you can. You're the only family he has right now, and he needs *you*." She placed her hands on his wrists and squeezed, then pulled away from him.

Looking over at his innocent nephew, he whispered, "I need him, too." He broke away from her and stared through the tiny window in the OR door. Waiting.

Finally, hours later, exhausted and mentally drained, Taylor was able to see Caroline. After a quick visit in the recovery room, he sought out Ian to get the details doctor to doctor. She'd have a long recovery ahead of her, that was a given, but they'd saved the leg with pins and bolts and a lot of other hardware. She'd learn to walk again, but it would be a lengthy process. Something about which Taylor was gaining new insight into.

Taylor entered the ICU. Putting one foot in front of the other required more brain function than he had at the moment, but he plodded along, rubbing a hand over his face, trying to wake up a little bit. Someone, one of the nurses probably, had set a relatively comfortable chair beside Caroline's bed, and Taylor collapsed into it.

A long sigh escaped him, and he bent forward, clasping his hands between his knees. Eyes closed, he stayed that way, listening to the background noise of the ventilator, the heart monitor, the sounds that were all familiar to him, but now took on new, significant meaning.

Life was so very fragile, and these machines were all that were holding Caroline together. The significance of that fact had escaped Taylor until now. Things like this happened to other people, other people's families, and *he* put them back together with confidence. He couldn't sit doing nothing by his sister's bedside, waiting for someone to fix her. Confidence this night was sorely lacking.

It had been just the two of them for so long. They helped each other, depended on each other, needed each other. And now Taylor was powerless to do anything except sit and wait. It wasn't in him to do nothing, and he ground his teeth in frustration.

Piper's words came back to him. *Alex needs you.* And he knew then that he had something to do to help Caroline. Ensuring that her child was safe and cared for wasn't nothing. Reaching out, he took her limp hand carefully in his. "I'm sorry, Caro," he said, adopting his childhood nickname for her. "I'm sorry you're here, but

Ian has fixed your leg, and we're just waiting for the rest of you to catch up. Don't worry about Alex. I'll take care of him as long as I need to." Pausing, he watched the monitor pulse away. The overhead light reflected off his watch, reminding him that the night was rushing by. He glanced at the timepiece and stilled.

The timer that he'd set weeks ago sped merrily along, obviously unaware that Taylor's life had come to a screeching halt. Time waited for no one and pulsed on regardless. He hadn't wanted to take Alex, he hadn't wanted the interruption of his lifestyle, the nuisance of it all. But as he watched the time count down to the end of his agreement, something knotted in his gut, sickening him. Piper was right.

He was afraid.

Reaching over with the other hand, he pushed the button twice. Once to stop the timer, and again to end the program. The watch face returned to its normal mode. He rose from his chair and gave his numbers to the ICU nurse caring for Caroline. "I'll be available should anything change. Otherwise I'll be back in a few hours." He needed some rest, and he was as certain as he could be that Caroline was stable. Putting his personal trust in his coworkers and friends was something he'd never had to do before. He received hugs from the staff as he made his way out of the hospital and their sympathy almost pushed him over the edge. He hadn't realized how many people genuinely cared about him.

He was humbled by their outreach. He was humbled by Piper.

Driving home, though only ten minutes away, was one of the longest drives he'd ever made in the predawn. He let himself in and walked to Alex's room first. Still clothed, the boy was sprawled on the bed, his mouth slack with sleep. Taylor knelt on the floor beside him as emotions he'd kept at bay for too long finally overcame him. "I'm sorry, Alex. I'll take better care of you from now on. I won't let you down." He stroked the dark hair, then left the room.

Piper lay curled on her left side on the couch, a spare blanket half on, half off. She must be exhausted after working her shift, then helping him. He'd been unfair, asking her.

Something behind his heart shifted a bit, piercing something that had lain hidden and dormant until now. Until Piper. Despite everything, could he be falling for her? Locking his heart away had been a priority in his life. He hadn't needed anyone. Hadn't wanted anyone in his life. Until Piper had breezed into it.

Something had begun to change. He'd begun to change. She sighed in her sleep and adjusted her position. The blanket slid off, revealing her long, long legs. She wore only one of his T-shirts that fell halfway down her bare thigh. Desire flared hot and heavy in him. Emotions raw, he scooped her up in his arms and carried her to his room.

"Taylor? What's going on?" she asked, her voice rough with sleep, and she blinked like an owl. Her arms slid around his shoulders. "Is Caroline stable?"

"Yes." He placed her in the middle of his bed and sat down beside her. This was where he had wanted her for a long time. And now that she was here, he just wanted to hold her.

"I'm so glad." Blinking sleepily, she moved closer

to him and pulled him against her for a tight hug. "I'm so relieved."

"Yeah, me too." Words wouldn't come, they lodged in his throat. The night of emotion had left him devoid of function, and he just wanted to hold her against him for what was left of it. "Will you stay with me? Let me hold you while I sleep a while?"

Piper's hand clutched the back of his neck, and she pressed her forehead to his. "Yes."

Taylor pulled the covers back, and settled with her against his side. The security of having her in his arms and the bliss of sleep overwhelmed him in an instant.

In the moments before becoming fully awake, Piper turned toward the heat source at her back. The cobwebs of sleep faded, and the events of the evening rushed back to her. *Taylor*. She was in his bed. The place she wanted to be above all others, but the circumstances that had led her to this place were unfortunate. As she tried to ease away from him, the touch of his hand on her hip made her pause. He turned into her back, bringing her against him. Waiting a moment, she hoped he'd settle back to sleep so she could escape, but as she tensed, waiting, she realized he was tense and waiting, too.

"Where are you going?" he whispered.

"I thought you were asleep."

"Until you moved."

"Sorry. Go to sleep, and I'll head home."

"Stay, please." He pressed a kiss to her cheek, her nose, her lips. "I need you, Piper. More than I ever have."

A tremor of responding need swept through her at his

words. She'd needed to hear them. Without answering, she turned to face him. The desperation in his voice, the raw emotion vibrating off him, the tremor in his touch lured her closer to him. Like the proverbial moth, she was going to get burned, but the light proved irresistible.

As she opened her eyes, the dim peach glow of the desert morning crept over the windowsill and bathed the room with its soft light. As she reached out to Taylor, she knew it was all over for her. She'd fallen in love with him.

Expecting his hands to be bold and demanding on her body, his gentle touch surprised her, unfurling soft petals of desire. Slow, drugging kisses and hands meant to tease and please roamed over her with tenderness, rousing her more than fast and urgent moves.

"You are so beautiful, Piper."

She returned his kisses with all the love she had in her. She might not be able to say the words aloud, but she could show him with her kiss, with her body, exactly how she felt about him. When she moved with him, took his body inside hers, there was a peace, a sense of belonging that she'd never experienced before. They fit.

Taylor sighed in pure bliss as he eased within Piper's soft body. A low shock pulsed through his system. It seemed that this was what he'd been seeking, searching for all of his life. The softness, the acceptance, the love that she offered as her hands crept up around his shoulders and pulled him tighter to her. Strength and energy eluded him as he lost himself in the joy of Piper's body. Arms trembling, he touched her, treasured her body and teased a quiet response from her.

Her soft whispers, her sighs of pleasure heightened

his own, until he lost himself in her. Pressing his forehead to hers, he watched her face. "Open your eyes."

As her eyes locked with his, he let go and gave himself completely to Piper.

The smell of food woke Taylor. The summer sun shone through the window, and he bolted out of the bed. Grabbing the phone, he called the hospital to check on Caroline. Relieved that she was still stable, he calmed down. After a quick shower and dressing, he followed the delicious smells coming from the kitchen.

Alex stood beside Piper and poured batter into a hot skillet. "Not too much, or you'll end up with one giant pancake instead of two normal-sized ones."

"Okay."

"Hi, you two." Taylor entered the room and headed for the coffeepot, which was almost full.

"Hi, Uncle T. Piper's helping me make you breakfast."

"I see that. Smells great." In fact, everything smelled great and his mouth watered in anticipation. He turned from the pot to admire the blush on Piper's cheeks, wondering if it was from the heat of the stove or a heat that he had generated that made her color. "I checked on your mom, and she's stable. After we eat, I'll take you over to see her."

"Okay." Alex picked up the spatula and checked the bottom of the pancake.

"Looks good enough to eat," Piper said, then jumped when Taylor's cheek brushed hers.

"So do you," he whispered, then straightened.

"Yes, well. How about I get out of the way so you guys can go see Caroline?" She held the plate while

Alex loaded the pancake on top of the pile. "I'm sure you don't need me here, getting in the way."

"Will you come with me? Us?" Alex asked, his eyes wide and uncertain.

"I'm a mess. I need to shower and change out of these scrubs."

"Please?" Alex implored.

Piper looked at Taylor who gave a quick nod. "Let's eat. I'll go home and change, then meet you at the hospital. Okay? I have to turn in my badge anyway." Having just spent an intense night with Taylor, she could use a break, to sort out her feelings that were about to spiral out of control and try to distance herself, to evade the allure of Taylor. Her nerves, her feelings were flayed raw right now. But as she looked at Alex, she knew she couldn't leave him with his mom in critical condition. She had a gap in her work life now anyway. There was no reason she couldn't help Alex out now, was there?

"Cool," Alex whispered, and carried the plate to the table.

Taylor said nothing, but watched the interplay between the two and accepted the plate set in front of him.

CHAPTER FOURTEEN

A SHORT hour later, Piper entered the hospital and followed the signs to the ICU on the second floor. The nerves she'd kept at bay earlier now flooded through her, and she had to stop before she rounded the last corner. Closing her eyes, she took a few centering breaths. This wasn't about seeing Taylor again. This wasn't about them as a non-couple, this was about being a friend to him, to Alex, and helping them through a tough situation. No matter how she felt, they needed her right now.

Raised voices pulled her from her inner pep-talk, and she stepped into the hall leading to the ICU.

Taylor stood nose to nose with another physician. Alex was backed into a corner by the door, his eyes wide and fearful.

"Hi, guys. What's going on?" she asked, and tried to project a calm energy toward Taylor who looked like he needed it. His face was red and his fists clenched at his sides. Testosterone fairly scorched the air.

"Dr. Jenkins here is being a butt-head."

Piper recognized Ian McSorley and knew he was a friend of Taylor. "I see. Is Caroline okay?" She looked between the two from Ian's amused expression to the thunder brewing in Taylor's.

"She has to go back to surgery," Taylor said.

"And you want to scrub in, right?" she asked, knowing without asking that was going to be the issue.

After a pause and a sideways glare, he said, "Yes."

"Bad idea, Taylor. You know that." Dr. McSorley folded his arms over his chest, and stared down his friend, the patience of a saint in his expression. "You are out of line with the request. Again. If our roles were reversed, you'd treat me the same, too."

"I'd cut you a break because you're a colleague." Taylor's eyes were narrowed and cold as he glared at Ian who only grinned, which seemed to madden Taylor further.

"No, you'd kick my ass out the door, which is what I'm doing to you."

Taylor flinched, dumbfounded surprise showing on his features. "Are you kidding me?"

Ian grinned and included Piper. "Nope. Will you take this guy out of here for a while or suture his mouth shut?" he asked her, and gave a charming smile which she returned.

"I don't know if that's included in my skill set." She glanced at Taylor and motioned Alex to her. "But I'll try."

"Can I see my mom now?" Alex whispered.

"Go in, Alex. Piper can take you." Ian gave the directive, but stepped in front of Taylor to bar his entry. "You and I need to have a man-to-man. In private."

Piper left Taylor and Ian to their conversation and escorted Alex to his mother's bedside. They spoke to the ICU nurse who apprised them of the situation. "She's stable now, so the doctor wants to go in and fix her wrist. It wasn't urgent last night."

"Is she awake at all?" Piper asked, and stroked Alex's hair.

"Yes, in and out. She's still got the breathing tube, so she can't talk, but I'm certain she'll hear you."

With an arm on his shoulders, Piper led Alex to the side of the bed. "Let's see if she's awake."

"Mom? It's me, Alex, again. I'm here with Piper. She's a nurse, Uncle T.'s friend." He touched her hand, and she slowly clasped his fingers. Pure excitement on his face, he turned to Piper. "She's holding my hand."

Tears flooded her eyes at Alex's hopeful words. Wasn't that what it all boiled down to in life? Hope? If things weren't the way you wanted them, there was always hope for change. If you gave up on hope, there wasn't much else to live for.

"That's great. Taylor's going to be happy, too."

The man's heavy sigh behind her alerted her to his presence. "She's doing better, isn't she?"

"Uncle T.! She's squeezing my hand."

Piper moved back to let him into the small space beside his nephew. "That's good. She's going to go back to surgery in a little while have her wrist fixed, so we'll have to leave in a few minutes."

"No! I don't want to leave her."

Alex's heartfelt cry squeezed Taylor's heart, and he reached out to the boy. "I know. I know. Neither do I, but for now we have to let the doctors and nurses take care of her."

"But you're a doctor, and Piper's a nurse. Why can't you take care of her? Please?" His watery gaze included

both of them, and Taylor pressed his lips together, unable
to form words. They wouldn't come out of his mouth.
He looked at Piper and held his hand out to her, needing
her help, needing her right now in this very emotional
time that he was so unfamiliar with. Depending on her
made him weak, but right now he couldn't find the
strength he thought he had. Jumping out of a plane with
a faulty 'chute would be better than this.

"We are, honey, but when our family member is a
patient, we're not allowed to take direct care of them.
It's kind of a rule."

"Why not? You're the best doctor and nurse ever!"
Alex cried, and his voice cracked.

Just then the anesthesiologist arrived to review the
chart.

"Come on, Alex. Let's go—" Taylor started.

"No!" He pulled away from them and clung to his
mother's hand. "She needs me, and I'm staying here
with her."

"It's okay, son," the anesthesiologist said. "You can
stay with her and hold her hand all the way to the OR
doors, okay?"

Alex nodded, and glared at Taylor.

"Why don't you and I get out of the way and give
Alex a minute with her?" Piper said, and tugged on
Taylor's sleeve. With another sigh, he allowed her to
lead the way out of the cubicle and to the coffeepot
provided for families. He didn't speak, but stared into
the depths of his cup.

"It's different, isn't it?" she asked, her voice soft and
full of compassion.

"What?"

"Being on the other side of things. Not in charge, not the one calling the shots, not the one fixing everything."

"Yes." He couldn't begin to explain how different it was. Having been there herself, Piper knew exactly what was going through him.

"Hurts, too, doesn't it?"

Taylor turned away without answering. Despite having made love early that morning, he didn't feel close to her at the moment. He didn't know what he wanted. Didn't know what he needed. Right now he just wanted to be left alone. Alone was what he was good at. Entanglements got him into situations like the one he was currently in. The allure of Piper was almost too much, he almost wanted to reach out to her, to tell her what he was feeling for her, but he just couldn't. Not right now. Maybe not ever. Maybe a bit of fresh air would clear his head. "I need to go for a walk, clear my head. Can you stay with Alex for me?"

Piper stared at him a second before she gave the answer that would tear her heart in two. "No, I can't."

At that, he turned to face her, shock on his face. "What?"

"No, I can't stay with Alex for you anymore." She dumped her coffee and tossed the cup in the trash. "I just can't, Taylor. I can't be around you, I can't be with Alex right now. I'm sorry. I just can't."

He stepped closer and took her by the arm. "I thought we were friends, Piper."

"Yes. We have been. We've been friends and lovers and now I can't be either to you." Tears swirled in her eyes, but she didn't let them fall. "I've got to figure out what I'm doing on my next assignment or where I'm going, what I want to do next."

Taylor dragged a hand through his hair. "What's going on? What's the matter with you? I *need* you right now. Don't you know that?"

"Yes, I know. I can't be with you just because it's convenient for you to need me right now. When this is all over, you won't need me anymore, and I can't live like that." No. She just couldn't do it anymore. The past was headed for a repeat if she didn't stop it now. If only Taylor had said he wanted her with him, wanted her company, her presence, her support, that would have been different. Wanted her, not needed her.

"Live like what?"

Her lower lip trembled, and she took in a breath before she buckled and gave in to him. "Loving a man who doesn't love me back." With a hand pressed to her mouth, she turned to walk away.

Taylor felt like someone had punched him in the gut, and for a second he couldn't breathe, let alone take in what she had just said. He was such a bastard. He didn't want to hurt her but, dammit, he needed her help right now. Needed her more than he'd ever needed anyone in his life.

"You...you love me?" he asked, not really expecting an answer.

Tears now overflowed her eyes and she didn't seem to happy about it. "Yes, Taylor. Fool that I am, I love you." Her lower lip trembled and she turned away from him.

With unnamed emotions shooting through him, he reached out a trembling hand and placed it on her shoulder before she walked away from him for good. "Piper, please."

She stopped, but didn't turn back to him. She waited and he felt every tense muscle in her shoulder.

"To say this comes as a shock to me is a gross under-statement. I don't deserve your friendship, let alone your love."

Finally, she turned to face him again, the hurt in her eyes plain to see. He hated that he had put it there, and he wasn't sure he could make it go away. Reaching out to her, he cupped her face so she didn't withdraw from him again.

"Will you please stay? I don't know what's going to happen between us, but I know if you leave we'll never know."

For a few seconds that seemed a lifetime to him, she stared at him silently, assessing the truth in his words. He didn't know if what he felt for her was love or not. But he knew that the thought of never seeing her again made him want to crumble to his knees.

"Do you think you could extend your assignment for just a little while?"

"Why? I can't just stay because there's an opening. Any travel nurse can fill the position."

Unable to answer right away, he simply breathed and looked at her face. Pain and hurt and somehow hope all were exposed raw. "For Alex. For Caroline. For me."

"Why?"

The word was harsh in his brain and the searing pain in his chest hadn't subsided. He opened his mouth, but nothing that made sense formed in his brain. She loved him, that's all that swam around in his mind. She loved him.

She took a defiant step forward, challenging him. "Tell me why, Taylor. I need to know."

"Because I need you, Piper. I need you. The right words won't come, but I need you." His voice cracked.

"Then I'll stay. For Alex. For Caroline. And for you. Until Caroline is out of danger, I'll stay. After that, I can't make any promises."

"Thank you, Piper." He took her hand and squeezed, wanting to drag her into his arms, but if he did, he knew he might not ever let go. "You don't know what this means to me."

"No, I don't. It's up to you to let me know that."

"I will. I'll make it up to you somehow, I promise."

"No promises you can't keep, Taylor." She withdrew her hand. "I'd rather have it honest and painful than be misled."

"I'd never do that to you, Piper."

"Time will tell. It's all up to you now."

Her arms went around him, and they held on to each other as emotions unnamed swirled around them. Taylor fit Piper against him and squeezed his eyes shut. Everything about her fit, he didn't care what she said about them being poles apart. In the important things, they fit. Not the little details that they could work out. And he couldn't let go of that now. Maybe not ever. "I don't know if I can give you more than that, but if you don't stay, we'll never have a chance to find out."

For long minutes they simply stood there and held on to each other. The noises of the ICU washed over and around them, but they seemed immune to the outside forces moving nearby. Finally, Piper eased back, tear smudges on her face, and she had left a wet mark on Taylor's shirt. She took a shaky breath and looked up at him. At that moment he knew he felt more for her than he had for any woman. He couldn't let go of that or his soul would never be the same again. Was that love? He didn't know, but he couldn't make himself let her go.

"I'll go call my company and see what they can arrange." She took another step back. "At this point, I'm only willing to stay until Caroline's out of the hospital and rehab, which will likely be just a few weeks."

"I understand." What she didn't say aloud was what he knew in his gut. It was going to be up to *him* whether she stayed beyond that. From here on out, everything that happened was on his head. Something shifted in Taylor as he looked at her. He knew she loved him. And he felt things for her that he had never felt before. Was that love? Was it simple lust gone wild? Or was it wanting to keep the loneliness at bay? He didn't know, but he damned sure was going to find out if this thing between them was going to survive the test of time. It was certainly being tested now, which didn't bode well for a long-term relationship.

"I'll go talk to Emily, too, and be back in a while."

"I'll be waiting for you."

She gave him a small smile and took the stairs to the ER.

Time ticked by slowly for Taylor as he sat at Caroline's bedside after the second surgery. Piper had successfully extended her contract for four weeks, starting in one week, which gave her a break of seven days in between. That meant he had five weeks to convince her to stay. Or she was going to leave for good. He knew that.

God, he just hoped that Caroline's recovery was un-complicated—no infections, no blood clots, no setbacks. He stared at the monitors, at Caroline's vital signs displayed in glowing green numbers, illuminating the dark of the room. Stable. The respirator had been removed and the tube taken from her throat so that she would be able to talk again when she woke. A simple nasal cannula provided the essential oxygen she needed. Though this was progress, he still couldn't relax, wouldn't give up his vigil at her bedside.

If only she'd wake up properly, he'd feel much better about her condition, know in his heart that she was going to survive and be his sister again. For so many years it had just been the two of them, depending on each other for support. If he lost her now, he didn't know what he'd do. Losing Piper would break his heart. If he lost Caroline, too, he'd lose his mind.

He rested his head on the edge of her bed and closed his eyes with a sigh. He was so tired, physically and emotionally. A tingling sensation began in his hair and tugged. He shot upright as Caroline's fingers moved with purpose. That was a fabulous sign of improvement. As he looked at her face, her eyes cracked open and held his gaze. She was in there.

"Hi, Caro," he said, and reached out to touch her face as a thrill of relief shot through him. "You're back."

Nodding, she tried to speak, but her throat wouldn't make words yet. Taylor reached over for a mouth sponge and wet it, brought it to her mouth to moisten it. "Hi," she said, finally.

Taylor spoke to her, filling her in on what her injuries were, what had happened. Tears overflowed her eyes as she listened. "Alex?"

"He's at rock-climbing camp today. He missed a few days, but I figured it was better for him to go than to hang around the hospital so much. I'll bring him by after camp." He left out the part where *he* felt totally incompetent in dealing with Alex's grief. Other than spending time with the kid, there was little he could do at the moment until they knew how Caroline's recovery was going to go.

Another nod and she closed her eyes, rested a moment, then opened them again. "Who's Piper?" she asked.

Stunned, Taylor stared at her. "You know about Piper?" he asked.

Frowning, she closed her eyes again, thinking. "I remember something. Soft. Warm. Loving."

Yes, Piper was all that and more. So much more, and he was beginning to see it, was beginning to not want to let go of it, beginning to see the change in himself. "She's an ER nurse who took care of you when you first came in. A friend."

"More." The frown remained, as she opened her eyes. "Isn't she?"

"Yes, she's much more." Taylor huffed out a shaky breath as emotions poured through him. He closed his eyes and pinched the bridge of his nose as he struggled to control himself. He couldn't appear weak in front of Caroline now, but he was so relieved. He needed to be strong for her, for Alex. Giving in to an emotional weakness was just plain unmanly. He couldn't. He didn't want to. But it seemed that his heart had other plans. Not long ago, he'd broken down with Piper, admitting things to her he'd never have done previously. A few deep breaths and clamping an iron will on the emotions he struggled to contain, he finally opened his damp eyes. "She's much more."

Caroline stared at him, her eyes clearer than they had been moments ago. "Tell me." She looked into Taylor's face. "You have feelings for her."

"Yes." He could no longer deny it. These feelings for Piper were stronger than anything he'd ever known. Sure, he'd had relationships, but they'd been the casual, no-strings-attached kind. What he felt for Piper was entirely different.

"Tell me, T." She squeezed his hand. "Who is she?"

With a nod, he looked down at their entwined hands. This was his big sister that he'd share his joys and sorrows with all through his life. How was he going to tell her he loved a woman but couldn't say the words? "She's wonderful, and...I think I'm in love with her." For the first time, he was able to admit that aloud and knew that it was true. The fear building in him nearly choked his throat closed. How could he ask Piper to stay when he was such a failure at relationships? How could he ask her to give him one more chance when he'd had more chances than he deserved?

"Taylor." The heart monitor revealed the racing of Caroline's heart. "*You're* in love? How?"

"Like you suggested, I kept my feet on the ground long enough to meet the right woman." Without any intention of having that happen.

"She loves you?"

"Yeah," he said, and looked away.

"That's wonderful."

"Not so wonderful. She's afraid she won't be enough for me, afraid of getting hurt, afraid of me wanting more."

"Is she right?"

Thinking for a second, Taylor didn't know how to

answer. "Sometimes I think she's right, but when we're together, it's magic. She grounds me, balances me, keeps me from staying in the clouds too long."

Caroline smiled at him as tears filled her eyes. "Then you need to convince her to trust you. I never had that with José and it drove us apart."

Taylor nodded, but fear cramped his heart. What if he couldn't say the right things? Then what? "I'm not sure I know how. I've never been good at commitment stuff." Exhaustion seemed to overwhelm Caroline as she struggled to keep her eyes open. "We'll stop talking now so you can get some more rest. You're doing better and the leg is healing, but you need sleep. My love life can wait."

She took a deep breath and closed her eyes, nodded. "Come back, bring Alex."

"I will." He leaned over and kissed her cheek as she succumbed to the mind-numbing sleep she desperately needed. As he stood, he thought about her words. Convincing Piper that she was enough for him, that she could trust him. His fear throbbed to the surface. What if Piper was right? Could he do that to her and walk away? He didn't know and didn't want to think about it right now.

As he left the room, he wondered if he could face the rest of his life without Piper in it. He had five more weeks to figure it out.

CHAPTER FIFTEEN

TAYLOR took a personal leave of absence from work. Just for a week. Maybe two. Who knew how long he was going to be caring for Caroline and Alex? His life had been completely derailed by his sister, his nephew and a woman he wanted as his lover. One had been foisted on him, one had been a family obligation he had willingly taken on and one had stolen his heart from out of the blue.

Unable to ignore the kitchen's deplorable condition any longer, he washed the dishes that had piled up over the last week. If this kept up, he'd have to hire a cleaning service. Caroline was eventually going to come home, but wouldn't be able to stay by herself right after rehab, so he imagined she'd come to stay with him until she was on her feet again. His sister and his nephew had nearly taken over his life, but he was okay with that now. In fact, he was looking forward to having them both here. The silence in the house was overwhelming, and he wouldn't be able to tolerate it for much longer.

Alex hooted from the living room, apparently finding some solace in shooting space aliens. The sound of normality made Taylor smile. This was the sound a happy family made. A pang of longing shot through him. Longing for what hadn't been but, more so, for what could be and wasn't. An image of Piper soft and dreamy whispered into his mind. The sound of her laughter echoed inside him, and he tried not to listen to the call of his heart. The phone was just inches away. All he had to do was call her. And what? Say he he'd been an ass? That he was wrong?

Trust. The simple problem between Piper and himself was trust. Caro had hit it right on. Neither he nor Piper trusted each other enough to reach out, both were afraid of being hurt. But at their ages, who hadn't been hurt more than once and painfully so? Taylor sighed, searched for any remaining dishes and opened the oven door.

And found the cake. It hadn't changed much in the last week, but just looked hard and dried. The icing as crusted over as his feelings had been until this summer. Until Alex.

Until Piper.

Welcome Home. The red icing words seemed to have a message just for him.

Home. It was what he had felt when wrapped in Piper's arms.

Home. It was what his house had felt like with Piper in it.

Reaching in with hands that weren't quite steady, he removed the cake and turned to find Alex standing in the doorway of the kitchen.

"What are you doing with that?" Alex asked, his eyes wide with questions. Reaching out, he stuck a finger in the icing, licked, then made a face. "I forgot about it."

Taylor glanced down at the cake. "I was going to throw it out. Doesn't seem like it's edible anymore."

"Letting cake go to waste stinks." Alex watched as Taylor tossed the cake into the trash and bundled it up to take outside. "You miss her, don't you?" he asked, wiser than his years.

"Yeah, but your mom will be home soon. She's healing well."

"I meant Piper." He shrugged and looked away from Taylor. "I miss her, too. She's cool." He returned to the living room and turned off the television.

Unable to speak through the lump in his throat, Taylor took the bag of trash to the Dumpster outside. He needed a moment alone to collect his thoughts, which had scattered at Alex's insightful statement.

The night sky had pushed daylight away. The stars, so visible in the high desert sky, popped out here and there, as if waiting for someone to see them. The sight, the beauty of the night sky, the loneliness of it, left a hole in his chest. This beauty had once been enough to fill him. Now he knew better. Piper was the one who had filled him, completed him, and Alex was right.

He missed her. Commitment and responsibility no longer seemed to be things that interfered with his life, but things that he needed and wanted in his life. Like Piper.

Piper packed up her unappealing lunch of leftover tuna salad and tossed it into the trash. She had a few more days to explore Santa Fe before her contract extension began. Surely there were wonderful places to eat, exotic foods to try, retail therapy to be done. Determined now not to waste her time off, she grabbed her keys, her purse and opened the door.

Taylor stood there with his hand raised. "Uh, hello."

"Hello." She paused. He looked as yummy as ever, but his eyes were as wary as her heart felt. "What are you doing here?"

"I wanted to talk to you." He lowered his hand to his side and shoved it into his trouser pocket. He was dressed casually, as if he were on the way to the golf course.

"I was just about to go out for lunch." That was direct without being rude, wasn't it? If he didn't want to join her it was an automatic excuse to leave. She wasn't testing him so much as giving him an opportunity to step up to the plate.

"Mind if I join you? I'd like to talk."

Looking into his eyes, she couldn't say no and a flutter of relief swept through her. He'd been through hell the last week or so with his sister's accident and continued care of Alex. He probably hadn't had a decent meal in that time, either. Green chile cheese fries were great, but it wasn't sustainable nutrition for anyone. Who was she to deny him a good meal now? "Sure."

"Where were you going?" he asked, and led her to his car.

"Nowhere special. I was just going to drive around until I found a place that looked good or I was too hungry to care what the food was like." Now, with him so close, her appetite for food had fled somewhat.

Taylor gave a quiet chuckle. "Let me take you to my favorite lunch spot." He started the car and headed out into the steady flow of traffic.

"I thought that was the hospital cafeteria," she said

with a teasing arch to her brows. The banter between them felt like old times, but with a certain amount of strain that just didn't feel right. Maybe there was no going back to what might have been between them.

"Hardly. This is a hallmark of Santa Fe. The original inn was built 400 years ago when this area was settled. The food there is outstanding and the atmosphere is whatever you need it to be."

"Take me to it."

After a short, quiet drive, Taylor parked and escorted her into a hacienda, a pueblo-style, wooden-beamed and stucco building that looked as if it had once been a private home on the outskirts of town. Gardens and private terraces offered a sense of privacy for a number of tables and the waiter led them to one of these secluded alcoves. Alone and nervous now, Piper took a seat. If they had still been lovers, this table for two surrounded by a tall fence veiled in lush ivy would have been a perfect place for a romantic rendezvous. But now she didn't know what they were, and the scene lost its charm. They ordered and a heavy silence hung between them.

"How's Caroline today?"

"How have you been?" They spoke at the same time.

"You first," Piper said, and sipped her iced tea. Relaxing with him over a casual lunch wasn't likely to be happening today. Being on her guard would save her from embarrassing herself by revealing things she wanted to keep hidden. For her own sanity, she had to protect her emotions from him. He'd already been too close to her for comfort.

"She's much improved, thanks. Out of ICU today,

and probably going to rehab by the end of the week." He picked up his water glass twice, but didn't drink. "So far no complications."

"That's wonderful. I was so worried when she first came in." Hands nervous, she fiddled with the napkin in her lap.

"How have you been, Piper?" he asked.

The tone of his voice was husky and low, personal and intimate, and she knew he wasn't talking about her work life or her sister. With him watching her so intently, she had the feeling that the rest of the world faded and it was just the two of them tucked away together. Almost afraid to look at him, afraid she'd reveal her feelings without words, she gave a quick glance and a shrug. "Okay, I guess."

"Piper, look at me, please."

Tears pricked her eyes as she glanced at him and looked away. Going to lunch with him had been a really bad idea, no matter how hungry she was or how brilliant the atmosphere. "I'm sorry, I can't. Not when you look at me like that."

"Like what?"

"Like you want to devour me, like you want me, and I know it's not true." She spared him a glance, then returned her gaze to her lap. "Maybe this extension was a bad idea. Maybe I should have left when my first contract ended." She sighed. "I can't be a casual lover with no strings attached. I want the strings, and I need the attachment. I can't be what you want, Taylor. I'm not built that way."

He leaned back in his seat as the server interrupted with a basket of freshly made tortilla chips and house salsa. "What way is that?"

"You know, Taylor. You know." Finally, she looked at him. "You're about danger, adrenaline and excitement. You're fearless." She paused and swallowed, the words sticking in her throat. "And I need to be safe."

"You're safe with me, I would never let you get hurt."

"No, I'm not safe." She would never be emotionally safe and stable around him. He was too volatile, too out there. He had the power to hurt her more than any man she'd ever known.

"I didn't mean for that rock-climbing thing to happen. It was an accident, you know that." Now he leaned forward, intense.

She leaned closer and placed a hand on his, waiting until he looked at her. "I wasn't talking about climbing. I was talking about my heart, Taylor. With you, I'll be forever fragile, never sure of where I am with you, and I can't live that way."

"Piper," he said, and took both of her hands in his and pressed his face into them. "I've never said this to another woman, but...I've missed you."

His voice cracked and the sincerity in his face convinced her that he told the truth. Could there truly be hope for them yet? Could she stand on the truth as he knew it and not get knocked down?

"I've missed you, too. That's what makes this so damned hard. We were friends and I miss that." She wanted desperately to believe in him, in what they could be together, but some part of her just knew it wasn't going to happen. Her emotions were a mess when it came to Taylor. Tears escaped her eyes.

Taylor pulled her close and kissed them away, then kissed her mouth as if she were the secret to sustaining his life. "I don't want to let you go, Piper. I'm not ready to watch you walk out of my life."

"I don't want to, either, but how are we going to make this work?" Concern filled her eyes and the tentative smile faded.

"I don't know. I don't know. But if we don't at least try to make it work, we'll never know, will we?" he asked. Tenderly, he pressed a kiss to the back of her hand and lingered there, as if savoring the smell and the feel of her skin. He looked at her as he pressed his cheek to her hand, his compelling gaze holding her captive. "Don't be afraid. Don't walk out of my life. Please." He sighed and looked down at their entwined hands. "Something has been missing in my life until now. Until you."

Piper stared at him for a few long moments without speaking, afraid to give life to the hope that had begun to bloom in her chest. "There are so many things I've been afraid to do since my parents were killed. I've been so wrapped up in making sure that Elizabeth was taken care of, that life was safe and secure, that I think I've forgotten to live my own life." She gave an abrupt laugh and reached up with one hand to touch his face. "I don't want to be afraid anymore, Taylor."

Taylor pulled her close for a hard kiss on her lips. "Stay with me, and you won't need to be afraid. Neither of us will need to be afraid or alone any longer."

"Where would you like these?" the waiter asked as he stood beside the table, holding two steaming plates of food.

"I'm thinking we need those wrapped to go," Taylor said, and let go of Piper who settled into her chair with a blush on her cheeks.

"Certainly. I'll be right back."

"Are we leaving?"

"We're going to take our lunch to your place where no one will find us for a while, and we can talk uninterrupted." He cupped the back of her head and brought her close for another drugging kiss.

She pulled back slightly and whispered against his lips. "Drive fast."

They made it back to her apartment and shoved the take-out into the fridge before Taylor pulled her against him. His hands trembled as he cupped her face and drew her mouth upward. The taste of her, the feel of her, the scent of her, all reached inside him once and for all, filling the void that had lived in him.

She was the answer. She was what he needed. She was what he wanted in his life to make it complete. Now he knew what she meant to him. He felt as if he'd jumped off a cliff and forgotten the glider.

Her hands clung to his waist and her breathing came in quick gasps as she answered his kiss. Eager pulses of want and desire spread through him, making his heart erratic and his palms slick. Wanting her skin against his, he had to push down the needs raging in him, reel in the urgency pounding through his body. This wasn't just about him. His feelings for Piper had changed. He knew she loved him. And he? Yes, he loved her, too.

"Piper," he said, and cupped his hands around her face. "Piper." He pressed his forehead to hers, needing to take a calm breath, to savor the feelings rocking his world at the moment.

"What? What's wrong?"

"Nothing, babe. Nothing at all." He kept her face

tipped up so that she looked at him, knew he spoke the truth. With his heart pounding the way it was, he could speak nothing else. "I want to make love to you right here and right now."

"Yes, I know." Her eyes went soft, her desire for him obvious.

"The first time I made love to you was for the pleasure of it. The second time was from need." He looked at her, pressed a small kiss to her nose. "This time is because I love you."

"What?" Tears overflowed again. "Don't tell me that just so I'll stay, Taylor. You don't need to do that." She started to pull away, but he held her tight, more certain than ever of his feelings for her.

"Listen with your heart, not your hurt. I love you, that's not a lie. It's the biggest truth of my life and it's been staring me in the face since we met. I just couldn't see it. I've missed you these last few days, and I've realized that my life and my home aren't the same without you. I want you in my life, Piper," he whispered.

"But—"

"No buts. We'll work it out. Somehow we have to. I love you, and I don't want to let you go. The rest is just details." He wasn't going to let go of her, he just had to convince her of it.

"I don't want to let you go, either," she said, and closed the gap between them. "I'm so afraid."

"Of what?"

"Of you. Of me. What we could have together and losing it. That scares me the most."

"Don't worry about what hasn't happened. When teaching people how to jump out of airplanes my instructor deals with a lot of nervous people. What he says applies here, as well. 'Open yourself to the possibilities, and just let go.'"

Breathless at the pain in her chest, wanting so badly to reach out to him, but afraid the fear would win, she looked into his eyes. Nothing except love, nothing except trust filled them. Could she do any less than honor him with her own love and trust? "I will."

She let go, and he caught her.

Clothing was removed by urgent, trembling hands and kisses were hot and deep. Naked, Taylor carried her to her bed and laid her on top of it, then pressed his weight down on her. Skin to skin, sigh to sigh, they loved each other in the most intimate of ways, drawing deeper into each other with each seductive kiss.

As Taylor eased inside Piper, he knew that this was the welcome home that he'd be wanting the rest of his life. Unable to control the want, the need, the urgency pulsing within him, Taylor guided her legs around his hips and buried himself deep inside her with a groan of satisfaction. When she cried out his name, he knew there was no other place he wanted to be. Seconds later his body responded and he found his release.

Aftershocks coursed through Taylor as he turned with Piper to settle her comfortably in his arms. "I love you, Piper." He pressed a kiss to her temple. "I've never said that to another woman. I've never been able to say the words until you."

"Taylor," she whispered, and turned his face toward her for a soft kiss. "With my heart, my soul and my body, I love you."

"That sounds like a vow."

"I guess it kind of is. When you truly love someone, you do make a vow to them and to yourself."

"Can you stay with me here?" he asked, his eyes suddenly serious. "Can you stay in Santa Fe and give up travel nursing after this extension is over?"

She bit her lip and stroked his face with her hand. "You really want me to stay?"

"More than anything. But you have to want to stay, too. We can make a home, build a life together. The kind that neither of us has had." There was vulnerability she'd never heard in his voice, in the soft stroke of his hands down the length of her back. The man with the magic hands loved her. Wasn't that a precious thing?

She sat up on the bed and knelt beside him.

"I can hear you thinking. What's going through your mind?"

She dropped her head and allowed the wave of hair to cover her face. "Can I trust you? Can I trust everything that you are, that you claim to be, to want?" Raising her head, she stared intently at him. "What will happen if things don't work between us? It will kill me to love you and lose you."

"There are no guarantees, Piper. Only trust will make it work. Between you and me." He met her gaze straight on. "I don't know how to tell you how much I feel for you. How I feel when you're with me. I just don't have the words in me. The only way is to take that leap of faith and trust what's in your heart." His gentle hand stroked her face. The energy flowing from him into her nearly broke her heart with its sweetness.

There was respect, there was humor, there was friendship, and there was certainly passion between them.

Were those enough of the right building blocks to have a forever love? "You're right. You're absolutely right." Without her clothing, bared completely to him, she stood at the end of the bed, holding a post for balance.

"What are you doing?" he asked, and sat up at the head of the bed, his eyes glowing as he watched her.

"If I fall, will you catch me?" she whispered.

"A naked woman in bed, are you kidding?"

"Be serious." This was the playful Taylor that she loved, but she needed more right now, just for a moment.

"I am." Taylor gave her a lingering glance to her curves, but the smile on his face and the look in his eyes let her know he understood her.

Without another word, she closed her eyes and let go, falling forward. She didn't get far, because Taylor caught her, pulled her close and turned her gently in his arms. "If you fall, I will catch you. When you stumble, I'll be there to help you up." His voice was a husky whisper in her ear. "But you must promise to do the same for me." A kiss to her cheek. "I want to build a life with you, Piper. Will you marry me someday soon?"

With emotion choking her throat tight, she nodded. "I will."

"I love you. The rest is just details."

They sealed the vow with a long, slow kiss.

EPILOGUE

Six weeks later

A BUNDLE of bright cheery balloons tied to the mailbox fluttered in the afternoon breeze. A "Welcome Home" banner adorned the threshold from the living room to the kitchen in Taylor's house.

"They're here! They're here!" Alex dashed out the door into the driveway and jumped up and down until Taylor pulled the SUV to a halt. Piper followed along at a more reserved pace, but she wasn't able to contain the smile on her face as she watched Taylor assist Caroline into a wheelchair. "What can I take?" Piper asked.

"There's a pile of stuff in the backseat you can bring in," Taylor said, and kissed Piper on the cheek. "Hi."

"Mom, Mom! You'll never guess what."

"What?" Caroline said with a laugh. Thin and gaunt from the lengthy recuperation, Caroline's pleasure at being with Alex was obvious. "Tell me what."

"Uncle T. got me a gaming system!" Energy and excitement sparked off Alex. With his mom home, as well, his life was complete.

"Oh, like you need another one." She turned to Taylor.

"You weren't supposed to spoil him so much." The playful glare she gave turned soft with affection for both of them. As the only men in her life, she needed them both.

"It has educational programming, too. Don't worry." Taylor gave her shoulder a squeeze of reassurance.

"There's even an exercise program for you," Alex said. "It'll make you stronger."

"Now I see your ulterior motive," she said, and pushed the wheelchair forward. "You've been talking to my physical therapist."

Piper held the door as everyone bustled through into the kitchen. Caroline looked up at Piper, adjusted the wheelchair to face her and held out her hand. "Hello, Piper."

"Hello, yourself." Piper leaned over and greeted her new friend and soon-to-be sister-in-law. "It's good to see you again. You look better now than in rehab."

"I'm very happy to be here." Caroline sniffed appreciatively. "Something smells wonderful."

"We made you a cake," Piper said, and drifted closer to Taylor.

"We?"

"Alex and I. Taylor did the decorating." She looked up as Taylor pulled her against his side.

Caroline laughed and placed a hand over her heart. "I never thought I'd ever hear that about my brother."

"Come into the living room, and I'll show you the exercise program, Mom." Alex led the way and Caroline followed. She gasped at the state of Taylor's living room. "What in the world happened in here?"

"It's home now," Taylor said, and let his eyes sweep the jumble that had once been a showroom.

"But…" Horrified concern filled her eyes.

"Don't worry, I'm not."

"I didn't want to take over your life, Taylor." Tears dripped down Caroline's cheeks. She was still weak and easily overwhelmed.

"You didn't. My life is more open than it's ever been, and that's a very good thing." He crouched down beside her chair and placed a hand on hers. "I wouldn't have had you hurt for anything, but this experience has been a life-changing one for me. One I needed more than I ever realized."

Alex approached. "You should have seen the couch before we steam-cleaned it," he said out of the corner of his mouth. "Grape soda."

"Oh, Alex."

"Caroline, it's really okay." Piper moved toward Taylor and slid her hand around his waist. "The Taylor you know is still in there, but he's made a lot more room for the rest of us in his life."

"Yeah," Alex said. "He even said I could get a dog! Is that cool or what?"

"Taylor, are you ill?" Caroline asked, a frown on her face, and she blinked at him as if seeing him for the first time.

"No." He looked at Piper. "I'm in love."

Alex made a rude sound in his throat. "Same thing."

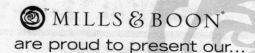

MILLS & BOON

are proud to present our...

Book of the Month

Pure Princess, Bartered Bride
by Caitlin Crews
from Mills & Boon®
Modern™

Luc Garnier has secured the ultimate prize –
Princess Gabrielle – a pearl beyond measure.
But will Luc be able to break through her
defences to make this not just a marriage
on paper, but of the flesh?

Mills & Boon® Modern™
Available 15th January

Something to say about our
Book of the Month?
Tell us what you think!
millsandboon.co.uk/community

MEDICAL™

Single titles coming next month

NEW SURGEON AT ASHVALE A&E
by Joanna Neil

Dr Ruby Martyn swaps her white coat for wellies and a pram, leaving her job at Ashvale to care for her adorable niece. But the A&E can't cope without her and neither can her boss, gorgeous doctor Sam! Convincing Ruby to return is important, but first on his agenda is winning her heart!

DESERT KING, DOCTOR DADDY
by Meredith Webber

Sheikh Yusef knows his kingdom will benefit from doctor Gemma's renowned approach to medicine, and the immediate connection between beautiful Gemma and his tiny daughter amazes him! As a man *and* a father, he knows what he must do: this sheikh surgeon will make Gemma his royal bride!

On sale 5th March 2010

millsandboon.co.uk Community

Join Us!

The Community is the perfect place to meet and chat to kindred spirits who love books and reading as much as you do, but it's also the place to:

■ **Get the inside scoop from authors about their latest books**

■ **Learn how to write a romance book with advice from our editors**

■ **Help us to continue publishing the best in women's fiction**

■ **Share your thoughts on the books we publish**

■ **Befriend other users**

Forums: Interact with each other as well as authors, editors and a whole host of other users worldwide.

Blogs: Every registered community member has their own blog to tell the world what they're up to and what's on their mind.

Book Challenge: We're aiming to read 5,000 books and have joined forces with The Reading Agency in our inaugural Book Challenge.

Profile Page: Showcase yourself and keep a record of your recent community activity.

Social Networking: We've added buttons at the end of every post to share via digg, Facebook, Google, Yahoo, technorati and de.licio.us.

www.millsandboon.co.uk

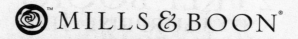

2 FREE BOOKS
AND A SURPRISE GIFT

We would like to take this opportunity to thank you for reading this Mills & Boon® book by offering you the chance to take TWO more specially selected books from the Medical™ series absolutely FREE! We're also making this offer to introduce you to the benefits of the Mills & Boon® Book Club™—

- **FREE home delivery**
- **FREE gifts and competitions**
- **FREE monthly Newsletter**
- **Exclusive Mills & Boon Book Club offers**
- **Books available before they're in the shops**

Accepting these FREE books and gift places you under no obligation to buy, you may cancel at any time, even after receiving your free books. Simply complete your details below and return the entire page to the address below. You don't even need a stamp!

YES Please send me 2 free Medical books and a surprise gift. I understand that unless you hear from me, I will receive 5 superb new stories every month including two 2-in-1 books priced at £4.99 each and a single book priced at £3.19, postage and packing free. I am under no obligation to purchase any books and may cancel my subscription at any time. The free books and gift will be mine to keep in any case.

Ms/Mrs/Miss/Mr _____ Initials _____

Surname _____

Address _____

_____

_____ Postcode _____

Send this whole page to: Mills & Boon Book Club, Free Book Offer, FREEPOST NAT 10298, Richmond, TW9 1BR